# THE LEGACY OF
# YANGCHEN

降击神通

# AVATAR
## THE LAST AIRBENDER

# THE LEGACY OF
# YANGCHEN

## F. C. YEE

AMULET BOOKS · NEW YORK

Cataloging-in-Publication Data has been applied for and may be obtained from the Library of Congress.

IISBN 978-1-4197-5679-5

Jacket illustrations by JungShan Chang
Book design by Brenda E. Angelilli and Deena Micah Fleming

Printed and bound in U.S.A.

10 9 8 7 6 5 4 3 2 1

Amulet Books are available at special discounts when purchased in quantity for premiums and promotions as well as fundraising or educational use. Special editions can also be created to specification. For details, contact specialsales@abramsbooks.com or the address below.

**ABRAMS** The Art of Books
195 Broadway, New York, NY 10007
abramsbooks.com

*For Karen,*
*who has seen my entire author career so far.*
*And to whom I'd like to show the rest.*

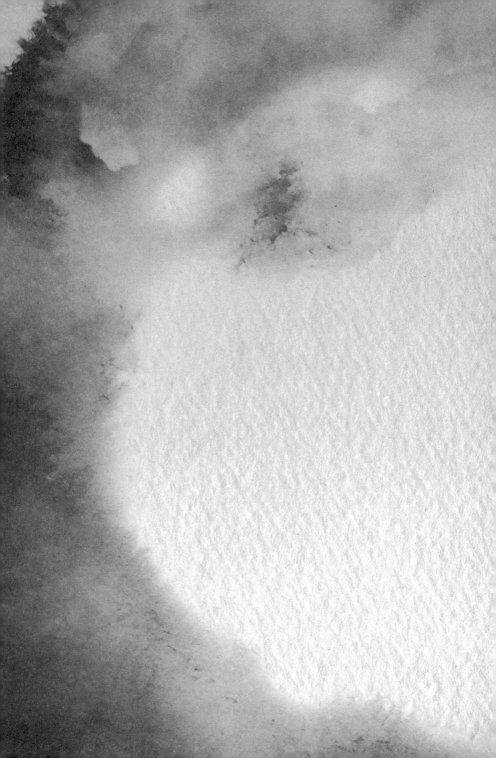

# DEPTHS

**CHAISEE UNDERSTOOD** from an early age that to be successful, you needed to be willing to go further than others thought possible.

To wit—the villagers of her little unnamed island dove for prized cucumber-sponges far below the glistening surface of the waters, where sunlight faded and ears threatened to burst. No one in the Mo Ce considered such a feat viable or worth the risk.

But Chaisee's people ignored the prevailing wisdom. Without the aid of waterbending, they trained their bodies to accept the pressure, their minds to embrace the signals that they were dying. Dive after dive, they forced their way farther into the depths and scraped their hands raw against the slimy spikes of the reef to come up with little puffballs of a creature that, once carefully killed and dried, would fetch a generous string of coins on the open market.

She and her fellow villagers willingly took on the often-fatal endeavor again and again so they might eat for another season.

And faraway nobles washed their faces with the cured exteriors of cucumber-sponges, the softest touch known in the Four Nations. A mutually beneficial agreement based on one party's willingness to torture themselves and the other side's complete distaste for the slightest physical discomfort.

As Chaisee grew older, she began to manage the village's books. She took over from her father the negotiations with haulers who came to collect the sponges, pearls, dried shellfish meat—the secret was to spy on other suppliers while using uncharted islands as stashes to control market prices. She had no reason to suspect her future would contain any disturbances to this arrangement other than the occasional monsoon.

The ship that broke the cycle arrived with battened sails and swooping foredecks. Strangely, it bore flags of both the Fire Nation and the Earth Kingdom. The party that came ashore in longboats was led by junior ambassadors from both countries. In front of Chaisee's assembled village, they read a proclamation decreeing that the inhabitants of this island would no longer be allowed to produce certain goods of the sea. By a vanishingly rare agreement between Earth King and Fire Lord, the exclusive rights had been granted to some merchant they'd never heard of in a faraway city that was completely landlocked.

*This can't be,* Chaisee's father had said, hushing her with a raised hand. Suddenly the negotiator again. *We protest this decision. You must at least give us the chance to formulate a response.* To buy time, he resorted to their island's customs of hospitality. *Let us entertain you tonight as honored guests. We can talk of bargains in the morning.*

The officials agreed. They needed to reprovision and take on fresh water anyway. While the ship's quartermaster negotiated the purchase and loading of supplies, a feast was quickly put together for the important visitors and their crew.

The general nervousness among the villagers ebbed as they shared good food and drink with the sailors around the burning fire in the square. The meal would remind these strangers that the island was home to families like theirs and that a measure of humanity should prevail over dictums sent from afar.

Chaisee did not partake wholeheartedly. She stayed removed and observed, as was her habit, which meant she saw in full when one of the sailors picked up a torch and flung it into the largest hut. Like one might offer a bone to a guard animal. She wasn't fast enough to stop him or speak out.

The building was the one used to store the drying cucumber-sponges, and in their raw state the dusty, porous bodies of the sea creatures were better than the best tinder. The roof blew out with a roar, spewing heat and flame and embers over the adjacent huts. The fire spread so fast that half the village was ablaze before the screaming started.

Chaisee remembered the reactions of the ambassadors who had obviously given the order, their faces lit by the blooming, dancing flames. They rolled their eyes, snorted in contempt, and departed as calmly as they came. Annoyed with the whole affair at best. Her father was too distraught, occupied with fighting the fire, to prevent the outsiders from reaching their longboats and leaving the shore unimpeded.

She watched the delegation go, understanding that a confrontation would have achieved nothing. The letters they bore granted them the power and voice of their rulers. There were no criminals here; her livelihood burning away was the law enacted. She might as well have tried to exact justice from the leaders of the Four Nations themselves. What fool could aspire to that?

*We weren't strong enough to keep this from happening,* she thought as her neighbors desperately tried to carry water to the fire in buckets, gourds, cupped hands, wailing as their futures dissolved into smoke. *We didn't have the right friends.*

Working yourself to the brink of oblivion was pointless if you couldn't defend the life you made. Maneuvers, deals, negotiations were simply dance steps. Pageantry. The true arbiter waiting at the end of the performance was violence.

Chaisee's ruined village was a kiln that baked the lesson into shape. She kept it in mind as she sought work on islands closer to the official Fire Nation archipelago. The form held hard and without cracks as she made her name in trade, mastering the codes of business spoken in every country while accumulating leverage over her partners and rivals alike. When the Platinum Affair clamped across the world, she was quick to see opportunity and predicted correctly how it would condense power even further into a few hands.

By the time she became eligible for the role of Zongdu in Jonduri, the war had already been fought and won. In the minds of the shangs, there were no rational choices other than Chaisee to lead the city. Her selection was unanimous.

In many ways, Zongdu Henshe, her counterpart in Bin-Er, was of a similar mindset as Chaisee. Though he was a fool who squandered information and resources with no regard for strategy or long-term consequences, he had successfully ground her plans to a halt by threatening to turn over everything he knew to the Earth King. He'd stolen the fruits of her labor, her means of becoming immune to harm in all the ways her little childhood village was not.

Henshe's waywardness had posed a greater threat than any of the brilliant men and women whom Chaisee had tangled with in the past. The wise could be counted on to do what was wise; there was no predicting the actions of a buffoon. But now Henshe was gone, and with him her assets. Chaisee had been left without a move. She could only sit and wait.

"Mistress." Chaisee's newest attendant announced herself, pausing on the warped floorboard by the door of the nursery. Each shift of the girl's socked feet produced a squeak like a pained bird. "Mistress, you have a—"

The baby woke. A scorching wail rose from the teak crib in the corner.

Chaisee rubbed her forehead, taking care not to cover her face completely. "I just got him to sleep!" She had to raise her voice, something she never used to do, in order to be heard.

"I'm sorry, Mistress, but you have a letter and—"

"Leave it and get out!" The attendant scurried over, laid the envelope on the desk in the nursery, and fled for her life.

She didn't see Chaisee drop her snarl as soon as she was gone. The girl would report back to Fire Lord Gonryu that her mistress was cracking under the strain, uncharacteristically showing more emotion. Perhaps frustrated by her child. Distracted, and therefore less of a threat.

Nothing could be further from the truth. Chaisee's son was a sharp reminder for her to stay focused. And his cries were a perfect deterrent to eavesdroppers. Taking her time, as calm as if she were listening to the serenade of a babbling brook, Chaisee opened the letter. She drew a chair over to the crib and rocked it gently while she read.

The message was nonsense. But it was written in a hand she recognized and contained hidden signals that let her know exactly where to find the person who'd sent it.

Her son quieted down, but she knew he would start howling again if she stopped rocking. Perhaps his skin was prone to rashes. A frustrating prospect, when she already bathed him with cucumber-sponges, which were much more expensive these days than back when she was a girl. She went through an amount that would have made her younger self gasp, but there was no softer touch she could resort to.

Chaisee folded the paper back up with one hand and looked around. The nursery she'd constructed in the mountaintop estate was dark and cool, a respite from the sweltering heat outside. But the entire house would pass to the next Zongdu of Jonduri once her term ended.

She'd have to leave this place behind soon and start over again. Those were the rules laid out by the heads of state, who never had to worry about moving on from what they'd built while they were still alive. The Avatar, young Yangchen, was like that too. She would be the bridge between humans and spirits for her own little eternity before she passed and a new Avatar was born.

There were a lot of powerful people in the way of Chaisee's ambitions, laying exclusive claim to permanence. They'd be sovereigns of their domains until the very day they died, never having to fear their status being stripped away, never knowing what it was like to be naked and vulnerable.

Chaisee could be the last person standing among them, if she chose the right path, proved herself willing to go to depths beyond reckoning, and remained a step ahead of the other players in a game that could reshape the Four Nations themselves. An outrageous folly, but one she had the means for. And the will.

She looked at the letter again and smiled. With the right incentives, anything was possible.

# ADORATION

"YOU ONLY WIN at keep-away because you're taller," Yangchen said. She remained motionless, not grabbing for the airball held within reach.

Jetsun pushed the wicker sphere closer to Yangchen's face. "Really. Nice excuse for never learning."

"I can't learn how to be taller! And it's not a fair game if you always start with the ball! We never switch places!"

The airball loomed larger, the moon threatening to plunge into the ocean. "Come on," Jetsun said. "Make a move."

As soon as Yangchen did, she'd give away some tell and Jetsun would react quicker than a hummingfly's wings, read her intentions, and retreat just far enough to make her think she still had a chance. "No. Not this time. Neutral jing."

"*Bwomp*," Jetsun said, pushing the ball lightly against the tip of Yangchen's nose.

That settled it. Yangchen shut her eyes. Jetsun couldn't predict which way she would go if she didn't know herself. She lunged blindly, flailing her arms randomly about, and only once she'd clapped her hands around the prize and successfully torn it away from her sister's grip did she open her eyes again. "Ha! Eat dust—"

Instead of the airball, Yangchen was holding on to a pulsing light, her hands lost in its undefined edges. Jetsun was standing a few feet away, deathly still. The older nun's eyes were blank and without reflection, anchored in the distance behind Yangchen. Her lips were blue. Yangchen had torn Jetsun's spirit from her body. No accusation, no voice told her so, but she knew beyond a shadow of a doubt.

She tried giving it back. The first instinct of a child who'd gleefully killed a bug but then regretted it. She pushed the light toward Jetsun. *Here. Your turn. False start. I'm sorry. Never meant to.*

But injuries couldn't be undone. No healing reversed time. As Yangchen advanced with the light, Jetsun retreated, floating just out of reach, never moving more than necessary to confirm Yangchen's crime.

*Take it back. Please, take it back.* Yangchen was no longer pleading with Jetsun but the spirits, the Four Nations, the universe. *Please. I'll do anything.*

As Yangchen gave chase, her feet splashing against emptiness, tendrils of mist enclosed Jetsun, as if her sister were being webbed by a spider-fly. A corpse shroud of fog, and only when Jetsun's mouth was about to be covered did she part her lips to say—

*"Aagh!"*

Yangchen woke with a start, her head snapping up from the desk. A paper came with her; drool had glued the document to her cheek. She swiped at her face, briefly thinking she was under attack, the victim of some kind of screening maneuver, until she regained her bearings.

The cold was the first sign, the cramped, drafty wood paneling the next. She was in the tiny room on the upper floor of the Bin-Er gathering hall that she'd commandeered for an office. Yangchen rubbed her eyes. This place was going to become her tomb.

Jetsun. There but not there. Of all the lives that could have haunted Yangchen in her sleep, it had to be her own. Jetsun's presence must have been a dream, not a memory, because in it they were about the same age. *I'm on the verge of catching up,* Yangchen thought.

The dream was accurate enough. One way or another, she was responsible for Jetsun's death by the severance of her spirit. The younger version of herself, the current version of herself, it didn't matter. It was her fault Jetsun had died.

A knock came at the door. "You were late before," Boma said from the other side. "Now you're very late."

"What do you mean before?" Her guardian normally eased her into the mornings.

She could hear Boma grunt, the sound of a sigh being plugged. "You asked for a few more minutes. I left and came back. The shangs are waiting." He lowered his voice. "So is the inspector."

Yangchen didn't remember the conversation. She must have been sleep-talking. She'd worked throughout the night above the room where the meeting was supposed to take place, napped on top of her documents, and she still wasn't on time. "Where's my staff?"

"You left it by your chair downstairs."

An important heirloom sitting there forgotten, for all to see. She swore at herself. *You're a mess. Get it together.*

She scrambled to get ready as best she could, gathering her hair and checking in a mirror that ink hadn't bled onto her face. Reluctantly she shed the blankets around her shoulders. She couldn't be seen clinging to comforts.

*Strength,* she told herself. *Control. Don't worry that you're walking away from your sister.*

Yangchen joined Boma outside the office and he followed her down the spiraling stairs to the ground floor. The main room was barred by double doors, and she pushed them open with air pressure. The gesture was more dramatic than she intended, her arrival announced by a gale of wind. Loose papers tumbled down the aisles. Gasps came from the seats.

And before Boma had to say anything, the people waiting for her in the grand hall stood as one. "The Avatar," he declared, trying to catch up.

The shangs of Bin-Er. The select group of merchants who controlled the flow of international trade to and from the city. "Apologies for my tardiness," Yangchen said to the assembly.

"No need, Mistress Avatar," replied Shang Teiin, one of the more senior representatives. "Your presence is a blessing no matter the circumstances."

Next to him, a woman wearing earrings made from pearls the size of grapes lowered her head. The dangling jewelry pointed to the floor as she bowed. "We're ready— We're *excited* to discuss the next phase of your proposals," said Noehi, who'd once made sport of mocking Yangchen when she thought she could get away with it.

Half a year had produced a marked shift in attitude among the powerful men and women who'd originally fought her efforts to aid the poor in Bin-Er. Afraid of being implicated in the disaster that led to three unimaginably powerful Firebenders causing havoc over the city, they'd seen the wisdom in partnering with Yangchen. If they failed to dance in tune together, the merchants would lose their heads for treason against the Earth King. And Yangchen would become one of the greatest failures in Avatar history—a history she could remember in excruciating detail.

"Shall we begin?" Noehi asked. Her gaze darted to Yangchen's empty seat on top of the central dais, and then to a man behind it at the recorder's desk, slightly off to the side. He was a heavily bundled official from Ba Sing Se whose brush moved faster than a master musician's fingers. As he glanced up from his pad of papers and made eye contact with Noehi, her lips twitched in fear.

*For the sake of the spirits, don't look at him like that,* Yangchen thought. *You're acting suspicious already.*

Inspector Gu watched silently as Yangchen sat down on her throne-like chair. She could feel his presence next to her, a hungry maw sucking in information to bring back to the Earth King. "Yes, let's," she said. She noticed her glider-staff leaning against the armrest, right where Boma had said it was, like a lonely stalk of grain. "I could use some tea as well."

One of the shangs' attendants scampered off to fetch refreshments. The meeting began in earnest. Besides needing to keep the secret of the balance-shattering Firebenders out of the Earth King's hands, Yangchen and the merchants were also on the hook for keeping business as usual flowing through the city.

So far, they'd succeeded. With the Avatar present to check the shangs' worst practices, Bin-Er was turning its reputation around and becoming known as a place of fair dealing. The population was growing faster than anyone had anticipated.

Yangchen rattled off the numbers she'd stayed awake last night preparing. "Based on my recent counts, the city needs at least four new wells, or else sickness will become an increasing danger"—she paused, considering Gu sitting behind her—"to prosperity. A plague, accelerated by a lack of fresh water, would certainly damage revenue streams."

She despised how she had to frame everything in terms of wealth lost and gained to appeal to her audience. But Szeto-like efficiency was what she'd promised. She had to deliver.

Shang Teiin stood up to respond. He adjusted the heavy cap on his head, a concession to his age and the cold. The flare of gold embroidery on its peak made him look like a candle. Yangchen forced away a pang of envy for the heavy fur cape around his shoulders. The hole she'd wrecked in the side of the building had been bricked shut, but a draft still snuck through the cracks.

"These measures are indeed wise," Teiin said. "But they're an unplanned expense. Expert benders who can reach the water table without disrupting the city above will not come cheap."

*This city is made of money, you stone-in-the-road.* Despite their survival hinging upon working smoothly with the Avatar, the shangs still found it in them to drag their feet. "If you're refusing, you can come out and say so," Yangchen said.

Noehi took over from Teiin. "It's not that we're refusing," she said. "It's just that we're a bit . . . stretched." The embarrassment written across her face told Yangchen she wasn't lying. "A large portion of our funds were tied up in arrangements and loans made with Zongdu Henshe. He still hasn't surfaced."

That was because Zongdu Henshe currently sat in a makeshift jail at the Northern Air Temple, sequestered from the world by the orders of Yangchen herself. If Henshe were free to roam, he'd sell the secrets of the Firebenders to the highest bidder the first chance he got.

"Henshe was the center of a web of promises," Noehi went on. "In his absence the strands have collapsed. Our outstanding dues to Taku, Port Tuugaq, and Jonduri are quite substantial. We genuinely don't have the cash on hand to afford another project."

Yangchen pinched her nose shut so she wouldn't burst out laughing. The shangs of Bin-Er owed money to their peers, like a farmer in hock. Why not? They'd made deals beyond their means, thinking it safe. And now people might not have water.

Servants returned with the tea. It came in the Yunoi style, served in the same large ceramic bowl the powder was whisked in. Yangchen stared at her drink, circling the green liquid around and around.

Teiin grew uncomfortable with her silence. "Avatar, perhaps we can delay the wells. The issue may solve itself, or perhaps there will be a—"

"Give me your hat," Yangchen said.

"I'm sorry?"

She looked up from her bowl. "I said, give me your hat."

Inspector Gu's brush stopped moving, a remarkable occurrence. Teiin glanced over his shoulder for another version of himself she might have been addressing. "Are you cold, Avatar? We could light a brazier."

The shangs behind him didn't dare make a sound. They kept their mouths shut out of confusion and fear.

"Master Teiin," Yangchen said, making sure she could be heard throughout the whole hall, "come up here, take off your hat, and give it to me."

*Do it or I will bring mutual ruin upon us all.* The silent declaration at the end of every sentence these days. Was the young Avatar mad enough to upset the delicate performance they'd crafted, over an item so trivial, to prove a point?

The chance couldn't be risked. Teiin pulled his cap off and shuffled forward, slowly, as if stuck in a greeting queue. "I meant no disrespect by covering my head in your presence—"

"Shh." Yangchen took the hat from him and put it in her lap before he could wring it between his bony hands and ruin the shape. Not done yet, she turned to Noehi. "Mistress. Remove your earrings. Give them to me. Now."

Noehi's hands went to the sides of her head. She snagged herself in her haste and winced. Once the jewelry was free, she brought it to the dais. On impulse, Yangchen drained her tea in one gulp and held out her bowl, still damp with dregs. Noehi hesitated before dropping the pearls into the vessel. They made a hollow clatter against the glazed surface, the sound of gambler's dice.

Yangchen rolled the pearls around, the twin spheres chasing each other like the koi of the Northern Spirit Oasis. In some ways, she was sitting for a portrait right now. Inspector Gu, and therefore the Earth King, and therefore the Four Nations, were watching.

So far, the message was clear. "You . . . would have us sell our possessions to cover the cost of the wells," Teiin said. *You're blackmailing us further.*

*I am.* Yangchen could leave it there, exerting her power without another word. She told herself behind drawn curtains and in empty rooms that she hated resorting to such measures. But how much could she claim to despise the rules of the game if she kept sitting down to play?

She jostled the pearls. They looked like the contents of a begging bowl, used to collect alms for survival. A useful poetic device.

"Wealth," she said, starting off slowly. "Assets. Baggage, burdens, sentiments, expectations. We cling to weights, afraid of being free." Yangchen shook the tea bowl the way one of her brothers or sisters might do in the streets of a town they'd never visited before, where they didn't have a local friend to rely on and a volunteer host was not forthcoming. A few shangs hesitatingly chuckled.

"It is always tempting to stand back and assume matters will sort themselves out," Yangchen said. "But I tell you now, there is no one left to wait for. It is we who must act."

An unprompted bout of selflessness from the shangs, in the magnitude she needed to pay for the wells, could tip off Gu that a suspicious deal was in motion. She needed to create a story that would cover her tracks and fit the image of a leader who appealed solely to people's better natures.

Yangchen reached over and took her staff that had waited patiently by the chair. Airbenders either crafted their own gliders or received them as gifts from treasured friends. Jetsun had made this one for her. Yangchen had complained about it being too big and unwieldy at first, but she'd grown into the length perfectly, as if her sister had been able to see her future.

She tossed the staff before her feet, purposely letting it clatter against the floor, a rough, uncouth sound. "I will sell my staff to help obtain the money we need," she said. "Surely it has some value as a relic."

Another gasp rippled through the room. Possessions of the Avatar belonged in the temples and shrines of the Four Nations, or at the very least in the treasure rooms of state palaces. Pawning her regalia was not supposed to be a thing Yangchen could do.

She saw the horror in Boma's eyes from all the way across the aisles. "Master Teiin, Mistress Noehi," Yangchen said. "You may have your belongings back. I cannot force you to join me."

*I am absolutely forcing you to join me.* Not only did the threat of the Firebenders remain, but like in Pai Sho, starting positions mattered. To refuse the Avatar would require action, snatching *back* the prizes from where they lay. What kind of monster would reach into the bowl of a pleading Air Nomad?

Yangchen's ungracious demands had happened moments ago, ancient and forgotten history. Teiin was quick to understand the dynamic. "There is a problem, Avatar," he said. He let his frown linger long enough so its transformation into a kindly, wrinkled smile could be noted by Gu. "You'll need more than my hat."

The old man was a good actor when he needed to be. He shrugged off his furs and laid them in a bundle next to

Yangchen's staff. Noehi followed, reaching at the back of her neck to undo the clasp of a pendant, but her elbow was bumped by another shang rushing forward with a purse heavy enough to bludgeon an ostrich-horse unconscious.

A wave of valuables piled in front of the dais as her audience found their giving spirits. Some of the merchants might not have grasped the significance of the ploy and were simply going along with the group. A few might have been genuinely moved. Yangchen spotted the servant who had brought her tea standing in the back, the girl's eyes shining as she bore witness to the Avatar's feat of inspiration.

Yangchen looked away before she made herself sick.

"Quite stirring back there," Inspector Gu said.

The pudgy, mild-faced man walked beside her down the hallway in private, as Zongdu Henshe had once done. This time she was the one bound to the city, the expert in its ways, and Gu was the visitor. "I don't think you'll have to suffer the loss for long though," he said. "I'm sure whoever ends up purchasing your staff will gift it back to you. The act would earn them much spiritual merit."

"No. I said I would go without it, and I mean to." Her whole message the first time she came to Bin-Er was that the powerful could make do with less. If she escaped through a loophole, the shangs would certainly follow.

And besides, the servant had seen her promise. She would tell her friends the story of an Avatar who'd laid down her wings for the good of the people, and from there the story would spread. Yangchen couldn't tarnish her own actions by flying over the denizens of the city like her word to them meant nothing.

Gu looked surprised she wasn't taking the easy route. "Won't that be inconvenient?"

"The purpose of life isn't *convenience!*"

Her voice rang out in the hallway with the vitriol of a teacher who'd been forced to repeat the same lesson over and over. But she'd never said those words to Gu before. The last time she'd railed against a life governed by expedience was to a person she thought was a friend. A true companion of the Avatar.

Yangchen rubbed her forehead with the back of her hand. The less she thought about Kavik and his role in creating this mire, the better.

"Apologies," she said to the inspector as they came to the exit on the side of the gathering hall rather than the main lawn. She tried to make her comings and goings as discreet as possible these days. "The demands of the city are many."

It was unclear how much Gu and the Earth King saw through Yangchen's lies to pass off the destruction in Bin-Er as the work of angry spirits, and therefore business best left to the Avatar. Recent memory helped her cause. She would never have guessed the disaster of Tienhaishi could have an upside.

Gu said something as she pushed her way through, with her hands this time, but his reply was drowned out by a crest of noise, the sudden release of tension like a loosed bowstring. The throng of voices struck them hard enough to make both the inspector and Yangchen flinch.

"*AVATAR! AVATAR!*"

Someone must have leaked that she was in town. Because a crowd, the biggest one she'd seen in Bin-Er yet, was waiting outside the building for a glimpse of the bridge between humans and spirits. Newcomers to the city mixed with old stalwarts, from across the Four Nations. A crop of uncovered heads, sprouting down the streets as far as she could see.

Yangchen blinked in the face of thunderous cheers. How long had they been there? She had been trapped by her duties in the gathering hall for the better part of yesterday. Had the towns-folk weathered the night cold just to catch sight of her leaving?

She raised her hand, slow and weak. *Please. Enough. I need to get through.*

The crowd took her gesture as a benediction. They surged in place, redoubling their voices for the woman who'd silenced the terrors in the sky those months ago. They wept joyously for the Air Nomad who'd lingered in the city and brought with her the boons of food and healing and care. *Avatar. Avatar. Avatar.*

"The city adores you a great deal," Inspector Gu shouted.

It was too late to rush back inside and go the other way. "This is . . . only a show of respect."

Gu did not look convinced, given they could barely hear each other. "I'm old enough to remember Avatar Szeto, and he was given plenty of respect. This is something else. Devotion, per-haps. Belief in Avatar Yangchen, who can cure all ills."

"Unwarranted."

As an official informant for the Earth King, observations were the jewels Gu provided his master. To get the best product, he'd prod at her discomfort. "Maybe not as much as you think. You've quelled the spiritual unrest over the skies, improved the lot of the commonfolk, and increased business in Bin-Er by a third," he said, as if two of those feats hadn't been frantic reac-tions to circumstance. "I don't know how you can sustain so many victories."

The roars crested. Yangchen could have confessed out loud and he would never have known. *I can't, Inspector,* she wanted to say. *My secret is that I can't.*

The money, the peace, the Firebenders hidden away deep in the mountains. Her successes were based off lies. Bin-Er was growing too fast for her to manage, its problems deferred, not solved. Sooner or later, she would be found out for a fraud, and this would all come crashing down.

Gu yelled something about staying behind and went back inside. Yangchen tried forging ahead, hoping to pierce the front lines, that the army arrayed before her might concede enough space for a getaway. But the crowd showed no signs of parting and grew only more frenzied as she approached. They were going to have their moment with the Avatar.

Yangchen did her best to put on a smile and pretend she wasn't trapped.

# AMONG FRIENDS

**EVENINGS TURNED** the bright walls and spirit-faced columns of Chief Oyaluk's feast hall a shadowed blue, the color of deep ice and marine caverns. Across the square, curtains of falling water shimmered like silken banners, backing a great fountain of ice that neither melted from the flow nor froze along its ridges. The temperature in perfect balance.

Yangchen never felt chilled in this place, not in the handful of times she'd visited. Oyaluk had been the only Chief of the Northern Water Tribe in her era, and she remembered his kindness when she was a young girl hiding behind Abbess Dagmola's robes, the Northern capital one of the first stops along the new Avatar's introduction tour across the world.

But the years marched on. As Yangchen assumed more responsibilities, the purposes of her visits had shifted away from mere goodwill. It was easy for the leaders of the world to smile at a child who asked for nothing.

She and Chief Oyaluk sat at the high table a few feet apart from each other. From her place of honor, Yangchen could sense the tension in Oyaluk's broad shoulders. She'd already rebuffed his attempt to talk during the feast. *After the tables are cleared and we're alone,* was her condition.

Until then, they stared straight ahead, nothing amiss in their expressions, and watched a solo performance from the Grand Master of Agna Qel'a. Sifu Akoak was young for his title, brash enough to risk weaving torrents of water between his elders seated down the sides of the square, demanding their stillness lest they be splashed. When the stream reached Yangchen, there was a murmur of concern, but she let the water play over her shoulders and added a sparkling twirl before sending the liquid on its way. An Air Nomad's good humor.

Sifu Akoak took his bows. Oyaluk stood and gave a speech of thanks to the spirits for their many blessings. His council members, for whom the Avatar was a familiar enough sight, were free to turn in for the night. The chief tilted his head at his guest of honor, a wag of his gray beard, as if to ask *Now?*

Yangchen gestured at the remnants of the feast. *Tables. Cleared.*

Oyaluk sighed. They waited still, for the elders of the North to file out and for attendants to take away every last plate and cup. The last to leave were the Thin Claws, the chief's personal retainers, stationed in the corners, girdled in ivory armor. Pride required them to obey Oyaluk's command for privacy with the Avatar slowly, grudgingly.

With only two people remaining in the vast dining area, the seating furs gone, the drums packed up, the hard ice surface resembled a competition ground. A time and place of Yangchen's choosing. "Now?" Oyaluk asked again, exasperated.

Almost. She bade the chief follow her to the center of the square, where she began to walk the circle, the basic exercise of airbending, one palm out farther than the other. Oyaluk glanced around them as he kept pace. A breeze followed her motions, sweeping the edges of the floor, taking the same path over the tables as Akoak's water. As she walked, the wind sped up until it overtook her to become a controlled cyclone. Had any debris remained, it would have been whipped dangerously across the ice.

Yangchen came to a halt, the vortex self-sustaining with minimal effort now. Inside the eye it was calm, but the surrounding winds rushed fast enough to form a barrier of noise. It would be impossible for anyone to eavesdrop on her and the chief.

Pak and Pik, who had behaved themselves throughout the dinner, surfed the currents of air with outspread wings, chasing each other in an endless loop. "You know I have secure rooms," Oyaluk said.

Rooms had walls, and walls hid people behind them. Sometimes in them. "I'm being more careful these days."

The chief shook his head. "I remember when you used to run after my nieces and nephews through the palace like that," he said, gesturing at the lemurs playing above them. "And now you're an Avatar as shrewd as any." He examined his hands, front and back, as if looking for evidence of the days gone by. "I was hoping that when you came into your power, you'd be fairer in your attentions. Not another Szeto."

She knew the accusation was coming, but it still stung. "I am not biased. I don't favor a nation."

"I know of your successes in Bin-Er and how much time you've been spending there. Earth King Feishan is skittish, unstable, and power-hungry. He is not the kind of person who should sit a throne. And yet you seem dedicated to strengthening his position. You're making him *money*."

Guilty. But not the only party. "I am catching knives that you and Fire Lord Gonryu dropped," Yangchen said. *Or rather hurled.* "Have you forgotten the two of you caused the Platinum Affair in the first place?"

The edges of his mouth drooped. "An act I regret every day."

As far as Yangchen was concerned, Chief Oyaluk owed her more than a pained grimace. He and the Fire Lord had meddled in matters outside their borders by backing General Nong's attempted rebellion against Earth King Feishan. They'd done it in *her* era, during the window of vulnerability when the Avatar was too young to have an impact on world affairs. Perhaps Oyaluk had made the decision while he watched the little visiting Air Nomad play with his family in the palace.

Yangchen knew Oyaluk was a reasonable man, a competent leader, decent at his core. Presumably Nong shared some of those traits and would have made a good Earth King, a founder of a new dynastic line of peace. But who could say for sure? Nong's body lay trampled into the dust at Llama-paca's Crossing, the site of his defeat in battle at the hands of Earth King Feishan the Skittish and Unstable.

Once evidence came to light that Nong had had official support for his failed revolt, relations between the Earth Kingdom, Fire Nation, and Water Tribe froze as cold as the heart of an iceberg. They would never recover, not without a continent-sized effort.

"Trading Feishan for Nong seemed brilliant at the time." The chief at least was contrite over his blunder. "Dare I say it was a move in the nature of your predecessor. Avatar Szeto manipulated the downfall of corrupt officials and the promotion of their better replacements as a matter of course."

*Salai's shoes.* The Earth King was not a provincial tax collector and none of them were Avatar Szeto. "It is entirely possible to outsmart yourself, you know. I've done so in many a lifetime." Oyaluk didn't know about her "gift" in full detail, but he knew she'd studied the written records of Avatars past. She and the chief were both well-versed in the history of mistakes and personal flaws linked to their offices.

"It wasn't even my idea to begin with," he confessed. She could tell he needed this moment of candor with someone who understood the weight he bore, leader to leader. Neither of them would ever make such admissions or excuses in public. "My most senior advisors informed me over a game of Pai Sho that Fire Lord Gonryu was inclined to throw his influence behind Nong and convinced me to do the same. They believed the two of us acting in concert would guarantee the plan's success. My representatives brokered the deal with Gonryu's behind the curtains."

"Over a . . . over a game of . . ." Yangchen clamped a lid over the fury boiling inside her until it reduced to a single grunt for the ages. *"Hmm."*

Oyaluk's story was remarkably similar to the one Fire Lord Gonryu had told her, also in confidence. Which meant neither head of state had come up with the plan to topple the Earth King. The folly had been cooked up by nameless men and women with contacts spanning the borders of the Four Nations. Figures in the background who thought grand strategy could be reduced to tile positions and numbers and who would probably never face accountability for being mistaken.

None of the lives Yangchen had lived could help her express the sheer frustration writhing in her stomach. The origins of the Platinum Affair had the finger smudges of the White Lotus all over it. This was exactly why she didn't trust the organization. Puppet masters who fumbled the strings didn't deserve applause for a worthy performance.

*What's done is done.* She had to move forward with the reason she'd come to the Northern Water Tribe, no matter how many Pai Sho boards she wanted to break over her knee right now. "There is a way for you to make amends," she said to Oyaluk. "At the upcoming convocation in Taku."

By the terms laid out in their charters, the zongdus of each trade city met every year to discuss business. Yangchen would represent Bin-Er in Zongdu Henshe's . . . conspicuous absence. But more importantly, the Earth King, Water Tribe Chief, and Fire Lord would arrive at the end of the weeklong conference to stamp their official seals on terms of renewal. Such convocations had been the only chance for face-to-face diplomacy between the leaders of the Four Nations since Yangchen had come of age.

"Those conferences are formalities," Oyaluk said. "During the last one, Feishan could barely stand to be in the same room as me. After completing his portions of the contracts, he knocked over the inkpots so my boots would stain."

"That was then. Like you said, he's been benefiting from my good work these days. He's richer. Happier. Now is the perfect time for an overture. Reach out to him in Taku and put up signs of good faith."

"End the Platinum Affair, you mean," Oyaluk said softly, as if remembering a lost dream. "Return the world to normal."

Yangchen nodded. Restoring open relations between the Earth Kingdom, Water Tribe, and Fire Nation would eliminate the need for shangs and zongdus and the many injustices that followed in their wake.

She'd come to realize the shang system was only a symptom of the underlying disease, a scab on the wound splitting each country from the others. Yangchen would stitch the oozing flesh back together with her bare hands if she had to. "We don't have to leave our mistakes uncorrected," she said. "We don't have to accept the ills of the world simply because they've lasted. Give me your support, and together we will make it so the Four Nations no longer have to hate and fear each other."

The task was large, monumental, but if Yangchen succeeded, the source of a deep and abiding suffering would fade from the world. *I could pass into the history books as an adequate Avatar,* she thought. *I could face my reincarnations without shame.*

In the long pause that followed, the trickling of water grew louder. Oyaluk made a little sweep with his fingers, asking for a refresh of the winds keeping their conversation a secret. After Yangchen obliged, he stood up straighter. The posture of a decision made.

"It won't work," he said. "You'll never get Feishan to swallow his pride. And he's not happier. If he claims to be in your meetings with him, he's lying. The Earth King wants retribution, not peace."

Yangchen wondered whose pride was the issue here. "You are speaking without basis."

Oyaluk debated with himself for a moment, as if deciding how much to reveal to her. "My advisors tell me that in the last few weeks, Feishan has been extremely agitated by a new piece of intelligence he's gained. Against all reason, he now believes the Fire Lord and I are responsible for the destruction in Bin-Er. As if we deployed some kind of weapon against him."

Later, Yangchen might look back on this moment as the greatest acting job she'd ever pulled off. She had only an instant to fight the thudding of her heart and cobble together a facial expression. Lips pursed just so, squint not too deep, voice, pause. The speed at which she responded was as important as the strength.

"Hah." No one would know how much work went into that scoff. "I don't see how you managed to anger the spirits over the city from an ocean away."

Part of the difficulty was remembering her own lies. Concocted events were like a vision she had to force herself into having, unlike the ones that grabbed her so easily in her sleep. "The Earth King's neglect of Bin-Er caused the sky fires to blossom.

They've stopped since I took over." The more she repeated the fake story, the deeper its roots would take hold. She hoped.

"It doesn't matter if Feishan is right or wrong about the cause," Oyaluk said. "What matters is he's moving troops and reportedly muttering about revenge as he stalks the halls of his palace. My Thin Claws have confirmed the former. One can hide their intentions in front of a seventeen-year-old Air Nomad who believes the best in people, but they can't hide thousands of men marching down a road."

Yangchen wanted to scream loud enough to disperse the whirlwind. The simplest explanation for Feishan's surge in aggression was that someone had leaked the truth about Unanimity to him.

The White Lotus knew about the existence of the Firebenders. More likely than not, one of them had betrayed their ranks. The secret society was supposed to be nationless, but it was made up of human beings with pasts and loyalties and ties of their own. Maybe the secret had been sold for money. As far as she knew, the organization didn't pay its members anything.

Worst of all, *she* was the reason why the White Lotus had such a complete picture of Unanimity. She was glad she'd kept the fate of the Firebenders hidden from them. *I never should have asked Mama Ayunerak for help in Port Tuugaq. I never should have asked* anyone *for help.*

"I have to respond," Oyaluk said. "I have to mobilize my own armies. If hostilities break out, the advantage will go to the side who strikes first, and the Water Tribe must be ready."

"Ready for what? Their chief to plunge them into a senseless conflict?"

"We're not Air Nomads, Avatar!" Oyaluk snapped. "Lest you forget, we can't all fly away at the first sign of trouble with our nobility intact! The rest of us have to survive down here on the ground!"

He wagged his jaw side to side and lowered his voice again. "I have to buy my generals as much time as possible by attending the convocation with a smile, lest I tip off Feishan. It's never pleasant to sit down with an enemy under false pretenses."

She knew the feeling well. Yangchen's words came out like they were fighting through mud. "You are racing toward a war you don't want . . . predicated on information you know to be false . . . while acting like nothing out of the ordinary is happening in the meantime." Her slowness wasn't born of disbelief. It was because she'd seen these exact events play out too many times to count.

"It's the only rational course of action. I know Fire Lord Gonryu must have rejected your proposal as well. Not out of any secret communication between us, but because he thinks the same way I do."

"Fearfully."

"Realistically. I wish the circumstances were different, Avatar. But they're not."

Out of deference he waited for her to end the discussion. The winds died down without her continued effort and the two of them became part of the outside world once more. Yangchen had come to Oyaluk's table with nothing to offer but the path to a better future. How poor a gift she'd brought her host.

She was tired and hollowed in a way she'd rarely been since her battle with Old Iron. It took so much work to raise the beam an inch. So slight a breeze to knock it crashing down.

"I'd appreciate privacy for the rest of my stay," she said, her voice raspy with defeat. "Thank you for hosting me. And for . . . hearing me out."

"Of course, Avatar." He sounded genuinely sorry. The most she could extract from him. "You will always be welcome in my hall."

Her exit was heralded by the babbling of water, the falling streams suddenly loud and penetrating. When she was halfway across the floor, the chief cleared his throat. She turned around.

Distance obscured Oyaluk's features. His shape against the night sky blotted out the stars behind him, leaving a gap of head and shoulders. He looked alone. Terribly alone. She knew he had the exact same view of her.

"My cousin Akuudan," the chief said. "Is he well?"

"He is." Akuudan had been one of the quartermasters guarding the funds the Water Tribe Chief and Fire Lord sent to General Nong. After he'd been captured by the Earth King's armies in the decisive battle, Yangchen had been the one to free him, not Oyaluk.

"He knows I couldn't get involved," Oyaluk said. "Had our link been discovered, he would have become too valuable a hostage. He would have become leverage. He knows this, right?"

Underneath, he was asking if Akuudan had forgiven him for making the choice of a ruler instead of a family member. Yangchen couldn't speak for her friend.

"You did the rational thing," she said. She turned again and walked away.

# THE SPIRIT OASIS

**BUSINESS OVER FAMILY** was a balancing act Yangchen knew well. She'd planned her North Pole visit so she could attend to both. Maybe she should have swapped the order. Prioritizing matters of state hadn't helped her with Oyaluk.

The search for her sister had brought Yangchen back to the Spirit Oasis, a tiered puzzle box. Water inside land inside water inside ice, behind an unassuming wooden door. The cove, cut into the depths of Agna Qel'a, had been created without the touch of human hands, possibly by Tui and La, the Moon and Ocean Spirits. Yangchen had better cause to believe the story than most.

As she crossed one of the arched bridges to the small green island at the center of the oasis, she was bathed in warmth. Underneath her feet, the waters were still and reflectionless, and her steps drummed against the planks louder than she wanted them to, announcing her presence.

She could smell the ever-ripe satsuma, the always-blooming osmanthus, the lush vegetation nurtured and kept at the peak of vitality by the energies of the oasis, heedless of the season and temperature outside. It was a good thing she hadn't brought Pik and Pak. They would have gorged on the fruits until the sacred site was barren.

The pool at the heart of the North was not a perfect circle. One lip bowed inward as if Tui and La knew people, with their needs and desires and weaknesses, would come to the edge of the water in search of guidance. The spirits had granted human beings a nice place to sit. Yangchen knelt down on the grass and pulled her legs under her into the lotus position.

The eternal koi swam in an endless loop before her, their wake lapping against the sides of their pond, their entire universe. Yangchen had drunk the customary tea brewed from leaves plucked from one of the bushes of the oasis itself, and borrowed vigor coursed through her veins.

She had to be present, vigilant. The Spirit Oasis was a place of ultimate peace. It could easily become a place of unspeakable danger.

Her knuckles met in her lap, touching arrow point to arrow point. *A fist opens or closes. It cannot do both at once.*

She had meditated to search for Jetsun in the Spirit World before, many times, always slipping through the veil with ease. She would relax, close her eyes, and then open them to the sourceless light, find herself standing in a verdant field or a welcoming forest. Spirits, silent and chattery, would greet her, great mute trees bowing solemnly at the trunk until their canopies brushed the ground, toadstools singing in five-tone harmony. A bestiary might gather, animal-shaped spirits flocking to Yangchen out of inquisitiveness, hoofed and winged creatures taking turns to nuzzle her outstretched hand.

The spirits who could and would talk required the most caution. Yangchen had thought about why they could be so unsettling, why so much judgment lay behind their eyes when they had eyes. Jetsun had given her the answer, long ago. Spirits rarely asked questions or struggled with discontent. They simply existed.

Which meant in any encounter, you were always the one bothering them. The fault had already been decided. Humans were intruders by nature.

This would be the first time she meditated at the Spirit Oasis using the clue the phoenix-eels of Ma'inka had dangled before her, the vision they'd tormented her with. *The fog. I need to find the fog.* Sometimes a traveler could cross over to a known location in the Spirit World if their determination and focus were sufficient. *Picture the fog.*

The skin on the back of her palms tightened, distending the arrows tattooed there. She couldn't shake the frustrations of the day. Business first had been the wrong decision.

Oyaluk's rejection of peace was a story immemorial. The Four Nations were always trying their level best to march off a cliff. And here she was, the latest Avatar attempting to drag them back from the edge. None of her past lives had succeeded in curbing the self-destructive nature of humanity.

*If a child given every comfort won't stop screaming, leave it in the field.*

Over her closed eyes, Yangchen's brow pinched. The strange, uncharitable koan bounced around her head, a flapping bird in search of the cage's exit. She wondered who let it in.

Then she remembered. It was a lesson from the pamphlet of Guru Shoken. The ancient philosopher whose works she'd been introduced to by Zongdu Chaisee of all people.

She made a little sound with her nose, ruffling the quiet of the oasis. Maybe Shoken was right. Maybe the world, blithely dancing along the precipice, needed to know what it was like to fall.

The common misconception about meditation was that you were supposed to completely erase the slate of your mind. Untrue. Thoughts were allowed to come and go. The duty of the meditator was to observe them until they passed, proving you and your mind's chatter were not one and the same.

But this idea, humanity being left to reap exactly what it sowed, stuck with Yangchen like a burr clinging to her robes. It lingered too long without her being able to sequester it.

She was still savoring the taste of vindictiveness when the physical realm tilted backward on its axis and the Spirit World swallowed her whole.

Yangchen tumbled along a patch of unknown ground, flailing without grace, her upturned robes trapping her limbs. An entrance this ungainly meant her body had passed through the boundary and not just her spirit.

She found her feet like an Earthbender: sensing the plane of ground and then lowering her center below her axis as soon as her feet touched down. Her roll turned into a skid into a crouch. She stood up and arranged her shawl back into place with one hand, on her guard.

She wasn't in the cheery meadows that had foiled her search so many times in the past. Nothing grew on the loose, rocky soil as far as the eye could see. The sky was the color of an angry sunset, a harsh, overdyed orange.

*Well, this is different.* Maybe the ugliness of her thoughts as she made the crossing had affected where she'd landed. She tried to take a step forward but sensed a tug on her leg like it was a lodestone needle. A nudge that threatened to become stronger.

Fight the unseen forces or follow them. For now, Yangchen chose the path of least resistance. She hiked in the direction she was allowed and soon found herself descending a gradual slope.

A sheet of white mist appeared around her ankles. When a shadow loomed over her path, she looked up and saw massive talons of stone curling in on her, each one a predator's claw the size of an Air Temple tower.

*The hand closes.* Jetsun, wrapped in gauzy vapor. Yangchen's own nightmares had laid out the carpet for her. She was on the right track.

The shawl around her shoulders felt heavier as she walked downhill, the scratchiness of her robes rubbing her knees raw. Her clothes were damp. From the mist, her own fear-sweat, both. The fog rose higher than her head.

Yangchen nearly ran smack into a sheer rock wall and, after feeling which way it twisted, came to realize she was entering the mouth of a canyon. *Never mind hands, what does a mouth do?* She fumbled along the wall for guidance, as if the rules of common sense still applied and she were navigating a simple maze. The other side could close on her faster than expected and wedge her into a trap. *It attaches to a throat. It consumes.*

Instead of slowing down she began to shuffle through the mist faster, switched to a light brush of her fingertips against the rock so she could jog. Not showing enough courage in the Spirit World was how she lost Jetsun. Suffering from the same mistake was inexcusable. Shoken would have agreed.

An outline of solidness flickered off to the side and she abandoned the canyon wall in pursuit. The mists were uneven and dotted with thinner pockets that wandered like floating strands in the eye. There the figure went again, meandering in the opposite direction.

Yangchen decided to take the risk and inhaled deeply. "Jetsun?" she called out.

The echo that came back did not belong to her.

Dozens and dozens of unfamiliar voices assaulted her ears. They could have come from the nuns of the Western Temple themselves and Yangchen still wouldn't have been able to recognize them through the sheer anguish twisting each one beyond the limits of what a human could produce. Inside the depths of the fog, people were being tortured to their wit's end.

The chorus of pain. She'd heard it before, when the phoenix-eels of Ma'inka had shown her a vision of Jetsun. Her sister's spirit was trapped in here somewhere. She was certain of it.

Yangchen immediately stepped forward, the balls of her feet digging into the ground as she spun full circle and scythed a blast of wind through the canyon. The white vapors parted, but nowhere near as much as they should have. The scant space she managed to clear was dotted with humans, silently stooped over by invisible yokes or with their heads thrown back in full-throated screams.

She ran to the nearest person, a man wearing strange, ornate nightclothes drenched in blood. As she checked him for injuries, he shook with glottal hiccups, choking on air. His braided queue frayed halfway down its length like severed rope.

Yangchen patted him down for wounds, focusing on his hands where the stains were deepest. "Tell me where you're hurt," she said. It occurred to her why his garments had struck her as odd. They'd gone out of fashion two hundred years ago.

He murmured, more gulping noises than words. "I didn't hear you," Yangchen said. She was on the verge of jamming her fingers into his mouth to check he hadn't swallowed his tongue.

"*I'm sorry!*" the man suddenly shrieked. "I'm so sorry! I didn't mean to!"

A child's apology after breaking something important. Yangchen let go of the man and slowly backed away. He wasn't injured. The blood soaking his sleeves wasn't his.

She bumped into someone behind her and wheeled around. A woman in plain farmer's garb stared at Yangchen, eyes wild with disbelief. "Nothing," she moaned. "It was all for nothing. Why did we— For *nothing*? How could we be such *fools?*"

The woman latched on to Yangchen, gripping her shoulders with the strength of an animal's bite. Yangchen wrenched free, nearly strangling herself with her collar. She tried to run back the way she came but at every turn was hemmed in by people from eras by and gone, shambling toward her, hobbled by their pain.

She could make out what they were saying clearly now. Cries of helplessness snagged at her like thorns. Hands reached for her as she fled.

*You can't deny me this! Not after everything I've done for you!*

*I lost him. He was right there and I lost him.*

*I will get what I'm owed! Do you hear me?*

*That was my last chance. That was my last chance. That was my last chance . . .*

The fog no longer granted her passage. It tugged at her face like matted cobwebs, bogged down her ankles like beach mud. Her exposed skin felt swollen and itchy. Instinct told her the vapor was squeezing through her pores and working its way under her fingernails. The fog was alive. It was trying to become a part of her.

Yangchen covered her nose and mouth and ran without breathing. But she could get only so far before her vision swam, threatening to plunge her into a dark sea. She keeled over into a crawl and dragged her body as far as she could. Her physical form had become a liability.

She always had to try to outdo Jetsun, didn't she? She'd lose both halves of herself instead of the one. She might laugh were she not trying to keep the fog out of her airways. By now she was sure it was a spirit, malign and hungering.

None of her predecessors had gone out quite like this, or else their memories would have bubbled to the surface. Avatar Yangchen shunned all fears, but she wasn't immune to the squeeze of shame and humiliation on the guts, the drumming of an out-of-control heart. Before she blacked out, she put aside her misgivings and begged for help from the people who had been sources of only pain and grief in her life.

*Save me,* she called out to her past lives through the Avatar State. *Please.*

# PREVIOUSLY

**˙ADMIT IT,˙** Kavik said as he drew water from the stacks of damp linen towels arrayed before him, bundling the moisture into a wobbling sphere. "This whole secret society recruitment pitch was just a way to get me to do your laundry."

"I can find better launderers in this city than you," Mama Ayunerak said. "I can also find more promising recruits for that matter." She flicked her wrist at a nearby barrel and sent twice as much water as he was bending over the towels, soaking them through once more. "Again. Drier. Add it to what you have."

Several of the neat piles fell over under the force of Ayunerak's waterbending but there was no point in complaining. The rule not to move the cloth at all applied to him, not her. So did the demand for speed. And thoroughness. And minimal motion.

Above his head came the footfalls of visitors to Gidu Shrine, residents of Bin-Er paying their respects to ancestors and spirits. He could hear thumps when they dropped to their knees to bow and could make out the faint claps of hands coming together before smoking incense. The existence of a secret basement had been a complete surprise when Ayunerak showed him his new home where he'd wait out the heat. The one time he'd run an errand inside the shrine, he'd broken in through the roof.

"Stop making that face," Ayunerak said. "You know this exercise could mean life and death."

She'd explained many times. Operatives of the White Lotus, and really any clandestine organization, needed to move without a trace. A Waterbender in a city not covered in ice and snow like Bin-Er would be forced to dry their surroundings after using their element if they wanted to keep their presence hidden. He'd kept himself from freezing to death once in the Blue Manse by bending water off his body but hadn't thought much about where it had landed.

"Do Earthbenders have to repack the dirt they use?" Kavik had asked. "Are Firebenders just plain out of luck if they burn something they can't hide?"

"Yes," Ayunerak answered without a sliver of humor. "We've lost people that way."

He believed her. Kavik had disposed of bodies in Jonduri and watched a man get murdered in front of his eyes. He'd do whatever it took to keep from getting stuffed into a packing crate or fed to shark-squids. He dried away. Dried his heart out. Dried like the wind.

"When I say *don't make that face,* I mean it," Ayunerak snapped. "You may have to bend under watch without being noticed and you don't want to give away signals. The little thing you do with your lips is getting worse."

Kavik didn't know he did a little thing with his lips, but he clamped them shut anyway and concentrated. Ayunerak was a tough sifu, but she was also the only support he had left in Bin-Er these days. His parents had been given passes to return home to Long Stretch in the North, where they remained safe and oblivious to the real business of either of their sons. As far as they were concerned, Kavik was still doing Avatar work. Not hiding in a White Lotus safe house until the authorities of the Four Nations lost his scent.

Under different circumstances, being tapped to join Ayunerak's friends would have been thrilling. An ancient society operating in the shadows, dedicated to philosophy, beauty, and truth? The chance to pull strings outside the confines of national loyalties to maintain peace across the world? Maybe Bin-Er hadn't been a force of corruption in his life, he'd allowed himself to imagine. The city had put him through so many travails to give him the skills necessary to serve a higher cause.

But it quickly became clear the White Lotus protected itself by walling off its branches from each other, keeping the right hand separated from the left. Kavik was the pinky nail, a new growth that could be trimmed as easily as kept. If the safe house was the port of call toward adventure, Kavik was stuck on the loading docks. He guessed Ayunerak was still arguing over his admission with her peers.

"The entire job is about waiting," she had said in a rare moment of sympathy. "In that sense it's no different than the petty errands you used to run for the shangs."

In the meantime, he trained next to empty planting pots, piles of desiccated bulbs, maintenance tools that hadn't had the rust knocked off them since before the Platinum Affair. Other goods with long shots of becoming useful one day. He left the safe house only under close supervision and had narrowly managed to avoid clawing his eyes out in fits of boredom-induced madness. The mildew smell barely registered anymore.

Kavik heard a particular pattern of thumps from the floor above. He paused in his task, recognizing the gait and who it belonged to. His fingers crooked, ready for a fight.

As soon as he saw the pair of feet at the top of the stairs, he launched the water he'd pulled from the towels, freezing the intruder's soles to the wooden planks. Lesson one of Ayunerak's combat training. *Hit first, preferably before the enemy even marks you as the enemy.* Do, the Firebender who ran the cook staff, pitched forward so violently he fell out of his boots, cursing Kavik's name on the way down.

Ayunerak reacted with blinding speed. She unfroze the very water Kavik had used—*lesson two, bend what your opponent is bending when you have no other choice*—and swept it in a lap around the room. She caught the laundry in a web of water—*lesson three, move your surroundings with your element when you don't have enough of your element*—and shoved it into a heap at the bottom of the stairs. Do landed in the cloth, unharmed.

He sprang to his feet and whipped a damp rag off his chubby face. "You nearly broke my ankles, you dunderhead!"

Kavik shrugged at him. Do, perhaps because he was about ten years older, had thought it fine to put a fire dagger to Kavik's throat the last time they sparred, close enough to leave a line of blisters. A little payback was in order.

Ayunerak made a *shut it* gesture at Kavik even though he hadn't spoken yet. "Why are you here?" she asked Do. The junior Lotus was supposed to visit only once every three days. Something must have been wrong.

He beckoned his superior closer and whispered in her ear. Ayunerak listened, her face set in stone. She didn't take any time to respond once Do had finished relaying the lengthy message. "Tell them I'll handle it," she said.

Kavik burned with questions. Who was *them*? Were they more powerful than Mama Ayunerak? How high on the rungs of ordinary society did the Order of the White Lotus reach? What was *it*?

Ayunerak gave Do a head shake toward the upper floor, indicating he should leave. The younger Lotus balked when he realized his superior's plans would not involve him, and he gave Kavik an incredulous scowl as he tugged his boots back on. Kavik couldn't resist giving him a wave bye-bye as he left.

The smugness was only for show; there was no guarantee Ayunerak would privilege him with any information. "What was that about?" he asked, tentatively.

She gave him a look from head to toe, as if she were comparing his growth to a chart. He didn't know how much he could have changed, planted below the surface of the earth. "I'm taking you home," she said.

*Home.* The Northern Water Tribe. "Is the heat off?"

"It most definitely is not."

One thing was clear—Ayunerak had sway. The brambles of the Bin-Er pass control office fell before the sharpness of her whispers, and the two of them were on a ship to Agna Qel'a the very next morning. Not once, from the march past the harbormaster's office to the nervous wait on the misty docks to the boarding of the sleek clipper, were they asked for names, fake or otherwise.

It hadn't been this easy for the Avatar. She'd been forced to sneak Kavik to the Northern Air Temple as a staging point just to get him across the waters. The discomforting thought of how much Yangchen had to do with so little made him seek the railing of the ship to feel the wind and icy spray in his face.

"You'd better get your stomach back for open water, and quick," Ayunerak said when she found him leaning as close as he could toward their destination. She thought he was seasick. "We're entering bubble-style, like I taught you."

In the hold was an umiak, open-topped and spacious enough to carry multiple people. When the clipper reached the drop-off point, still out of sight from shore, the crew lowered the boat into the water with Kavik and Ayunerak inside. The two of them shoved off with bending alone, no paddles. Speed would be more important than endurance.

The umiak slid over the waves without a sound. Up ahead, a raised promontory of ice stood guard over the coast. The natural tower was a watch post they'd have to sneak by.

Ayunerak was already in position, riding in a crouch, her arms gripping the sides. Kavik did the same, getting as low as possible. "Ready," he muttered.

Momentum carried them forward while she counted down quietly until the right moment. "Roll," Ayunerak commanded.

Together they leaned sharply to the side, yanking on the starboard edge, unbalancing the craft. The bottom of the umiak rose up and closed over them like a giant snapper-scallop protecting its pearl. Kavik hung on tight to his seat.

Ayunerak did the same, only she had the harder task while they capsized. She hauled the prow deeper into the sea using her weight and bent a pocket into the water around them with her free hand. The entire hull dipped below the surface and trapped the breathable air. They hung upside down in a little cocoon of her making.

"Get lower," Ayunerak said over her shoulder, her voice strained. "And get us back up to speed."

Blood was already rushing to Kavik's head. Lower relative to the boat, she meant. He flattened away from the delicate barrier protecting them from an entire icy ocean and pushed the umiak along in a series of one-armed thrusts.

They traveled inverted below the watch post, gliding across a mirror world hidden from view, their sky dark and deadly. Nothing under them but a fall into the clouds. Kavik's shoulders burned and the lashings he held on to cut into his fingers until they were numb. Their silence could have fooled another passenger into thinking the trick of stealth effortless, when in reality they were trying with all their might not to die.

Ayunerak lost her grip for a moment. The air bubble calved; Kavik caught a face full of seawater and hacked burning salt out of his throat as he leaned farther back in the hull. The ice wall loomed ahead, a ghostly blue stripe painted across the inky water, and he thought he spotted the entrance to the secret tunnel they were aiming for. A hole shaped like a jagged crocus.

But Ayunerak's muscles were shaking under her parka. They had to get there, now. Kavik grabbed the sides of the vessel with both arms and kicked ferociously, bending with his feet, an act less common for their style. The water behind them formed a sideways spout and propelled them forward. He'd seen the Avatar do this maneuver straight into the sky with her native element.

They regained their lost speed and then some. More air sheared away, leaving them with nothing to talk through. The last thing Kavik heard from Ayunerak was a garbled *"Up! OUR up!"* but he had no control or vision right now. He had to trust the senior Lotus would land them on target.

He heard the snap of a thin ice crust giving way and suddenly the umiak lurched out of his grasp. He slid along a frozen ramp that twisted and turned like an intestinal tract before landing on an open patch of hardpack, ocean water puddling around him.

They were in a cavern in the ice wall, lit by oil lamps. The boat lay off to the side, the hull shredded. Kavik looked up to see a young woman with a long braid rushing over to them, her hands already covered in water like a medic. "You dolt!" she cried at Kavik. "You could have killed the Executor!"

"No," Ayunerak said. She sat upright and cricked her back. "He made the right call. We would have been caught had he not acted quickly." She gave Kavik a nod approaching respect.

A rare gift. "This wasn't the first time I've had to rush an entry." Kavik sorted away the fact that in her distress, their contact had let slip Ayunerak's title within the White Lotus. He'd figure out where *Executor* fell in the organization later. "I'm okay too, by the way."

The young woman scowled and hunched closer to her superior, as if she could section off Kavik with her shoulder. "Our friend . . ."

Ayunerak rolled back the spilled seawater and used it to close the tunnel behind them. "You can say 'the Avatar,' Ivalu. We're with inside company. Did her meeting with the chief take place?"

"Yes but"—Ivalu glanced one more time at Kavik before continuing—"we lost sight of her a day ago."

"Is she not in Agna Qel'a anymore?" Ayunerak remained measured, but by force. She preemptively gestured for calm from everyone in the cave. "She made it past our watchers?"

"I don't believe so," Ivalu said, though she didn't sound completely sure. "Her bison and lemurs are still here, and she didn't come with a glider."

Something about the statement didn't make sense to Kavik. "Hold on," he said. "How do you know where her lemurs are?" Pik and Pak were tiny flying horrors. They came and went as they pleased and could disappear into the skies. They could hide in crevices and attack unseen from any angle.

"They're hovering around the back court of the chief's temple, just yowling and scratching at the ice," Ivalu said. "They haven't moved since—"

"Since a day ago?" Ayunerak's stare was an accusation. "You do know where that wall leads, right?"

"We're not fools; we checked to see if she was meditating at the oasis," Ivalu said. "She's not there."

Kavik still couldn't let the twinge in his gut pass. They had to have been talking about the Spirit Oasis. Children in the Water Tribe grew up listening to stories about the cove's warmth and wonder and beauty. Some of those tales, however, were cautionary. The rash child who wandered in without respect was always taught a lesson.

Kavik once had his own brush with perhaps-spirits. Years ago, after he and his brother, Kalyaan, got lost in a great blizzard, only surviving by the skin of their teeth, they'd told their parents afterward the route they were sure they'd trekked through. His parents had the same reaction as Ivalu. *But we checked that path on that day. The weather was clear. We couldn't find you . . .*

"Her body," Kavik said. "You mean her *body's* not there."

The lamplight flickered. Ayunerak's shout echoed through the cave. "We have to go! Now!"

Kavik had been to the capital of the Northern Water Tribe a few times as a child, for the New Moon festivals. The towers of Agna Qel'a had been and still were taller than any Middler building he'd ever laid eyes on. During daytime celebrations, sunlight would bounce off the fish-scale roofs and faceted walls like a shower of jewels. Artisans shaped entire blocks to honor the places where they were born, their elders, their legends, carving and freezing stories into the walls, delighting the citizens with the malleability of water.

Now, as he and Ayunerak and Ivalu raced through the streets under the faint moonlight, the multistory residences, blanked by shadow, seemed to lean in over him, giants paying a keen, unsettling interest in the bugs at their feet. *Would they make it in time? Could they scuttle fast enough?*

Ayunerak led them through alleyed twists and bends with the main streets only partially in view, slivers of the canals passing by. They must have been taking the route that least exposed them to guard patrols. Even with the Avatar's life potentially in danger, they sacrificed speed for secrecy.

A hands-and-knees scramble through a short tunnel deposited them into a courtyard. Kavik had to tear his eyes away from the massive palace rising into the darkened sky. He was trespassing on royal ground, and he didn't know the punishment they'd face if caught. There'd been no warning stories about this kind of situation growing up.

Ayunerak brought them to a wooden gate in the ice wall. Two shadows clutched at the handles, hissing, and Kavik thought that a pair of malevolent imps had been ordered by the higher spirits to guard the passage. But it was only Pik and Pak.

As soon as they saw Kavik, they launched themselves at his face. It took more willpower than he'd ever exerted in his life not to scream and flail wildly. They sniffed his hair, seeming to recognize him, and jumped up and down on his shoulders.

They might have been asking him to hurry. "Stay here," he said, before feeling incredibly stupid. Yangchen talked to them all the time, but he assumed their responses were due to some kind of Avatar-powered connection, not because they understood speech in general.

To his surprise, they let go of him and went back to perching on the gate. Ayunerak ordered Ivalu to keep watch. When she opened the circular door, a rush of warm air struck Kavik in the face. He leaped through quickly out of habit, not wanting to waste heat. Ayunerak followed and closed the barrier, plugging them inside.

Without needing to be told, Kavik lowered his head. He and Ayunerak pressed their hands together and quickly muttered out words of deference, protection, and acknowledgment that they were merely human. He kept going for as long as his elder did, and when she fell silent, he opened his eyes.

Before them stretched a pond as clear as glass. Only brief flashes across the surface betrayed the presence of water. A thin falling stream at the far end paused at an ice shelf halfway down before completing its descent behind a green island steaming with life. The bow-shaped archway of the Spirit Oasis beckoned them across the distance.

No one else was here. Were they too late? Too early? Wrong entirely? He started forward but was held back by Ayunerak. Her answer was always to wait.

The steady hiss of the waterfall made Kavik feel like they were trapped in an hourglass. The air inside the cove was thick and hard to breathe. He wiped sweat off his forehead with his wrist.

The motion revealed Yangchen lying on the island.

The Avatar, right there, when a second before she hadn't been. Kavik had to pass his hand back and forth a few times to make sure he hadn't somehow conjured an illusion by accident. The only explanation he could think of was that he'd just witnessed her return to the physical realm from the Spirit World.

Her body suddenly jerked, her elbow dragged upward as attached to a rope.

"Something's followed her," Ayunerak said. *"Something's followed her through."*

A prickle crawled over Kavik's skin. Yangchen flopped over, her head lolling. Her eyes glowed, casting light through the cavern. Through the radiance, he saw a spray of mist shaking this way and that, anchored to the Avatar but struggling to break free. The vapors bloomed and coiled into an opaque, soupy mass that dragged Yangchen back and forth over the grass.

There wasn't enough room for two people on either of the thin walkways extending along the edges of the cove. Kavik and Ayunerak took one each, racing each other to get to the Avatar.

Kavik arrived at the island first and stumbled through the unnatural cloud, waving his arms. He reached Yangchen and tried to haul her to safety, but an umbilical connection resisted him. Ayunerak ran across the opposite bridge, stripping water off the ice wall, and slashed a liquid blade at the fog that had congealed above the central island. The pull on the Avatar didn't slacken.

Yangchen convulsed in his arms. As Ayunerak tried to land blows against their intangible foe, Kavik looked around, desperate for an idea.

His gaze landed on the sacred pool at the heart of the oasis, said to be like no other water in the world. Surely, he'd be forgiven in these circumstances, no? Yangchen was the spirits' Avatar as well. They needed their end of the bridge as much as humans did.

*By every oath ever sworn, I am sorry for this.* Kavik pulled water from the tiny pond. He nearly caught one of the eternal koi in his bubble and winced as it flopped back into its home with a splash. Once he'd borrowed enough, he threw it over the Avatar like a blanket.

He'd only thought to shield her. But as soon as the water came between her and the fog, a silent twist doubled him over. He covered his ears, but it didn't help. The mists screamed with a voice he heard in the marrow of his bones.

His own tears blinded him. By the time he looked up again, the grayness was gone, as if the whole attack had been a shared hallucination. There was no rift in the oasis that he could see.

He heard coughing behind him. Kavik turned to see the Avatar sitting upright. The sacred water from the koi pond that had repelled the hostile spirit was just an ordinary puddle now. Yangchen flung the damp end of her long hair out of her face. Her jaw dipped when she saw her rescuers.

There was a weighty pause. Kavik had never been in the presence of such a concentration of wisdom and authority. The Avatar, Master of all Four Elements, and the Executor, senior member of the White Lotus. Both of these women had the power to shape the world.

"You know, this is why spiritual journeys are taken with *partners*," Ayunerak said to Yangchen in the exact same tone she used to lecture Kavik about the nuances of blotting water from paper. "Basic safety."

Yangchen lay back down and rolled away onto her side. "You're not my boss," she muttered.

# COMING TO THE TABLE

**THE SUMMIT TOOK PLACE** in a private home, a small apartment along one of the branch canals. Kavik didn't know if it belonged to the Avatar or the White Lotus. Given how unfriendly the two sides seemed, the room would probably never get used again after tonight. The location had been exposed to the enemy.

A shame, because the inside was comfortable and warm, a far cry from the cellar he'd been hiding in. Kavik claimed the corner mattress, a double layer of finned caribou fur, since no one else would. Yangchen and Ayunerak were both reluctant to sit at first, but eventually they took places opposite each other on a thick rug in the center of the room.

For a while, there was quiet. It had been a long day for everyone. Exhaustion reigned.

"Does anyone want to explain what that fog was?" Kavik finally asked.

"A spirit." Yangchen examined the angled designs formed by the yarns. "I think it . . . invades the mind somehow. Forces its captives to relive their pasts."

She smiled bitterly. "Lucky for me I have too many pasts. Too many worst days of too many lives. I might have glutted it and been spat back out into the physical world."

"What were you doing?"

"I was searching for someone trapped inside. I wanted to free them from their suffering."

"And was this single lost soul worth risking the life of the Avatar?" Ayunerak interjected.

Yangchen's eyes flicked upward, blazing with fury. She swallowed the retort she so obviously wanted to give and changed the subject. "You've joined the White Lotus," she said to Kavik.

She made it sound like an accusation. "I had no other choice," he said. "The Thin Claws were hunting me down and I still needed help getting my parents out of Bin-Er. The White Lotus extended their hand. They're protecting my mother and father in Long Stretch as we speak."

He exhaled hard. This next part would be difficult. "The only thing I had to trade for our safety was Unanimity." He could hear Yangchen grow still. "I told them what I knew about the Firebenders. Chaisee. My brother. They know everything that happened up to the point when we last spoke." The pain of their parting conversation, Yangchen telling him he was no companion of hers, should have sunk to the floor of the sea by now.

Kavik pushed it down again and steeled himself for the Avatar's anger, but it never came. At least not for him. "I can't blame you for that," she said. "I did the same thing once, thinking the White Lotus could be trusted to keep a secret for the greater good." Hostility rolled off her in waves. "Instead they leaked information about Unanimity to the Earth King."

"That's a baseless accusation," Ayunerak said. "And a violation of our sacred vows of neutrality."

"Really? Then tell me why Feishan is suddenly afraid of a weapon powerful enough to topple countries!" Yangchen rose in one fluid motion of airbending, her element lifting her high off the floor before she landed on her feet. "Your organization is either corrupt or incompetent! Which is it?"

"We will conduct an investigation as to how the Earth King could have come about his suspicions." Ayunerak's voice was level. "We all know *you're* not corrupt."

Yangchen bowed formally to them; blood had been drawn from both sides and now the proceedings were over. "Thank you for saving my life," she said, icier than the waters they'd passed through. "Now if you don't mind, I need to go figure out how to keep the Four Nations from backsliding into chaos over a power that should never have seen the light of day. A situation I believe everyone here is partially to blame for."

Her parting shot was aimed at Kavik. "Some more than others."

He wasn't going to argue that point. "Please, wait," he said. "We sought you out for a reason. Finding you in the Spirit Oasis wasn't part of the plan, but we did need to talk."

Yangchen wasn't listening. She was already by the door and there was no time left to broach the topic smoothly. Ayunerak stood up. "Take the kid back!"

Outrage alone stopped the Avatar from leaving. She turned around slowly. Kavik knew she wanted them to see her say no.

"Another trade," Ayunerak said, needing to work fast. "The White Lotus wants one of our own posted by your side, and Kavik is a known quantity to us both. In return for letting him travel with you again, we'll help you end the Platinum Affair. That is your ultimate goal, no? Restoring peaceful relations between the Four Nations."

"It *was* my goal!" Yangchen shouted. "At this rate I'll be lucky not to preside over a collection of ruined cities with arbitrary lines drawn between them!"

Kavik needed a moment to process the exchange. He'd already known about Yangchen's distaste for the poverty and exploitation of the shang system. He assumed by establishing a presence in Bin-Er, she was simply focusing on the sickest patient, like a doctor. She'd declare victory once she fixed a few problems, then move on.

But her aims went farther up the chain, as she was fond of saying. He could see her logic—if political tensions were the reason behind a corrupt arrangement and continually threatened to fester into real violence, then best to attack the problem at the source. The heads of the Four Nations.

His former boss was after big quarry. Yangchen was trying to undo history itself.

"It's not too late to work in concert," Ayunerak said. "We'll speak peace into the ears of Chief Oyaluk and Lord Gonryu while you do what you can with Feishan."

"Call it a hunch," Yangchen said, batting her eyelashes. "But I have the distinct feeling that the last time the White Lotus tried to influence world rulers through secret whispers, it didn't go so well."

Ayunerak's methods weren't working. "Can we talk?" Kavik asked Yangchen while he still had the chance. "Alone?"

She made the deep, scoffing snort he remembered so well. "What makes you think you of all people can convince me?"

"I can't. I just want to catch up."

He had the feeling she only agreed because it gave them both the chance to dismiss Ayunerak. They did it in tandem, as if they'd rehearsed it, both opting for the silent head-tilt toward the door. Revenge must have been a long time coming for Yangchen, because judging from the smirk on her face, she took as much glee from the moment as he did.

Kavik's current boss narrowed her eyes and shuffled outside. He caught a grumble about the attitude of ungrateful children as she passed.

Once she was gone, he didn't wait. "I'm sorry," he said as soon as the door closed. He'd never truly apologized when they last spoke. "I'm sorry for everything. Letting the Firebenders get away the first time. Sneaking up on you in the oasis."

*For betraying you.* He couldn't spit those words out. He had to make a different confession instead. "They want me to spy on you. If you let me travel with you again, I'd be sending reports on you to Ayunerak."

Yangchen rolled her eyes. "I gathered—thanks."

"Is it so bad to have someone watching over your shoulder? Look at what happened tonight. Ayunerak wasn't wrong; journeying alone is dangerous in either world, spirit or human. The White Lotus could help you if you played along with them."

Back when they still worked together, Yangchen would occasionally display a perfect memory for someone else's words down to the mood and inflection. She did it now, crossing her arms in sullen mockery of Kavik, even lowering her voice in a passable impression of his. *"I value my freedom."*

He'd forgotten how good an actor she was. And how infuriating she could be. "Fine, waste of time, I get it," he said. "Can you at least tell me how our friends are doing?"

Yangchen threw her head back and laughed. "Like I would *ever* reveal anything to you anymore about Unanimity!"

This conversation was going so sideways they were threatening to end up in the Spirit World. "Not the Firebenders, you flying hog-monkey! I mean our actual friends! Tayagum, Akuudan, Jujinta! Are they well? Are they alive?"

Her expression turned pensive. "They're fine." She wasn't so cruel as to deny him that information. "But they're not happy about having to lie low. Akuudan and Tayagum built a life for themselves in Jonduri, and it's no longer safe for them there. You cost them their home, Kavik."

That hurt. That arrow he was obligated to take in his guts. The pain was the price of knowing they were unharmed. "This is why I want back in," he muttered. "I need to face them again. Jujinta too. I need to let them all have their say. When somebody just vanishes on you, for good or ill . . . it eats away at you."

Another scoff, but weaker this time. Less pronounced. His argument, born of Kalyaan ditching their family in Bin-Er, had penetrated her defenses. She tapped her foot and looked around the room. "I could give you a blessing of forgiveness on their behalf and then you could be on your merry way."

The salve for his conscience wasn't hidden under the mattress. "You could. But that's not what I'm asking for."

The Avatar opened her mouth to lay down her final verdict. But before she could speak, Ayunerak barged back inside. "Narrowly avoided a patrol," she said. "We're still clear for now, but either way, this little spat has gone on long enough. The White Lotus knows Feishan's on the verge of declaring war upon the rest of the world and that the leaders of the other nations will reciprocate.

"You need our influence to ensure cooler heads prevail," she said. "And if that doesn't appeal to you, I'll give you one last ultimatum. Either the kid's an Avatar's companion again, or else Oyaluk's forces inevitably catch him on this very trip. And then all those precious secrets inside his head become compromised."

"Wait, what?" Kavik said. "What's that supposed to mean?"

Ayunerak ignored him; she was only addressing Yangchen at the moment. "I can't get Kavik out of Agna Qel'a safely," she said. "Currently, I don't have the resources to extract a secondary asset. The only way he doesn't get pinched is if you fly him out of the city under cover."

"Wait a second!" A flush of outrage crept up Kavik's neck. "You brought me here without an escape route? *On purpose!?*"

"Typical," Yangchen said. She rubbed her eyes, a sign she'd reached the limits of her endurance. "The saying in Pai Sho and generalship both is *Prior to the battle, break the cooking pots.* Make a bad move on purpose to force the hand of enemy and ally both."

Ayunerak didn't even have the decency to look smug about her gambit. Putting Kavik's life in danger was merely an inconvenient but necessary step in the recipe she was following. "The Avatar will make faster progress ending the Platinum Affair, and the White Lotus will get assurances from a source both sides know well. Our pride keeps us from cooperating and that's an emotion only kings and fools can afford. Those of us who work from the shadows aren't supposed to make decisions out of pride."

She'd finally picked the right choice of words, because Yangchen briefly made the face of a patient forced to drink sour medicine. No one here was happy, nor were they friends. The start of a true compromise.

The agreement couldn't be spoken out loud; it was too fragile and would have collapsed under its own weight. A howl of wind and the chill that crept through the walls reminded them that whatever their human concerns were, the temperature had fallen too far. Venturing outside right now posed the risk of freezing.

So as not to break the spell, each of them silently picked a corner of the room to curl up in for the night. Kavik drifted off to sleep with a bleary vision of the Avatar hugging her knees, her gray eyes wide open under her troubled brow.

## TWO WEEKS EARLIER

Nearly every conversation Kavik had with Ayunerak in the Gidu safe house was held over a game of Pai Sho. Breakdowns of his performance during bending training—Pai Sho. Updates on the events of the outside world—Pai Sho. And now, mission briefings could be added to the list.

"This plan of yours will never work," Kavik said as he placed a sacrificial Rose tile. "The Avatar's not the forgiving soul you think she is."

"I'm well aware the girl can hold a grudge," Ayunerak said. She laid down a Boat, far from where the local infighting took place on the board. "I give it three chances in ten of success. Well worth pursuing."

Kavik had to think about her move for a while. Not only was it a bizarre play, bereft of any meaning to him, but the section of the grid she'd dropped her piece in was so worn from age and use, the grid lines were difficult to see. The board had been stored in a chest under several layers of waxcloth, and the dark, fine-grained wood it was milled from might have been older than the shrine itself.

Maybe there was no point to the move, and it was merely a distraction to make him waste his energy. "The trick is we'll be forthright about it," Ayunerak said. "We'll admit your purpose is to be her White Lotus liaison. If she accepts, she's going to do everything she can to keep her most important secrets from you, especially the location of Unanimity."

The scenario had been flipped upside down. Yangchen *had* trusted him implicitly, once, because she knew he wasn't a plant. "We're going for persistence here, not cleverness," Ayunerak went on. "She's human. She'll make a mistake and let some information slip. Or she'll drop enough clues for you to fit together, bright young man that you are. Feel free to loosen her guard however you can. Give her that little pout and melt her heart if you have to."

Kavik cut off the Boat tile from the main formation by laying his Chrysanthemum down with a hard snap of his pointer and middle fingers, loud enough to be considered a rude act in the context of a serious game.

Ayunerak was unfazed by his annoyance and his line of play both. "Once you're able to confirm the location of the Firebenders, you send me a message immediately," she said. "One of our teams will move in to extract them from the Avatar's control. And then your end of the bargain is finished."

When he didn't respond, she glanced up from the board. "You look awfully troubled for someone who's doing a service for humanity." She placed another tile but kept her finger over the design, preventing him from seeing what it was. "Do you think destructive power of that scale should remain under the control of an impetuous child?"

*I'm her age, and you're relying on me to snatch it away from her,* Kavik thought.

Ayunerak pulled her hand back to reveal her society's namesake piece. From its position in the center, the White Lotus tile could dominate the near spaces in each quadrant. Played too early, the move would have been so terrible that the only conceivable purpose would be a signal to the opponent. She'd saved it for midgame, where it could distort the final shapes of the board unchallenged.

"The Avatar is right about one thing," Ayunerak said. "The rulers of the Four Nations cannot get their hands on those benders. But neither does that mean she can be trusted to make the final call on how to deal with them. Someone has to act with wisdom and foresight when the leaders of the world aren't up to the task."

"You."

"Us, Kavik. You're inside now, as inside as it gets." Ayunerak stared into his eyes, as if to check his depths for resolve. "The quicker we get the Firebenders into our custody, the sooner we can focus on extracting your brother from Chaisee's organization."

Kavik's price. Neither side had come to this arrangement out of the goodness of their hearts. Ayunerak wanted a plant who could recognize the Firebenders by face. Kavik refused to cooperate unless she promised safety for his family. His entire family.

The fact that Kavik had to deliver first made it clear who had the advantage in the bargain. "The chances she takes me back are worse than three in ten. More like slim to none."

"But if she does cave, you'll have more of her forgiveness than you think. Consider it from her perspective." A smile crept across Ayunerak's lips. "What kind of monster would betray the Avatar twice?"

# MISTAKEN IDENTITY

**KAVIK HAD SUFFERED** a downgrade. The last time the Avatar snuck him out of a city, she'd provided him a false identity, given him a plausible fake job, and arranged transport through security checkpoints. An expert display of clandestine travel.

This time she rolled him up in a carpet.

Her departure at sunrise was going to be celebrated in full view of Chief Oyaluk and his closest advisors, she'd explained. It would have been rude and suspicious to sneak out without a formal farewell. The vast array of gifts she was obligated to accept by custom would be the only chance to get him onto her bison.

So Kavik played the waiting game again, tucked between the treasure piles, bound as tight as the filling of a stuffed seaweed roll. In so many layers of woven buffalo-yak wool, the heat was unbearable. He couldn't scratch his nose with his arms pinned to his sides.

Through the muffling of the fabric, he could hear bits of Yangchen's parting conversations with the chief. By the time she got to wishing good health upon the new litter of snow leopard–caribou cubs in the royal stables, it was clear she was dragging her feet on purpose.

"Oh, just fling it anywhere on the saddle," she said to the loaders when asked about the carpet.

Kavik had to suffer through a hard bump on the shins and an extensive round of final blessings before they took flight. His instructions were to count to five hundred before revealing himself, but he wasn't going to wait for that. He knew exactly how fast Nujian could climb into the sky.

He wriggled and rocked back and forth, inching himself out of the carpet roll, and got stuck halfway. "I could use a little help here."

Yangchen sat in the driver's position, presenting her stiff back. "Reins" was all she said.

"You can fly him without your hands! I've seen you do it!"

She didn't respond. Kavik squeezed himself through the binding and collapsed on the broad saddle. Pik and Pak immediately settled on his face, one atop his forehead and the other squatting over his windpipe. Perhaps because he'd helped Yangchen at the Spirit Oasis, they chittered at him in a calm, friendly series of clicks instead of trying to rip his nostrils off. "I missed you both too," he muttered. A blatant lie.

He brushed the lemurs away and got to his knees. "That's the closest I've ever been to the Chief of the North. My parents would never believe my luck if I told them." He waited for her to offer a jibe about how fortunate it was to be considered part of the furnishings, or something hearkening back to their first encounter when he was stuck in the ice of the Blue Manse. "Between you and him, I've met a lot of famous people so far. Maybe I can sneak up on the Fire Lord while he's sleeping and—"

"Let's get one thing straight." Yangchen tilted her head back, staring at him upside down over the curtain of her dark, cascading hair. Despite her silly posture, there was only cold contempt in her expression. "I am *tolerating* your presence for now. Don't go assuming everything's back to normal." Her eyes crinkled into a smile as welcoming as desert mud crack. "How's your brother?"

"I don't know." Kavik ran his hand over his brow. "I don't know where he is. Assuming he's still working for Chaisee, then he has to keep up the act. If she ever found out that Zongdu Henshe planted him inside her organization, she'd . . ." He'd seen what Chaisee's association did to spies. The victims whose bodies he'd been forced to dispose of in Jonduri probably hadn't even gotten the worst of it.

Yangchen dropped the grin and turned around to face him normally. He knew she'd only brought up Kalyaan as a barb, a reminder that she hadn't forgotten whom Kavik had betrayed her for. "Ayunerak said she'll help me look for him once the time is right," he said. There was no downside to telling the Avatar this portion of the truth. "But I don't have any way to keep them to their promise."

A deep grunt came from Yangchen's chest, the most sympathetic sound she'd given him since their reunion. "Then you might find your bargain pushed back until the next era. The one thing the White Lotus is good at is waiting."

Kavik believed her. Many a night he'd lain awake underneath the shrine, thinking about the different employers he'd had over the years. If Yangchen had been the one giving him her word, she would have moved quickly and not stopped until the job was done. For the Avatar, the right time to act was always *now*.

The wind blew harder and turned his sweat into pinpricks. He found his parka hidden among the supplies and put it on. "I'm no expert flier, but aren't we going the wrong way for Taku?"

Yangchen stifled a yawn. "We have to stop by the Northern Air Temple to drop off these gifts from Oyaluk; they help fund the village and hospital."

Kavik had to keep himself from appearing interested in their destination. He watched Yangchen, trying to tell if her nonchalance was feigned. "I'm looking forward to seeing the mountains again," he said, prattling on as blithely as he could. "Catch another sunset."

, This Northern Air Temple happened to be the most likely place to find leads on the Firebenders. "Convenience," Ayunerak had explained. "Convenience and logistics. The Air Temples are the territory the Avatar has the most control over, and the Northern one is the closest to Bin-Er. I'd say there's a seven out of ten chance she's keeping the Unanimity benders somewhere in the vicinity. If so, your job would be to pinpoint their exact locations. The Taihua range is too big to search by hand."

For someone who favored Pai Sho so much, Ayunerak certainly liked to speak in terms of dice throws rather than certainties. "She's from the Western Temple," Kavik said. "She could have brought them to her home."

A frown inched its way across Ayunerak's face. "Due to an unforced error on my part, she doesn't consider the Western Temple leakproof anymore."

There was another possible fate for Thapa, Yingsu, and Xiaoyun. "You don't . . . You don't think she killed them, do you?"

Kavik had asked purely as a hypothetical. He didn't really believe the Avatar would take the convenient way out of her dilemma. He was merely considering every angle.

But Ayunerak answered him seriously. Not from the perspective of someone who looked at Yangchen and saw an Air Nomad but as someone who evaluated the Avatar as a world power. "She wouldn't. You don't waste assets in this game. Punishment and retribution are for amateurs. The three of them are as safe and sound as can be."

Justice seemed to have no place in the conversation. Thapa, Yingsu, and Xiaoyun had wrecked a quarter of Bin-Er and terrorized its residents. Did their crimes matter at all? Or could anyone's wrongdoings be washed away provided they were valuable enough?

The sun crawled higher. Kavik spent most of the day watching Nujian's shadow pass over the sea and ice below while Pik and Pak surfed the bison's invisible wake, gliding and bobbing through the air. This part, the peaceful, quiet hours in between destinations, he didn't miss as much.

Yangchen kept pushing the pace without a break. By evening, she had shrunken inside her robes with tiredness. He'd caught her nodding off twice and offered to take the reins but was refused each time. "We have to set up camp," Kavik said once light began to fade.

"We can keep going. Nujian's not tired yet."

"But you are. Did you sleep at all in the safe house or have you been awake the entire time since then?"

No answer. Kavik sighed. She hadn't changed her habits since he'd watched her thrash in the night at the Northern Air Temple, freefalling through a forest of airball pillars. "Come on. Even Great Yangchen needs her rest."

She huffed and made a click with her teeth. Nujian responded to the signal by descending toward a series of islets, landing on the flattest one without needing to hear a command. Kavik lowered the tent rolls down from the saddle and jumped to the ice. He'd set up shelter, but not before he did something very important.

He walked around to face Nujian, letting the bison see and sniff him. "I'm sorry," he said. He stroked the bison's snout and got an appreciative grumble. "What I did wasn't right. I'm glad to be back riding with you."

Yangchen scoffed. "That was more heartfelt than you were with me."

"Can't hear you, busy making up." Kavik pressed the side of his head against the fur of the Avatar's companion he liked most. Nujian knocked him back, but only to get enough space for an affectionate lick.

They set up tents and a small stove in between. The preserved searoot they ate for dinner was bland and chewy, but there was dried fish for Kavik, a sign that she'd thought about him while packing. Despite herself, Yangchen couldn't help but consider the needs of others.

He watched her stare into the coals after their meal, her chin on her knees, the flicker reflected in her eyes. The heat wasn't enough to stave off the chill. "Help me clean up?" he asked.

"No."

*Okay then.* She'd never treated him like a servant during their first mission, but if she needed to get some pettiness out of her system, so be it. He melted a sheet of water to toss over the embers, but before he could put out the fire, Yangchen spoke again. "I'm done, Mesose," she said. "I'm done cleaning up after them."

The water hovered between his hands. Her voice had aged decades, sounded as if someone had fitted the wrong gauge of strings to a zither. "They take with both hands, and they pay only with blame. They find your edges and then they dwell there. Work a hundred miracles? You're worthless for not performing a hundred and one."

Her posture had changed too. She was no longer curled up and tense like a troubled young girl. She looked down her nose at the fire, head cocked to the side, a guru about to banish a student permanently without a second thought.

"Yangchen?" The name came off his tongue with difficulty, a reminder of how infrequently he said it out loud. She was always *her, you, the Avatar.* The too-close presence in his face or over his shoulder. "Avatar Yangchen. Is that you?"

No answer.

Ayunerak had briefed him on the scenario. *She doesn't have a strong wall between herself and her past lives. She might slip into a memory, and it might turn ugly. Play along if you can but restrain her if you need to.* Like he could handle the world's most powerful being losing control a few feet away. He was out of his depth here.

"I'm so close to giving up on them," Yangchen announced. She pulled back her lips and ran her tongue over her gums as if discovering how much she liked the bloody taste of the truth. Kavik could have sworn her teeth were sharper and more crooked than they were moments ago, but that had to be the glint of the coals playing tricks on him. "I'm so tired of fighting on their behalf. Human beings choose their own misery, over and over again. Tell me why humanity deserves an Avatar, Mesose. I could handle the blame, the finger-pointing, if I just knew why."

Kavik cursed to himself. He had to assume the cover of this Mesose person, but he'd never heard of them before. He frantically tried to think of which group, which nation, which faction her past companion might have belonged to, before realizing the exercise was moot.

The truth applied across eras. "I can't," he said. "I can't tell you why we're worthy of a protector. You have to believe we are."

Immediately he wished he'd done better. He wasn't a poet. Yangchen, or the person inside her, chuckled. "That's it? That's the only reason? Blind faith that people can change?"

Her laughter grew louder and choppier until it became a glottal howl. She threw her head back, rolling as if to tip off the edge of a platform. She beat her chest with her fist hard enough that he thought she might crack her breastbone.

Terrified, Kavik threw the water he still held over the stove, quenching the coals. He wasn't sure if it was safe to wrest the Avatar out of her memories by force, but he couldn't bear to watch her in this state. The life that had trapped her was full of pain.

The hiss of steam silenced Yangchen quickly. She blinked and coughed, wiping froth from her lips. "What just . . . oh."

She saw Kavik frozen in place and sighed. "I suppose you were briefed about my 'gift.' "

He nodded slowly. "Well?" she snapped, interpreting his fear as scorn. "How embarrassing was it? What'd I say?"

"You don't remember?"

"Not always."

"You, uh, whined a lot. You were playing some kind of game I didn't recognize, and it must have been a competition because you were whining and complaining to an official judge." He put on a smirk. *Kavik* could be a role as much as any other sometimes. "It was pretty pathetic, I have to tell you. You just kept going and going."

Yangchen exposed her teeth in a scowl, and he squinted at them, but in the moonlight they were the same as always, pearly and straight. "That one might be new," she said. "I guess I can't be a good sport in every life."

She tried to rise and stumbled. Kavik caught her by the elbows. "You need rest," he said. "We both do."

"Just get me inside my tent." She leaned more weight on him, threatening to collapse in his arms. Kavik managed to get her past the entrance and ease her descent into her blankets.

Yangchen drew her covers over her shoulders. Something about the gesture made her look ill, like one of the patients in her own hospital, and Kavik's feet refused to move for a while.

What exactly was he doing? Guarding her from hostile birds? It was strange he hadn't left and stranger yet that she hadn't dismissed him. "I'm going," he said, in case she was still awake.

He turned to leave but stopped when he felt a slight tug on his leg. Kavik looked over his shoulder and down at the Avatar. "Thank you, Se-Se," she muttered softly, her eyes closed.

Before he could respond, Yangchen's hand fell to the ground, limp, and she began to snore.

# STOMPING GROUNDS

**THAT NIGHT** might have been the first one in any of their shared travels where the Avatar had gotten more sleep than Kavik. He couldn't remember her bunking down peacefully on Nujian's saddle, in the Northern Air Temple, the Jonduri safe house, anywhere they'd rested in proximity. Despite the lightness of her step, Kavik would always hear her scurrying about late into the night.

He'd stayed up this time, fretting over what he'd heard. Did the White Lotus know there had been at least one past Avatar who'd been so close to turning their back on humanity? Was that even a past life? Mesose could have been someone born of this era, a survivor of Tienhaishi perhaps. If so, the violence in her throat could have been aimed at the Four Nations of today.

Which meant *that* was the person he was going to have to cross a second time.

He kept his distance from her as they flew, sitting as far back in the saddle as he could. He wasn't sure that kind of rage could dissipate in a single night. It was more akin to a generational curse, a haunting that made wide swathes of land taboo to enter.

*That might not have been the only Avatar disappointed with us, ready to end it all.* Most of an iceberg remained under the surface, its shape and mass never to be discovered. The thought chilled him worse than the wind. His teeth clicked against each other.

"Did you say something?" Yangchen asked, swiveling her head back sharply.

"No," he squeaked. He didn't want to ask who Mesose was, in case the name reminded her of misplaced trust and fitting punishments.

The discomfort between them made for a quiet trip. They passed over the strait without incident and flew into the Taihua Mountains. Yangchen started the descent early, weaving them between the gray peaks and skirting the rocky hillsides.

The low, winding flight path might not have meant anything. But it could also have been a sign she didn't want to give Kavik a sweeping overhead look at the terrain. As if she were keeping the Firebenders somewhere in the surrounding area as Ayunerak had theorized.

*Or she just likes breezing through valleys and Unanimity is on the other side of the world.* He needed to be patient. The White Lotus wanted certainty, not half-baked guesses.

When the village that supported the Northern Air Temple came into sight, Kavik immediately recognized the stone hospital nestled into the slope. But it was no longer the only large structure in the settlement. Several hasty construction projects had sprouted up since he'd last been here, lopsided storehouses of wood and clay, new hutches with straw roofs, dugout pits so deep and wide they had to be communal root cellars. The narrow walking paths were stuffed with people squeezing past each other.

He watched a team of workers unload lumber planks off the back of a sky bison, an unusual display. "The village is bustling," he said.

"There are a tenth more people living here than the arable land can support, and the number keeps growing," Yangchen said. "At our current rate of alms collection, grain reserves will be exhausted in two years. The rock springs don't deliver enough water for everyone, which means the newcomers have to rely on snowmelt. One dry winter will spell utter disaster."

Yangchen turned and gave him a hard smile that was all squint. "But yes. It's *bustling,* as you say."

Kavik peered down below again. She wouldn't have hidden that information from anyone who'd come to the mountains seeking to live in a town growing under the auspices of a hardworking Avatar. But neither would she have turned them away. Even from a distance, most of the faces seemed happy and content, unconcerned about a heavy balance of borrowed time coming due.

*Because their Avatar would think of something.* Kavik watched her chew harder on her lip the closer they got to the center of the village. The puzzle she worked on might never be solved.

The people in the street spotted her, or maybe they recognized the pattern of fur on Nujian's underbelly. A riotous cheer went up. The townsfolk paused their work, stopped in their tracks, put down their burdens. Slowly at first, and then quickly, they followed the Avatar's bison, hurrying to meet her when she descended to the earth. The flow of heads through the street reminded Kavik of grains of sand spilling down the neck of an hourglass.

Yangchen sucked in a breath through her teeth. "I'm going to be mobbed. You have to get out before we reach the landing area."

"Yeah, right. How am I supposed to *wait no no no—*"

Airbending as sure and strong as a pair of solid hands grabbed Kavik by the middle and flung him over the saddle's edge. Because of how close they were to the hillside, he didn't have far to fall or much time to scream. Instead of a hard impact against the rocks, he bounced off a cushion of air and slid all the way into a thatch of bushes, his feet higher than his head.

"Stay hidden!" Yangchen called out, her voice fading as she flew away. "I'll find you later!"

Kavik blew a clump of fallen leaves off his face. Things were turning back to normal faster than he thought.

Navigating the streets without drawing attention was easy since nearly the entire town had emptied to go catch a glimpse of the Avatar. Kavik shuffled past stalls and parked wagons, his hood pulled over his head. It was the freest he'd been allowed to move about in a long time and worth disobeying the Avatar.

He examined the new lines of construction running higher up the slopes. A teahouse with flying eaves in the southern Earth Kingdom style. That was new. Over there, a kitchen with its chimney puffing thick smoke from an oven blazing away. It would have looked like a promising scene, except Kavik knew the cost of that smoke.

Fuel was hard to get in the North, and they weren't that far from the North, relatively speaking. Sure enough, the woodpile next to the kitchen quickly went from chopped logs to bundles of thin branches to twigs from the gangly little bushes that grew along the road to the village. The townsfolk were denuding the mountainside for things to burn.

He could see the seeds of Yangchen's distress. The place was starting to look more like Bin-Er.

Lost in his thoughts, he bumped into a child who'd run into his path. Kavik looked down, half expecting to see the little monk who'd conned him out of a whole silver for a tiny fruit pie. Instead, it was a kid from the Earth Kingdom staring back, sunburned and curious.

The boy's mother hurried over. "Lan, don't wander into the street," she scolded. The young woman leaned over to pull her son away. When she glanced up under Kavik's hood, she frowned. "Do . . . I know you?"

Kavik held his breath. This was the woman he'd helped Yangchen save from the brink of death in the hospital the first time he'd visited. He shook his head.

"No, I'm sure we've met before." She straightened and tried to take more of him in, tucking a strand of hair behind her ear. She bit her lip. "You don't live in the village, do you? We would have bumped into each other."

Neither Yangchen nor Ayunerak wanted him noticed by locals who weren't Air Nomads. He had to cut this short. "In a hurry," he grunted before turning around and fleeing into the teahouse. The sign said it was closed but the door wasn't locked. He could stall with the owners until the woman went away.

Inside, he scraped his feet against an entrance mat and let his eyes adjust to the dimmer light. The Avatar could have remembered to tell him the monks had found the kid, he groused to himself. This whole time his lingering memory of the woman they'd saved together had been tainted with failure and the screams of a parent who'd lost a child. Not something he ever wanted to hear again.

"Can I help you?" The deep rumble of the shopkeeper was muffled by Kavik's hood.

Right. He was pretending to be a customer who'd overlooked the sign. "Tea, please," he said. He pulled the cover back from his head.

He'd gone dull, Kavik decided. Hiding in Bin-Er, not working, had made him lose his touch. He should have recognized the proprietor's voice even through layers of fur.

Because it belonged to Akuudan. The big man stood behind the counter. He'd been in the middle of wiping it down with a soaking rag, but at the sight of Kavik his hand skidded to a halt.

Tayagum and Jujinta sat at a table near the wall as if they had some long-standing tradition between them of meeting for snacks and stimulating conversation. Tayagum's blocky chin fell in surprise. "What the— What are you—"

Kavik had squandered his rehearsal time. He should have come up with a plan for running into the three people he'd worked over as badly as he had the Avatar. He was at a loss for what to do.

Jujinta, on the other hand, must have known exactly how he'd treat the moment, because without hesitation or changing his expression he drew a knife and leaped over the table at Kavik, blade-first.

# DEAD GIVEAWAY

**JUJINTA'S SILENCE** was louder and more off-putting than any war cry. Kavik barely managed to twist out of the way. His former partner's knife plunged deep into the doorframe instead of his stomach.

Extracting the blade would take a great deal of effort. Normally that would mean the threat of a weapon was over, but Kavik had fought alongside Jujinta before. The weapons portion was never over.

Sure enough, Jujinta released his grip on the first dagger and spun around, a fresh glint of steel sliding out of his sleeve into his other hand for a backhand stab. Kavik reached across the room with his waterbending and the wet rag flew out of Akuudan's hand. He froze the cloth over his vitals like a plaster just in time to catch the point of Jujinta's second knife.

The two of them tumbled to the ground. Jujinta landed on top and leaned into the pommel of the dagger. Kavik struggled to maintain his armor of ice and cloth against the pressure.

"Come on, you can do better than that," Tayagum said.

Kavik realized with some dismay he was talking to Jujinta. "I know how to stab someone, thank you very much," Jujinta said calmly. He hammered the end of his knife with his free hand and the ice cracked inside the fibers of the rag.

"This isn't funny anymore," Kavik said, his teeth clenched. He couldn't be sure if Jujinta was using all his strength, but *he* certainly was.

"You just don't get the joke," Tayagum said. "Give it time."

"Enough." Kavik heard Akuudan lumber over from behind the counter. Jujinta's weight suddenly vanished as he was hoisted away by the back of his collar like a scruffed croco-cat. "The Avatar must have brought him here. No crossing him off until we find out why. From *her*."

Kavik peeled off his makeshift layer of protection and leaned back on his knees. In a way, he was grateful they didn't want to hear an explanation right now. It saved him from having to dance around the subject of the White Lotus. "I see you're all doing well. Nice new place of business. The market for establishments without customers must be growing."

"Go eat coals," Tayagum snapped. "You think you can talk to us after what happened? You just pop in, having fun on your grand adventure, and turn on whomever you like. No sweat off your back if a mission goes sideways in a foreign land! We *lived* there! Do you understand?"

*That was their home,* Yangchen had said. The guilt that had been curdling inside him came back up wrong, a defensive spray of bile. "I never intentionally revealed your connection to the Avatar! If anything, the message I left with Jujinta saved your lives!"

"You mean the message you tricked me into delivering," Jujinta said, quiet where Kavik had shouted. "You used me like a pawn to do your bidding, only to turn on us in the end."

"I had to! Or else my brother would have been exposed and killed! I had to decide between duty and family. I–I'd make the same choice again a thousand times."

He wasn't sure why he'd stuttered.

Akuudan let out a sigh. "I get it." Tayagum looked at his husband like he'd grown stripes, but Akuudan shrugged. "The kid picked blood. I wish more people thought the way he did." His weariness seemed to take root in some tragedy of the past, but now was not the time to ask.

"Do you know if Chaisee ever found him out?" Jujinta asked.

"I don't. I haven't heard from him since then. If he's smart, he got as far away from her and the association as possible."

"Agreed," Jujinta said, nodding thoughtfully. "Though death would certainly be a kindness to your brother if she found out he was a spy. Pieces of him would be draped across the entire island as an example to—"

"Thank you, Juji. I never would have remembered without your help." Jujinta had been inside Chaisee's organization far longer than Kavik and had undoubtedly seen more of her cruelties. "Best-case scenario is he's laying low, like I had to."

"Like we still *are*," Tayagum said. "No one's sob story changes anything. In fact, I think you're running another con on us right now."

Kavik had only made it into Jonduri by getting past Tayagum's suspicions first. He didn't have passphrases to vouch for himself this time. Brazenness would have to do. "Like Akuudan said, I'm here with the Avatar's blessing. So, what do you say we all relax, take a few deep breaths, and wait for her to arrive? Break out the nice calming tea, if you've got any in stock."

He got up. Kneeling was for the contrite, and the goal here was to avoid looking like a plant desperate to get back into the team's good graces. To that end, he drew an enraging smirk across his face, one that had started scuffles in Bin-Er when he needed to create a scene. He was rewarded with furious scowls.

Kavik's former comrades surrounded him like a containing wall, their suspicions boxing him in. His mission with the White Lotus was going to grind to a halt if the Avatar kept them this close by. In fact, that had probably been her plan all along. Yangchen never intended to lose out on the deal with Ayunerak and was counting on this close circle to protect her most valuable secrets. Tayagum made an *I'm watching you* gesture, pointing to his own cold glare before turning his forked fingers upon Kavik.

Fine. Kavik looked around the room at the narrowed eyes, flared nostrils, squared stances. He would outsmart every single person here if he had to. He was already thinking of the first message he'd have to send the White Lotus informing them the mission was going to encounter stiff resistance when he heard the thunderous crash.

Their heads all jerked in the direction of the sound. Kavik had flown into town with Yangchen under a clear blue sky; the noise couldn't have been the weather. "You've got to be kidding me," he muttered.

Another cracking boom. An explosion echoing through the mountains. Not right up close, but not far away either. The four of them in the teahouse knew more than anyone exactly what that sound was.

*Okay*, Kavik thought as he ran out the door, the other three close on his heels. *Maybe not that stiff.*

# GRAVITY

**AFTER DROPPING** Kavik off, Yangchen slowed Nujian's flight down considerably. If the crowd below rushed too fast to greet her, it could quickly transform into a lethal stampede. It was easy to trip if your attention was focused on the clouds.

A monk from the Northern Temple swooped around the bend on his bison and fell in beside her. "Avatar," Mingyur said, bowing his round, dimpled head. "Welcome back. Are you here to check on the guests—"

Yangchen lifted her hand. "Please, Brother," she said. "We'll talk about them later, in private."

He nodded and loosened his reins so his bison, Fengbao, could playfully butt against her younger brother Nujian. They came from the same parents but in different litters, separated by a few years, and while they didn't get to see each other often, their bond remained resolute.

While Fengbao chomped on Nujian's ear, eliciting a bellow, Mingyur glanced over the saddle behind Yangchen. "I see Chief Oyaluk was as generous as ever." He pursed his lips and for a second she thought Kavik had left an obvious trace of his presence behind. "What happened to your glider?"

She didn't want to deal with his reaction. "It's there, somewhere."

"You really should keep it closer, for your own safety. I make sure my men always have their staves when they're on duty."

She appreciated the vigilance. Despite his cheery nature, Mingyur was a skilled fighter and a natural pick to lead the squad of Northern monks who guarded the members of Unanimity.

Yangchen watched the bison siblings lock horns. Her smile slowly faded.

Mingyur was barely five years older than her and still hadn't received his arrows. He wasn't some grizzled mercenary like Thapa and the other members of Unanimity he watched over. He didn't have "men" and he should never have had to order his brothers to remain armed at all times.

The Northern Air Temple had been infiltrated by thoughts and languages of the other nations. And it was Yangchen's fault. She didn't have guests; she had prisoners. By bringing them here, by prizing a fellow Air Nomad's ability for violence, she'd opened the gates to such behavior. Every move she made took her further away from the person she was supposed to be.

She pressed the heel of her hand against her nose until it hurt. Abbot Sonam was afraid becoming jailors would corrupt the monks, but Yangchen was losing her grip on herself the fastest.

Ahead was a grassy slope underneath the surrounding cliffs that often served as her touchdown point. Yangchen pulled Nujian away from Fengbao. The growing crowd cheered and clapped as she descended. She had rarely felt less worthy of applause.

After landing, she tossed Nujian's reins to a handler and slid down to the grass on a ramp of air. Below her, people from every nation packed the tilting field, expectant. Breaths bated.

Yangchen used to be able to visit the town without having to come up with a speech each time.

*Not in the mood. Not in the mood. Not in the mood.* "Friends!" she said, her smile warm and wide so they could see it from the back rows. "It heartens me to see you prosper in my absence." Behind her audience stretched the newly constructed portions of the town, erosion already forming gaps between the floors of the huts and the earth underneath. She could spot new refuse piles grown waist high. "I . . ."

*I what?* Sooner or later there would be nothing left to say. She felt like a bird searching a dry plain with a nest of hungry chicks behind her. *Feed us words, feed us wisdom, feed us forever.* "I . . ."

The tremor in the earth reached her feet before her ears caught the sound of the explosion.

Shamefully, her mind went to the wrong places first. The lies she'd have to tell to smooth this complication over. An entire village would need to be convinced they heard nothing. It was a freak storm. It was a spirit. The old, frayed standby that still seemed to work.

Another part of her branched off into sniveling hope. Maybe Xiaoyun or one of the others had demonstrated their ability, once, as a lark. A little prank between prisoner and guard to alleviate the boredom. Everyone here was a friend, no?

The second blast, louder than the first, put reality back into the forefront. One of the Unanimity Firebenders was on the loose. Maybe they all were.

A scraping, chalky sound came from over her head. It grew into an oceanic hiss. The villagers who had lived at this elevation long enough knew *that* noise, the roar of a familiar, deadly beast, and they screamed. *Rockslide*. The explosions had unsettled the mountains.

Boulders the size of hay bales tumbled down the cliff, generals leading a charge, waves of gravel and dust following close behind. Yangchen leaped, air spouting herself up the sheer face, and the largest chunk of rock slammed into her back. She blunted the impact with earthbending and dug her heels in, halting its roll.

Bracing the load with her shoulders alone, she flung her arms out to the sides. A wall shot out of the cliff to the left and right in successive pieces like a series of drawers yanked out of a medicine chest, one after the other. The rest of the rockslide struck the barrier and Yangchen's jaws clashed together from shock. Something thin and jagged cut the inside of her lip. A fragment of her own tooth knapped off by the pressure.

She spat the flake out and struggled to raise her head. The townsfolk underneath gazed in horror at the doom the Avatar held back. Had it been a single boulder, several, she could have managed, but the original fracture lines must have extended across the cliff face. Her control over the wall lessened the farther away it ran. If her outstretched arms wavered the slightest bit, the whole structure would collapse.

"Help me!" she shouted to the people below. She knew some of them could. "Earthbenders! Any benders!" Water could be frozen into extra support. A Firebender could blast apart some of the debris provided they were powerful enough. "Help me!" she shouted again.

Did the people of the village decide one by one, or all at once? Did they look around for a leader, a first mover who gave them permission, or were they struck by the same inspiration simultaneously? Yangchen had plenty of practice reading an audience, and she concluded they all made their choice at the exact same time. The little discrepancies were purely physical. The ones who could move their limbs faster did, and the rest weren't far behind.

To a man and woman, the townsfolk turned and fled.

She allowed herself to understand. If they reached their houses and got their families and possessions to safety first, then what did it matter if the Avatar faltered? They had to look out for themselves. They were obligated to prioritize the well-being of those closest to them. The villagers knocked each other over in their panic, creating the stampede she'd taken pains to avoid earlier.

*Avatarhood was a prize beyond kingship*, she'd once read in an ancient philosophical treatise. A single lucky life out of a generation triumphed in the greatest game of chance in the world. The rocks crushed Yangchen further, slowly folding her in half.

Off in the distance she spotted an incongruity, a tiny portion of the herd going the wrong way, coming closer. Kavik. And behind him Jujinta, Tayagum, and Akuudan. Kavik flung people out of his way with the technique of a wrestler, doggedly trying to reach her. He searched the hillside with his gaze until it landed on Yangchen's. She couldn't hear him yell but could see him mouth the words. *Hold on. We're coming.*

Yangchen inhaled through her nose and inflated her lungs. Keeping the breath inside her helped lock her muscles in place and the wall stopped shifting.

Her only chance to keep the earth at bay was the Avatar State. But the sudden release of energy might send the elements flying everywhere.

A slam reverberated through the barrier, but in the same direction she was pressing. Nujian took the weight of the cliff with his massive head, buttressing the stone. He paddled forward with his tail, fighting with airbending stronger than any normal human's.

His roar reminded Yangchen that she would always have at least one companion who'd come to her aid. Nujian had flown straight to her in the middle of unloading; half of the unsecured gifts had tumbled off his saddle.

She'd been searching for support in the wrong places. Had she looked up in the sky, she would have seen the line of Air Nomads speeding toward her on their bison. They swooped low and followed Nujian's lead, each mighty animal propping up a section of the wall, a ramming contest against the mountain itself.

The pressure on her back disappeared. Her people had bought her a moment's respite. "Hang on just a bit more," she said to Nujian. Yangchen sprang off the cliff, spinning to face the peak, and while in freefall, clothed herself in the power.

Each of her predecessors would have described the Avatar State in their own unique way. Coming home to the welcoming arms of family. Rising above the treetops like a giant. Becoming truly, completely unfettered, breaking free of stubborn chains. For Yangchen, it was the gratification of seeing her will embodied without question. While the energies remained within her grip, she could shape the stuff of the world.

The landslide. She tilted her head. So tiny. Forcing the accumulated rubble back, against the natural flow, was academic. The surprise of the monks. Did they not know how far she was above them? She compressed the rocks, tightening them into a form that resembled the original mountain well enough, visibly shrunken though. A memorial to her deed.

From inside the whirling sphere of air, the elements obeyed her; everything obeyed her. Only humans remained stubbornly wayward. Were they so special? She examined the villagers scurrying below her feet, and yes, the Airbenders as well. *Look what I can do without them. Look how weak they are without me.*

The thought came as it always did when she remained in the Avatar State for too long. *I could stay here. I don't have to go back.* She had no idea what that meant, not going back, or if such a thing was even possible. All she knew was that the temptation to find out grew stronger each time.

Another explosion. Yangchen detected the flow of air shifting around her like a wayfinder using the current to sense the presence of an island over the horizon. Her first impulse was to be annoyed. Affronted. A power to rival her own shouldn't have existed in this cosmos. *She* was supposed to be the only winner in the ultimate game of chance.

And then her frailties caught up with her. Like they always did. Panic was a human emotion, and it washed away the trappings of the Avatar State like ice water. The Firebenders were loose. She'd brought them here, close to one of the few homes her people had. A settlement of helpless villagers lay close by. Any damage would be on her head.

The rotating winds that kept her effortlessly suspended died down. Yangchen plummeted, a harsh jerk back into her surroundings, and she hastily caught herself with an air spout. Nujian's saddle gave her a platform to land on. She dropped to one knee, masking her drained strength with a pose.

*That was a bad one.* In the fields near Port Tuugaq, there hadn't been people around to spur the feelings of contempt and disdain that so easily came with unchecked power. There was no such thing as humility in the Avatar State. Her arrogance hadn't spiraled out of control that badly since Old Iron.

Mingyur flew closer, cautious. Yangchen stood up in the saddle to show him she was herself. "Gather the others and evacuate the townsfolk to the flat zones," she ordered. The Northern

Temple had long-standing contingency plans for earthquakes, but they weren't designed to handle so many people. The task would require every Air Nomad and sky bison on hand.

"The guests," Mingyur said. His moony features scrunched in worry. If a member of Unanimity had broken free, several of their brothers might be hurt or worse.

There was no end to Yangchen's culpability. She forced herself to remain impassive. "I'll deal with them."

"Alone?"

"Go!" she snapped. "Now!"

Mingyur rolled Fengbao away to organize the rescue effort before more of the mountaintops shook loose. Nujian turned his head as far as he could to look at his human companion. Despite the mounting chaos around them, her bison remained steadfast, resolute.

Yangchen flicked her gaze at the little squad still trying to make its way toward her. Nujian never needed reins or words to understand her intentions. He plunged toward the village street, trusting her to surf atop his saddle. Yangchen cut the remaining lashings with slices of air and blew the rest of the valuables over the side to free up space. Mingyur was right. She did need backup, and from people who knew how dangerous Unanimity could be. Her assets were meager in that department, however. Tayagum and Akuudan she would trust with her life, but Jujinta she'd met only a little while ago. She hadn't vetted him herself.

And then there was Kavik.

*Kavik.* She wanted so badly to blame him for the mess they were in right now. But he hadn't been in the village long enough to have anything to do with the explosions. Beggars couldn't be choosers; she needed all the bodies she could find.

That made four people she could rely on in this situation, one of whom wasn't even on her side. *What an embarrassment of riches,* Yangchen thought as she flew toward her team.

Had they more practice working together, Yangchen could have picked up her companions in one swoop, a matter of trust and linked arms. For now, she had to settle on landing Nujian in the street and tossing the four men, each a different size and weight, into the saddle with air spouts. To their credit they didn't complain about the rough handling.

"Why are we going that way?" Kavik shouted after Nujian took off for the Air Temple proper. He pointed in the direction of the isolated, winding valley that ran deeper into the Taihua Mountains. "The explosions are coming from over there!"

She ignored him. "You two," she said to Akuudan and Tayagum. "Find Abbot Sonam and tell him what's happening. Do what you can to set up a perimeter in case this is a full-blown attack. I'll see to our loud friends."

"What about the . . . uh . . . other . . ." Tayagum normally didn't stumble over his words.

She realized what he was trying to say without giving away too much. And he was right. The noise of Unanimity could have been a diversion to extract a different prize. "Jujinta," Yangchen said. "I need you to head into the visitor's quarters underneath the temple and check if anyone's disturbed the fourth room in the main hallway. Even if there's nothing wrong, stand guard outside the door until I come."

Kavik muttered to himself, taking in the meaning of her commands. "Another target that's not the Firebenders . . ." His eyes suddenly goggled out. *"You mean to tell me you've been keeping Zongdu Henshe prisoner here this whole time!?"*

She didn't mean to tell him anything at all. But Henshe's disappearance would have been the subject of much gossip in Bin-Er. Yangchen cursed Kavik's sharpness, a quality she'd once admired when he still worked for her. The White Lotus was going to have a field day with this information.

At least now she could drop the pretense. "Watch Jujinta's back," she told Kavik. He nodded, waiting for more. "And do what he tells you."

His lips pouted in frustration at being relegated to a secondary role. *An act,* she reminded herself, performed by a flawless actor. Kavik was merely playing the sincere, jealous team member eager to climb back into her good graces. She might as well have been giving orders to Mama Ayunerak.

*Avatar companionship isn't tenured,* she thought as she dropped the four of them off at the temple landing walkway and reversed course into the mountains. *Sometimes you have to start over from the beginning.*

# SECOND OPTION

**WATCH JUJINTA'S** *back*, Kavik groused to himself. *I* made *Jujinta.*

"Don't step on the mittened hermit crabs," Jujinta said as they sprinted across the gold-edged walkway that led inside the Northern Temple, like Kavik hadn't already been a guest here and eaten under its roof long before his partner ever laid eyes on the place.

A gong began to sound, an offset beat of one, one-two, one, one-two. Kavik guessed the pattern was the code for a rockslide, bad enough to require all hands on deck. The great entry hall was already empty.

They reached the ferocious bison fountain at the back. Kavik hoped he could gather some water there, but the flow had been stopped and the pool was dry. Maybe it only ran during certain seasons. A young monk bounded out of the arch leading to the cloisters, in a hurry to join his brothers and help the village.

Kavik recognized the kid from his previous visit; he'd been tromping up one of the many sets of temple stairs when they'd run into each other. The monk skidded to a halt. Kavik was about to ask directions to the lower-level visitor's quarters and if water could be found along the way before realizing the Airbender hadn't stopped for him.

"Master Jujinta!" The monk bowed deeply at the waist, waiting for orders.

"We're fine; help the others outside," Jujinta said. The command might as well have come from the Avatar herself, given how the kid sprang off again. The gong kept beating its summons.

Kavik found himself deeply irked. *"Master" Jujinta?* "I hope you know where you're going." *He's been staying at the temple longer than you; that's all.*

"I do." Jujinta took a turn through a door Yangchen had never bothered to show Kavik. Locks were a rarity in the temple as far as he'd seen. "This is the only way for Henshe to make an escape without diving off a sheer cliff face."

They descended into a network of passages carved into the stone of the mountain itself. In the dark recesses, Kavik thought he spotted a formation of men and women waiting to ambush them. His heart leaped up his chest. But it was only more statues in more alcoves. Air Nomad aesthetics still prevailed below the surface.

The likenesses of the past temple elders had been awe-inspiring the first time he'd seen them, swept clean by the breeze, sunlight cradling their serene expressions. A connection to the past he could appreciate.

But now they filled him with dread, like he was being stared at by corpses. Worst of all were the empty spaces yet to be filled. He could hear Yangchen's voice in his head, playing it off in a flippant manner like she so often did. *That's where I'll go when I die.*

And there was still no water around. He remembered the monks carried it everywhere by hand as a practice, to know the weight and be grateful, like that boy upstairs had been doing when they first met. In Kavik's opinion the Air Nomads didn't have to be so humble all the time. A running tap would have been useful at the moment.

Jujinta led him into a wooden corridor that curved along the lines of the mountain. Beams of light shone through grease paper windows, and an indigo carpet woven to extreme lengths out of showmanship muffled their footsteps. Those were features that normally weren't present elsewhere in the temple. It was as if the monks had tried to make outsiders comfortable here.

*Probably not* those *particular outsiders, though.* Five men stood in the hallway. They weren't monks. They'd made a good attempt to dress like the villagers, in thick weathered clothing rolled in mountain dust. Tayagum's instincts had been right. Zongdu Henshe was attempting a breakout.

"You shouldn't be here," Jujinta warned. "This is a restricted area."

The term sounded jarring, and it wasn't because of Jujinta's unvarying pitch. There weren't really that many restricted areas inside the Air Temple, in a hard sense. Air Nomads were told the circumstances of a secret or sacred place. And as individuals, they chose not to go into the places that weren't meant for them. Kavik remembered a monk telling a story over dinner that he'd once stumbled into a conclave of visiting abbots performing an incense ritual. They'd merely sent him off with a quizzical glance, not even pausing their chant to yell at him.

The men didn't move. "Headkickers," Jujinta snarled, brimming with contempt for his former occupation. He drew a knife slowly from the sheath at the small of his back.

*Something's off,* Kavik thought. Hard hitters and professionals wouldn't have blanched at the sight of a blade the way they did. One of the men, skinny and sunburned like a farmer, raised his hands. "Hold on." His voice trembled. "No one said anything about knives."

The leader puffed out his chest in a desperate attempt to look larger. "Shut your mouth, Hosung. All of you, stay put and hold your ground."

"I'm not dying for a couple of silvers! I'm going home!"

Kavik stepped in front of Jujinta before he spilled blood on holy ground—if the guest wings still counted as such. "Wait. Are you hog-monkeys actually from the village below? Did somebody pay you to come here and delay us?"

"He knows!" Hosung shrieked. The wide-eyed man burst through the line of his comrades. Kavik stepped to the side and let him run by.

Jujinta, however, stuck a thick arm out, solid as a tree branch, and clobbered the man in the throat. Hosung's own momentum sent him cartwheeling to the floor. His face bunched the carpet in several waves before his limp body skidded to a full stop.

The rest of the group were faced with a choice. They had to decide who was more intimidating, the dead-gazed killer behind Kavik, or their quickly deflating leader. "I think you lot should get down on your knees, put your hands on your heads, and close your eyes until we get back," Kavik said.

The temple was such a spiritually enriching place that the qualities of the Air Nomads were bound to rub off on its visitors. With quiet grace, the intruders from the village freely chose to accept his invitation.

Kavik felt like he had a hair caught in his throat. An itch he couldn't swallow.

Between his days working for hire in Bin-Er, his stint in the Jonduri association, and his White Lotus training, he'd come to learn that players of the game, *the* game, had their own individual styles. The Avatar was a studier, someone who liked to prepare as much as possible and know things others did not. Yangchen put in great effort in advance so she could contain damage and prevent loss of life, the equivalent of a Pai Sho player who'd memorized every relevant opening move to shorten the games.

Zongdu Chaisee, if the rumors floating through the White Lotus were true, was the complete opposite. A fiend who held on to her secrets through atrocity. She'd lace your seat cushion with powdered toxin and wait for you to collapse over the board. Victory through being the lone survivor.

Causing a landslide as a distraction and packing the hallway with fools from the village to buy time for an escape was its own distinct, callous signature. Cruel by way of shocking indifference. Had Hosung and the rest been a bit braver, they could have gotten killed. Kavik supposed it was a fitting attitude for Zongdu Henshe, who'd cared only about his short-term goals and nothing else beyond.

The itch in his craw turned to nausea when he saw the two monks slumped against the wall, bleeding from the head. *Someone is going to answer for this*, he thought in a fury as he raced over.

Kavik knelt down and checked their wounds. They'd been given a hard thump each but thankfully were still alive. Behind them, a door barred from the outside had been forced open.

Guards and locks. Of course Yangchen would have taken precautions. Jujinta pressed his back to the wall and flicked the door open wider without exposing himself. His caution was warranted. Getting the drop on an Airbender was no mean feat.

The room revealed itself to Kavik in slices. Fluttering papers, strewn books. A bed that hadn't been made. A puddle of blood on the floor. Zongdu Henshe lay in the corner, his glassy, unblinking eyes staring up at the ceiling. The Avatar's prisoner was dead.

Jujinta immediately went to the small window. It wouldn't have been the most comfortable exit, but someone limber enough could conceivably have squeezed through. "No scuff marks of a grapple on the ledge," he said. He stuck his head out and the winds ruffled his hair. "I don't see anyone on the cliff. No pitons or rope left behind. I couldn't climb this face unaided."

Kavik patted down Henshe's corpse, pausing briefly to reflect on the last time he'd handled a body with Jujinta in tow. Poor Qiu. Kavik had been sick for hours after that. Now, here he was, taking liberties like a grave robber. What had happened to him? Maybe exposure to the Avatar and the White Lotus had sanded away his decency like grit blowing across a stone.

He had to keep going and determine the cause of death. He was flummoxed for a minute until he realized it had happened not from the front or back, but sideways. The former Zongdu of Bin-Er had been stabbed in the armpit with a very long, very thin weapon that was nowhere to be found in the room. The wound was a neat lung-heart-lung channel, the way you'd place an arrow for an ideal instant kill on a finned caribou.

Kavik surveyed the room again. He spotted a detail he'd missed the first time. Over by the bed, the pool of Henshe's congealing blood met the edge of another puddle, this one purely water, the edges where the liquids joined a swirling pink. The murderer had tossed aside his melting weapon and hadn't bothered to dry the scene of the crime properly before making his getaway.

He stood up, his hands on his head, sucking on his cheeks in dread. It wasn't Henshe's style that Kavik had found familiar. For all his talents and ingenuity, Kalyaan sometimes liked to cut corners.

# THE DUEL

**YANGCHEN HAD TO CHOOSE** from three different isolated huts dotted throughout the range outside the temple, one for each member of Unanimity. Unreachable except by flying, the little plots of land had originally served as hermitages for monks who wanted to practice meditative solitude. She'd turned them into holding cells for the Firebenders.

Apparently, there was nothing about her culture she couldn't corrupt. Yangchen set aside the philosophical issue for now. She felt rather like the mark in a shell game. Choosing one location meant temporarily abandoning the monks in the other two.

Those "follow-the-pebble" games were usually rigged. She took a moment to gather herself as Nujian sped below the ridgeline and tried to remember the plunge into the Avatar State she'd just taken. The heightened sensitivity through her amplified airbending. A shockwave from one of the explosions had struck her skin, ruffled her fine hairs. The detail she wanted was there, but at the time it had been awash in the ocean of scorn for the very people she was trying to save.

Yingsu's hut. Her best guess would have to do. A nudge with her heel, and Nujian veered into the eastward fork of the valley. *I need to be right,* she thought. The shadows cast by the overhangs fluttered like insect wings and gave way to blinding sun. *Please, just this once, let me be right—*

Nujian stopped short and she lurched forward. Her eyes adjusted to the light. Ahead, the hermitage where some of the most venerated Air Nomads had laid their heads throughout the centuries had been turned into a smoking ruin.

Her bison refused to move forward, his instincts for danger taking over. Yangchen frantically looked for her fellow Airbenders. There, lower down. She spotted Yingsu pressed against the side of a large, jutting outcrop.

The powerful Firebender had her arm wrapped in a chokehold around the neck of a struggling young monk. The rest of her guards lay strewn among the rocks, their orange robes standing out like blood splatter against the gray gravel.

A foul, thick rage that needed no past life to fuel it leaked from Yangchen's lips. She vaulted off Nujian and directed the air spout behind her, funneling herself downward at her enemy like a streaking meteor.

Only a single gesture, caught almost too late, diverted her path. Yingsu glared angrily at the bodies scattered around her and pressed a finger to her lips. *Shh.*

She wouldn't have been telling the dead to stay quiet. Yangchen pulled up at the last second and slammed into the mountainside, cushioning the blow with earthbending. She crawled out of the tunnel she'd created like a singing gopher. One Firebender and six very alive Air Nomads stared at her in shock. "Idiot!" Yingsu shouted under her breath. "You just gave away our position—"

Next to them the mountain erupted sideways. A blister of flame spread across the slope and would have consumed them had Yangchen not airbent against it with as much force as she could muster outside the Avatar State.

Heat enveloped them like the walls of an oven. The monks stayed low and covered their heads. Yingsu maintained her grip on the one who screamed and babbled in fear, preventing him from leaping into the flames out of panic.

The explosion passed but the dust remained suspended in the air. Yangchen coughed, her lungs muddy. *"What is going on!?"* She could barely hear herself speak.

Yingsu threw the monk she held down to the ground so his brothers could deal with him instead of her. "Thapa's somewhere on the other side of the valley," she said. "He probably already got Xiaoyun, and now he's trying to kill me."

There wasn't time to question why the Firebenders had turned on each other or how Thapa had escaped his own prison. Nujian floated behind the safety of the bend. Yangchen curled her tongue and whistled for him to pick them up.

Yingsu guessed her intentions as soon as the first shrill note hit the air. She quickly reached out and clamped her hand over Yangchen's mouth the same way she'd manhandled her erstwhile jailer. *"No!* You want to give him a big furry target?"

Common enemies made for strange friends, and Yingsu seemed to have thrown in her lot with the Avatar for now. Yangchen had to trust the Firebender knew her former comrade's capabilities better than she did. But Nujian was still the only escape, and they had to move before Thapa could get off his next shot. She slapped away Yingsu's arm and turned her attention to the slab of rock they hid behind.

The swirl of her wrists resembled the motions of her native element more than earthbending. She split the largest chunk of stone into two plates wider across than she was tall and set them spinning on their edges. "Follow the cover for as long as you can!" she ordered the monks.

Their confusion cleared up once she sent the rocks rolling in two different directions. Her brothers from the Northern Temple were done; she wasn't going to risk their lives further. A shove of air got their feet moving toward Nujian. They crouched low and tried to keep up with her moving screen.

Yingsu went to follow them, but Yangchen pulled her back in the opposite direction. The Firebender scowled but was forced to scurry with her behind the second bouncing disk. The point was to make Thapa choose. Hopefully he'd hesitate.

Ahead lay a series of clefts in the slope, a web of natural trenches that looked like better cover. But they lay too far ahead. Yingsu knew it. "We're not going to make it before—"

Yangchen grabbed her collar again and yanked her down into a shallow ditch that barely concealed the tops of their heads. The stone continued to roll. Right as it reached the fissures, another fire blast shattered it as easily as a brick flying through porcelain.

From wherever he was hiding in the distance, Thapa launched a sequence of furious attacks against the grooves cut into the mountain. The feature of the landscape was visible across the distance. Yangchen had been counting on it.

"He thinks we're in there," Yingsu muttered. "And he's expending energy with each shot. Nice trick."

Deception over protection. The only barrier separating them from instant death was some wavy grass. Out of the corner of her eye Yangchen caught a glimpse of Nujian flying back toward the temple, a full complement of Airbenders on his back. At least she'd gotten them out.

Because beyond that victory, she hadn't really thought through her next steps. A shower of dirt landed on her face. She and Yingsu might be buried alive at this rate.

What Unanimity did wasn't bending, she decided with surprising, genuine hatred. It was a perversion. The air shook from the unnatural act and vibrations raced from the ground up her spine. She understood the one monk's jabbering breakdown. The sensations overwhelmed the eyes and ears, an assault through the very channels an Airbender trained to keep open.

The sizzling sound of ash descending to the earth faded away. Yangchen counted through the quiet, the number reaching higher and higher. "Is he done or is he trying to bait us into moving?" she whispered to Yingsu once she reached fifty. She didn't want to bend them to a better position in case an errant plume of dust showed Thapa exactly where to aim.

"What do you think?" said the Firebender.

Then they were going to be here for a while, sharing this ditch side by side. Yingsu hardly fit, given how tall the woman was. "Ironic," Yangchen said. "Not long ago you were the one who got closest to killing me."

"If only I'd succeeded. Then I wouldn't be trapped here." Yingsu had been the most stubbornly silent of the prisoners; this was more than she would normally speak in weeks. She had a strange voice with no upper register, as if she were eternally mocking a foolish grandfather. "And it was plenty long ago. Time passes so slowly in these mountains I nearly set my own hair on fire out of boredom."

*You should have taken up a hobby like Thapa.* A breeze rustled the weeds and Yangchen seized her opportunity. While the vegetation along the hillside remained briefly in motion, she craned her neck and built a picture of her surroundings in a flash. The skill took practice and was especially prized by, well, the White Lotus. Sometimes Yangchen wondered if their animosity was due in part to how desirable a recruit she would have made.

As soon as the wind died, she hunkered back down to safety. A wrinkle along the opposite hillside gave their enemy a wealth of comfortable options to hide in, a reverse slope defense. His superior position was likely the reason Yingsu hadn't wasted effort shooting back yet. "How do you know it's Thapa out there and not Xiaoyun?" Yangchen asked.

"Blast pattern." As Yingsu stared at the sky, her long features turned into a snarl. "Plus the fact he's always been a backstabbing rat-lick son of a worm. I warned your flyboys as soon as I heard the first explosion."

So she'd saved their lives. Yangchen began to laugh. She covered her mouth and there was nowhere for the giggles to escape but through her nose as snorts.

"What's so funny?" Yingsu demanded.

"Well, you know . . . Chaisee picked a bad name for the three of you. *Unanimity?*"

The Firebender scowled. "Codenames don't work if they contain meaning about their subject. They tossed out 'Skyflower' and 'Drumbeat' for that very reason."

She smoothed long strands of hair off her forehead as if trying to clean a knife she wanted to use soon. The braids she once wore had long since come undone. "This whole scheme was busted from the beginning. Ever since I got off that ship and saw Henshe's stupid grinning face."

"Oh?" Yangchen said carefully. "You weren't supposed to?"

"No. We were originally going to deploy in—" Yingsu realized she was giving away information, the very act she'd spent so long in the mountains trying to avoid. She thumped the back of her head on the ground and made a face.

Preserving the honor of her masters hadn't paid off in the slightest. "No," she finally muttered. "The plan was always to make a mess out of Taku, not Bin-Er. We had maps of the city memorized and everything."

Yangchen nearly bolted upright out of the ditch. *Taku.* She swallowed the thumping of her heart. "Why did you switch it up?"

"I don't know. We had a date we were supposed to be ready by, but the boss-boss came along and said we were shipping out early. Way early."

Chaisee's lieutenant. Kavik's brother. "Was the boss-boss a Water Tribe man with eight fingers?"

"No, just a— Come to think of it, he did always wear gloves even though it was too hot. How did you know?"

How indeed. Special Avatar powers. Zongdu Henshe had called in a favor from his planted agent Kalyaan to deploy Unanimity in Bin-Er against Chaisee's wishes, when she'd been saving them for a special occasion. "What date were you supposed to be in Taku?" she asked.

Yingsu's answer confirmed Yangchen's worst fears. The same day as the end of the convocation. Chaisee wanted to bring her weapons to bear in Taku when Chief Oyaluk, King Feishan, and Lord Gonryu would all be in town at the same time.

Thapa sent another blast into their side of the valley, close enough for the pressure to churn the contents of Yangchen's stomach. In a cityscape, the explosion would have been a building the size of a temple courtyard gone, erased from existence along with anyone inside. No bodyguard in the world could protect their charge from an attack like that.

Henshe had tried deploying Unanimity to halt an army and terrorize a citizenry. He'd nearly succeeded but had lacked any real strategy or vision. The true ideal use of this technique was the guaranteed elimination of a few key people. The feather's weight that moved a wagon's load.

"Enough of this nonsense!" Yingsu shouted over the ringing in their ears. "It's him or us. Are you going to handle Thapa or do I have to?"

For a moment Yangchen thought she was asking her to take the air from Thapa's lungs like she'd done to capture him in the first place. She almost replied that she couldn't create the void from this distance. But Yingsu had never experienced the technique herself, so she couldn't have known about it.

She wanted the Avatar to take care of the problem the old-fashioned way. "I need him alive!" Yangchen yelled back.

"You only need one of us alive."

Yangchen looked at her. She'd said it so easily, like a trusted advisor of many years. "You only need one of us to interrogate, and I've already cracked," Yingsu repeated. "Any more prisoners are unnecessary complications. The current situation kind of makes my point, does it not?"

Yingsu might have spurned her former comrade for a turncoat, but now that he'd made the first move, she was ruthlessly willing to pay him back in kind. "Thapa's not a misunderstood pawn; he's a piece of filth and a loose end. Elevate me for a clear shot and I can make sure he never hurts anyone again."

There was no nonlethal version of Yingsu's specialized firebending. "You're hesitating," she said when Yangchen didn't answer. "Hesitation gets people killed."

Throughout her lives, Yangchen had heard the adage more times than she could count. Mostly from weaklings pretending to be strong. Children who thought they were adults. Amateur historians who divided the actions of her predecessors into good and bad with a dull cleaver, hacking merrily away without much thought, really praising themselves with each blow.

She still didn't move. Yingsu glanced over Yangchen's shoulder and shook her head sadly.

Yangchen followed her gaze. Against the clear blue sky, contrasted for all to see, was an orange-robed figure flying toward them on a glider. Mingyur.

He'd left Fengbao behind, probably to help carry villagers to safety, but now that was done, he was going to help his

Avatar come flame or high water. He wasn't going to abandon his sister. Yangchen could picture the doggedness on his round face. Running into the fleeing guards and hearing their account would have only made him more determined.

"No!" she screamed at him. "Stay back!"

"He's the distraction we need!" Yingsu said. She spoke quickly in escalating pitch, trying to outrace the moment. "Either he dies alone and buys us a chance to live, or all three of us go down! You know what you have to do!"

"Mingyur!" Yangchen tried to stand but the Firebender held her back. She was the panicking fool now, the main liability. *"Mingyur!"*

"Don't trade yourself for nothing!" Yingsu bellowed.

Futile gestures. Hadn't she always railed against them?

And yet breaking free of Yingsu's grip and launching herself into the air was the ultimate pointless act. She wasn't going to reach Mingyur in time no matter how hard she tried. She could send her countryman off to oblivion with the knowledge of just how much she cared. Not enough to avoid the choices that doomed him, but enough for her to extend him her hand. As if she had something valuable to offer.

Her mind painted another picture. A dual portrait that spanned the valley. The Avatar, eternally trapped between earth and sky. Thapa grinning because she'd given him everything he wanted. Because she'd broken cover, he could follow her path in reverse and pinpoint where Yingsu was hiding. Her weakness had sealed the Firebender's fate as well.

Yangchen always found that time slowed and thoughts quickened in moments of agony, punishment for those who are too aware for their own good. *"Drumbeat" would have been a fitting name,* she thought as she heard the faint *pop-pop* sound that had heralded destruction over Bin-Er.

A seed of heat began to blossom not far away, infinite promise stemming from a singular, immeasurable point. "Skyflower" was a fine choice, too. *I can't protect them all.* It was a mistake to believe she ever could.

As the fire bloomed in the air, wrapping the side of the valley in light like a sunrise, Yangchen was left with one final thought— that things might have been different if she had her glider.

# MITIGATION

**THE EXPLOSIONS** had long since stopped. Kavik waited in the hospital with the others. He knew the Avatar would come straight there to provide healing. If she was still alive.

One by one the injured filed in. He forced himself to look. Walking wounded, mostly the young and old, or people on the smaller side. The villagers who would have been trampled most easily. Thankfully no dead yet, at least, not beyond Henshe. The Airbenders who had been struck down outside his room were awake and resting in the corner. They'd groggily reported seeing nothing before an impact to their heads knocked them out.

The murdered zongdu was certainly going to be a . . . conversation. Kavik scuffed his foot along the floor. Tayagum and Akuudan were still helping with the cleanup, which left Jujinta hovering over his shoulder, vigilant. The Avatar's last order to stand guard no longer had a target with Henshe dead, and it seemed like Jujinta needed an outlet. Kavik was the prisoner now.

He wanted to explain he had nothing to do with the assassination. But any excuses would have fallen flat. One didn't have to go that far back in time to find Kavik's hand in shaping this disaster.

The side doors to the hospital, big enough to accommodate a wagon backing in, flew open with a crash. Yangchen shuffled inside. Draped over her shoulders was a much larger monk. She bypassed the queue of people waiting to be healed and laid the man on an open bed, setting him down in gentle, deliberate steps.

"Cordon," she said to Jujinta while she shucked off the top of her patient's robes. To Kavik she barked, "Water like last time. Now."

She was in her heightened state, her focus as sharp as the edge of a snapped glass. Jujinta pushed back the disappointed crowd to create more space. Kavik found enough clean water from several waiting buckets and surrounded the Airbender's body with the liquid, lifting him up so Yangchen could inspect the damage. He kept his mouth shut, fearful that a single wasted breath might tip the scales the wrong way.

"His lungs are ruptured from a shockwave," she said as she moved to the other side of the bed. "They've collapsed like empty waterskins inside his chest. Keep him elevated and steady. Do *not* move."

Kavik nodded. He waited for Yangchen to take some of the water and use it to apply her healing abilities. They'd worked as a team this way before, him providing the bulk movements, her the skill and fine manipulations. There would be a gentle blue glow and underneath, the shared feeling of life on the mend, a rush more heady than any Kavik had experienced.

Yangchen stabbed the man instead.

With a short, crisp hammer of her fists, two sharp points of water pierced into his chest. Kavik yelped and nearly dropped the patient. It was as if the Avatar had wrapped his fingers around a knife and guided the blade into a target she wanted to assassinate. She made sure they'd both be judged for the crime.

Wisps of blood and bubbles of air floated from the tiny puncture wounds, upward through the layer of water Kavik struggled to maintain. Yangchen spread her arms and expanded the cocoon, then contracted it. A wheezing sigh came from the still unconscious monk.

Kavik could feel the man's breathing return, weak but steady. Yangchen circled her hands and two dots like temple fireflies danced over the small incisions, sealing them. The familiar glow spread from there and the Avatar, while not relaxing completely, appeared like she could see and hear beyond a narrow tunnel again.

The most dangerous phase was over. The spectacular feat had been performed. What remained was work. Without needing to be told, Kavik kept the patient encased while Yangchen applied the familiar shimmer to the water and ran her hands along the energy pathways of the Airbender's body.

Kavik tried to remember if he'd met the man during his first visit, but the effort rang hollow. *This would be just as bad if he were a complete stranger.* Yangchen had once told him that a person didn't rise in value simply because you knew their name.

"When we're done, I need to give you a briefing," he said once it seemed like she could spare a bit of concentration.

Her eyes mostly stayed with her hands, but she was able to glance up at Kavik periodically. "Tell me now. We're going to be here for a while. Is it about our guest in the visitor's wing?"

No one was close enough to hear them, but still. "I don't know if this is the best time to go into the details."

"I said tell me now."

Kavik winced. It wasn't like she was holding a pillow to wring or hurl if she became upset and momentarily lost control. She was cradling a human life in her hands. *Mingyur.* The name came rushing back. Mingyur had led the blessing for Kavik's table before they ate their simple dinner of toasted barley and butter tea.

Over the knot in his stomach he gave her the full story, down to the bones. During the chaos of the rockslide, Henshe had been crossed off, likely by Kavik's brother, Kalyaan. Kalyaan had bribed a group of villagers to serve as a distraction and escaped out the window down the mountainside. He was a skilled enough climber and Waterbender to have pulled off the daring escape. An honest testimony from someone who knew the man well.

Yangchen was silent for a while. Kavik kept a close eye on the water to make sure she didn't squeeze the remaining life out of their patient by accident, but his worries were unfounded. The Avatar remained completely calm. "Sounds like I should have hired him instead of you."

Kavik swallowed the lump in his throat. Out of the corner of his eye he saw two teams of stretcher-bearers try to reach the back of the hospital unnoticed, the section he knew to be the mortuary. The bodies they carried were too large for the stretchers and they had to struggle with the long limbs extending past the shrouds.

One of the cloths snagged, and before an attendant was able to replace it, Kavik distinctly saw the cold, lifeless face of Xiaoyun. From the other stretcher, a mass of undone braids dangled low enough to sweep the floor. Yingsu.

Two members of Unanimity were dead. The third unaccounted for. Any plans the Avatar or the White Lotus might have had for the Firebenders were in complete disarray.

A hubbub grew louder in the hospital. He'd missed its origin, but several people were trying to shove past Jujinta, and one of them, a man whose mustache was so black and glossy it looked glued on, made it through. Kavik assumed he was impatient for medical attention. He was lucky Jujinta played by a different set of rules in public, or else he would have needed his spine straightened in addition to whatever minor wounds he had.

"Hey, buddy!" Kavik nudged ineffectually at the line-skipper with his foot. His arms were busy keeping the water afloat. "Wait your turn!"

"I'm not injured; I'm the village captain." The man smoothed his mustache with thumb and forefinger as he spoke. "I need to know what happened to the gifts from the Northern chief."

Kavik had to shake his head a few times before those words fell into an arrangement he could understand. The treasures Chief Oyaluk had granted the Avatar. The goods he'd stowed away in. "Why?"

"We needed those alms to fund the village expansion. There was supposed to be a whole saddle full of valuables and instead we've got one wrinkled carpet and a bunch of camping gear!"

"I had to cut them loose," Yangchen said.

Kavik turned his head to look at Yangchen behind him. Her eyes remained on Mingyur, her hand on his wrist. She continued to pat her hip.

"You did *what?*" The captain tried to get closer to her, but Kavik shuffled back and forth, staying in between them. "Where? Where did you toss the cargo? Don't tell me you dropped it in the mountains!"

Yangchen didn't respond. *Tap. Tap. Tap.*

The man opened his jaws wide and went for a double-handed swipe against his facial hair. He must have been in some real distress. "Avatar, we need you to find those gifts. If not you, the other Airbenders."

"Are you kidding me right now!?" Kavik sputtered. His arms were starting to ache from holding up the water. "Go look for that stuff yourself!"

"Avatar." The man was shorter than Kavik and bounced on his toes, trying to get Yangchen's attention over Kavik's shoulder. He wasn't going to speak to a flunky when the person obligated to help him was right there. "Avatar. Avatar! You'd better have a plan to fix this—"

Yangchen clenched her fist. That was all the motion she needed. An invisible hand of wind carried the village captain out the side doors of the hospital and hurled him screaming into the sky.

"Made me lose count," she murmured without looking up.

Kavik didn't have time to be stunned. Yangchen had flung him into the air on many occasions, to infiltrate and extract him from tricky situations. Or simply whenever she was in the mood for pranks.

But no matter how off guard she caught him, he could still always tell she had his safety in mind, an adequate cushion prepared. Not so with the village captain. The man was in for a hard landing if Kavik didn't react fast enough.

He raced out the side of the hospital, taking the water meant for Mingyur with him. *Quick quick quick.* Ayunerak had trained him to grasp his surroundings in an instant, but with a landscape restricted to the basement of a safe house, they'd resorted to household objects on tables, covered by a sheet. No peeking by the honor system.

The hillside next to the hospital had changed since he'd last been here. Ramshackle hut. Loose bricks. Refuse pile. *Refuse pile.*

Kavik billowed his element like the sail of a ship and shoved the mound of garbage underneath the falling man, just in time to soften the impact. His control over the water burst, soaking the poor sap to boot. The smell was atrocious.

He ran up to the flattened pile of browning fruit cores, barley straws, discarded hearth ashes. The man struggled to right himself like a flipped turtle-crab. He was dazed but he wasn't hurt. "What the— Did she just—"

Kavik thought about letting the truth sink in. Maybe the village captain would come to a new understanding and learn to straddle the delicate line, taking a more cautious, possibly more correct approach to his relationship with his Avatar in the future.

Or maybe he'd simply lose his mind. Knowing human beings, the odds went pretty sharp in one direction.

"I told you to wait your turn," Kavik snarled. He twisted his face into a mask as intimidating as he could make. "Next time you taste the ground instead."

The village captain blinked as he put two and two together. He was wet and an angry waterbending outsider stood before him.

"She's going to hear about this," he muttered. He wiped his lips furiously with the back of his forearm. "Mark my words, she is going to hear about this!"

The man ran off down the hillside, hacking and spitting the whole way. Kavik watched him go, wondering if he'd really saved Yangchen any trouble in the long run.

The Avatar and her team met in a chamber of the Air Temple dedicated to ceremonies of candlelight. Around them, banks of little clay bowls no wider than coins lay filled with butterfat and cotton wicks. Kavik knew from the tour that novices would sometimes train in rooms like these, brushing their airbending over the hedgerows of individual flames, attempting to sweep them gently in one direction and then another without snuffing them out, like rubbing patterns into the nap of fabric. Storied masters of the past could spend hours in here without letting any of the lights flicker a bit, their control over the air so complete that they stilled the eddies and whorls of natural breezes until the flames froze in place.

In Kavik's opinion the octagonal room felt like a hallowed place and should have been forbidden to the uninitiated. But apparently, they still hadn't found the limits of Airbender tolerance. He, Jujinta, Tayagum, and Akuudan, interlopers all, crowded the center of the floor while Yangchen stood at the head. She had completed her investigation and was ready to debrief her team.

The gathering was decidedly not like old times. Even before the truth of Kavik's betrayal reached the others, their discussions in Bin-Er had been limited to frantic bursts of strategizing as best they could under a rain of fire. There had been no quiet moments to take stock.

Now the silence was too thick, a blanket in summer. "Is Mingyur going to make it?" Kavik asked. The Avatar wouldn't have left his side if there was more she could do. Either he was on his way to recovery, or he was . . .

"He'll recover," Yangchen said. "I don't know if he'll ever hear again though."

She was exercising great control. The flames of the lit candles were as tall and solid as claws. Tayagum went next. "Are the townsfolk questioning the explosions?"

"No, luckily. If they do, we can pass the noises off as cascades and other rockslides easily enough. The mountains are often home to strange noises. Yes, Juji?"

Jujinta had his hand raised, full extension, elbow locked. He put it down once he'd been called on. "Should he be here for this?" He motioned at Kavik.

"I believe so." Her slow, deliberate response would make it seem to the others like she was rubbing Kavik's nose in the continued aftermath of his poor choices, and not using the opportunity to align information with the White Lotus. "About six weeks ago, Thapa, after developing a rapport with his guards, convinced one of them to take a written message to his mother to assure her he was okay," Yangchen said. "Curse the soft hearts of my people, right? All of our efforts, undone by a letter to family."

*Why not both*, Kavik thought unhappily.

"Before agreeing, the guard read the letter and found nothing that would disclose Thapa's whereabouts, and he left it at a message post in Jang Hui for further conveyance," Yangchen continued. "But based on his recollection of the contents, I believe it contained coded instructions for Chaisee to rescue him. I don't think Thapa's actual mother, whoever she is, had the resources to survey the mountains, prepare a net under his cliffside hut, and coordinate his jump into a freefall dive during a guard rotation. I found the rigging they left behind. Quality work."

Kavik knew exactly who could have pulled off such a complex operation at Chaisee's behest, but he stayed his tongue.

"What happened to Thapa's guards?" Akuudan asked.

"He took it easy on them." Yangchen's bitterness was strong, considering mercy was a quality cherished by Airbenders. "He only blew up enough of the mountain to stun them and cover his tracks. The first explosions. I'm less certain of events after that, but my theory is his rescuers also scouted the locations of the other Firebenders. Thapa betrayed them all and killed the other members of Unanimity."

"Wait," Akuudan said. "Xiaoyun and Yingsu—"

"Are dead. Thapa managed to get Xiaoyun first, by surprise, and then Yingsu . . . The three of us took a series of hard shots. I chose to save Mingyur instead of her."

The candles flickered for the first time. Kavik saw regret in the Avatar's face. Guilt for feeling regret. The one person who might blame Yangchen for preserving the life of her brother Air Nomad over an important asset was herself.

"By some miracle none of Yingsu's or Xiaoyun's guards were hurt as badly as Mingyur," she said. "But I couldn't prevent Thapa's escape. The search teams are coming up empty and our chances of finding him before he gets clear of Taihua aren't good."

"I don't understand why Chaisee would want to get rid of two of her most valuable assets," Tayagum said.

"She probably didn't," Yangchen said. "I believe Thapa went rogue for a moment there. He eliminated the other Firebenders to make himself the sole prize in this game. He was valuable before, but now he's priceless." She swallowed hard. "I suppose he did us a favor."

"Killing your teammates to get a raise," Kavik muttered. "Not even in Bin-Er."

"Chaisee's smart, but no one can predict everything," Yangchen said, almost with a degree of sympathy for the zongdu. "Tell everyone what you told me about your brother."

The rest of the team took Kavik's theory rather well. They already hated his guts; there was no need to show him how much a second time. True professionals, all.

"Why would he kill Henshe if they used to be friends in Bin-Er?" Tayagum asked. "Does backstabbing run in your family?"

"Because it helps Chaisee," Kavik said. "Henshe could have testified about her plot to the Earth King or another ruler. My brother chose his second boss over his first."

"Not only is our enemy a step ahead of us, her underlings are, too." Yangchen shielded her eyes from some unknown harshness. "We're the last cart in an ostrich-horse–drawn train, rolling through the droppings."

The Avatar truly had a way with words. "What's our next move?" Kavik asked.

"Yingsu gave me a piece of information before Thapa took her out," Yangchen said. "Chaisee was saving Unanimity for Taku, not Bin-Er, and she was going to unleash them during the convocation with the Earth King, Fire Lord, and Water Tribe Chief. With Thapa freed, her plan's most likely back on. She only needs one Firebender to do permanent damage to the world."

Yangchen looked around at her team. "We have to go to Taku and remove Thapa from the board. The four of you know what he looks like and are the only ones I can trust on this matter. Yes, Juji, that means Kavik too; we need every resource we have. You can put your hand down."

Jujinta did as he was told, but he still had more questions. "Taku's much bigger than Bin-Er. And the only reason we were able to find any of the Firebenders to begin with was"—his lips juddered, so unwilling was he to give Kavik any kind of praise— "was *this person* over here giving us a head start. Could we not enlist the Airbenders who guarded Thapa?"

"I don't think we can count on support from the Northern Temple." Yangchen sounded like she could have elaborated but didn't.

Akuudan sighed. His chest contained enough air to blow out a small section of candles. "I'm too old for frontline work," he grumbled.

"Aw, sweetie." Tayagum bumped his shoulder against his husband's. "It'll be like when we met on the job, before the Platinum Affair and the stint in prison."

"You two were quartermasters," Kavik said. "Supply managers." Despite thinking Tayagum and Akuudan were scrappers when they first met, he'd learned they'd managed to avoid any of the painful work and since revised his opinion. "The toughest action you probably ever saw was dishing out stew." The two men simply shrugged, as if he had their measure.

"Can I have the room?" Yangchen asked. "Kavik, stay behind for a bit, please."

The excessive politeness in her tone made it seem to the others like she was really going to give it to him in private, to make sure he knew a horrific fate was in store if he tried to cross them again. Tayagum and Akuudan shuffled out of the chamber without complaint. Jujinta's gaze bounced back and forth between Kavik and the Avatar, the rest of his expression as unchanging as always.

"He's not a threat," Yangchen assured him.

"She could trounce me with both hands tied behind her back," Kavik said. He wasn't being sarcastic.

It took both of their testimonies to get Jujinta to leave. Yangchen waited a while before speaking. "Was that enough?" she asked.

"Enough what?"

"For your report to the White Lotus." She began walking in a circle around him, her eyes downcast. "You have to tell them everything you observe, don't you? You're the go-between. The errand runner."

The flames of the candles tilted as she passed them, bowing their heads. "You can report back to Ayunerak the sheer magnitude of my failure. How she's right—I'm an incompetent child who should never be trusted with world affairs."

He thought about denying the claim, but it would be no use. Based on how poorly the meeting in Agna Qel'a went, she already knew too much of the White Lotus's perspective.

Yangchen's voice was flat, as if she were delivering an account to a magistrate. "I mean, I lost Henshe, a valuable witness. I let two of the most valuable assets in the world die at the hands of the third. I nearly cost the village and the Air Temple more lives." Her slow, measured steps ticked each item off the list.

She wanted him to be an echo in the canyon, to throw her mistakes back in her face. He wasn't going to indulge her. "Ayunerak has her own work to grade before she starts on yours," Kavik said. "As for me, my opinion here isn't worth the breath I would need to give it."

Yangchen frowned. "That's not quite the same as not having an opinion."

"I know. I can keep my mouth shut and still do my job. Remember that's part of the deal with the White Lotus as well? Helping you?"

Her lips softened and then puckered the way they did whenever she was genuinely surprised. Kavik could have been convinced that for a moment, she forgot she hated him.

The candles flickered from an additional presence. He turned around, expecting to see Jujinta lurking about. Instead it was Abbot Sonam, the elderly monk who led the Northern Temple.

Sonam bowed his head, tufts of white hair forming a halo around the base. "Master Kavik," he said as if he were in the presence of an honored guest. "Thank you yet again for your efforts in the hospital. You have a knack for healing."

"I don't really know how to heal," Kavik said. He still lacked formal training in the art.

"Sometimes the greatest medicine is providing the right assistance at the right time," Sonam said. "Mingyur is awake and doing well."

"We should go see him," Yangchen said.

Sonam raised his fingers. "There's no need. Avatar, I have a quest for you. A matter of great urgency."

Kavik found the abbot's behavior a little abrupt. But Yangchen seemed to know what the old man was on about. "He can stay," she said, suddenly weary and resigned. "Tradition dictates a witness."

Sonam gave a solemn nod. "Sister Yangchen. The community of the Northern Air Temple desperately needs a boon only you can provide. After you next leave these sacred grounds, our existence depends on you returning with treasures of great importance."

"O elder," Yangchen said. "I devote myself fully to this cause. What shall I retrieve from the four corners of the world?"

"A blue panda lily," Sonam said. "The shadow of a breeze. The sinews of a spirit. And most important of all, the material possession that will fill the emptiness that lies in every human being."

Kavik's head began to sway. This couldn't mean what he thought it meant.

"When you see me next, you will see these jewels," Yangchen said, stilting over her vow. "So I swear."

"Thank you, Sister Yangchen." The abbot bowed deeply, the arrow points on the backs of his hands touching at his waist. "Carry the love of your people with you always." Sonam stood up, wiped the tears from his eyes, and left without another word.

Kavik didn't wait for the abbot to get farther away because he didn't care who heard him. "No," he said. "No, no, *no!*"

"You guessed?" Yangchen said. She'd stumbled from the blow a little there, but only a little. She was as calm as could be.

Kavik didn't need the ritual explained to him. It was a demonstration that Airbenders were passive even in the wording of their punishments, the least amount of violence spoken into being. The task Sonam had given her was poetic and impossible and could mean only one thing—Yangchen had been exiled from the Northern Air Temple.

"This is bull-pig!" Kavik shouted. "You're the Avatar. Overrule him!"

Yangchen made a gesture for him to lower his voice. "I'm an Air Nomad. A member of my people. The abbot is responsible for the safety of this community and I'm not going to disrespect my own traditions by undermining his authority." She ran her tongue over her teeth. "Besides, you're getting worked up over nothing."

To lose your connection to your home wasn't nothing. He told her so. "Relax," she said. "If you're worried about the village, I can still look after the townsfolk from afar."

She was almost smug about the turn of events. Finally, the castigation she'd been waiting for. "What is wrong with you?" Kavik said. "Why are you acting like this?"

"Because it doesn't matter. There are other temples I can lay my head at. Please, quiet down."

"The sunset from the tower. Your sister's favorite place—"

*"I SAID IT DOESN'T MATTER!"*

Her bark extinguished the candle flames. The light vanished, replaced by smoke. Yangchen's features were blanked out in the darkness, and the hallway lamps outside cast her heavy silhouette in the frame of the entryway. It was like she had an alcove to herself already.

No artist who loved her would have rendered her like this. "I need to be held accountable," she said, sounding like the void. "If I can't be an Airbender when it comes to my actions, I can at least be an Airbender when it comes to the consequences."

There was nothing he could say. "Go rest up," she ordered Kavik. "We've got a lot of work ahead of us."

Four days had passed since Thapa's jailbreak and the assassination of Zongdu Henshe.

Kavik hadn't seen Yangchen once during that time. He loitered in the teahouse with the others and waited. Occasionally

Akuudan or Tayagum would declare, unprompted, that she was probably making further preparations. She was fine. All was well.

On the night of the fifth day, Kavik waited until the others were asleep and snuck out the back of the teahouse. Since Jujinta adamantly refused to let his guard down until Kavik was unconscious, he had to use a trick—several.

He knew what he snored like, because Kalyaan had made fun of him for it often enough by mimicking him perfectly, according to their parents. Forcing air through his nose just so, he kept his eyes shut and tossed convincingly until Jujinta relented and sought his own bed in the teahouse.

Once he was the last person awake, he slipped from beneath his covers and froze a skeleton of ice braces under the blanket, making it look like he was still there. He'd get back before it melted completely and could dry the evidence. A small sheet of ice to form a bridge over the squeaky planks in the floor, and he was outside, free.

The skies were clear. He crept along the streets of the village, avoiding the illumination of the moon and stars, but couldn't resist the occasional glance upward. In the mountains, the celestial bodies looked close enough to pluck from the sky.

He reached the outskirts where the absolute newest arrivals sheltered in hutches and lean-tos thatched with straw until more permanent lodgings could be found for them. Avoiding the families, he wove between the travelers who were alone until he saw a tent with a circle drawn in the dirt in front.

He covered the mark with his foot. "Warmer than usual this time of year," he said to the person inside.

"Underestimate the night at your own risk," came the response through an opened flap.

"You know, you may be right." *I recognize your voice, Do,* Kavik wanted to snap. *This is stupid.* "Can I come in and take a rest? I could . . . trade you a tale . . . from my homeland."

The White Lotus passphrases were probably as old as Ayunerak. "Certainly. The wise man always appreciates swapping stories with an interesting stranger." The tent opened all the way.

Kavik crawled inside. Once he'd closed the flap completely, he knew he could talk without concerns of being overheard. The fabric was an ingenious blend that muffled sound; Ayunerak had demonstrated it in the Gidu safe house.

Do sat hunched under the slope of the tent. "Spoor of the spirits, we have to update those codes," Kavik said.

"We have people who've been stationed for years without meaningful contact, and changing the passphrases too frequently would leave them in the cold." Do rolled his eyes like Kavik was completely new to the game. "What's your report?"

Ayunerak had given him a few names in the White Lotus qualified to speak and listen for her and Do was one of them. But Kavik still wasn't fully comfortable. Part of him was inclined to side with Yangchen when she suspected a leak in the organization.

He put aside his misgivings and told the older man everything that had transpired since he'd arrived. "Huh," Do snorted. "This is what happens when we let children sit at the big table."

*The next time we spar I am going to shove an icicle so far up your nose, you'll get brain freeze.* "Unanimity is gone," Kavik said. "The Avatar ordered me to deliver this message. She needs help from the White Lotus to keep the leaders of the Four Nations far away from Taku. If the convocation proceeds as planned, Chaisee will have the opportunity to decapitate the entire world in a single stroke."

Do pondered the situation. "But if it doesn't go as planned, Chaisee will suspect we're onto her and withdraw the Firebender. We'll never get as good a chance to find and take control of him." He shook his head. "No. We can't give the leaders any warning that something's amiss."

Kavik couldn't believe what he was hearing. When pushed to the line, the Avatar would always focus on minimizing harm over seizing victory. "You're mad. The White Lotus is willing to gamble with the fate of the Four Nations?"

"War is a known quantity," Do said. "This Firebender and his technique are not."

Do, whom Kavik had never taken very seriously before, went calm and still the way only a true fanatic could. "The White Lotus is an ancient organization," Do said. "It has seen conflicts come and go. Rulers too. What it cannot abide is an unchecked power running rampant across the world. We already have one of those, and you know her well."

The man who delivered food and updates to the Gidu safe house would have been smug about putting the new recruit in his place, but this version was dispassionate, steady, and much more frightening. "We have fought for balance longer than you can imagine and have histories you could never dream of," Do said. "Our best results have always been achieved by maintaining a grip on a few vital reins of power while scorning all else. Whoever controls Unanimity at the end of this struggle will have the means to reshape the world to their liking. We can't let it fall into anyone else's hands, even if it means risking the life of a monarch or two."

"And if everything goes to pieces in Taku, what will the White Lotus do then?"

Do's response was immediate, generic, and true. A hammer that could be applied to any nail. "We'll watch the crisis unfold from a distance and adopt the best position to help the Four Nations in the aftermath, as we have done for generations. Do you believe Ayunerak would tell you differently?"

No. The problem was the Executor would say the exact same thing. He could hear Do's speech in Ayunerak's wizened voice, as if her spirit had possessed him. Maybe after reaching a certain age, a person came to treat conflict as a reoccurring expense, costly but bearable so long as relative comfort and stability could be maintained behind the front lines. Yangchen would have abhorred such thought. Kavik could see why she didn't get along with the organization.

"You're not to leave the Avatar's side in Taku," Do said. "If she finds leads on Thapa there, we want to know about them."

"You're spying on your ally instead of your enemy," Kavik said. "That's completely backward."

"We don't have a plant embedded with our enemy. I'll relay the Avatar's message to Ayunerak, but don't expect our strategy to change. Now get out of here before the Avatar notices you're gone."

Kavik got up and squirmed his way out of the tent. The flap closed behind him. He breathed in the crisp mountain air and looked up at the inky night sky.

On the way back to the teahouse, he suddenly came to a standstill, his boots embedded in the gravel. The frustration he'd been holding back came pouring out, and he swung his fist at the empty air, connecting with nothing.

*Do what we tell you. We know better.* Kavik had been hoping for things to start making sense when he joined the White Lotus.

But so far, it had been no different than living with Kalyaan.

# BAD COMPANY

**CHAISEE DID** not enjoy watching poor table manners.

Thapa ate like a ravenous beast, pinning roasted joints of meat to his plate with his hands and tearing the flesh off with his jaws. He wiped his fingers on pillowy bread buns before consuming those too and took large gulps of wine to help swallow the unchewed chunks of food.

He looked up with one eye, his teeth still embedded in a cricket-goose leg, and saw Chaisee's disdain. "Cut me some slack," he said. "This is the first taste of meat I've had in months."

Chaisee pushed a stack of napkins across the table. It was a good thing the former zongdu Dooshim wasn't alive to see his inn host such an uncouth guest. The luxurious resort, built on stilts over the middle of a flowing river, catered to exclusive clients, the kind rich enough to skirt the restrictions brought on by the Platinum Affair. She'd secretly bought the business after Dooshim passed away and had vacated the entire premises to ensure the security of her recovered asset.

Once cleared of other visitors, the inn made a fairly good location for clandestine meetings. The nearby waterfall ensured a low level of background noise to foil casual eavesdroppers, and the heavily perfumed air might have thrown off a poorly trained scent-tracking animal. The only access points were two long bridges spanning the banks of the river, and those were easily guarded.

"I'm told you exercised some initiative." Chaisee refilled Thapa's winecup and allowed herself a pour as well. Now that her son was delivered, she could have the occasional drink. "I detest initiative."

"Sorry, *Mother.*" As far as Chaisee knew, they were about the same age. Thapa waited. "That's it? I thought you'd be angrier."

"You don't know what I am."

He pulled a platter of steamed fish topped with slivers of ginger and scallion closer to himself. "I know you're down a couple of assets," he said as he got to work with a pair of spoons. "Look at it this way. I saved you the drudgery and expense of paying them. Now you have the honor and pleasure of paying *me*. Plus a bonus for showing . . . an enterprising attitude."

So his time among the Airbenders hadn't rubbed off. Shame. Chaisee greatly respected Air Nomad culture and was an avid reader of their philosophers. She wondered if the young Avatar had finished the *Works of Shoken* she'd gifted her.

She blinked as Thapa carelessly flipped the fish to get at the other side. "I think thirty times our original agreement will do," he said. "For a start."

"Is that what Henshe promised when he diverted you to Bin-Er?"

"Nah, I had to extort him. You and I, on the other hand, are true business partners. I'm the only person who can provide the services you need in the time you require. And you're the only one who can pay me—oh wait. You're not."

He shoveled spoonfuls of silverskim into his mouth and fixed her with his gaze. "I suppose the Earth King or the Fire Lord might be interested in my talents, enough to start a little bidding war. The Water Tribe Chief too, though I hope not. I'd hate to be stuck in the cold."

Thapa slowed down the pace at which he chewed and swallowed. Not out of concern for fish bones, but to make sure she was looking back at him. Causing revulsion was the point. "Face it. If you want sparks to fly over Taku, then you have no other choice than to bargain with me."

Chaisee decided that prisoners enjoying new freedom ate the same way as sailors on shore leave. What concern did they have for the mess they created? She remembered wanting to raise her voice at the ungracious visitors that fateful day on her home island, but her father had told her it wasn't their right to command a guest. Tradition demanded they remain obsequious, servile.

Some of the sailors feasted obliviously, spurred by the open air and the simple lifestyle of their hosts to cast bones into the sand and manners to the wind. Others, when they noticed her watching with disapproval, applied an edge to their raucousness like Thapa did now, a show for the tight-lipped young girl. The greater the mess one caused, the more power they exerted. An attitude she found many across the Four Nations adopted even when they didn't realize it.

"No," Chaisee said. "There will be no new deal. Not because I can't afford it but because I won't allow it. I don't do business with people lacking in character."

Thapa belched loudly. "Too bad. I was hoping to stay until I finished dessert. The monks did baked goods better than anyone else in the world and I think developed a sweet tooth."

He stood up and shoved the entire table aside with a single sweep of his arms. The legs skidded across the floor. A waterfall of plates cascaded over the corner.

No barrier separated her from Thapa. She'd ordered her guards to leave them alone. The hulking Firebender glanced at the door, someone accustomed to checking for witnesses before acting, and then at her. "Last chance."

Chaisee didn't get up.

Grease dripping down chins, light from the cookfires glinting off the fat. The cold ashes of her family's hut, sifting through her toes. What kind of home could vanish so easily? No home at all. The only foundation you could trust was one you'd built yourself. Thapa took a step closer.

*"Upon fickle whim, the mind invites its masters,"* Chaisee said. She snapped her fingers.

Her asset stopped moving. *"The eyes and ears, four gates to block the conquering truth,"* Thapa responded.

For a while Chaisee said nothing. Therefore Thapa did nothing. He stood there, silently, awaiting command.

"Lower your head," she said. He did as he was told, bowing. "Lower. More." The big lummox had all the height Chaisee lacked. Once their heads were level she looked into his eyes, spreading his lids apart with her thumb and forefinger. His pupils had dilated; he didn't seem to be faking.

Chaisee sighed. She considered that Thapa might very well have done her a favor by murdering the other two Firebenders. He'd always taken to the conditioning the best out of the three, and his treacherous nature didn't matter when she could force his pliancy. Henshe had lacked this guarantee of Unanimity's loyalty, and that was why he'd been doomed to fail in Bin-Er. The idiot deserved whatever betrayal Thapa had inflicted upon him.

The plan was back on track. But she needed to make absolutely sure there would be no further exercising of initiative.

"Pick up that knife and stab yourself in the thigh," Chaisee said. "Don't hit an artery. And you can speak naturally." She hadn't fully tested if he was capable of passing undetected in this state or if people would notice something off in his speech patterns.

Thapa made a gesture with his fingers, a signal for a bribe. "I'll do it, but it'll cost you."

Chaisee stared at him.

"Kidding, kidding," Thapa said. Her asset found the knife by his feet. He plucked it off the floor and held it in a reverse grip, the sharp point facing down and toward the meat of his own leg. "How many times?"

# THE OATHBREAKER

**KAVIK THOUGHT** he knew rich from the times he'd infiltrated properties owned by the Bin-Er shangs. But he was wrong. Teiin and Noehi and the rest of them were inexperienced campers bringing too many possessions on a hike, worried they wouldn't have enough luxuries to sustain them.

From the aerial view alone, the wealthy of Taku had no such concerns. The roofs were tiled with expensive slate that had to have been earthbent one by one into the right shapes, the streets were as smooth as smoked leather, and the fountain in the center of the square was literally gilded from base to peak. Above the busy commercial and residential sectors, Taku's famous Old Town climbed the inclines of tiny Mount Wuyao like creeping ivy, tendrils of stately, aristocratic bungalows lacing across the slope.

He finally understood why the shangs of Bin-Er fought to grow their balance sheets with such tenacity. Taku was a measuring stick they were desperately trying to catch up to. Or it was the consolidated holder of all their debts. There was no reason the rival city couldn't have been both.

Kavik pulled back from the saddle railing and looked around. The procession of monks who'd joined them acted no differently than the one that had taken them to Jonduri. The Airbenders were relaxed and happy, cracking jokes and trading stories. Either word of the Avatar's exile from the North had been kept from them, or they'd been asked to pretend like nothing had changed.

Kavik found either prospect immeasurably heavy inside his chest. This wasn't Yangchen's arrival. This was her farewell journey.

He could see only her back, her hands on the reins. He was afraid of who might show up once they landed and she turned around to face him, Yangchen or one of the Avatars past who'd walked longer upon the ground and didn't share her invincible resolve.

"We're descending," she said. She sounded like herself. The bison dipped and the cheering of the crowds below grew louder.

Kavik could only sit. Wait. Watch. Like his job entailed.

Five Airbenders entered the bland, dingy white house in Taku's international district using a back-alley door hidden behind a jook cart. They'd successfully escaped the throngs of Taku residents surrounding the Avatar's official lodgings with the aid of the monks who'd run a screening pattern using distracting, weaving movements. One last favor from the Northern Temple.

No one had paid them any mind. Air Nomads might be a sight worth seeing, but not when you could lay your eyes on the pinnacle of Airbenderhood. The poor suckers in the crowd might be waiting in the street outside that magnificent, currently empty mansion for a very long time.

Kavik didn't mind that he wouldn't be staying in the finest accommodations the city had to offer. As far as safe houses went, this one was positively posh. The communal room was clean and dry, and there looked to be a kitchen and bathing area in the back. The place reminded him of his parents' house in Bin-Er.

The door shut behind them. "I think I have a headache," Kavik said. He threw back his orange hood, inhaled, and gagged. The scent of flowers reached up through his nose all the way to the back of his skull. "Did they add extra perfume to the petals?"

They'd nearly been smothered by the waves of blossoms thrown by well-wishers and blessing-seekers. The residents of Taku had stolen and multiplied the greeting celebrations from Jonduri. "This town doesn't spend silver when it can spend gold," Yangchen said.

Tayagum and Akuudan shrugged off their borrowed Airbender vestments. Wearing the clothes of the temple felt like a special crime to Kavik. Of course they'd all been ordered to put on the Air Nomad disguises by Yangchen, but the act had to be some kind of offense in normal circumstances. Defrauding of the wind and spirits, four counts. Punishment was merited.

As if to agree with him, the air suddenly began to shake, a crash of brass that vibrated through the house down to its foundations. Kavik flinched from the noise, but then so did the others. They'd all learned to fear strange sounds coming from the sky.

Only the Avatar remained unmoved. "The great gong of Taku," she explained to her startled crew. Another bone-rattling clash nearly drowned her voice out. "During daylight, it sounds off every hour on the hour."

The anticipation of a third strike that never came was worse than the actual noise. "We have to listen to that repeatedly?" Kavik asked once his eardrums stopped bouncing.

"The only true wealth is time," Yangchen said. "I'm taking a bath first to wash the perfume off. Don't bother me for at least an hour. Maybe two." She stomped down the hallway to the other end of the house, her normally featherlike footfalls doubled in weight.

"She's taking it well," Kavik muttered.

"Taking what well?" Tayagum snapped.

*Had she not told them?* The truth of her exile suddenly burned like a hot coal in his hands. "Working, uh, with someone who turned on her." *How could she not tell them?*

Tayagum looked like he was about to unleash a tirade but clenched his teeth back together when Akuudan put a hand on his shoulder. No need to rehash the recent past. "Come on," Akuudan said gently. "Help me scrounge up something for dinner. I'm thinking ocean kumquat and komodo sausage."

"Fire Nation food?" Kavik was slightly confused.

Akuudan pointed with his chin at Jujinta. "We like him better than you." He gathered Tayagum about the waist and together they went off to the kitchen area.

This was the first time Kavik had come to grips with his former partner, alone, since returning to the fold. "So . . ." He scratched the back of his neck.

Jujinta hadn't moved to take off his disguise. His glower, completely devoid of any warmth, was a jarring contrast to the Airbender robes underneath. Someone had sawn the head off a temple statue and replaced it with the visage of a fearsome spirit who scared children into obeying their parents. "Look at you!" Kavik said brightly. "New boss and everything. How's it working out?"

"It has been the most glorious experience of my life." Jujinta rubbed the bridge of his nose where the skin turned paler as if to check if his scar was still there. The old wound was a smear across his face, like he'd tried to remove a surface blemish and scoured flesh off instead. "Every moment in the Avatar's service is a guided step along the true path. By following in her wake, I have been blessed with certainty in all I do."

"As long as you're happy." Come to think of it, Kavik hadn't seen him perform his symbol-carving ritual once since their reunion.

"Yes. *As long as Jujinta is happy, then no harm done. He doesn't know any better.* That's what you were thinking, right?" Kavik wanted to protest but was cut off. "Let me tell you something. My happiness wasn't worth the chaos you let into the world, and neither was your brother's life."

Back in Jonduri, Jujinta spoke like each word cost its length in gold bar. To have him cut with so many remarks was almost an honor. "I've heard you claim you used to be an accountant," Jujinta said. "Then you should know every person has two sides of the ledger. You can start feeling better about yourself once your existence is a net gain."

Kavik puckered his lips. Philosophy lessons from his former partner. "I suppose a lecture is much better than threats."

"Oh no, I just haven't gotten to those yet." No one in the world could have said so with less affectation than Jujinta. No archness, only fact. "I know you left the inn at night to meet with someone. I told the Avatar the next day and she explicitly ordered me to drop the issue. That's the only reason I didn't track down your contact and put a blade in their spine before doing the same to you."

*There* was the Jujinta he was best acquainted with. Kavik put on a mild smile while surreptitiously feeling around him for water. There was some farther down the hall, a growing mass. The Avatar's bath? He glanced around Jujinta's torso for his favored draw locations, the ones he knew about at least. The loose Air Nomad robes did a good job of hiding them.

"I don't know who your new masters are, or why the Avatar accepts the situation," Jujinta said. "But if you betray her again, I'll kill you. If you hurt her or anyone else on the team, I'll kill you. If your death would further the Avatar's goals, I'll kill you."

He paid back the respect by watching Kavik's hands for waterbending motions. "It can be slow or fast," he said. "Not every wound needs to be fatal right away. Your spirit might benefit from additional time to repent in your final moments. Pain can be cleansing."

"I don't think the Avatar would approve, Juji."

"She wouldn't know. You'd simply vanish. One less problem for her to worry about."

Likening him to Qiu, the man whose body they'd dumped in the ocean together, seemed like an intentional low blow to Kavik. So he answered with one of his own. "Well, keep walking this path of truth. Maybe one day you'll be able to look your brother in the eye."

Kavik was surprised as the words spilled out his mouth. He didn't know he could be so mean. Jujinta reared back and then settled into his feet again. "I can't believe I touched a bow for you." He sounded more disgusted than anything else.

Akuudan poked his head around the corner. "Hey, one of you knuckleheads come help me. The floor's greasy and this is a job for younger knees."

"I would be happy to scrub away the filth so it is never seen again on the face of this earth," Jujinta said. He joined the others in the kitchen.

Akuudan might have noticed something amiss, but then again, Jujinta's declaration of war against caked-on oil was close enough to the way he normally spoke. Kavik had successfully shed his team like the last man standing at hide-and-seek. He'd won, but the losers got to keep each other company.

He was grateful, to an extent. If the shunning continued, Kavik would be in an ideal position to run his mission for the White Lotus, unobserved. His life would be much easier.

He just hadn't expected it to feel so lonely.

# MATTERS OF PRIDE

**YANGCHEN FORGOT** sometimes. The problem with clandestine affairs was how easily they were wiped out by aboveboard power moves. Spycraft could be like a fight between an owl-wolf and the sick gemsbok-bull it was hunting. The outcome was irrelevant if the entire herd got spooked and trampled both the participants.

The table she sat at was a harsh reminder that in daylight, money was still the most powerful weapon available. *"Feast,"* said Zongdu Iwashi, the man who ran Taku. He tipped over the row of Sparrowbones tiles in front of him to reveal a neat sequence of symbols. His clean-shaven face oozed with glee. *"Guru Ascends the Mountain,* single colors, double-double."

Yangchen watched Kavik sputter, no grounds to protest. He'd just lost a sum large enough to fund a fully kitted merchant voyage between here and Port Tuugaq in a medium-sized ship. "Perhaps Master Lio could start playing more defensively," she said through her gritted teeth. She was glad she didn't have to feign calmness here.

"I thought it was a safe discard!" "Master Lio," who'd seriously oversold his gambling skills, wiped his brow. The fake identity Kavik wore might have been one extra layer too many, causing him to sweat. "It's humid," he mumbled in excuse.

It was indeed muggy inside the sumptuous parlor above the Taku gathering hall. Iwashi's collection of scrollwork was going to warp prematurely, and some of his miniature trees would never thrive in the moist conditions. He'd purchase new ones instead of caring.

Iwashi was about fifty years old, short, broad, and bald. He'd already made his fortune several times over in the mining business and was only a tourist as far as zongdus went. Unlike Henshe, who desperately needed the title to advance in society, Iwashi treated his job as a lark and was content to walk alongside the lumbering behemoth that was Taku's wealth. He could give it a prod every now and then while calling himself its leader.

The hands-off attitude Iwashi took toward being Zongdu of Taku apparently gave him plenty of time to master other pursuits at the highest level. "Therein lies your problem, Master Lio," he said. "By seeking safety, you become predictable. Prey in a burrow, with no recourse but to wait until you're dug out of your hole and slain."

Yangchen glanced to the side. Large paned glass doors opened to the balcony and offered a view of the harbor. In the distance, pleasure vessels bobbed in the waters. Iwashi's own pride and joy, the *Bliss Eternal*, was easily distinguished by the giant green banner trailing from the stern.

"Is there something that interests you down by the docks, Avatar?" asked the fourth member of the group.

"Yes," Yangchen said quickly. "I need to know when Master Lio's luck will come sailing in, because right now I think it's dropped anchor somewhere over the horizon."

Iwashi slapped his knee. Kavik shoved his tiles back into the center of the table, his lips a thin line. The dig at his expense was the fastest deflection away from the water that Yangchen could think of, but it wasn't helping his mental state any.

She couldn't blame Kavik for being rattled. Not when Zongdu Chaisee sat between them. "I wouldn't be too harsh on your companion," Chaisee said. "He might be bleeding money, but at the end of the day, it's only money. Not a matter of life and death."

"Bunk," Iwashi said. "Look at the phrasing you just used. *Blood.* Sanctimonious fools always claim that you can't put a price on human life, but you absolutely can. How much food does a person eat over eight decades? How much does medicine for a fatal disease cost? A magistrate declares compensation when a farmer's hippo-ox tramples the neighbor's child. Money *is* life. Money *is* death."

He suddenly leaned across the table corner and loomed close to Kavik's ear. The stretch of his neck coupled with his smooth head gave him the appearance of a cave eel. "I'm *killing* you, Master Lio," Iwashi said while Kavik stared down at his own lap. "Not with a knife in the dark, but in broad daylight. That is what your debt means."

The Zongdu of Taku gestured into the distance as if asking his victim to behold the waiting void. "If you were to run right now, duty, honor, and law would deliver you right back into my hands. I don't think your entire life's labors could encompass the sum you currently owe me. I'm killing you and anyone you might have hoped to support."

"Iwashi, that's enough," said Chaisee. "Don't be a churl."

"Merely a metaphor." Iwashi withdrew to his own seat, human once again. "But is it enough? What say you, Master Lio? Do you think you can recover from such devastating losses?"

Kavik didn't look up to meet Yangchen's gaze. She could have answered for him and signaled their retreat. This was their chance to withdraw. The fortunes of Bin-Er had been disemboweled, but if they held their guts in as they ran and didn't trip, they might escape.

But they still hadn't received the signal from the others. Jujinta, Tayagum, and Akuudan should have been finished at least an hour ago. Had they been caught? Were she and Kavik buying time for dead men? Or were they merely dawdling?

Yangchen's jaws stuck halfway open, a gate rusted to uselessness. She couldn't push a decision out. With nothing but silence on offer, Kavik interpreted her will as best he could. "No," he whispered. "I can keep going."

*Hesitation gets people killed.* Someone had told her that, once. Iwashi's claim was no poetic device. The funds for the wells she'd been planning were long gone. Money for shelter, warmth, food—gone. She and Kavik were gambling with lives and losing.

*This plan was a mistake,* Yangchen screamed in her own head. Only the breeze she stole from the window kept her from sweating like Kavik. *What was I thinking? What in the name of the spirits was I thinking?*

# BAITED

### LAST NIGHT

"I know what you're all thinking," Yangchen said to her assembled team. Night had settled over the safe house. She held the cup of tea in her hands close to her face, even though it was on the verge of blistering her finger pads. "We have six days before the Earth King, Fire Lord, and Water Tribe Chief arrive in Taku. Chaisee won't be as careless with her asset as Henshe. Five people can't possibly cover enough ground to get a direct visual confirmation on one man before it's too late."

The team stood around a flimsy table they'd hauled out of storage. The map of Taku they loomed over was marked up with a grease pencil, each smudge a location where Thapa could set up to inflict catastrophic damage. There were simply too many ideal hiding spots. The map was as dotted as a pox victim.

Succeeding with the same game plan as they had used in Bin-Er was always going to be unlikely. Not only did Taku present a larger, less familiar jungle, but the convocation itself was a problem. The merchants had boosted their private security contingents for the week, which meant the streets were filled with a lot of oversized benders, fighters, and hired toughs of all stripes. Thapa's distinctive build was no longer so unique.

"No luck turning back the heads of state?" Tayagum asked.

"None." She avoided looking at Kavik. He'd relayed her plea to the White Lotus, but there had been no response yet, and as far as the latest news was concerned, Feishan and the other leaders were still on their way. "I've exhausted my channels with them—pushing any harder risks causing another international incident. We're on our own."

"If we can't defend with our numbers, then we need to attack," Jujinta said.

"Precisely." She noticed the annoyed little pout Kavik made when she praised Jujinta and tucked it away for later. "With the right records, we can narrow these locations down to a manageable set."

"Stealing information from Chaisee isn't going to be easy under these circumstances," Tayagum said.

"We won't have to. We can count on her to do the smart thing in this scenario, which is to make her preparations through an intermediary. Zongdu Iwashi."

If the woman had one exploitable pattern, it was that she liked using her peers as patsies. "From her perspective, Iwashi is the ideal agent. He can set up any arrangement she might need in Taku. And she can demand the favor in a face-to-face talk without creating a written trail leading back to her."

Yangchen drank her tea in gulps, pain smearing over her tongue. While the others had their own cups, she'd laced hers with leaves used in the special brew that visitors to the Spirit Oasis drank. Whether she was allowed to have it outside of the ritual was a gray area, but it was much stronger than normal tea and she needed every bit of energy she could muster. "From *our* perspective, Iwashi is a much softer target."

"How much softer?" Kavik asked.

She put the empty cup on a curling corner of the map. "It'll be like scoring on an empty hoop. I guarantee it."

"Zongdu Iwashi has many great loves," Yangchen explained to her assembled team. "Cicada-cricket fighting, penjing gardening, sailing. Especially sailing. This year's convocation has been scheduled during a very inconvenient season for him. The winds are favorable for ships and normally he'd be on the water as much as possible. During these months he even sleeps on the boat at night and handles what little work he does while at sea."

"So all of his important documents will be in his little floating office," Tayagum said.

"The *Bliss Eternal* is anything but little, but yes. Once the convocation finishes for the day, he's going to be eager for an evening jaunt around the coast. His personal security will follow him."

"We hit the boat before his evening cruise," Akuudan said. "Seems straightforward enough."

"It would be, except there isn't a good window during business hours. Based on the maintenance and resupply schedules, we'd have to strike after the convocation adjourns but before Iwashi himself reaches the docks."

"Exactly how long have you been preparing to go to war with the Zongdu of Taku?" Kavik asked.

Bin-Er was supposed to be only the first stop on her campaign to challenge the shang system as a whole. But she'd gotten sidetracked, to say the least. "Whoever starts playing the game first wins. Are you honestly surprised?" He shrugged and shook his head.

Yangchen picked up where she'd left off. "As I was saying—Iwashi's hobbies. There is one pursuit he loves even more than sailing. The only thing that could keep him from his beloved ship after a day of boring meetings." She paused and looked around. "Sparrowbones."

She sensed everyone's interest sharpen immediately. The gambling game was practically Jonduri's national sport. "Iwashi is an absolute fiend for Sparrowbones and has been known to challenge random players on the spot if he thinks they'll put up a decent fight," she said. "Unfortunately, I don't quite measure up, at least not by myself."

Yangchen swirled her remaining dregs of tea, scrambling any fortunes hidden in the leaves. The future was made, not read. "Now tell me. Which of you four happens to be the best player?"

Hours later, Yangchen and Kavik snuck out of the safe house and made their way to one of the main avenues that spanned Taku. The plan required them to start their day in the Avatar's official lodgings. Moving as a pair through the side streets was much faster than going alone when they could watch each other's blind spots.

They relaxed once the sounds of nightlife filled the air. The warm glow of lanterns painted the walls of the international zone an inviting orange, while the sizzle and chop of food stalls punctuated the lively conversations taking place along the sidewalks. One corner was lined with shadow puppet stages. Artists smeared hide cutouts against mulberry paper screens using sticks of rattan while the audience on the other side cheered and booed their favorite characters from old folktales.

Yangchen grabbed Kavik's arm and tugged him along when he dawdled, broad grins on both their faces. They ran past turning heads, giggling, and made it to the side of the guesthouse where the Avatar was staying for the convocation. A quick air spout elevated them both to the second-story window of her official quarters. They undid the latch with fumbling hands and tumbled through together.

As soon as they were inside, they dropped their smiles and separated all the way to different corners of the room. Yangchen firebent flame into the lamps and looked around. There was an enclosed, three-sided bed, carved with lattices as fine as the lace of a noblewoman's dress. A lotus-shaped censer hanging from the ceiling spilled sweet fragrance over the furnishings, and the dressing table held an array of combs. She snorted when she realized it—they'd put her in a wedding suite.

Kavik circumnavigated the walls, dragging his spread fingers along the surface to check for hidden apertures. He finished his rounds and faced her again. "Clean," he said.

"No errand runners threatening to burst out and hold me hostage?"

His wan grimace was especially sad compared to the expressions he'd faked so well earlier. "Not unless they can bend solid wood."

They both stood with their arms held close to their bodies, unwilling to relax. "Tomorrow's a big day," Yangchen said. "Are you sure Chaisee isn't going to recognize you?"

"You already asked."

"I'm asking again. In case you didn't feel like you could tell the truth in front of the others."

She could have ordered him closer into the light so she could examine his eyes, check his pulse, watch the flush of his skin, but he seemed so thin right now, one of the paper shadows from the street plays that could only move along a single plane. A nudge in the wrong direction would distort his answer.

"What you really mean is, did my brother rat me out? Did he burn me?" Kavik took longer to think about his response than he did when she'd asked back at the safe house. "The answer is no. He'd have nothing to gain by it."

Thanks to his last-minute confession, she knew the story of what happened in Jonduri. Kalyaan had facilitated his entry into Chaisee's association and sent him home to Bin-Er with his cover intact. In a way, he'd protected his little brother as well as himself.

Yangchen was satisfied, as much as she could be given the circumstances. But then Kavik added one last unnecessary stamp to his testimony. "I'm Kalyaan's family," he said. "His blood. He'd never play games with my life the way you would."

*You think we're playing games here?* she wanted to snap. *Is that it?* But he had a point. Kavik had never truly volunteered his services. In Bin-Er, they'd bargained with each other from a blackmailing down to a transaction. Claiming she didn't know how dangerous the Jonduri mission was made Yangchen either callous or incompetent. Both, really.

Companions throughout the eras were willing to make any sacrifice for their Avatars. But Kavik vexed her. How much could she really ask of him? How far could she push him in the name of service and still live with herself?

There was no exit now; their fates had been twined. She wished she hadn't spoken to him so harshly when they'd parted ways in Bin-Er. It had been satisfying to slap him across the face with the label of *asset* and deny him genuine companionhood, but lashing out hadn't been worth it. A little absolution back then might have led to an easier current state of affairs. Kavik giving of himself freely, like a devoted friend. Yangchen responding with grace. Instead, the two of them had gone and made things complicated.

"I think you should go to sleep first," he said. "The people you become . . . It's better if they have someone to talk to."

Yangchen blinked. Right. The very small circle founded by Jetsun and the nuns of the Western Temple had expanded to include Kavik. There should have been some anger inside her at that, her vulnerability exposed to another outsider, but she couldn't find it. Kavik seemed to get a pass where Ayunerak didn't. "Are you sure you don't want to lie down for a bit?" she asked.

His eyes darted to the bed, the only place to do so other than the floor. "I'll be fine." He went over to the writing desk in the corner of the room and seated himself in the yokeback chair before finding a pencil and paper in the drawer. "I need to do some tabulations to make sure I'm remembering the figures cor-rectly. You're sure Taku uses Omashu-style rules?"

"Iwashi does. That's where he's from."

"Perfect." He steadfastly refused to look up from the desk. "Good night, Avatar."

Yangchen stood there for a while longer. She didn't know exactly what she was waiting for, or why she needed to stare at the top of his head. So she went to bed. Shielded by the carved enclosure, she stripped off her outer robes, tucked herself under the covers, and closed her eyes.

The only sound in the room was the rasp of his pencil. She could tell from the glide over the paper that he had a smooth and steady hand. The soft scratching filled her ears like com-forting plugs of cotton. She would have liked to have lain there, listening to him work, but before she knew it, she was fast asleep.

"Avatar, breakfast!" The maid's cheery voice pierced the morning silence. She didn't wait for a response and burst into the room. "Avatar, I've— Oh my!"

Yangchen rose from her bed, the covers falling from her shoulders to reveal her in a state of undress. Kavik woke with a start and nearly tumbled from the chair he'd slept in. While he was fully clothed, the fact remained that a gentleman caller had slept overnight in the young Avatar's quarters.

Yangchen quickly wrapped her blankets around her again in a makeshift cloak and shuffled over to the maid, crowding her back out of the room. The warm scent of porridge sweetened with mountain honey rose from the tray between them. "Mistress . . . I'm terribly sorry. What was your name again?"

"Guaba." The maid, who was shorter, tried to peer over Yangchen's shoulder without hiding it very well. *What nation is he from? Is he handsome?*

"Mistress Guaba, I know what this looks like, but I assure you nothing untoward is going on. Master Boma, my usual guardian, was not able to leave Bin-Er, and sent his grandson Lio in his stead to serve as my escort. No, I mean—yes. Escort."

Guaba nodded with what she thought was a blank expression. "Shall I bring more food?"

"No, this is fine."

"You'll share then." The glint in the maid's eye was sharper than the sunlight knifing through the crack in the curtains. There was only one spoon.

Yangchen forced a smile. "Please exercise discretion. I wouldn't want my fellow dignitaries getting the wrong idea." She wrested the tray out of Guaba's hands, turned around, and closed the door with her back.

Kavik had collected himself by then. "Smells good," he said. "Did she buy it?"

Gossip was universal, but for some reason servants were stuck with the bad reputation for it. "Between the people who saw us in the street and good Mistress Guaba, you have a solid cover." The more a story embarrassed a powerful person, the truer it appeared. "Come on. Let's eat."

The maid would have been disappointed to find out nothing scandalous occurred with utensils and mouths and the combinations therewith. Yangchen and Kavik simply took turns, passing the bowl to each other between slurps.

The symbol of Taku on the doors to the council hall remained one last barrier. Yangchen looked up at the bronze-plated floating gardenia, and above it, the gong tower that pierced the skyline. She wasn't looking forward to how loud the next strike would be this close. "Are you ready?"

Kavik tucked his satchel of papers under his arm and warmed his face up with his palms, rubbing his skin back and forth. "Let's go."

She pulled a rope attached to a bell, ringing it once, and the floating gardenia split down the middle. They were greeted by the harsh screech of chairs sliding over the floor. The businesspeople of Taku knew their manners and stood up to receive her without being told. They'd arrayed themselves in two wings with a long aisle down the middle.

Dozens of curious eyes landed on Yangchen and Kavik. *"Now would be good,"* she whispered out of the corner of her mouth. He might not have gotten enough sleep.

"The Avatar," he announced, taking on Boma's role. "Master of the Elements, Bridge Between Humans and Spirits." Yangchen started forward but he wasn't done. "Protector of Bin-Er and Defender of Tienhaishi. Benefactor of the Taihua Mountains, Healer of the Sick and Caretaker of the Hungry."

He might as well have thrown in "Captain of the Western Novice Airball Team" while he was at it. *Too much.*

*"I'm giving you your due,"* he whispered back. As if the entire assembly were in on the prank, the prominent men and women of the city began to clap. The noise was foreign to her. Applause was for a job well done; supplicants didn't clap for their benefactors, and neither did politicians for their opponents.

She was about to say as much, but Kavik cut her off. "You do good work. Shut up and bask for a moment."

They walked down the aisle toward an elevated section of floor. Yangchen fought the urge to shield her face as she passed much older men and women putting their hands together for her like she'd stunned them with a vocal performance. Somewhere around the halfway point, she realized the other strange component here was that these people weren't hiding knives in their glances. The shangs of Taku were no more or less greedy than their counterparts in Bin-Er, but at least they weren't trying to stab her under the table. As far as she knew.

Kavik kept making small circles with his arms as if he were physically scooping the praise atop her. *Isn't she something, folks?* Her embarrassment was sweeter than their breakfast honey to him, judging by the grin smeared across his face. "You're going to pay for this," she muttered.

"Sure, right after you—"

The retort died on his lips. Kavik's face sifted into a dignified frown. They'd reached the end of the hall. On the elevated section, there was a long table with four settings of prominence. Three of them were already filled.

Kindly old Zongdu Ashoona of Port Tuugaq raised his hand in greeting. Having recently recovered from a lingering illness, he was bundled in furs despite the heat and smelled faintly of medicine plasters. In the middle was Zongdu Iwashi, resplendent in the Kolau silks of his home city, his shiny head looking like an egg in a nest too small to hold it.

And at the far end stood Zongdu Chaisee.

The woman who ran Jonduri returned Yangchen's gaze with a relaxed, easy blankness. She was reminded of the ascetic practice where gurus crossed their legs and faced a wall for hours, days on end to contemplate the nature of emptiness. In Chaisee's case, the wall might have blinked first.

"Welcome, Avatar!" Iwashi said. "Or should I call you zongdu? You've represented Bin-Er quite magnificently these past months, or so my spies tell me."

His language didn't rattle Yangchen; everything was a jest to this man. Until it wasn't. "I hope by the end of this convocation you will call me friend."

"Oh, how well put! I don't think it will take that long." Iwashi turned his attention to Kavik. "Who is this fine young fellow?"

Next to her, she could sense Kavik's tension as if it were her own muscles screaming. The air around him practically vibrated. Overtly, the nervousness of a new companion unused to the grandeur of world business.

But Yangchen knew the true cause of his anxiety even if Kavik would rather die than admit it. Deep down, he wasn't as sure of his brother's loyalty as he'd professed.

Definitely *too late now.* "This is Master Lio, grandson of my usual guardian, Boma." Yangchen made sure not to favor any of the zongdus with her eye contact. "He will be serving me on this trip."

The twitch of Iwashi's lips, a squashed smirk, revealed he'd already heard the rumors from Guaba or some other busybody from the street last night. A minor victory. The more important ruse was the frequent letters she had Boma send over the years to nonexistent relatives in each nation and most major cities. She'd counted on some of them being intercepted by official border censors and enemies the likes of Chaisee, and now, thanks to Boma's prodigious and cosmopolitan fake family, she had a wealth of covers for any agents she needed directly by her side.

Chaisee tilted her head backward at a small group of men and women sitting behind the table, off to the side. They wore much plainer dress and clutched reams of documents like Kavik. "He can join the other attendants." She made no sign of recognition and if anything, sounded impatient to start business.

Kavik visibly relaxed. Yangchen's practice of littering misinformation into the sea had finally paid off. *You also got his friend Qiu killed the same way, you fool.* She took the chair once meant for Zongdu Henshe, another man who shouldn't have fallen under her watch.

She had to play this well, or else so much would count for naught. Yangchen settled in. "Shall we commence?"

"How have you not murdered someone in broad daylight at one of these meetings yet?" Kavik whispered in her ear.

He'd mimicked the other clerks and secretaries who'd stepped forward and delivered pieces of information to their seated masters when called upon. Bent at the waist and lips screened from the audience by a cupped palm. "Just like . . . 'Bam! Rock to the head.' There's your point of order for you."

Yangchen snorted, turned her head to the side, and made her own tunnel with her hands. "Power of imagination."

A lot of work for a simple reply. Every aside between a zongdu and their support staff had to be masked, every challenged claim backed up by figures, and every figure judged for relevancy. "We haven't done anything but listen to people complain about things we already know," Kavik said. "Is official Avatar business always this terrible?"

It had actually been worse before Szeto, who'd codified procedures that became widely emulated across the Four Nations. "This is how the meat gets butchered," Yangchen said. "Bettering lives requires good decisions, not cheering contests. Any progress on your end?"

Kavik glanced back at the pool of assistants. A dozen eyes immediately turned away like a school of fish changing direction. "I've been 'caught' with my waitbook at least twice. It's not like I have to pretend being bored."

The setup was in motion. Most of the zongdus' staff members were accustomed to pulling double duty as watchers. The Avatar might have done the same had she not brought her "special friend" to a real meeting with real stakes instead of a professional. Foolish, but what could you expect of a child?

Aside from Yangchen, Chaisee had the fewest clerks. One man and one woman, who seemed to share their mistress's patience and discipline. They sat lance-straight with their hands on their knees. While the other attendants occasionally gossiped with members of a different entourage, these two spoke to no one idly, not even each other.

And strangely, whenever Chaisee motioned one of them over, their faces shifted like sliding puzzles into rigid smiles wide and tall enough to wrinkle their cheeks. Yangchen recognized the man from her first visit to Jonduri from the scar over his eyebrow, but upon Chaisee's summons, he transformed into a different person, vacuous and giddy. Once his task was completed, he sat back down, and any traces of emotion vanished.

Chaisee must have coached them to show exaggerated emotions or none at all. A useful technique in front of so many people. Fluctuating between extremes gave nothing meaningful away.

"I don't want to reach the end of today's itinerary wondering if we've snagged him," Yangchen whispered to Kavik. "Drive it home. Aggressively. But make it look natural."

"How exactly?"

"I don't know. Show some initiative."

Kavik frowned. "Aggressive and natural-looking are completely opposite cues."

"No, they're not." She demonstrated with a quick, gentle puff of air in his ear. No bending. Just her lips.

Kavik turned so red he could have lit the hall in the dark. He clambered back to his chair and nearly stubbed his toe on the small step in between.

Everyone noticed. He noticed everyone noticing. He tried to hide by tucking his face into his papers, but his ears glowed like coals over the pages. Yangchen grinned openly, more icing on the ruse of their "special friendship."

Was she being a bully? Perhaps. But she'd never told Kavik taking him back was going to be completely free of punishment.

Kavik ended up waiting longer than she expected. The meeting reached its doldrums, the midway lull when the participants were struck by how little they'd accomplished.

"I'm sorry," Zongdu Ashoona said. He rubbed his eyes with the corners of his wrists. "Remind me again who the party of the second part is for this clause."

"*You,*" Chaisee snapped. She was the only participant who hadn't flagged in the slightest. "Are you a 'yea' or a 'nay'?"

Ashoona coughed and rubbed his chest. "I lost track. We're going to have to start the contract over." A groan rippled through the merchants in the audience.

The screech of Kavik's chair as he stood up was like the cry of a hunting bird, alarming partly because of the unexpected direction it came from. Until now, no attendant had been bold enough to speak unprompted.

"If I may," he said. "The Honorable Zongdu of Port Tuugaq, based on the previous sums discussed, the order of seniority in which the share agreements are applied, and the voyage success rates of the past two years, will achieve with a 'yea' vote a seven in ten chance of profiting the equivalent of five thousand four hundred and twenty-three standard ingots of silver, weighed against a three in ten chance of losing eight hundred thousand, six hundred and sixty-seven. A tremendous hidden risk masked by a paltry reward."

"You kept a running tally?" Ashoona said.

There were no notes in Kavik's hands. He recoiled from his elder's frown, fearful he'd overstepped. "In my head, yes, though it would be wise if someone checked my calculations."

A fury of clacking abacus beads was the only sound that filled the hall for a good minute. Iwashi's accountants got there first; one of them leaned into his master's ear and whispered. "Master Lio is right," Iwashi said. "Down to the last ingot. Impressive."

Kavik bowed deeply. "Please excuse my impertinence; I was only trying to act in good faith. It didn't seem right to let a business partner mistakenly deal into a closed Thirteen Ministers."

Iwashi's eyes lit up. *Got him,* Yangchen thought.

"Thank you, my boy," Ashoona said. "I appreciate your honesty."

"A brain paired with a handsome face," Iwashi said. "I thought Airbenders were supposed to be immune to earthly charms, Avatar." The Zongdu of Taku smirked while his servants made sure his joke went appreciated.

*Laugh it up,* Yangchen thought. *We're about to rob you blind.*

# HOOKED

**"I'M SO GLAD** you and Master Lio could join me, Avatar," Iwashi said as he led their unlikely little group along the gallery of shuimohua works. They came upon a forest of daggerpines captured on unsized mulberry paper with inky, flowing strokes. "The game really comes to life when playing against your peers, and there aren't many people in this world who can stand on equal footing with a zongdu these days. Ashoona's refused to touch a tile ever since I trounced him at the last convocation."

Though the others were loath to admit it last night at the safe house, Kavik was their best option for keeping Iwashi distracted. He'd learned the rules for Sparrowbones while infiltrating the Jonduri association and apparently humiliated its champion within a matter of days. "He's the best player I've ever seen," Jujinta had admitted, sounding like a reluctant witness sworn to tell the unpleasant truth. "If the plan requires beating Iwashi, he's your man."

Kavik didn't need to defeat Iwashi; he just needed to stall him. So far, the operation was proceeding smoothly. The invitation to a private, after-business game had been procured and the others were preparing to move on the *Bliss Eternal,* the ship vulnerable without the presence of her owner.

The one complication they couldn't fully plan for was the fourth member of the party. The most likely scenario was that Iwashi would select the most skilled member of his retinue to match against her and Kavik, but there was no guarantee whom he'd round out the table with. Anyone present in the meeting hall after business concluded was a candidate.

And that was how Yangchen found herself walking down the hall arm in arm with none other than Zongdu Chaisee.

*A marriage of convenience,* Yangchen thought as they paused to admire the landscape hanging on the wall. At least Chaisee helped by playing her part well. *The Zongdu of Jonduri and the Avatar? Why, they got on famously. Hard workers both, common interests. Lent each other books.*

"I must say, Avatar." Chaisee patted the back of Yangchen's hand like a convalescing grandmother even though she was still in her thirties. "I do so admire how you've brought the Bin-Er shangs in line. News reaches my ears of their unprecedented desire to serve the common good." Her smile was as faint as the brushwork depicting the wind blowing through the tree trunks. "Why, one might almost think they were suddenly afraid of you."

"People are capable of great change." *You make my skin crawl.* "When tended to properly, the common good serves us back. Teiin and Noehi and the rest simply came to the truth."

Oyaluk had the right of it; making nice with the enemy at close range was difficult and unpleasant. The two of them were able to fill a certain amount of neutral territory with congratulations over the birth of Chaisee's baby, who waited for her back in Jonduri under the care of house staff. But on every other subject, Yangchen couldn't help but feel that all their statements were as loaded as crossbows. "You're too modest," Chaisee said.

She leaned over to examine the corner of the painting, dragging Yangchen with her by the elbow. "What they saw was the value of quietude and compliance in . . . Apologies, one moment."

The zongdu reared back, forcing the Avatar to match her movement again. "Iwashi," Chaisee called out. "You've been had. This painting's a fake."

"Hmm?" Iwashi had guided Kavik farther down the hallway toward a weapons collection, as if decorative broadswords could only be truly appreciated man-to-man.

"Bizhimao signs her work with the *cat* radical, not *hair*," Chaisee explained. "You and the forger might be the only two idiots in the art world who don't know that."

Iwashi sucked on his teeth and ran a hand over imaginary hair. "Doesn't matter if it's not real; people only need to think it so. I'll sell it to a greater fool the first chance I get."

"So you're keeping it forever then," Chaisee said.

"Ha! Good one! And to think I only have a few more convocations before your term ends. I don't know what I'll do without your scintillating company."

Yangchen had never seen two zongdus interact behind closed doors before. She found the casual banter unsettling. Not only did it completely overturn the picture she'd built of a stoic, humorless Chaisee, but watching her and Iwashi act cozy in secret rankled Yangchen's sense of fairness. Merchant leaders always played up an image of ferocious business rivalries, a world of never-ending cutthroat competition against their peers, but Chaisee and Iwashi made the reality seem more like a backroom club where senior enough members patted each other on the back and scoffed at the idea of fulfilling their surface-level duties.

No wonder Yangchen didn't get along with the White Lotus. She could already hear Mama Ayunerak admonishing her for bringing her emotions along. *Don't be a child. This is how the meat gets butchered, without personal feelings coming into it. Yes, we're all playing the game against each other, but you're not supposed to take it* personally.

They reached a dead end. "Not those doors; that's my office," Iwashi said. "We'll be playing in the parlor. Better views." He pulled on a latch and slid a screen wall to the side, revealing a sitting room that framed the ocean in large glass windows spanning from floor to ceiling. Rows of shelves held scholar's stones and miniature trees, many of the specimens pruned and trained in the cascade style, branches spilling over the edges of their containers in green waves.

"What the blazes is that?" Kavik yelped. He pointed to the center of the room.

Squatting over the floor was a large table covered in blood, rivulets of brownish red cascading over the edges. A pattern of slaughter covered the top, as if the platform had served as an altar where dozens of victims had been sacrificed.

"Dramatic, isn't it?" Iwashi said. "Bloodlacquer. A product exclusive to Taku, refined from the resin of itchleaf trees. Looks and smells like actual blood in liquid form and dries to a durable coating. I told the artisan who made it to surprise me with his impulses. I think the fellow might be hiding a few dark secrets."

He glanced over at Yangchen. "Oh dear," he said. "I'm sorry. I understand how the goriness could be upsetting to an Air Nomad's sensibilities."

Yangchen hissed into the flat of her hand. She couldn't care less about outward appearances. The table underneath the varnish had been carved from the heart of a purple rosewood. A wave of nausea coursed up her throat when she saw the growth rings peeking through the coating, too many to count. An unfathomably old man of the Foggy Swamp had been cut down while still alive to make Iwashi's statement piece.

Acid etched the back of Yangchen's tongue. Something ancient threatened to burst out of her, whipped into a frenzy by the destruction of a being that would have weathered the ages had it not been for a single tiny pest whose entire lifetime barely registered as a mote of dust in comparison.

Old Iron. The giant spirit would understand her rage. The giant would approve if she reached out, closed her hand around Iwashi and simply *plucked* him, like one would a biting insect—

Kavik reared back into her, hard.

Chaisee caught Yangchen before she tripped on her robes and fell over. "Mind your employer's presence, Master Lio!" she snapped.

"Pardon!" Kavik bowed deep in apology. "I just lost my bearings for a moment." He glanced up at Yangchen. "I . . . seem to be okay now?"

She leveled her breathing. Abbess Dagmola's counting patterns, sped up. She squeezed back into herself and hoped the skin of Avatar Yangchen would hold. "It was only a slip," she said.

Iwashi laughed condescendingly. "I'm glad my tastes could inspire such awe. Come, sit."

He positioned Kavik across from Yangchen, himself and Chaisee to her right and left. Iwashi reached into a compartment and pulled out a set of standard bamboo-backed tiles, plainer than she expected. "Before we start, the stakes," he said, resting his elbows on the tray, his chin cupped in his hands. "I find anything less than a silver ingot a point not worth the time spent."

Yangchen laughed. She'd been ready to squander her entire diplomatic expense budget for this distraction, but thousands of points could change sides per round. The amount Iwashi was talking about could ruin a wealthy household in a single stroke of bad luck. "I think we might need a friendlier bet." She winked, mouth open in an exaggerated grin. "Air Nomad, in case anyone forgot. I don't have money to my name."

"Nonsense," Iwashi said. "You control the budget of Bin-Er, do you not? Just take what you need from there."

"Gambling with public funds—"

"Happens all the time," Iwashi finished for her. "What do you think we were doing down in the meeting hall? We made bets on which projects would pay off and which ones wouldn't. Tell you what. I'll sweeten the deal with the greatest treasure from my collection. If you end up ahead in money won at the end of the session, you can have the extra prize on top."

He got up and walked over to a long, narrow cabinet on the wall, probably for his tree varietals that needed shade. "Again, Air Nomad," Yangchen said. "Valuables and possessions mean little to—"

Iwashi opened the wooden cover to reveal a glider-staff.

*Her* glider-staff.

The wings had been spread like the sides of a gutted fish, held open by pegs between the ribs. Storing it for display like that would cause damage. The paper was already warping in the humidity, creases developing in the wrong spots.

"I bought this at a Bin-Er silent auction," Iwashi said. "Given how much I paid, I hope you can confirm the provenance. I seem to be a sucker for counterfeit items."

Yangchen couldn't see the nicks and wear patterns from this distance, but she could feel them. She knew where the shine of the lacquer had been buffed away by her grip, which of the tail pins needed replacement. She hadn't gotten around to a proper maintenance session with her glider before losing it. Iwashi raised his eyebrows, expecting an answer. "That's mine all right," she said. "Or it used to be."

Kavik was halfway out of his chair and openly fuming. "Lio," she said quickly, before he ruined the plan by making a scene. "It's all right. I donated my staff to raise funds for Bin-Er and Zongdu Iwashi came by it honestly. Just . . . rather faster than I expected."

"Oh, believe me, I snapped up this beauty as swiftly as I could. Though, if it is yours, why is the name *Jetsun* carved into the tip? Someone you know?"

Yangchen grimaced. "The mark of the maker."

Iwashi ran his thumb along the butt end, picking at the characters with his nail. "Maybe I should sand that off; I don't want people getting confused." He glanced at Kavik, who knew about Jetsun. "My boy, if you're that mad, then all you need to do is play well. I'm offering the Avatar's staff on top of my portion of the stakes. This is your chance to give a fine present to your boss."

"Interesting," Chaisee said. "I feel compelled to match." She reached behind her neck and undid a clasp, drawing out a single black pearl on a string, large and lustrous enough to turn the head of Mistress Noehi herself. "This specimen is the result of my first successful dive as a youth. The night abalone where I grew up would very rarely produce pearls of a unique color, but only in the island's most dangerous waters."

"Right, this mysterious home island of yours that no one's ever visited in years," Iwashi said. He turned to Kavik, looking for an audience. "She probably cultured it from a common Jang Hui clam. I'm surprised the dye doesn't rub off on her skin."

"Hold on," Yangchen said. She was getting swept up in a pace she didn't want to maintain. She needed the game to happen, but siphoning funds from Bin-Er wasn't a risk she was willing to take. People's lives depended on that money.

"Avatar," Kavik said. She followed his glance to the window and with a great deal of consternation realized Iwashi's ship was visible in the distance, the distinctive square banner of the *Bliss Eternal* fluttering in the wind. A single lull in the distraction and the zongdu might remember where he really wanted to be at this hour.

"With your permission, I'd like to play," Kavik said. He leaned back in his chair and gave Yangchen the cockiest grin she had ever seen in her life. "Trust me. By tomorrow morning Bin-Er will be richer, and you'll be soaring through the air on your glider once more."

"See?" Iwashi hooted. "Master Lio has the right attitude. Don't take any of this too seriously."

Despite the exhortations, one real and one fake, she *was* considering her options seriously. Sparrowbones was a game of mathematics over bluffing and drama. Even though Kavik was playing the role of a suitor trying to win his date a carnival prize, he was still genuinely the best number cruncher she'd ever met. He could likely keep the game even for as long as they needed, especially with her help.

"Fine," Yangchen said, exasperated the way anyone would be with an overconfident partner. "Let's begin."

With an expert flick of the tray, Iwashi dumped the tiles out facedown. The four players reached in with both hands for the shuffle. The clack of ivory filled the room. "So," Iwashi said. "Anyone have gossip to share?"

"The Saowon are up to no good again," Chaisee said.

Yangchen's fists fell to the table. She took a deep breath. "What do you mean?"

"My sources tell me they're refortifying the old strongholds across Ma'inka." The Zongdu of Jonduri spoke idly, as if informing her friends that the market was short on oranges. "Not for a war now, but for much later in the future. It's a very long-term play but smart, given how they've been locked out of the highest level of Fire Nation politics. I approve."

They couldn't. The Saowon wouldn't be so bold or so stupid. "Perhaps your sources are mistaken," Yangchen said.

"No, it's true," Iwashi said. "I sold them the stone. Good Earth Kingdom granite. For some reason they were afraid of quarrying their home island."

Yangchen wanted to hurl a fistful of tiles at the wall. She'd bought the spirit-stricken clan so many chances to simply live, and they couldn't. They couldn't stop striving, couldn't stop seeking advantages. Her deal with the phoenix-eels had made the clan social pariahs, shut-ins, and so they'd decided to turn their houses into citadels. *We're not breaking your rules,* she could imagine Earl Lohi saying.

"I'm sorry," Chaisee said. "I should have advised you to leave them to their fate when you visited me in Jonduri. You can't ask people to change. No lesson is ever truly learned except through pain."

"New leaders always have too much faith in humanity," Iwashi said. "I remember when I first took this job. I was very much like the young Avatar."

"Don't flatter yourself, Iwashi," Chaisee said before Yangchen could unclench her teeth. "She actually works hard."

"Hey!" Iwashi said with mock offense. "Despite my current reputation, I was quite active and generous early on. I was the very picture of a committed politician at first."

"Forgive me for speaking out of turn . . ." Kavik said.

"My boy, you can relax. We're all equals in the game. You want to know what happened?"

Kavik nodded. Iwashi began to stack tiles into the treasure pile, the distinctive pyramid shape they'd draw from throughout the round. "The problem came after I threw the city a particularly indulgent Grave-Tidying Festival," he said. "You'd swear the entire population of Taku was hungover the next morning.

I went out for an early stroll, and everywhere throughout the streets people ran up to me with smiles on their faces. They told me how much they loved the celebrations, the food, the fireworks. How much better my festival was than any of Zongdu Wonseok's."

He caught something in Yangchen's face she didn't realize she was giving away. "The young Avatar knows where I'm going with this. She knows exactly why I became so upset."

Iwashi stopped moving to see if Yangchen would jump in. When she didn't, he smirked. "Their praise," he said. "The nature of their praise offended me down to my very bones. They *graded* me. Like I was some sort of schoolboy with cake crumbs on my face. Who did they think they were, believing they had the right to judge their benefactor?"

With his arms outstretched and his fingers hanging down, he looked like a caricature of a vengeful, neglected ancestor, coming slowly after his irresponsible progeny. "Wonseok was a good zongdu by every conceivable measure, but the residents of Taku were comfortable smearing his name and stamping upon his work. You should have heard the filth they said about him! Your neck would turn red!" Iwashi shook his head. "No. I glimpsed the future that day and realized no matter how much of my spirit I poured into the job, people would talk about me in such terms. I decided then and there not to waste a mote of energy on croaking insects."

"You got scared of criticism that hadn't even happened yet," Yangchen said. *That's what we do here, right? Rib each other.*

But the noise that was supposed to be a scoff came out of her throat like a swallow of discomfort. Iwashi smirked, as if he knew he'd struck a nerve. "Maybe. But I was right. Once the afterglow of the festival wore off, I was blamed for an increase in street pests. Turns out the citizens had littered food everywhere during the celebration; the animals had gorged on the refuse and multiplied faster."

The clacking ceased once the treasure pile was finished, making Iwashi's voice cut through the room like a knife. "Avatar, your Saowon problem isn't actually with the Saowon, the Fire Nation, or any of the nations. The true problem with the world lies deep inside humanity itself, and despite your best efforts it will never be fixed. Mankind is a poor investment. A barren field. The less you do for it, the better."

Yangchen spoke slowly, categorically. "You are wrong, Iwashi. You are wrong, and you always will be."

Iwashi glanced downward. "Well, part of you agrees with me. Or else your left little finger wouldn't be twitching so."

She snatched her hand back into her sleeve before she could control herself. Wrong move. The looks from the older members of the table were full of pity. Kavik seemed excessively worried, like she might abandon her entire worldview because of a single misinterpreted tell.

Iwashi could score points off her in frivolous debates all he wanted. In fact, the lengthier the better. She composed herself and turned to Chaisee. "Our hosts presents an interesting argument about human nature," Yangchen said. "Do you have one of your own?"

"I believe I mentioned it already." Chaisee helped herself to the capstone of the pyramid. "Build your hands, everyone."

Compared to mythic, ancient Pai Sho, Sparrowbones was a newborn, having sprung into the world a generation or two before Szeto. Yangchen learned the rules herself when she was younger, not through a past life. Had her immediate predecessor ever allowed himself to indulge in frivolous pursuits, he would have enjoyed the pastime, she thought. The game embodied the current age of money quite well.

In Pai Sho, a victory was a victory; there was no concept of "by how much." But in a standard four-sided Sparrowbones match, the winner of a round could profit off any number of losers across a wide range of points. You couldn't see your opponents' tiles—you could only infer them.

Iwashi took the first draw. Yangchen and Kavik made eye contact; their primary strategy was still on. The two of them would exploit their numbers advantage by racing toward low value combinations, ending rounds early with "coward hands," and trade meaningless sums back and forth to stall the conclusion as long as possible.

*"Feast,"* Iwashi said. He tipped over his rack. "Ah, Master Lio, that's bad manners to keep drawing after the game is over," he said as Kavik reached for his first tile.

Iwashi was met with blank stares. He gestured at his revealed combination. "Closed-ended *Stars in the Darkness*, worth three thousand points, doubled for a self-drawn completion, redoubled for going out on my first turn. That's twelve thousand points, more than the ten thousand table limit. The game is over, and everyone here owes me some silver, I believe."

He snatched Chaisee's pearl and stood up from the table. "We'll sort out the transfer of funds later. Now if you'll excuse me, I need to head down to the docks so I can catch the last hour of favorable winds."

"Iwashi, I haven't even gone yet," Chaisee said.

"Tough. That's the beautiful thing about Sparrowbones, isn't it? All the skill in the world can be nulled out by a bit of luck, just like in the real world. Look at the Avatar and Master Lio, Chaisee. They're not complaining."

*A bit of luck.* Iwashi had managed to land the highest scoring combination in the game in one deal. "The odds,"

Yangchen whispered. "The chances of this happening were . . . were . . ."

"Lio," Iwashi said. "Tell the Avatar what the chances were."

Kavik needed a moment to find his voice. "One in three thousand seven hundred forty-four," he croaked.

"Eh, so more than a bit," Iwashi said. "Anyway, the sea calls me. You're all welcome to join me on my boat." He walked over to the window, undid the latch, and threw it open to let in the sea breeze. "That is, unless you want to keep playing. Open stakes, no table limit this time."

Yangchen gripped her robes at the knees, somehow already beaten into the universal posture of the debtor. The salt air stung her nostrils. They hadn't consumed enough time. Kavik stared at her, wide-eyed and waiting for orders.

She'd been hustled. She was the fisherman, yanked underwater by her own line. The Zongdu of Taku had found his greater fool. "We can continue." She and Kavik could still try their team strategy to avoid further damage. Maybe even win something back.

Iwashi turned around, framed by the sea and sky. "Very good." He retook his seat and began shuffling the tiles. "I don't think you have too much to worry about, Avatar. My previous win was a fluke. It's not like victories of that magnitude happen every round."

# *LANDED*

**"FEAST," IWASHI SAID.** *"Four Gales.* Twelve hundred points. No doublers this time, unfortunately."

Yangchen's jaw was sore from clenching her teeth. Acting was no longer a concern here. "How . . . do you keep . . . *dealing into him!?*"

"I don't know!" Kavik wailed. He was on the verge of tears. "That many consecutive melds should happen only once in every fifty thousand games!"

"Ah, you see, there's your issue." Iwashi sipped the tea a servant had brought him. "You have an overreliance on numbers, Lio. You need to learn to read the flow. Luck is a fickle guest. Though plenty of 'rational' men and women may deny it, the tides of fortune are a very real force." He gestured at Yangchen with his little finger; the rest held his cup. "Much like the spirits."

*Curse this game,* Yangchen thought. Curse this game and its stupid names for countless winning combinations that found their ways into Iwashi's hands over and over. The Zongdu of

Taku had preyed upon Kavik especially, scoring hit after direct hit upon her so-called expert.

Both Yangchen's and Kavik's losses came at the expense of Bin-Er. They couldn't continue like this or else the city would become a silent Tienhaishi, its residents sucked dry by the debts she'd signed on their behalf. Yangchen drew her hands over her face, using the motion to peer at Chaisee.

The Zongdu of Jonduri, who'd somehow managed to remain relatively breakeven throughout the carnage, caught her looking and shrugged. *Leave me out of this,* her frown seemed to say.

Pity from her worst enemy. Yangchen would rather be locked in a staring contest with Thapa.

"Can we— Can we take a short break?" Kavik pleaded. He mopped his brow. "Just for a few minutes."

"But of course," Iwashi said. Kavik got up and stumbled to the sliding door, not the window, the wrong way if he needed air. He nearly pulled the frame out of its slot, amusing Iwashi rather than angering him, and lurched down the hall.

"Excuse me." Yangchen withdrew from the table—more chuckles from her host—and chased after her partner.

She caught up to Kavik around the bend of the art gallery where he leaned against the wall. Maybe he was sick. That would have explained his disaster of a performance. "What is going on?"

"Can they hear us?"

The hall was empty but just to be sure, Yangchen spun the air around them. The indoor version of the trick she'd used with Chief Oyaluk was less effective but would have to do; the window Iwashi had opened was her cover.

Kavik straightened and turned around. The sheen of panic on his face was nowhere to be found. Other than the sweat beading on his skin, he was as calm as could be. "Iwashi's cheating," he said.

Yangchen opened her mouth to shout, but nothing came forth. She was caught somewhere between complete surprise and disgust with herself for not considering the possibility. "He's cheating," Kavik repeated. "He's elbow leeching, edge reading, wall gliding, every dirty trick in the book."

"Sleight of hand?" *That simple?* "I would have seen him—"

Kavik gave her a quizzical look. *No,* she reflected. *I've been distracted.* The table, her glider, Chaisee's presence. Iwashi had fooled her.

Kavik skipped the opportunity to call her out on it. "He was only testing the waters at first," he said. "I wanted him to think he could keep getting away with it. When we go back in there, I need your help to reraise the stakes as high as we can."

*"Are you kidding?"* Yangchen shouted under her breath. "If he's been cheating the whole time, that's our chance to catch him in the act so we can annul our losses!"

"Getting caught isn't going to faze him." Kavik set his jaw. "Iwashi is a hypocrite and a bully. He was never interested in a fair game or a test of skill; he just likes to hurt people. He can't handle a real battle where he faces losing."

Kavik took Yangchen's hand. "I've said I hated Bin-Er in the past, and maybe that's still true. But it's my city whether I like it or not, and I'm not going to let its people be robbed by a thief who doesn't even need the money. Didn't you tell me once that we have to fight for complete strangers as hard as we do for our friends?"

It wasn't like him to make grand gestures. Yangchen halfheartedly tried to pull her arm back, but his grip remained firm. Kavik gently spread her fingers and put them on his neck, over his pulse. His heartbeat was as slow and steady as the changing of the seasons. He moved closer.

"Have faith in me," he said, staring into her eyes so she could see his pupils. "I can beat him."

He was telling the truth. Or at least he believed so with all his heart. Yangchen grunted and looked away. "Your skin is clammy."

"I know. I had to wait for that too."

They made sure to start—and hide—their argument well before reentering the parlor.

*You had to show off, didn't you! Had to look like a big man and get my glider back!*

*Well excuse me for trying to defend your honor!*

An embarrassed couple would speak in whispers, so they kept their voices low. Yangchen found it ironic how their fake quarrel had nearly the exact same content as their real one.

*It was just a run of bad luck; I can come back from this with a few hands. Please. I'm begging you. The treasures Chief Oyaluk gave you; those are easily worth at least five more rounds—*

The best answer here was no answer. Yangchen slid the door open again, signaling the end of the protest. A sullen, hangdog pair they made. "My friends, I don't think we can play any further," Yangchen said through her forced grin. She remained standing at the threshold, as if she wanted to bolt right now. "Consider this our declaration of surrender."

A high-risk trap. If Iwashi acquiesced and sent them on their way, they'd be utterly sunk. "I can give you credit," he said. "I'm sure you're good for it."

Kavik began to speak, but Yangchen elbowed him in the side. "Thank you very much but no. The temple elders always warned us not to gamble. I think this has been the perfect cautionary tale."

"What if I paid out gold to your silver?" Iwashi said.

The surprise that followed was genuine. They'd wanted to raise the stakes, but neither of them had considered Iwashi would go so far. *He's not putting himself at risk in his mind,* Yangchen thought. *He latched on to his opponent's hope and wants to inflict more pain.*

Thanks to her earlier lapse, the zongdus knew what Yangchen looked like when she froze; she did her best to give them another show. In contrast, Kavik acted as quickly as a drowning man reaching for driftwood. *"Yes!"* he said. "Yes. Your sportsmanship is appreciated." He raced back to his seat and motioned to Yangchen hopefully.

He did "hapless desperation" so well. If Yangchen didn't know better, she might believe Kavik's greatest desire in the world really was to redeem himself in her eyes. She sat down furiously, if such a thing were possible. Chaisee gave her an almost sisterly headshake, the kind of warning a woman gave to her junior. *Your funeral.*

The four of them pushed their tiles back in once more for the shuffle. Yangchen chewed on her lip. They could still lose, even with the knowledge that Iwashi was cheating, even with the advantage he'd spotted them. They built the pyramid again. She was sorely tempted to monitor Iwashi and catch the motions she'd missed earlier, but if she stared too intently at his hands or avoided them in excess, she might signal they were onto him.

A flashing sensation like a needle's touch, there and gone. She almost turned her head to chase it. *What was that?*

A stack collapsed and tiles spilled toward Iwashi's edge of the table, a miniature landslide. "Foul," Kavik called out. "Your losses are doubled this round."

"I'm aware of the penalty for upsetting the trove, Master Lio, thank you," Iwashi snapped. He looked flustered as he shook out his wrists. They restacked the tiles.

There it was again, the familiar pull, this time on Kavik's side. A broad smear instead of a dot.

Suddenly it dawned on her. Yangchen glanced at her partner. Kavik's frown of concentration revealed nothing.

"Have you two been able to enjoy the nightlife yet?" Chaisee asked. "I've been falling asleep at sundown, but Taku is a wonderful city for the young."

That kind of question would have normally come from their host. "Erm, yes," Yangchen said. "We saw a shadow play. *The Lost Slipper.*"

"I didn't care for it," Kavik said without looking up.

Until now, he had assiduously stayed out of the conversation. His lack of rank combined with his massive losses made keeping his opinions to himself the fitting choice. The corner of Chaisee's mouth turned up in interest. "Oh? That's one of the few plays with any maturity and realism."

"The poor man dies in the street and the evil minister trips over the corpse, embarrassing himself in front of the king," Kavik said. "Is that supposed to be a satisfying, ironic ending? I hate tales like that. Why is the humiliation of the strong considered a good enough trade for the lives of the weak?"

Iwashi still had no comment to give. Maybe he hadn't heard them at all. His teeth were exposed in rage at the state of his starting tiles. *A fair draw isn't as much fun, is it?* Yangchen thought.

"Such is the nature of the world, young Master Lio," Chaisee said. "Barring a freak occurrence, power consolidates. It doesn't disperse." She took her last tile. So did Yangchen.

That left Kavik as the last person to complete his starting hand. He picked up his tile and lifted his thumb to see the design underneath. "I suppose that's why I've stuck with this game through ups and downs. Everyone starts on equal footing."

Kavik used the piece he was holding to knock over the rest of his tiles in a sweeping cascade, as smoothly as if he were strumming a chord on a zither. *"Feast,"* he said. *"Flight of Returning Swallow-moths.* Ten thousand base points, doubled for self-drawn, doubled for my first turn, then doubled once again on Zongdu Iwashi for his trove penalty."

Chaisee whistled. The Zongdu of Taku trembled, mustered himself, and grinned. "Congratulations on your luck finally arriving."

Luck had nothing to do with it. For a brief instant Kavik had frozen some of the tiles together using his own sweat and the ambient humidity in the room. Not enough to stick them like glue and leave evidence of what he'd done, but just enough to make Iwashi botch his sleight of hand.

The same subtle waterbending technique let Kavik manipulate the pile as it was rebuilt by sticking the ivory surfaces to his frosted skin. Had she not been able to waterbend herself, Yangchen would have never noticed him arranging his own victory.

They had to keep playing. Kavik was right; they had to keep their opponent at the table. They weren't out of the hole yet. "Thank you for the lesson about flow, Zongdu Iwashi," he said. "I think the currents are about to change."

If Kavik's floundering act was good, his *punch-me-in-the-face* arrogance was masterful. Iwashi tightened up like a sea prune in vinegar. "We'll see," he said, his once-dripping flowery speech trimmed down to the bare minimum.

Yangchen needed to do her part in annoying their host to the point of committing murder. She and her partner were a team, after all. "Can you be a dear and fetch the waiter?" she said to Iwashi. She smiled sweetly and pointed at his drink. "I'd like one of those. With a slice of lemon."

Iwashi unbuttoned the top of his collar and ran his finger around his neck. "Hot as the blasted Fire Nation in here," he complained.

That was Yangchen's doing. Once she understood how slippery tiles were to Kavik's advantage, she'd increased the temperature in the room steadily. Even Chaisee dabbed at her temples with a kerchief. Perhaps another Firebender could have caught the Avatar in the act, but hey. It was good to be special sometimes.

Her turn. She could push for a quick, certain win on this round but at the expense of landing a knockout blow. While thinking about it, she took a sip from her drink.

Her lips met solid ice. Kavik had frozen the contents of her cup. *Don't end,* he was telling her. He had something better up his sleeve.

A bead of sweat on the back of her neck pulsed, goosing her skin and nearly making her yelp. She scowled at Kavik, but he pressed on her with waterbending again, then once more. *Give me a three tile.*

Yangchen palmed a three of mountains—Iwashi wasn't the only one who could perform sleight of hand—rubbed some condensation from her drink on the back and flicked it under the table at Kavik.

He wasn't ready. The panic in his eyes subsided only once he realized she'd frozen the tile to his trousers. He squinted at her for taking the unnecessary risk.

"Oh, would you two stop making eyes at each other and just play?" Iwashi snarled.

Yangchen laid down her discard. "Apologies. This *is* a big hand, isn't it? If Lio wins with any double, he gets back everything we've bet so far *and* the points difference in gold ingots. Bin-Er could have eight wells instead of four."

"Or a spectacular Grave-Tidying Festival of its own," Chaisee helpfully suggested. "You made yours sound so nice."

The teasing had bored fully into Iwashi's head. He wavered over his discard before selecting a five-leaf, the safest option according to the information available on the table. Even Yangchen could sense his capitulation.

"It almost pains me to do this," Kavik said. "*Feast. Swords in the Armory,* eight thousand eight hundred—"

"I know how many points it's worth!" Iwashi shouted. He was so frazzled he leaned over and swept all the tiles back into the pool before Kavik could show off his winning combination. For all anyone knew, he could have been making up his claim to victory. "Again!"

"Iwashi, maybe we should stop," Chaisee said. "A wise player knows when to quit."

*"We're not stopping in the middle of a rotation!"*

The Zongdu of Jonduri rubbed her forehead. "You said that two rotations ago." The shame and embarrassment her peer should have been feeling was bouncing off him and striking her.

Yangchen looked at Kavik. There was always this risk, too, of becoming trapped in a vortex of money flowing back and forth to no end. That was why the signal they'd settled on with the rest of the team was one that could not be ignored. "Do I smell smoke?" Kavik said. He sniffed the air. "Does anyone else smell smoke?"

"Look!" Yangchen pointed out the window. Down by the docks, a thick column of black smoke rose from the largest wooden object in the waters. The *Bliss Eternal,* now ablaze.

The game was officially over. So was the mission. And Yangchen discovered that when it came to screaming, Iwashi was almost as good as she was.

# ANONYMITY

**YANGCHEN AND KAVIK** left the meeting hall in solemn silence. It didn't feel right to celebrate when their host was so clearly devastated.

But before they left, Kavik did make a point of taking Yangchen's glider-staff off Iwashi's wall, carefully closing the wings, and presenting it back to her with his own two hands. And then, in another show of gallantry, he tried to give Chaisee back her pearl.

She'd refused. "To the winner go the spoils. Avatar, hang on tight to your companion. A worthy partner comes by once in a generation."

In the street, Kavik offered Yangchen his elbow, his face serenely happy. Their cover allowed the gesture, and so they linked arms under the setting sun.

The lanterns went up for the city's night market. They'd already seen most of Taku's entertainments yesterday, so the only stop they made was to boo the ending of *The Lost*

*Slipper* so loudly that the puppet handler quickly improvised an alternate outcome where the dead hero was revived by a kind passing doctor and the evil minister dedicated his life and fortune to repenting. The audience clapped much harder than last night.

Once they reached an alley, they split and broke for the safe house in separate directions. Yangchen began her tail-throwing routine slowly, sticking with ordinary turns, but soon she picked up the pace, darting through shadows and leaping over fences. She felt the need to outdo Kavik even though he couldn't see her. She hadn't been lying when she'd complimented his moves in Bin-Er.

Her glider justified the extra flourishes, the vaults, the leaps. She'd missed its balancing weight, the sense of security in her hands. When she approached the safe house, she twirled herself to the roof entrance with the wings collapsed in staff form for the sheer joy of the unnecessarily difficult feat.

As she let herself in through the hatch, she heard Kavik entering on the ground floor. She ran down the stairs and met him in the hallway. He must have taken an athletic route home as well, because he was breathing as heavily as she was. They squared off and drank in each other's grins, their faces flushed and glowing, no words to bridge them.

Yangchen broke the stalemate. She threw her arm around Kavik's neck and yanked him into a headlock. "We did it!" she crowed, mussing his hair as hard as she could. "*You* did it! You utter fool! I can't believe you pulled it off!"

Kavik whooped and lifted her into the air, a skilled wrestler's counter. "Tell me you saw his face when you pointed out the boat! I'll cry if you say you missed it!"

He spun her round and round while they laughed. A fall backward would have been ugly, but what did they care? Not only had the mission gone right for once, but they'd won their city enough money to put its troubles at bay for a good long while. Yangchen was still squeezing Kavik in glee when the door opened again and Akuudan walked through.

He peered at them. "You need to grip him lower under the chin or he won't pass out," he said to Yangchen.

"Like *this!*" Tayagum said, appearing next. He leaped onto Akuudan's back and snaked his arm affectionately around the bigger man's collar. Akuudan kept a stern face up but made sure to support his husband's weight while glaring at Kavik, presumably for touching the Avatar.

"I take it your end of the mission went well," Yangchen said.

"Buttery smooth," Tayagum said as he got down.

Kavik snorted. "You took your sweet time."

"We finished within parameters." Akuudan pulled out a roll of notes; it would contain a copy of the ledgers Yangchen had instructed them to search for. "Not only did we have to impersonate the resupply crew, but we had to pick several locks, stay ahead of the roving maintenance shift, hide in a bulkhead, and make the arson look like an accident."

Now that Yangchen saw it, the two men's clothes were torn, stained, and a little sooty. They'd been through an ordeal. "Felt positively young again," Tayagum said with a big grin. "You, on the other hand, just sat your lazy behind in a chair and played a game for a few hours. My grandmother could have performed your half of the mission."

Yangchen wanted to correct him after everything they'd been through at Sparrowbones, but it was cute watching Kavik sputter in indignation. "Where's Jujinta?" she asked.

"Here." Jujinta shut the neglected door behind him with an accusing click. "I finished the tail sweep. We weren't followed. To my knowledge."

He looked around and Yangchen could tell he was bothered by the jovial mood, how close each pair stood to each other. "Did everyone have fun?" he asked. "Was that a requirement I missed?"

"Hey, come on." Yangchen reached out and took Jujinta's hand while holding on to Kavik's. The former partners could barely stand the secondhand contact and tried to pull away, but she stood firm, an anchor with many chains.

"We're a team," she reminded them. The auras of sheer loathing the two boys had for each other clashed in the middle like a storm front, with eddies of mild disdain from the older men toward Kavik thrown in for good measure. But who better to ride the invisible swells than her? "We put aside our differences and work together because . . . because . . ."

Her attempt at a rallying speech faltered. She couldn't say that in contrast to the zongdus they acted without self-interest, not with Kavik as part of the group. Free will wasn't the reason they'd all come together either; Akuudan and Tayagum would have preferred their peaceful retirement in Jonduri had they not been burned.

*We work together without bringing emotions into it?* Jujinta's iron shell was really a boiling cauldron threatening to spill over any moment. "Just quit complaining and work together!" Yangchen said. "I shouldn't have to play babysitter on top of everything else!"

At least with this group she could be honest about her thoughts. Kavik clapped slowly at her oratory prowess. "Words for the ages," he said. "Truly."

Yangchen wasn't bothered by his sarcasm, but she wasn't the only person in the room this time. Suddenly she had to switch from pulling Jujinta closer to pushing him away so he didn't gouge Kavik's eyes out with his bare hands for insulting the Avatar. Akuudan and Tayagum passed over the chance to show any maturity whatsoever and suggested areas below the waist to kick.

Her hair got caught in the scuffle. As Yangchen tried to untangle herself from the clawing and scrabbling, she cast a prayer into the future. *May my successors keep less ridiculous company,* she pleaded with any spirit that would listen.

"You need to get along with Jujinta," she said to Kavik on their return trip to her official lodgings. The stolen notes were tucked safely in her robes. Her staff rested firmly in hand. It was time for the Avatar and Master Lio to rest for the night.

They passed a corner strewn with lettuce leaves from a cart; Iwashi had been right about the city's littering problem. "I used to." He shook his head and brushed the side of his nose, as if genuine affection were a stinging insect. "What do you care, anyway? I'm not part of the team. Did you forget I have to report all of this back to the White Lotus?"

She'd assumed so before they'd embarked on the mission, and she'd remembered again on the way back to the safe house. But in between there had been a genuine gap where Kavik was her companion only, and not the agent of another party trying to take advantage of the Avatar.

Any lapse was her fault, but she found herself peeved at Kavik regardless. Like he remembered the entire time. "You were the decoy," she reminded him coldly. "And you performed your duty. Tell Mama I give you full marks; you're real senior Lotus material."

"Glad to be of service," he snapped. "I'm always available when one of your plans nearly ruins an entire city."

Yangchen grimaced, wondering how they'd flipped from basking in triumph to taking shots at each other. Kavik knew she was keeping the prize of the mission on her person. Would he go for the notes? There was no serious way he could overcome her in a face-to-face confrontation, but he could sponge the information with a trick if she wasn't careful.

She'd never been spied upon with both her knowledge and consent before. The openness of the struggle made for a bizarre set of rails, forcing them both down a single path. Their best option was to keep cooperating, no matter how reluctantly.

She quickened her pace. Instead of keeping up, Kavik followed a few steps behind, looking for all the world like the victim of a spat. As they came to the mansion of her official quarters and marched through the common area, the whispers of the servants were as loud to her ears as shifting sands.

When they reached her room on the third floor, she'd had enough. She stepped through her door, laid her staff in the corner, and faced Kavik. "Look," she snapped. "We're not children. Stop sulking, come inside, and we'll talk about this."

"Yes, please," said a voice from deeper in the room. "Let's."

Yangchen turned slowly. The collision of her heart into the walls of her chest had left as quickly as it arrived. Whoever it was that snuck into her room, they'd missed their moment to attack. A raise of her fingers lit the lamps on the tables.

The intruder, a Water Tribe man, sat in the chair Kavik had slept in, resting the side of his head on his fist.

No introductions were necessary. While there wasn't much of a family resemblance in a physical sense, Yangchen could see the connection as clear as day. Kavik's fake smarmy grin, the mask he put on to infuriate, deceive, and project complete confidence in his lies, had been modeled entirely off this man's natural expression.

Even his body language, the slouch of indifference, was already familiar to her. In every aspect of his mannerisms, as if doing so were some kind of good luck charm, Kavik had desperately tried to copy his older brother, Kalyaan.

But now, in the presence of the genuine article, he'd withered. Kavik's shoulders rounded in a preemptive flinch, a student caught cheating by his tutor. Kalyaan gestured behind them. "You forgot to close the door."

In his haste, Kavik slammed it shut, sending a loud bang through the room. Kalyaan snorted and shook his head, and in the span of those few moments Yangchen suddenly could imagine what it was like to live with such a person, to spend years in the presence of someone who held an invisible measuring stick over you, to carry the weight of their superiority.

"The Avatar in the flesh," Kalyaan said. "What's the proper procedure here? Do I bow? Grovel? Ask for a blessing?"

"You stay where you are and don't move," Yangchen said. She clenched her fist behind her back, winding up for one of the many ways she could take him down.

"Easy now; I didn't come here to fight. I have a plan in place for if I don't walk out of here safely on my terms, so let's try to keep the peace, eh?"

"What are you doing here?" Kavik asked, his voice small and hoarse.

"I need to talk to your boss for a bit. Stay if you want; I don't care."

Kalyaan turned to Yangchen. The slight movement coupled with his singular, tunneling gaze was all it took to dismiss Kavik, push him to the side, out of mind. The grown-ups would take it from here.

She stilled any motion of her body toward the notes in her robes. She didn't know what he knew yet, and there was no need to give away a detailed confession in response to vague accusations. "Does Chaisee know you're here?"

"No," Kalyaan said. "And she doesn't know who Kavik is, so you can both rest easy on that front. I'm not a monster who would betray his own blood." He leaned forward in her chair. "Consider this a courtesy call between two professionals in the same trade."

Two, not three. Another slight against Kavik. Once, Yangchen had commiserated with Kavik about the complex nature of older siblings, but in the span of a few words she'd concluded that Kalyaan and Jetsun were nothing alike.

"I know about your grudge against the shang cities," Kalyaan said. "I know about your little adventure this afternoon. Bankrupting Iwashi through his favorite game? Good stuff. There's a certain flair to letting your enemy hang themselves." He nodded appreciatively, as if the whole exercise had been run solely for his pleasure. Everyone could be relieved; the customer was happy.

If Kalyaan thought the Sparrowbones game was the entire mission, then he'd missed the move on Iwashi's boat. Or he was simply using the same tactic as her, lingering within the realm of common knowledge until the other side gave away more than they had to. "So glad I measure up," Yangchen said with a slight courtier's bow.

Kalyaan scrunched his lips and shook his head; she'd presumed too much. "However, I wanted to warn you—antics like that won't work on Chaisee. You need to back off her trail before someone gets hurt."

"Like in Bin-Er?" Yangchen said. "Like Henshe was?"

"Exactly!" Kalyaan's smile shone bright and pure, as if he'd nothing to do with those events. "Henshe, may he rest with the kindest spirits, created that mess because he stuck his nose where it didn't belong. There are plenty of fights you can pick as the Avatar. Let Chaisee win and stick to marks like Iwashi and the Bin-Er shangs. The adults can handle running the world."

Kalyaan gave more compliments than Ayunerak, flew a different banner, but ultimately his tack was the same. Everyone wanted to write history, but there was only so much ink to go around. "I'm not rolling over for your boss," Yangchen said.

His eyes narrowed. "You should. She may have more Firebenders than the three you know about. The woman's good at keeping secrets."

Yangchen sucked in her breath too quickly and he noticed. "You're bluffing," she said to cover herself. "You don't really have a plan to get out of here." She took a step closer. An airspout into the ceiling would knock him out with the least amount of noise; the only difficulty would be avoiding permanent damage to his neck.

"Before you attack me, why don't you take a look out the window?" Kalyaan said. "I won't bolt. We both know I couldn't escape your clutches through bending alone."

Yangchen grimaced; the lashings of flattery worked well to keep her off balance. She stepped carefully around Kalyaan, watching him. He remained seated, true to his word. "Two blocks down, right side. The benches by the sweet wine vendor."

She reached the window. The evening's neighborhood shop stands were busy setting up under the lantern lights. Steam wafted from dumpling carts while noodle hawkers laid down their carrying poles and mixed fresh batches of sauce. Some of the food and drink sellers dragged stools and long tables into the street to give their patrons a place to rest.

A small gathering had formed by a banner advertising a ginger-flavored concoction to ward off the heat, and as Yangchen ran her eyes over the drinking customers, her first impulse was to expect Thapa providing overwatch. Threat plus distance would have equaled the hulking Firebender staring back at her, ready to blow up the entire floor.

What she saw was so much worse.

"Isn't it annoying when an amateur tries to play the intelligence game?" Kalyaan said behind her. "He probably fancies himself the hero of a play. The royal in disguise who walks unseen among his citizens. Must really get his juices flowing."

Sitting on the bench, dressed in commoner's clothes, was Earth King Feishan.

The most powerful man on the continent sipped his drink and cast his gaze around the street, unrecognized by the pedestrians flowing around him. Yangchen swore, openly and floridly. "I know, right?" Kalyaan said. "His Majesty isn't supposed to be here this early. He's been snooping around the city under cover, searching for signs of collaboration against him by the shangs, the zongdus, the Fire Lord, the Water Tribe Chief. Poor fellow is so wrapped in the shroud of paranoia that he thinks everyone's against him and so has to confirm every imagined piece of evidence himself."

Whoever started playing the game first won. The Earth King shared the same mindset as the Avatar, the two of them more alike than Yangchen wanted to admit. "I've got a man posted on Feishan right now," Kalyaan said. "One who doesn't mind spilling royal blood. Do you think I'm bluffing about that?"

He might have been, but at this point it didn't matter. The Earth King was too big a liability. If Feishan disappeared anonymously into the gutters of Taku, a hole would burn through the map, starting in Ba Sing Se.

*Someone,* Yangchen begged into the void. *Anyone. Please. Just give me a break. For once.*

"Sifu is on the lookout for trouble," Kalyaan said, enjoying her distress. "If he catches us fighting, we both lose. What do you say to a truce? I know this mansion isn't your only base. I could easily root out your safe house in Taku and raze it to the

ground, along with the team you've probably got hidden inside."
He flipped his head to the side. "But I won't."

His sheer arrogance was a weapon in itself. A few supremely
confident words, and now she had to doubt her craft, re-
examine how well she'd covered her trails. "And what would
you want in return for this act of goodwill?"

"I want you to stop messing with my brother's head."

Kalyaan leaned forward. The casualness and geniality
he'd addressed her with, so like the joshing between zongdus,
drained away with the motion. "What you're doing to him is no
better than blackmail. You're holding a knife to his conscience,
and I don't appreciate it when people threaten my family in any
shape or form."

Yangchen's eyes darted to Kavik, but he'd become unread-
able, forged his features into determined blankness. She'd never
seriously entertained the thought that he might crave her forgiveness. He'd always been working one end of a bargain or
another, first for her and then the White Lotus. She'd come to
accept that. She needed to believe that.

Because if Kavik was risking himself out of sheer guilt,
then his brother was right, and she really was extorting him
without end.

"I protected Kavik in every way that you didn't," Kalyaan
said. "I got him far away from Chaisee, out of danger, like an
older brother should. Only for you drag him straight back into
the jaws of the beast! You're a hypocrite, Avatar. If you were
worth anything, then your companions would follow you by
choice. Not because they owe you."

Yangchen searched for a response to fling back, only to find
her quiver empty, her tongue robbed. Kalyaan rose from the
chair and stretched, protected by an armor more impenetrable
than any layer of elements. He sidled over to Kavik and threw
an arm around his shoulder, giving Yangchen a side-by-side

comparison of the two brothers. While both were handsome, Kavik's squarer jaw lent earnestness to his face, a tempering softness. Kalyaan was all knives. Grip the wrong end and you got what you deserved.

"This fellow here is the real reason I sought an audience with you tonight," Kalyaan said to Yangchen, shaking his younger brother back and forth. "If you have any decency whatsoever, you'll stop using him as a piece in your game."

Kavik stared at the floor, trembling. No shield could hold forever.

"Wait until I pass Feishan and turn the corner before you or the Avatar move," Kalyaan whispered into his ear. "Tael's out there waiting for me. You remember Tael, right? You know how jumpy he can get. Like this!"

Kalyaan punched him in the stomach.

Yangchen jolted in surprise. It took her far too long to process that the blow was fake, Kalyaan's fist lagging behind his shoulder.

But Kavik didn't even flinch. His lack of response could only have been the product of conditioning, years of childhood games with familiar, uneven rules. *I get to do what I want. For you to attempt the same means you lose.*

Kalyaan disappeared down the hallway the opposite way Yangchen and Kavik had arrived, an outrageous act in itself. The lower floors were full of staff. They'd notice an intruder. She was almost tempted to call him back and offer help in escaping. Instead, she waited by the window and watched the Earth King, the only person whose reaction mattered right now.

Defying all logic, Kalyaan emerged in the street below, completely unimpeded. No one chased after him or raised their voice. He must have scouted her quarters better than she had, moved completely within people's blind spots. Kavik's brother had skills she could only dream of.

He strolled by Feishan without attracting attention. Soon after he disappeared into the next block, a thin man sitting behind the Earth King got up, dropped some coins on the table to pay for his untouched drink, and followed.

Both Kalyaan and this Tael person, whoever that was, had managed to get within arm's length of the ruler of the Earth Kingdom. An assassin's dream. Only then did Yangchen believe this visit had been a personal matter for Kalyaan, hidden from his boss, because Chaisee might have taken that opportunity.

Yangchen wheeled around. "We have to go after him," she said to Kavik. "He's got a big head start, but if we work together—"

"It's no use," Kavik said quietly. "He's gone. We'll never find him, not unless he wants us to."

They didn't have time for this. "I have my staff now; I can follow him from the air. You fell for it."

"But *he* won't!" Kavik shouted. "How many times do I have to say it? He is better than me! He has always *been* better than me! *He always will be!*" He rammed his fist into the wall. His knuckles met the good, solid wood with a crunch. He punched the wall again, harder, and a third time for good measure.

Yangchen knocked him to the floor with a gust of air, too slow to protect him from himself. He curled up on his side, cradling his hand, holding the seed of his pain.

She pulled the nearest water to her so hard the porcelain flower vase shattered in place. Dropping to her knees beside him, she tugged on his wrist. He fought her until the agony became too much to bear, and she wrested his injured hand free.

His fingers were already a swollen mess. The misalignment in his knuckles struck her deeply. Earlier today she'd watched him put on a masterful show of dexterity, and without immediate attention he'd never be able to perform to that level again.

The water glowed as she began to mend the wounds and seal the fractures. She wouldn't be able to stop halfway. If there had ever been a chance to tail Kalyaan, it was gone now.

As she healed Kavik, she had to consider the possibility that he'd hurt himself on purpose to let his brother get away. She didn't know what to believe, when not long before she'd risked an entire city's well-being for the chance to reclaim a small bit of her connection to Jetsun. There was no weakness as great as family.

# KEEPING PACE

**YOU DOLT.** *You blockhead. You utter ninny.*

Though Yangchen's healing was flawless as usual, Kavik's hand still throbbed. Phantom pains, mixed with embarrassment. *Here's the newest agent of the White Lotus, throwing a tantrum in front of the Avatar. You cost her the chance to chase down Kalyaan.*

The briefing in the safe house washed over his ears. A blob of sound that might have been his name. "Hey. *Hey!*"

Kavik snapped to attention. "Is there a problem?" Yangchen asked. She looked at him from across the map table. Her phrasing was stern but the concern in her eyes was gentle.

The rest of the team's, less so. "No." He put his arms behind his back so she wouldn't catch him rubbing his knuckles again. Jujinta tracked the movement with his eyes, as if taking mental notes for an upcoming prizefight. *Delicate hands. Good to know.*

The two of them had already informed the others about Kalyaan's visit and the Earth King's presence in Taku. They'd handled it rather well, all things considered. "Your entire family can rot in the same pit as Feishan," Tayagum had said.

Kavik sometimes forgot the Earth King was responsible for Tayagum's and Akuudan's imprisonment. "Take that back," he'd replied. "My parents are very nice."

Yangchen had immediately spent the night after Kalyaan's visit analyzing the notes they'd stolen from Iwashi's books on the ship. The freshness and value of the information would deteriorate quickly since the longer they waited to capitalize, the higher the chance Chaisee realized Iwashi's string of misfortune was no accident—assuming she hadn't already.

That was why Yangchen called the meeting shortly after dawn. Kavik had been hurled awake by the sound of that infernal gong whose reach seemed to penetrate every corner of Taku. He was tired.

But the dark bags under Yangchen's eyes indicated she hadn't so much as napped, and Kavik could tell from scent and temperature that she wasn't drinking the same tea as them. Something stronger.

She quaffed her special brew and set the cup aside. "As I was saying. The records we nabbed from the *Bliss Eternal* narrowed the possible locations for Thapa to be hiding in down to a manageable number." Yangchen paused and angled her head, a brief moment to acknowledge something going right for once. "But there's something else I learned. Chaisee doesn't only lease property from Iwashi; she charters his ships as well. According to his logs, small vessels occasionally used to leave Taku carrying supplies while returning empty. They never made port in any of the other shang cities."

"Sounds like he's just trading on the side to avoid paying his dues on the customs revenue," Kavik said. "Like the Bin-Er shangs were."

"The goods aren't valuable enough," Yangchen said. "We're talking cheap foodstuffs, clothes, the bare necessities for survival. I have a hunch that these ships provisioned a secret location where Chaisee trained the Firebenders."

Tayagum frowned. "That's a big hunch. I didn't reach that conclusion when I transcribed the notes."

"You haven't spent as much time as I have studying the false names Iwashi uses for his counterparties," Yangchen said. "I've been thinking about this day and night. It takes time and effort to develop bending prowess. Bitter work from both student and teacher. Turning Thapa, Yingsu, and Xiaoyun into weapons would have required a proportionally huge commitment of resources."

Yangchen spread a different map over the first, a rendition of the Mo Ce and its neighboring seas. "The Port Tuugaq testing range I discovered a while ago wasn't set up to house anyone for an extended length of time. Chaisee must have an isolated large-scale operation somewhere else under her control, and an uncharted island in her home territory would be the perfect fit."

She began to mark up the paper. Her strokes crossed the waters between the shang cities, back and forth, lines thickening with each round trip. "The prevailing winds keep merchant ships leaving Taku primarily within these corridors. And *these* are the most common Air Nomad flight routes. I hate to admit it, but we rarely deviate from them because we can travel in straight paths. Convenience rules us too."

By the time she finished scrawling, a distinct patch of sea in the shape of a triangle remained unmarked. "Here," she said, tapping the center with the tip of the pencil hard enough to blunt the lead. "Process of elimination."

"What are you proposing; that we drop the plan and leave Taku to search open water for an island that may or may not exist?" Kavik said.

"I admit it sounds daft," Yangchen said. "But after Bin-Er, I couldn't pursue Chaisee as hard as I wanted because she hung the threat of more Firebenders over my head, and last night Kalyaan did the same. There very well might be other members of Unanimity out in the world. I need to know if this ordeal ends with Thapa, and I can't pass up the chance to find out."

"I agree with the Avatar," Jujinta said. "We should go look."

"You always agree with her," Kavik snapped. "You're about as useful in these planning sessions as an iguana-parrot."

Akuudan calmly put his hand between them, both to block their view of each other and to remind him how much bigger his fist was than theirs. "Where would we find the time?" he said to Yangchen. "You're needed in Taku."

"In a bit of luck, I have at least an entire day off. A messenger came at dawn. Iwashi's called for a temporary adjournment of the convocation. He's not feeling very well and needs to rest."

"Ha!" Tayagum grinned at Kavik. "You broke another man's spirit so badly he had a physical reaction. Good work."

Kavik grimaced and flexed his fingers behind his back.

"We still need to watch for Thapa," Akuudan said. He peeled the sea chart away to examine the city map of Taku again. "With how these locations are arranged, we could get away with two people on the stakeout. How do you want to split the group?"

Yangchen paused; Kavik understood the decision wasn't as trivial as it sounded. More protection and safety on this impromptu sea adventure meant fewer eyes in Taku. She responded by encircling him and Jujinta with an arm each, like bales of straw. "We'll handle the search for the island. Me and the boys. It'll be a bonding exercise."

She squeezed them hard enough to make Kavik's eyes water. "You two will be on your best behavior, won't you?" she said, her smile more dazzling than the early morning sun.

They had to leave as soon as they could, Yangchen told them. A lot of ocean to cover and not much time.

The real reason for an immediate departure was more complicated. Yangchen needed to plumb the secrets of this supposed island before Kavik had a chance to meet with the White Lotus and give them the information. His double agent status forced her into hurrying; nothing he could say would work to slow her.

Everyone split up to prepare for their next task. The Avatar flitted back and forth between the members of her squad, overtaken by a frenetic energy. When Kavik quietly suggested to her in the kitchen that she rest and leave the work to them, she rebuffed him. "Both Iwashi and the White Lotus are wrong," she'd said, her voice lowered to keep the conversation in one room. "Neither Sparrowbones nor Pai Sho encapsulate life, because enemies in real life don't take turns with each other."

She handed him the empty cups she'd cleared from the table. "Chaisee's been forcing me to stand still, and other people have paid the price for my inaction. No more. We need to determine her true strength once and for all, and we're not going to accomplish that by resting."

Kavik wanted to tell her she was blaming herself unfairly and consequently pushing herself at an unhealthy pace. But it was too late to express such concerns at this stage, when the Zongdu of Jonduri sat across the table and Kalyaan dropped by for friendly visits. The right time would have been long before the convocation. *I could have spoken up had I stayed by her side as a real companion,* he thought with a pang in his chest.

"For now the game is a race," Yangchen said. "We don't get to determine what we think is an appropriate speed and then stick to it. The answer to how fast we should go is *faster.*"

She stormed away to check on the others. Perhaps he only imagined her fatigue. The leads provided by Iwashi's books might have reinvigorated her.

Kavik began to pour out the cups into a bucket so he could wash them. Ayunerak had ingrained in him the habit of cleaning up after himself for operational security; a dirty dish could reveal how long ago the occupant of a safe house had used it. But then he stopped.

One of the clay drinking vessels contained the remnants of the Avatar's tea. She'd packed the cup with leaves nearly to the brim, certainly not how it should have been served. A hunch of his own scratched at his skin, demanding attention.

Kavik looked around, not wanting to be accused of scandalous behavior, and took a small sip of her dregs. It tasted like regular tea. A little on the grassy side, peppery even, but not unpleasant. *She just likes this blend, whatever it is,* he thought. He'd been suspicious over nothing—

Between one heartbeat and the next, Kavik's pulse became thunder.

His hands trembled. His face grew hot. He was more than alert from the brew; he felt maddened. Her drink had to have been tenfold stronger than his, and she'd been downing it all throughout the night and morning.

"When you're done in there, can you bring up the travel rations from the storage room?" Yangchen called out to him from around the corner. She sounded perfectly normal, and not like her veins were about to burst.

Kavik couldn't reply without his voice shaking. The best he could manage was a gargle of acknowledgment before needing to lean against the wall. He thumped his fist a few times until his bearings returned and hurled the damp bolus of leaves into the waste bucket like it was poison.

The Avatar was putting a physical and mental strain on herself that would have sent a normal person to a hospital bed. He needed to tell the others so they could force her to slow down, to stop before she—before she—

*She'd never forgive you. Impede her plans again and see what happens. See if she'll keep you around.*

Kavik jammed the heels of his hands into his pulsing eyeballs. She wasn't an ordinary human being, he told himself. He had to believe in her, the same way Jujinta and the townsfolk around the Northern Air Temple did. "First door on the left," she called out again, annoyed that she couldn't hear her commands being followed with promptness.

His vision cleared enough to find the storage room. Kavik stumbled inside and groped through the darkness, searching for the supplies. The Avatar had made it perfectly clear what she wanted. It wasn't up to him to second-guess her.

# BONDING

**AT LEAST** Nujian looked spectacular as usual. A day of frolicking in the wilds outside Taku had rejuvenated the Avatar's bison. He came to them by bounding over the meadow, enjoying the contact of his six feet on the earth. The grasses shook at his impact.

"Not so loud," Yangchen said to him. She wore a gray city-dweller's outfit for the mission and had wrapped her head in a scarf. "You're going to draw attention."

Nujian huffed, slowed to a trot, and tossed back his woolly curls, fallen leaves woven into his fur like the embellishments of a landscape painter. Despite the scolding, the very first thing he did upon reaching them was to nuzzle his Airbender. Yangchen leaned into the touch, her eyes closed.

Kavik could sense the strength they drew from each other. Yangchen barely ever touched Nujian's reins and often spoke to him as if he were a sibling rather than a beloved steed. It must have been nice to be able to rely on someone so completely.

Right now, a different sky bison wearing Yangchen's normal saddle slumbered in Taku's stable, pampered by grooms and handlers who were most certainly on the payroll of the zongdus. The switch had been prepared in advance in case they needed to leave Taku without anyone knowing; Nujian had never entered the city.

So encased in deception were they that even the Avatar's bison had a body double.

At least Kavik could look forward to some quality time with the best member of the team, the one who knew a grudge couldn't live forever. He extended his arms as Nujian approached. "Aww, there's my big fluffy— Hey! *Hey! That's cheating!*"

Jujinta, using his innate talent at producing hidden objects out of thin air, held up an apple that had distinctly not been part of the supplies. Nujian veered away from Kavik and cozied up to the filthy briber, rumbling until he got his treat.

The expression in Jujinta's eyes as he scratched the bison's ears was colder than the teeth of an ice saw. *That's right*, his dead, soulless gaze said to Kavik. *I will take everything from you.*

"Sure, keep wasting valuable time," Yangchen said. She'd already leaped onto Nujian's withers. "Just remember I can turn him against both of you with a word."

That ended the showdown. Kavik and Jujinta climbed into the saddle without another word. Some threats were too horrific to ignore.

Kavik could admit to understanding Iwashi's obsession with boats this time of year. The weather was absolutely stunning. Had he similar means as the Zongdu of Taku, he also might have chosen to idle his days away in these waters.

Gone was the stifling humidity of the coast, replaced by a warm, pliant breeze. The ocean rolled and foamed beneath them, a layer of confection spread as far as the eye could see. The only thing ruining the flight was the company.

"Will you stop doing that?" Kavik said as Jujinta slowly, unnervingly rotated his head back and forth over the saddle edge. Yangchen had assigned them a direction each to monitor. "Staring at the same patch of open water more than once is pointless. If you didn't see it the first time, you're not going to see it the next."

"You search in your way, and I'll search in mine," Jujinta said. He made another swivel, taking deliberate care to blink at regular intervals. "Besides, only a fool trusts his first glance. The sun glare, a large swell blocking a portion of the horizon. You may have already let our goal slip by in your carelessness."

Kavik rolled his eyes and leaned back. He tapped his foot against the saddle. Once, twice. Finally, he scowled and turned to look behind them. There was nothing, of course.

He'd been skeptical of this plan from the start. Drawing conclusions about the existence and location of a secret base from gaps in records felt flimsy to him. He preferred positive confirmation, direct evidence. Perhaps he would have been more convinced had Yangchen allowed him to read the stolen notes, but there was no way she was going to reveal more information to the White Lotus than necessary.

"Can you drop us close to the water?" Jujinta asked her. "Really close?"

Yangchen clicked her teeth and Nujian rolled sharply to the side. Kavik had to hang on to the rail behind him to keep from sliding across the saddle. Jujinta leaned down as they descended, reaching for the water's surface, until they got close enough for him to skim his fingers along the waves. "Anything?" Yangchen shouted over the slicing hiss.

"No." Jujinta withdrew his arm and shook the saltwater off. "I thought I'd give it a try."

Nujian leveled his flight path and reascended. Kavik considered what he'd just seen. They should have brought Tayagum if they wanted to read the currents; he was the most experienced sailor. "You know how to wayfind?"

"I guess not well enough," Jujinta said. "You don't need to look so surprised. I was born on an island. I have as much affinity for—" He cut himself off.

"Ha!" Kavik said. "You were going to say you had as much affinity for the water as me before realizing how stupid you would have sounded. It's a good thing we didn't put you in front of Iwashi. He would have picked his teeth with you." He settled back into his seat and waited for a comeback.

"So I'm not the best talker," Jujinta said quietly. "I'm not as quick-tongued as either of you."

He'd withdrawn into himself, his lips pressed tightly together. His posture, tense to the point of nearly shaking, reminded Kavik of how he'd carried himself before the warehouse job in Jonduri, when the other members of the association mocked and cheered against him in the knife-throwing contest. He'd forgotten to resume sweeping the horizon back and forth.

Kavik caught Yangchen glaring furiously at him over her shoulder. Right. He couldn't spar with his former partner the same way he did with the Avatar. Threatening to kill each other was somehow fair game, but not making fun. They wouldn't have asked Jujinta to playact any more than they would have assigned Kavik to knock out an enemy at range.

He sighed. "You know, even back in Jonduri, I don't think I recall you mentioning where you grew up."

"Because I didn't," Jujinta snapped. "My people don't reveal secrets to outsiders."

"At this point we're not exactly outsiders anymore. You already know my dirtiest piece of laundry and it's good manners to reciprocate. Come on. Spill."

Everyone imagined themselves a fortress. But if there was one lesson Kavik had learned from his conversations with marks, it was that a retreat behind walls was often a plea for relief. Apparently, Yangchen agreed, because she let go of the reins to join them in the back.

She tucked her feet under her in a lotus position. "Sharing stories with people who care about you can sometimes ease the burdens we carry. A secret released is like a shouldered stone, dropped into the sea."

Jujinta eyed them both warily, unsure of how to deal with a two-pronged assault of friendly interest. His jaw twitched, a series of false starts that seemed like they would build up to the real one.

But the winds shifted. Jujinta shut like the lid of a clam, arms folded over his chest. "There's no point in talking about my home," he said. "Because I can never go back there again."

Kavik scoffed. "*Never's* a bit strong, don't you think? If you've got heat on you, it'll die down eventually."

"I agree; time heals many a rift," Yangchen said. "I'm sure that once you're ready, you can return—"

"I *can't!*" Jujinta roared. "What part of that do you two not understand?"

They'd pushed too hard. Jujinta never raised his voice, most certainly not at the Avatar. "I can't simply declare things fixed!" he said. "If something happens, and it's your fault, then it's your fault forever!"

The furrow in his brow caused the scar over his nose to deepen. "You!" he said to Kavik, brimming with resentment.

"Just sauntering back into the team's good graces without a care. I know you think you can talk your way out of any situation, but you can't. You don't get to speak a new reality into existence just because it suits you."

He turned to Yangchen. "And with all due respect, Avatar, *you* are welcome anywhere in the world. You don't know what it's like to be severed from your roots!"

Yangchen's face went pale. Jujinta didn't know that she'd been exiled from the Northern Air Temple. Nor could he have known Kavik wasn't safe in Bin-Er or Agna Qel'a. He'd flung his knives blind and caught them both dead center. A consummate trick-shot artist.

No one spoke. To think, the three of them could have bonded over how similar their circumstances were, had the truth not been such an impossible gulf to bridge.

Nujian grunted, mercy-killing the conversation by alerting them to a flock of seabirds up ahead. Frigaterns. The gray birds sliced into the wind like the tip of a weathervane. Several of them carried small fish in their beaks.

That had to mean a nest was close by. The Avatar's hunch was correct; somewhere up ahead was land. Celebrations were in order.

Nujian's looming bulk set off a frenzy of cawing from the frigaterns. "We should have placed bets," Jujinta said over the noise.

# CIRCUMSTANTIAL EVIDENCE

**THEY DEBATED** the merits of a scouting flyover and quickly decided against it. "The place could be crawling with Firebenders the likes of Thapa," Yangchen said. "We don't know for sure."

So they settled on a low approach, skimming the waves. The island grew nearer, expanded, a thickening green brushstroke atop black volcanic sand, the painter's perspective. Kavik gripped the saddle rail, his knuckles nearly bursting through his skin as Nujian swung from side to side in a serpentine pattern. He thought it was the motion making him dizzy and nauseous until he realized he'd been holding his breath and counting until the noise came. Unanimity had baked a terror into his bones that he wasn't over yet.

Yangchen landed Nujian on a stretch of beach barely wider than he was. "You can't come charging in if you hear explosions," she said to her bison once their feet were firmly on the ground again. "You understand me? No heroics this time. It's too dangerous."

Kavik wasn't sure if her companion got all of that, but better safe than sorry. The forest of thick-trunked lava palms came up to the edge of the shore, dense as clasped fingers, and blocked any view of the interior. To venture farther, they'd have to duck inside a bowed arch dripping with vines.

"I feel like we're encroaching on the domain of a spirit," he said as he filled a skin with seawater and slung it over his shoulder.

"We're not," Yangchen said. "No vengeful beings on this particular island."

"Are you sure?"

"Pretty sure."

They tiptoed over the web of roots crisscrossing the forest floor, line abreast, him and Jujinta guarding the Avatar's flanks. Kavik found comfort in moving together. Their physical coordination almost made them look like a real team.

The going was slow. Because of the humidity, moss had grown over every surface, coating the trees and rocks in a jade fur. The sun, sieved through the canopy above, dappled the forms of Kavik's mission partners as they crept through the trees, giving them the shifting light-dark-light forms of tiger-dillos.

He noticed over Yangchen's head and slightly behind her, in her blind spot, a pair of green-and-black-plumed birds he didn't know the name of. The idea that they were following the Avatar would have been ridiculous had they not been moving in complete unison with her. Whenever she took a step, they took a little hop along the branches to keep up. Step. *Hop.*

Kavik waved at Yangchen. "Are those birds following you?" he whispered. "Do you have food in your pockets or something?"

As soon as she looked behind her, the birds flew down from their perches and landed on her shoulders. They chirped sweetly and fanned their tails, revealing a spot pattern that resembled a winking face.

The sight of nature flocking to the Avatar was amusing, but also not. Disrupting the animals around them could give away their presence. Yangchen frowned at her new disciples until they got the message and flitted away into the forest.

"Don't worry," Kavik said. "I won't tell Pik and Pak you've been cheating on them."

She rolled her eyes at him and kept going.

Yangchen suddenly raised her fist again. Not to tell Kavik off, but to call for a halt. "What is it?" Jujinta asked quietly.

"There's a clearing ahead."

Kavik peered as far as the crowded growth would allow. "How can you tell?"

"The wind blows differently. Careful now."

Jujinta reached under the back of his shirt and drew a long, wicked dagger. Kavik removed the stopper from his waterskin and placed his thumb over the opening. For once they weren't trying to out-brandish each other. Their leader, who had the sharpest senses, took point and they fell in behind her.

Sure enough, the forest eventually gave way to an open expanse, a swath of combed, tended land within the tangle of trees. About a dozen long huts lay in rows. Kavik noted several of the roofs in disrepair, the woven fronds eaten away to reveal bamboo poles jutting out like the ribs of carrion.

They waited to see if anyone came or went. No one did. Yangchen hefted a rock and earthbent it with scorching speed at a distant tree. A hollow *thunk* reverberated through the clearing.

Still nothing. No one came to check on the noise.

"Stay close to me," Yangchen whispered. They ventured toward the nearest hut and peeked through the door. Inside was empty except for an internal scaffolding of bamboo that lined the walls.

"Storage?" Kavik guessed.

"Barracks," Jujinta said.

The rest of the huts contained the same sets of frames. Assuming Jujinta was right about the beds, this complex could have slept a hundred people. "There can't be that many Thapas running around," Kavik said. There simply couldn't. The Four Nations would lose their collective minds. There would be no stable footing if Unanimity could be had by the dozen for cheap.

"Let's keep searching before we draw any conclusions," Yangchen muttered. *Let's not dive into the nightmare scenario before we have to.* The world could stay whole and unbroken for just a little longer.

Only one building in the camp stood out, a double-length lodge that capped the rows of huts. One half of the interior was clearly a training floor where fighters and benders could practice forms and spar. The other end was a jumble of bare bookshelves, broken jars, wooden poles of varying lengths. He picked up a potsherd and sniffed the curved, stained inside surface.

The odor had faded, but he could still detect the once pungent bajitian and mustard seed. Ingredients for dit da jow, "hit medicine" used to numb and toughen knuckles ruined by punching. The same kind of wounds the Avatar had treated on him, but with the damage tempered into the bones instead of undone. Based off the remaining trash, the occupants had gone through the herbal remedy like water.

Kavik looked at the room again, with different eyes. A training floor was nominally a respected space where students could make a noble effort to hone their skills. Even his dingy

Gidu basement counted as a hall of learning, under Ayunerak's tutelage.

This place gave him the impression of a factory instead. An assembly line that made injured people. The product could be moved from one end of the building to the other for maximum efficiency.

There was no dignity of a sifu's touch he could discern here. Only output.

"Look at this." Jujinta held up a large scrap of paper. The remaining corner of a scroll that had likely been pulled from the wall in haste. On it was the depiction of a human arm, naked, marked up with lines like a butcher's guide of where to cut. The drawing ended at the shoulder, along the tear.

Yangchen took the paper from him and examined it closely. "This is a very old, very archaic Air Nomad acupuncture map. The energy pathways follow our ancestral theories about chi movement. There's a lot of overlap with common medical knowledge, but some important differences as well." She flopped it back down like an old man reading a newsletter over his morning tea. "Chaisee shouldn't have this."

"You told us she collects rare books," Kavik said.

"She shouldn't have this," Yangchen repeated. "I've never seen one of these diagrams outside a temple before."

"There's more ground to search," Jujinta said, his gaze shifting to the door.

They circumnavigated the clearing in single file instead of treading on the soft earth where they might leave tracks. As Kavik brought up the rear, he saw that he hadn't imagined it earlier—Jujinta was antsy. Nervous even. His movements were unusually stiff and slow. Kavik managed to tap him on the shoulder without getting sliced open, a troubling sign in itself. "What's wrong? You look like you swallowed a horse-bug."

Jujinta grimaced. "This is a cursed place," he said under his breath, not wanting Yangchen to hear. "We shouldn't have come."

"The Avatar said there aren't any spirits around."

"Spirits, no." Jujinta's nostrils flared as he looked up at the trees. "It's the echoes of people I'm worried about . . ."

He spoke with such quiet certainty that the hairs on Kavik's neck stood on end. The empty beds. Suddenly the wind through the branches took on the rustle of voices. The birds had been silent for too long.

*"Psst."*

Kavik nearly jumped out of his skin. *Screaming fleas.* "I said stay close," Yangchen hissed again. She beckoned them over to a footpath leading deeper into the woods. It hadn't been used in a while; new shoots of grass sprouted in the worn dirt.

They followed the trail like the winding banks of a river. The jungle here was so thick they had to squeeze sideways through the trees at times. The path became a lifeline. If they lost sight of the thread, they might never make it back to the entrance of the maze.

The Avatar, still in the lead, disappeared around the bend of a thicket. Then Jujinta vanished. Suddenly Kavik was alone. In his haste to catch up, he slipped as he took the corner and for a brief moment the hands that caught him felt like they would drag him into the sky.

Thankfully, the palm over his mouth belonged to Yangchen. She kept it there so he wouldn't make any noise of surprise at the large temple of black stone sitting right in front of them.

The greenery had cloaked the edifice as well as any ambush predator. Jointless, giant blocks of hardened lava rose higher than a Taku apartment. No vines or wayward branches touched the construction, as if the jungle recognized the aberration in its midst.

Jujinta was right. Customs had been created for places like these. *Avoid the shoals. Stay clear of the pits. Do not go near the black building.*

"We need to look inside," Yangchen said.

Kavik knew it, despite the screams of protest from deep in his marrow. They searched for a door.

The pitted stone made it difficult to see edges in the masonry. They almost missed the entrance on the first pass. A tunnel low enough to force a crouch. "Why would you go to so much trouble to build this structure and not bother with a full-sized door?" Kavik wondered out loud.

"Because you don't want anything to escape," Jujinta said. "Light. Sound. People. Perhaps the Avatar should wait outside for her safety."

"Perhaps the Avatar should upend this entire building with earthbending and shake the contents out like a basket," Kavik said. "For all of our safety."

A weak joke, to keep the unease at bay. But Yangchen answered honestly. "I don't know if that's called for yet." She opened her hand and a flame rose from her skin. Carrying it like a torch, she ducked inside the stone.

The walls of the tunnel were unsettlingly damp, as if the stone breathed and perspired. They shuffled along quickly; there was no advantage to lingering in such a vulnerable position. Jujinta's limbs blocked the Avatar's precious light. As the rearguard, Kavik had to frequently look over his shoulder at the entrance shrinking behind them. He imagined that someone who'd fallen down a well might enjoy a similar view.

Suddenly the tunnel opened into a larger room, and they

could stand again. Yangchen sent the flame in her hand to a spot on the wall. A mounted torch, used up halfway but with enough wood left to burn.

The fire revealed they had the room to themselves, except for a large pile of scrap metal sitting in the center. Light reflected off jutting angles. Kavik walked over and leaned closer without touching.

Iron hoops. In assorted sizes. Some of the rings were only as big around as a pumpkin, and others were so large they'd been broken down into quarters to fit through the tunnel. While they'd been tossed into the heap without care, like a collection of cheap bangles, Kavik noticed the pieces could have been arranged in a continuous line from smallest to largest, without duplicates.

"What do you make of this?" he asked the others. Maybe a cooper had been searching for an ideal barrel size through trial and error.

"I don't know," Yangchen said. "But there's something underneath."

She was right; buried under the metal was a cloth-covered object, probably a chair judging by the shape. Yangchen began to pull the rings off and throw them into the corner, pausing only to examine her hands with distaste. "They're greasy."

Kavik helped her. The iron was indeed slippery with animal fat, as if the pieces had to slide against a moving component. Once the last ring had been pushed aside, he wiped his hands on a corner of the cloth before yanking it away.

He needed a moment to fully comprehend the object he'd just unveiled. "Oh no," Kavik murmured. "No, no, no."

It was indeed a chair. But the feet were bolted to the floor. The legs, armrests, and back had leather restraints to fit around the body of the occupant. The seat had been stained dark by foulness. The ends of the arms were grooved and splintered where fingernails had gouged into the wood.

Kavik retched. *"Leave,"* Yangchen barked protectively, as if she might quarantine her companions before the taint of evil reached them. He barreled out of the tunnel, holding his sides, until he tripped over grass.

After emptying his stomach of the travel rations, Kavik rolled onto his back and tried to scrub his face with sunlight. He was tempted to open his eyes and let them fry to get the image of that chair out of his head.

Jujinta emerged from the tunnel. A single cough was all he needed to muster himself. He thumped his fist on the stone, upset, but in the manner of an experienced general surveying his losses. "We shouldn't have come," he muttered.

Yangchen stepped out. Without a word, she motioned them away from the building's edge. Then she turned around and slammed her foot into the earth.

Roots snapped. Gravel sizzled. The black stone, the whole massive structure, sank straight down, lowered by the Avatar's power as smoothly as a bucket on a winch.

*Wait,* Kavik wanted to shout, *the evidence.* If they buried the traces of Chaisee's crimes, there'd be no way to make her answer for them.

And then his rational voice took over. Evidence of what? Presented to whom? Was there a fair and impartial judge waiting in the wings? Could they go to Feishan and ask for the Earth King's law to be applied here?

Kavik watched the sinkhole fill, too sick to be impressed. Loose, leached soil covered the stone, a giant grave. Once the act was done, Yangchen exhaled and wiped her face, showing the exertion of a feat that would have normally required the teamwork of several masters. She took the time to press her hands together and chant, reciting a prayer of warding and protection repeatedly, pleading with the spirits to leave this foul place at a distance.

Kavik agreed. Certain evils needed to be buried and never disturbed again.

# PRIMARY SOURCES

**COMPARED TO** the horror behind them, the sea was a clean break, a place to bathe Kavik's mind if not his body. *My element*, he thought. *Thank the tides.*

The water came in gentle waves. Patches of dark coral stretched below the surface. Breadnut palms clustered along the edges of the sand. Their fruits could have been turned into a bland, gluey porridge, but only unripe, inedible specimens hung from the fronds.

"I don't get it," Jujinta said. "This is just a cove."

Kavik knew what he meant. Chaisee's trails had led them here, which meant this place must have factored into her plans. But the beach was idyllic. Fish swam, crabs scuttled over the rocks. He doubted very much that outdoor relaxation was part of the Unanimity formula.

Yangchen pondered the foaming whitewater. "Maybe our hosts can tell us the significance of this location," she shouted, loud enough to startle both of her companions. "If they can forgive us for trespassing."

Kavik thought she was backtracking, that the island really was home to spirits, until the very human noise of footsteps came from behind a tall flowering bush. He whirled around and drew a blade of water from the skin at his side.

A boy, around twelve or thirteen years old, stepped into view, followed by a girl of the same age. Their clothes were tattered and salt-eaten, their cheeks sunken with hunger. They looked like the victims of a shipwreck.

"Did you know they were there the whole time?" Jujinta whispered.

"No," Yangchen replied. "Not until after we reached the shore."

Kavik re-formed the water into a less threatening sphere, holding it to the side with one hand while reaching out with the other. "Hey," he said, risking a step forward. "We're not going to hurt you."

"Don't," Jujinta warned.

The girl and boy didn't seem to like Kavik getting closer. But their eyes were drawn to the fresh water. They licked their scabbed lips. "Are you thirsty?" he said. "Here, we can share. Easy now."

As he neared, he must have moved too quickly or made an unfriendly face. The girl lunged forward as fast as a viper and punched him with a single knuckle right in his palm.

A pinpoint shock ran through Kavik's body, up his arm, crossing his chest, and all the way to his other hand. Numbness followed like rain surging through a gutter. The only reason he didn't scream was because his lungs were caught in the path.

The water he was bending fell to the sand, his control over it gone. His shoulder drooped low enough for the skin strap to slide off. The girl grabbed the pouch and fled along the beach, the boy chasing after.

Kavik found the breath to howl as he twisted about, trying to regain the sensation in his arms. Yangchen grabbed him and forced him to sit. "Are you okay?" She ran her hands over his body and came away confused. "You don't feel injured."

To her, maybe. *"What the flying frog was that!?"* The impact had dug between muscle and bone, straight into the gaps of his body. He didn't know he had gaps in his body.

"I've never seen such a fighting technique," Jujinta said, with way too much admiration for someone who had just downed his mission partner. "But I told you not to get near."

"How bad is it?" Yangchen asked Kavik. He knew what she was asking; she could try to give him more extensive first aid but at the cost of pursuing the girl and boy.

He got to his feet. The numbness had begun to clear, but slowly. He tried extracting water from the damp sand, but only a pathetic tendril rose to meet his efforts. The punch had weakened his bending somehow. If the effects were permanent—

He didn't want to think about the possibility. "I'll walk it off," he growled.

While the two children might have been trained in arcane methods of combat, they were fortunately novices when it came to evasion. They'd fled over the beach and left tracks.

The feeling in Kavik's arms gradually returned as the Avatar's team gave chase, and so had some of his bending. "A good sign," Yangchen said, though from her lilt she clearly had no benchmark to compare to. She, Kavik, and Jujinta followed the footprints around a small scarp.

On the other side was a grotto. The sand was littered with rotting breadnut cores and a large bed of ashes that once held a campfire. He suspected fresh water might have sometimes trickled down the dark grooves in the rocks above, but today there was none. The boy and girl were survivors on their last legs.

Despite that, they were already halfway up the scarp. "Please get down from there," Yangchen said. "Before you hurt yourself."

The pair probably realized how vulnerable they were caught out on the cliff surface like ice geckoes. They slowly clambered back to the sand. Kavik's waterskin hung over the girl's bony shoulder, already empty.

"We have more," Yangchen said. "Food too. You must be hungry, no?"

They didn't respond. "We want to help you," Kavik said. "Tell us what happened here."

Still nothing. Silence was the smartest play, Kavik had to admit. These kids didn't know who he, Yangchen, and Jujinta were, friend or foe. They might all be standing on the beach for a while.

Yangchen reached behind her head to undo her scarf, willing to reveal herself to gain their trust. *I'm the Avatar. I'm here to help you.* Jujinta put his hand on her elbow. "Wait," he said. "Allow me to speak to them in a language they understand."

He advanced on the children. Kavik suddenly remembered the first time they'd met, when Jujinta had casually inserted a blade into another errand runner during what was supposed to be a friendly bout of target practice. "Juji, no!"

Too late. The daggers were already in his hands.

*Thk-thk-thk.*

The first knife buried itself into a peach-sized chunk of driftwood twenty paces away. The target bounced into the air from the impact, and the second knife struck home before it landed. The third was just for show, a big rude gesture to the governing laws of the cosmos. The block of wood landed neatly on the new tripod that kept it elevated off the sand.

Jujinta had juggled an object from afar, using only the points of his blades. "See that?" he said to the stunned children while their mouths still hung open. "Most people don't know what it takes to pull off a feat like that."

The girl and boy eyed Jujinta nervously. His trick, meant to disarm, could have been interpreted as a threat not to run. "But every remarkable talent represents dozens of people who couldn't make the cut," Jujinta said. "You sharpen a sword but discard the grindstones. I know because I grew up on an island just like this one. I know what goes on in these sorts of places. I could tell right away that we three are cut from the same cloth."

In the span of his speech, he'd managed to get close to them without suffering a paralyzing jab. "Now." Jujinta clapped them both on the shoulder. "I could behave like the people who ran this camp and promise we'll only take one of you to safety, whoever proves more useful to us, and leave the other to rot. I'm sure you're used to such competitions."

Yangchen started forward in protest. "I won't, though," Jujinta said. "We're going to rescue you both. And once we do, neither of you will have to answer for the horrible deeds I *know* you've committed to survive."

The boy and girl began to shake. "We'll pretend none of this ever happened," Jujinta said into their ears, as gently as if he were crooning them to sleep. "You just need to answer my friends' questions. And then all will be forgiven."

The kids broke down sobbing. "Merciful spirits, Juji," Kavik muttered under his breath. That had to be one of the cruelest displays of manipulation he'd ever seen.

Jujinta turned around to face Kavik and Yangchen. "Ask away," he said. "You two are better at talking."

The girl's name was Hsien and the boy was Raitei. They hailed from different villages along the Natsuo Island chain, where national boundaries were blurry and work was hard to come by. They'd answered the call of a visiting unmarked ship recruiting men and women across the archipelago. Age and fitness didn't matter, only the willingness to make sacrifices for their families. The voyage would be made entirely down belowdecks. Benders like Raitei stood to earn extra.

"We must sound like rubes," he said, sullen.

"On the contrary," Yangchen said gently. "We understand completely. You didn't have much of a choice."

Once they arrived at this unknown island, they'd been separated into groups. Those who couldn't bend, like Hsien, were forced to train their bodies until they broke. "We practiced our striking on each other," she said.

"After you punched me back there, I couldn't bend," Kavik said. "They taught you how to do that through sheer trial and error?"

"You held your hand out and stood still," Hsien said. "I don't think I could have hit you if you were moving."

A pattern emerged in her story of the recruits being separated into multiple little divisions, like a plot of farmland dedicated to different crops. The few Earthbenders present had been marched deeper into the volcanic interior of the island for some unknown purpose. They never returned. A randomly selected group was assigned to practice "herbalism" on the leeward side of the island where strange flowers and bushes grew. They never returned.

The non-benders of Hsien's group who couldn't keep up physically were taken away, one by one. Admitting you were injured was a mistake they quickly learned to avoid, but one you could induce in others. "We hit each other harder and harder," she whispered, wiping her eyes. "Anything to avoid ranking last. They told us the washouts got sent home with less pay. We didn't question it— We couldn't—"

"We understand." This time Jujinta, speaking with enough

conviction for the three of them. Yangchen and Kavik hid their winces.

"It was all for nothing," Raitei muttered. "Several months ago, the camp runners up and left. New recruits stopped arriving. So did the supply boats."

That roughly coincided with Henshe's debacle in Bin-Er. Chaisee might have decided to cut ties in case the island was discovered and a trail led back to her. "There were only two dozen of us remaining by then," Raitei said. "Once it was clear we were on our own, the adults scavenged a couple of rotting longboats and tried to flee."

"We wanted to go with them, but they wouldn't let us," Hsien said. "Not enough space."

*Sweet spirits*, Kavik thought. "They would have come back for you, right?"

Raitei was too young to give him such a condescending look. "It didn't seem to be their biggest concern," he said sarcastically. "Serves them right though; a storm struck that very night. We're probably the only two survivors."

The brutality of this place had infected the residents. A special strain of fever Chaisee had exhumed from the soil. "What group were you in?" Yangchen asked Raitei. "How did they train you?"

"I was part of the Firebending group." He looked around at his audience with golden eyes and got up from the sand. "As for our training, maybe it's better if I show you."

He led them back around the promontory to the section of the beach they'd first arrived at, the tiny slice of paradise with its clean sands and blue waters. Raitei beckoned Yangchen closer, having long since made her as the leader, and whispered.

Whatever he said made her turn pale. She broke into a run toward the water and before Kavik or Jujinta could advise caution was already splashing up to her waist. With a powerful leap she dove in the rest of the way and disappeared under the surface.

Her body became a distant blur, as swift as a silverskim, and then he lost sight of her. Before he had the chance to fear for her safety, a flash of light rippled through the water, as brief and bright as the fireflies Yangchen had once shown him in the Northern Air Temple. The wind picked up at his back, and he recognized the movement of air as suction, the rush to fill a void. Space began to open in the sea.

Kavik had seen the Avatar cut open waves before, but she'd done it from the shore with bursts of angry airbending, the way a normal person skipped stones across a pond. This time she'd let herself be swallowed by the beast before exploding it from within. A tidal roar rose in his ears.

The gap in the ocean widened enough for him to spot Yangchen pushing apart walls of water, the workpiece initially resisting but then conquering the jaws of the vise. The seafloor unveiled. Coral reef became walkable hedgerow.

"Are all Waterbenders that powerful?" Hsien murmured.

Even more remarkable than creating the field of dry land was the minimal motion Yangchen needed to maintain it. *Stay*, the hand behind her said to the entire ocean, though the surface was twice her height. With the other, she knelt and picked a dark object off the sandy floor. Kavik thought it was a strand of long kelp until the links fell into place, dangling from her grip.

A chain. Yangchen pulled until it held, one end anchored into the rock. The other end terminated in a loop. A cuff.

Kavik searched over the exposed sand and saw the regularity he'd missed before, the work of human beings. A grid of iron points like the one Yangchen knelt over, bolted into the shore, evenly spaced. Ten by ten.

"They had us firebend underwater," Raitei explained. "Not to produce flame; that would have been impossible. The point was to fight against the surrounding pressure and exert as much force and will as you could in a single burst."

*Like an explosion.* "The chains," Kavik said.

Raitei stared blankly over the horizon. "The initial breakthrough only comes if you really, truly believe you're going to die."

Yangchen walked back to the group. The sea closed behind her neatly, as if the elements were afraid of making a mess in her presence. Her face was murderous.

She strode right up to Raitei. His knees buckled. "I don't know any more!" he said, afraid of the titan that had come from the sea. "This was just the first step. There's more to it, but I never got that far."

"Then who did?" Yangchen demanded. "How many?"

Raitei wiped his mouth like a pickpocket under interrogation by the law. "Only three of the surviving recruits were chosen to keep going. I guess you had to have big lungs or something. They were all huge."

Kavik described Thapa, Xiaoyun, and Yingsu to him. "Yes," Raitei said, nodding. "That's them. The camp handlers took them away on a ship, a proper ship, long before the rest of us were abandoned. I still remember the guy with the long ears grinning at us and waving farewell. Smug rat-pig."

"No one else?" Kavik asked.

A glint of resentment in Raitei's eyes, born of rejection. "No one else."

Information made for strange coin. Raitei had flipped them

the key to their bindings, changed their understanding of the world. Knowing where Unanimity ended meant they could finally break free of their standoff with Chaisee.

Only Thapa remained. The last tile they needed to complete their hand. They could *win.*

"Let's get off this spirits-forsaken rock," Yangchen said.

As she led Hsien and Raitei away, she tossed Kavik a small dark object that he'd missed her picking up from the seabed. He turned it over, thinking it a normal rock until he saw the lips of the black shell clamped shut.

A night abalone.

# THE PRICE

**"YOU CAME HERE** on a flying bison?" Raitei asked.

He was more suspicious than Hsien, who'd been immediately entranced by Nujian and was already petting the soft fur on the top of his nose. "Befriend an Air Nomad and their companion, and sometimes you can borrow one," Yangchen said. Technically the truth.

They climbed aboard and took off. The island couldn't recede into the distance fast enough. Soon Hsien and Raitei, both exhausted, fell asleep in the back of the saddle.

Yangchen watched them slumber. "She was developing weapons," she murmured. "Chaisee was making tools through mass-production, a numbers game where she discarded the failures. Unanimity was just her biggest success."

The Avatar looked up, eyes blazing. "She needs to pay for this. She doesn't get to walk away clean. She doesn't get to see her plans fulfilled."

"What will we do with the children?" Jujinta asked.

"Find their families, if they have any." Yangchen flicked her head to the side. "But that's not perfectly safe, is it? Chaisee might come back for them. Especially Raitei. Even if he never mastered the full technique, he'll be the last, closest person in the world to Unanimity once we neutralize Thapa."

"He'd become worth his weight in platinum several times over," Jujinta said.

Yangchen sighed wearily, and Kavik remembered she needed sleep too. "The smartest move would be to hide them until the heat dies down," she muttered. The irony seemed to weigh on her heavily. That was exactly what Ayunerak had done with Kavik. That was also what Yangchen had done with the Firebenders, to disastrous ends.

Kavik wondered how Hsien and Raitei might handle being sequestered from the world yet again. Yangchen had mentioned that Thapa enjoyed his isolation in the mountains well enough, while Zongdu Henshe considered the same furnishings outrageous, a crime against his person. Kavik gripped the saddle rail and looked toward the island, diminished to invisibility. He supposed it was all a matter of perspective.

They couldn't land in Taku, especially not with their new passengers. Yangchen guided Nujian to an empty road on the outskirts. One end led to the heart of the city, and the other to a small town where hopefully an inn or some other lodgings could be found.

Nujian took cover behind a green knoll for his landing. Once his paws touched the grass, Yangchen helped everyone disembark. Raitei crawled to the top of the small hill and looked around, surveilling the area in case anyone had spotted them. *Smart kid,* Kavik thought.

"We're going to help you," Yangchen said to Hsien with firm pats on the girl's shoulders. "It's going to take a while, but we're going to make things as right as we can. I know we haven't told you much about ourselves, but I promise we're on your side."

"Answer me one question," Raitei said. The road must have been clear, because he stood up tall, backed by the sunset. "Are you going to take down the people who ran the camp? Are you really going to bust Chaisee?"

Yangchen took her headscarf off and shook her hair out. She was the Avatar, an avenger revealed in full, and a strong pride shone in her eyes. "I swear on the spirits that we're going to bring her to justice. By the time we're done, she won't have a square inch of dirt to her name."

Raitei nodded. The light caught his face, and his expression made Kavik realize many things at once, multiple insights cramming their way through the crowded door of his mind, speeding his thoughts but slowing his body.

They were all at fault, him, Yangchen, and Jujinta. They'd made a complete hash of their operational security on the return trip and spoken their secrets out loud. Raitei had been feigning sleep the whole time; Kavik had never been surer of anything in his life. Raitei had heard every word.

Kavik started a scream, the limited space in his throat preventing him from forming a better warning. What was it Akuudan had said once? Yangchen was too trusting. She'd assumed Raitei had asked about Chaisee out of a need to see his torturer punished.

Instead, he'd been confirming whether Yangchen planned to ruin his golden opportunity. Raitei was an immensely valuable asset, they'd so carelessly revealed, but only to the right people, the ones who'd brought him to the island and made him suffer in the first place.

Enough money could heal any wound. The boy inhaled sharply through his nose and his stomach caved in on itself.

Kavik dove at Yangchen, meaning to tackle her and Hsien to the ground. He hadn't made it a single step before knowing he'd doomed her, pulling her attention toward himself when she should have been paying it to the threat. Had it been Thapa or even Kalyaan standing on the hill, she would have reacted like lightning. But this was a child she'd saved, and her guard was no more raised against him than it would have been with one of her patients in the hospital. Jujinta caught on to the situation, but as fast a draw as he was, he wouldn't be fast enough.

The Avatar wasn't out of companions though.

Nujian rammed into Raitei, throwing his shaggy mass between his Airbender and the danger. Kavik heard the *pop-pop* drumbeat of the Unanimity technique, but there was no explosion that followed, no fire, only a muffled *whump*. Nujian's long, woolly curls fluttered as if taken by a breeze.

And then suddenly more bursts, rapid, too many. A shriek that could have been Raitei or Yangchen or even Jujinta. Kavik collided with the Avatar and they fell to the grass, dragging Hsien with them.

Kavik immediately leaped off Yangchen and scrambled around to the other side of Nujian. Raitei lay faceup, his lifeless eyes exposed to the sky. A single, small wound in the middle of his forehead, no bigger than the punch mark of an awl, trickled blood over his skin, as if the pressure of his technique had failed to project past his skull and sought a channel of escape.

Nujian groaned. His forelegs dropped to their knees, then his rear legs, and finally his middle, a felled forest. The great beast shuddered, closed his eyes, and was still.

"*Nujian!*" Yangchen slid on her knees to her bison's flank, glowing water already in her hands, but there was no visible burn mark, no wound to attack. Yangchen frantically moved the healing water around Nujian's bulk, looking more and more with each passing moment like a mason trying to repair a dam in the middle of bursting. Nujian's rumble, the huff of air through his nose that had always been present in the background, was silent. There was no task to be done, no feat to perform. He was gone.

The water slipped through Yangchen's fingers. She gasped, searching for air to breathe, and when she found it, she cried softly, the quietest noise Kavik had ever heard her make. He slumped to the ground in shock while the Avatar buried her face in Nujian's fur and wept.

# AFTERSHOCKS

**KAVIK BEGAN** his tail-slip route at the Avatar's mansion. He left at a morning hour that was neither notably early or late and joined the growing crowd of Taku residents on their way to work.

Where Bin-Er was concerned primarily with raw goods, Taku seemed to traffic in refined, crafted items produced at the sharp end of a master's chisel or distilled to essence in crucibles, the results of concentrated heat and effort and tooling. Medicines and oils, three different cures for every ailment, paper matched to only one kind of ink—who knew what manner of disaster would occur if the fibers touched the wrong color—woven garments for degrees of weather between perfect and too perfect.

After twisting and turning and a quick change to the way his hair was tied, Kavik entered a dumpling house that catered to elderly folks who had time to spend the morning sipping tea and reading bulletins. He didn't understand why the most popular dish seemed to be plain wrappers without filling, rolled into little cylinders and barely touched with black bean sauce.

Perhaps the citizens' tastes were so enlightened that flavor was an unnecessary distraction from true eating.

He slid into a booth already occupied by two people. By sitting on the same side as Do, opposite Ayunerak, the three of them could somewhat pretend to be a family, two younger, very distant cousins come to pay respects to their matriarch.

The Executor of the White Lotus had made it in person. Sneaking into Taku was less arduous than climbing the Taihua Mountains for someone her age, but Ayunerak's presence also marked the fact that they were running low on time. The boss tended to show up once your back was against the wall.

"You should order some food," Ayunerak said to him. "We do have an expense budget, limited as it may be."

"I'm not hungry." Kavik hadn't eaten much since they lost Nujian, had avoided certain foods. He wanted to mourn in the limited way he could under the circumstances.

But the demands of the world hadn't ceased. Ayunerak lifted her teacup, and the breath of her nose blew away the steam. "Then report."

He thought he might have trouble recounting events. Surely the thorns would stick in his craw and cut him on the way out. But facts poured out of him swiftly, each one as distant and manageable as a number in a ledger. Speaking like a historian far removed lessened the ache. It helped that Yangchen already knew he would share information with the White Lotus. Some baseline level of disloyalty was expected.

The one part he left out was Hsien. The girl had been glad for the chance to leave her life behind and stay at the Western Air Temple for a while, maybe indefinitely. Kavik wanted to give her respite from being treated like an asset, and there was little risk in letting her roam free without the White Lotus's knowledge. It was unlikely that the strategic balance of the Four Nations would ever be swayed by hand-to-hand combat.

Once he'd finished, there was a pause. Which way would his audience land? Kavik wondered. Show a scrap of humanity at no cost, or get right down to business?

"You . . ." Do rubbed his temples. "You lost the last Unanimity Firebender. You discovered a priceless new asset, one that could have changed the entire game, and you lost it in the same day. You bleeding little twerps dropped the one ball you could not afford to drop."

Maybe Kavik's expectations had been too high. For all Raitei's sins, he was a person, with his own needs and decisions. Had they considered him as such a little bit more, they might have been able to prevent his and Nujian's deaths. "A child is dead, you scum-sucking tick. He's not an *it*."

Ayunerak lifted her fingers, as if she could order a truce from a nearby waiter. Kavik had to assume this location was secure since the White Lotus had chosen it. "The boy's circumstances are tragic, to be certain. But had you managed to keep him alive and turn him to our side, we would have had more options. We could have helped develop this child's skills in a safe manner."

They had just listened to Kavik explain at length how the development of said skills relied on cold-blooded torture. He smacked the table with his palms. "Do you care at all about stopping Unanimity? Or do you just want to own it?" The White Lotus seemed flat-out envious of Chaisee.

"Both," Ayunerak said. "I know you don't like it, but such is the reality of the world. The best outcome we can hope for is that this ordeal ends with a neutral party firmly in control. And for good or bad, there isn't a more unbiased and experienced set of leaders than the White Lotus."

Kavik didn't bother to hide his snort. He might have been a full inductee, but he didn't owe his employers a sycophant's devotion.

They had Do for that. "You think the Avatar's a better choice," the older man said. "You're not that hard to read. You think everything would be free and easy with the Avatar holding the reins."

Kavik expected him to speak ill of Yangchen like he'd done in the mountains and was already thinking about which liquids to spite him with. Or maybe he could just coldcock him in the jaw over the table.

But Do's tack changed unexpectedly. "You can't put that much on a single person," he said in a voice approximating gentleness. "A single person breaks. A single person suffers the loss of a dear companion and becomes distraught. A lone human being can never be truly rational or detached."

How reasonable his explanation of the Avatar's shortcomings. "The great advantage of the White Lotus is that it has no form or shape or outward appearance," he said. "The Avatar has to act in accordance with her form, which limits her options. You think your faith isn't a burden on her?"

Kavik thought of the adoring crowds, the nagging village headman. Mingyur on the stretcher, needing healing. He'd sprung Jujinta on Yangchen without her approval. And if he tried to consider how his own continued presence weighed on her . . .

In a twisted way, was the White Lotus the only group of people in the world trying to make Yangchen's job easier? He wasn't sure. He wasn't sure of anything these days.

"Our own efforts to find Thapa aren't bearing fruit," Do said. He made a little credit-seeking gesture with his shoulders. *See? I can admit we're not perfect.* "Locating him may come down to you and the Avatar, but apprehending him is our task alone. So is custody."

"What about Feishan? Are we going to just let him wander the streets playing investigator? He's one of Chaisee's possible targets."

"She made him before we did," Ayunerak said, frowning. Another slipup by the home team. "She's had plenty of time to do him harm but opted not to, which means she's content to exploit his presence until the right moment. To her, he's the perfect means to hamper our operations."

That would explain why Kalyaan gave away the Earth King's identity for free. Weaponizing the threat of a mutual loss only worked if both sides were aware of the possibility. "Chaisee is not Henshe," Ayunerak said. "She won't be careless with her assets. She knows she realistically has one shot left at causing maximum destruction, especially now that Thapa's the only member of Unanimity remaining."

The end of the convocation, when the Fire Lord and Water Tribe Chief arrived in an official capacity. Presumably Feishan would have to throw his costume away and don the mantle of Earth King again, at which point the highest value targets within the Four Nations would be publicly assembled.

Every single player at the table was watching the same hourglass run out of sand. It drove Kavik mad that they could wait. He wanted to break cups, hurl a chair, splash ink. "My brother."

"Your brother the phantom," Ayunerak said. "We would have liked to have found him too. But his craft is impeccable. Better than our best."

Kavik could only laugh. Somehow, after everything that had happened, Kalyaan still ended up immune.

Blessed. His brother was simply blessed. Hadn't that always been the case?

Kavik knew the atmosphere was wrong the moment he stepped into the safe house. He raised the sack of buns carefully like a shield. "I brought breakfast." A weak cover for his outing but the best he could do.

Akuudan stood in the entranceway alone, the first guardian at the gates to a realm of punishment. He took the bag from Kavik and tossed it aside. "Come on," he said. "She wants to see you."

The safe house was not large. But walking down the hallway with Akuudan behind him, blocking his path to the easiest exit, put Kavik on tenterhooks. The big man had always been the kindest member of the team to him. Perhaps this was an attempt to get him to lower his guard. If so, it wasn't working.

Before Kavik left the restaurant, Ayunerak had asked him how the Avatar was holding up. He thought it a wildly unfair question. The lifetime bond between Air Nomad and bison was sacred and famous across the Four Nations. *The loss of her boon companion? Oh, she's toughing it out, a real trouper, that one. Thanks for asking; I'll pass along your condolences.* "I don't know," he'd settled on.

His true feelings on the matter were harder to explain. Ayunerak had been the one to inform him about Yangchen's tendency to slip into the mantle of her past lives, but only in the sparse terms of someone who'd read reports. He was the one who'd seen Yangchen lose her kindness in a moment of distraction, fire and exhaustion the trigger.

Neither he nor the Executor really knew how the mysteries of Avatarhood worked. And in his ignorance Kavik secretly feared that Yangchen, out of anyone in the entire world, had a solution to her grief. Withdraw and let "someone else" handle affairs. *She's not doing well, and I'm scared that she'll turn into a completely different person.*

"Not there," Akuudan said when Kavik reached for the door to the planning den.

The only remaining portion of the house was the Avatar's own sleeping quarters. The dead end. Every professional instinct screamed at him not to enter a room with the escape routes cut. *These are people you worked with, people you ate with.* But what did that count for in the end? Yangchen could see chains of events reaching into the past like no other human being, talked about their significance often. And there was no way to follow the path to Nujian's death without tracing over Kavik's name several times.

He stepped inside and was surprised to find the floor packed, every single member of the team present. The cramped space made him realize how unusual the privilege he'd enjoyed ever since breaking into the Blue Manse was, to be alone with the Avatar where she slept. Even while she slept.

No longer. Tayagum and Jujinta flanked Yangchen while she sat on her bed, half-dressed, her long hair tangled. She clutched a blanket around her shoulders despite the warm Taku weather. Her unkempt state looked less like the self-neglect of mourning and more the carelessness of a ruler among her servants. *You're not worth the effort of looking presentable.*

She raised her head and Kavik flinched. Thinking she'd fully retreat, whether away from Taku or herself, was a faithless idea. The cold, hollow person in front of him was still Yangchen.

"I keep thinking about what your brother said to us that night." Her voice was scratchy as if she'd been crying, though he hadn't heard a single peep from her through the walls of the safe house. *"Let Chaisee win."* She exhaled through her nose into her cupped hands. "Is that what he told you in Jonduri when you turned on me? To let her have what she wants?"

*It's fine. Nothing bad will happen.* Kavik had let the products of that cursed island into the world because he'd given in to Kalyaan's persuasion that the Avatar's attempt to stop Unanimity was ultimately of no consequence, not worth endangering the family. The lump in his throat was too large to speak around. "More or less" were the words that should have come out. By going along with his brother, he'd gone along with Chaisee. He'd let her abominable investment bear fruit.

Kavik struggled to respond. The fury of the others was deafening. He wondered if Yangchen had told them about the White Lotus.

No, he decided. They all had plenty of reasons on their own to hate him. Every single member of the group had given up a portion of themselves in this fight. Home. Honor. A lifelong friend.

Only one person in the room hadn't paid the heavy price. Him. And looking into the Avatar's gray eyes, which had suddenly become stone walls raised against any attempt to fathom her thoughts, Kavik was certain that was about to change.

# BEREAVEMENT

**BEFORE DETACHMENT,** *grind flour, sweep the floor,* went the saying. *After detachment, grind flour, sweep the floor.*

Yangchen looked up at the Taku convocation hall, the sharp jut of its steeple, the blue sky beyond. The work would wait for you, no matter the ragged tear in your spirit. Work would be a lover in your bed as you wept, ever present and steady, cradling you when you woke up soaked in your sweat, unsure of how long you'd lost consciousness. *You still have me. You always have me.*

The obligations would still be there as you lost weight, startled yourself with the sharpness of your ribs, be there to remind you that you needed to eat, even just the bare minimum to keep your body moving forward. *You can't serve me if you don't have your strength.*

Yangchen had swum the tides of grief before. It didn't matter how much you begged for relief. It didn't matter how nakedly you showed your weakness. The world, the work, would flay its due from your hide, ripping off long bloody strips. It would attach sticks to you like a puppet and force you to keep up the motions. As long as your outline was visible against the light, then good enough.

*You did it so well before with Jetsun,* said the voice, all the voices, the collective voice. *Can you do it twice? We won't take no for an answer.*

She pushed open the doors to the hall and stepped inside. Entering was no longer a ceremony. Walking down the aisle, haggardness in her steps, made her feel like one half of a terrible marriage, the value of the contract more important than either of its participants. The zongdus sat at the table, each lost in their own preamble. Iwashi rested his eyeballs against his fists, still hungover from his financial losses. The sooner the convocation was over for him, the better. Chaisee briskly flipped through page after page of notes, all eras in time the same to her.

Ashoona watched a thin trickle of medicinal tea drip from a silver strainer into his cup. "Where's your companion?" he called out.

Yangchen stilled in the center of the hall. The blink she took was slow, long. Her hand had drifted to her stomach. She had to lower it to her side again willfully.

*He means Kavik.* "Ka—"

The world, already slowed, froze around her. If she ever had to pick a moment in her life that best espoused the lack of mercy she received as the Avatar, it would be now. Mistakes were simply not allowed.

Iwashi glanced at her, the only one to. "Lio . . . won't be joining us today," she said. *Avert catastrophe, and we will grant you a reward as lasting as a morning dewdrop.* "He's reconciling a few discrepancies in our books. Nothing serious."

"It can be hard to keep up with a sudden windfall," Chaisee said as she licked her thumb and bent another page. "The amount of cash you took from Iwashi would overwhelm any single accountant."

Iwashi glared daggers at his seat neighbor, the stumble from Yangchen forgotten. That was the funny thing about teasing, wasn't it? It was fine until it hurt.

Ashoona waited for Yangchen to finish her trek and haul herself into her chair. He served as the oblivious smiling barrier between her and Chaisee, blocking their line of sight to each other like the trees of an orchard row. Yangchen could lean forward or back a smidge and take a good look at the person who'd ripped her in half and then half again, who'd rendered an island of people into slag to get at the ore.

"Today's agenda is light on business," Ashoona said. "We have to prepare for ratification."

Chaisee tilted over the table, the first to break the seal. "That's when the Earth King, Fire Lord, and Water Tribe Chief will arrive." She took a long pause, just on the cusp of knowing. "To give their stamp of approval to our work."

"Of course," Yangchen said blankly.

Since this was the Avatar's first convocation, Chaisee insisted on spelling out the details, even though Yangchen, as a diligent student, would have read about them. Soon, the first of the security details would arrive, advance bodyguards from the Water Tribe, Earth Kingdom, and Fire Nation. Brocade Guards from the Pohuai Depot, the Fire Lord's palace elite, possibly even the feared Thin Claws of the North. The mood in the city would change considerably. Taku was going to have so many dangerous, vigilant people in it that even a dropped pin would be too sharp and swift moving an object to pass without scrutiny.

Only once the city had been deemed safe would the heads of state set foot inside. The tensions of the Platinum Affair hadn't subsided in the least. Rulers didn't simply show up out of the blue, Chaisee explained.

"I was wondering," Yangchen murmured.

Given how poor the current relations were between Chief Oyaluk, Fire Lord Gonryu, and Earth King Feishan, they'd do little in Taku but stamp their official seals on the policies the zongdus had drafted and leave. Then the cycle of business and shangs and goods and trade would continue. From now until forever more. In sickness and health.

"Realistically, that leaves this afternoon as the last session we have to make any substantive policy changes," Chaisee said to Yangchen. "What do you think?" Her manner was relaxed, friendly. "Do those events make sense?"

It did. The entire explanation had been one long reminder to Yangchen that she was officially out of time. Feishan's presence undercover was bad enough, but once security details arrived in Taku, operating a team would become impossible. Thapa was still nowhere to be found. Chaisee had successfully run down the hourglass.

She'd won. One Firebender to nothing. An empty board was all that Nujian's life added up to.

"What do I do?" Yangchen asked, her thoughts snagged. Chaisee had described separate entry processions for the leader of each nation, intending them as a threat—*look how vulnerable Oyaluk and the others will be in the open street*—but in her head Yangchen couldn't escape her bison's love of parades, how he'd bounce happily through the streets. "Walk out the gate and then back in again?"

The burst of laughter came from every direction in the hall, hammering into her ears like nails. Yangchen forgot herself, forgot her surroundings, could only hear people laughing at her loss, and suddenly she was six again, about to lash out in the way children lashed out, only she was the most powerful being across the Four Nations and the one person who could reliably get her to calm down was also gone, which was a shame because when the Master of Elements lost control, the entire world suddenly became very sorry and *meant it—*

"Avatar Yangchen!"

She came to, halfway out of her seat. A lapse in her perception like scissor-cut paper, the printed design matching so long as she remained perfectly still. Blinking, she looked around.

The assembly was still present. Not blown away by a gale force wind, not even mussed. She could only assume from the petering chuckles around her that she hadn't lost time. *Still trapped in the same joke.* She played her motions off as needing to smooth her robes under her and sat back down.

The shout had come from the end of the hall. "Apologies," said a young woman, one of Iwashi's attendants who glanced nervously at the courier standing by the cracked doorway. "You have a message."

Yangchen could hardly blame her for being on edge; Jujinta could intimidate without a word. He pressed an envelope into the woman's hands and slipped back into the street. The servant, not wanting to be the center of attention any longer than she had to, raced down the aisle and delivered the sealed note to Yangchen.

The wax broke off with a flick of her nail. Yangchen read the few short lines scrawled on the paper and refolded it quickly. "Is there a problem?" Chaisee asked. "Not bad news about Master Lio, I hope."

She sent the letter from her team into the air, where it consumed itself in a burst of flame. Members of the assembly gasped in surprise, but Chaisee, who'd seen her dispose of a message before in such a manner, watched the specks of ash fall to the floor with nothing more than an expression of mild interest.

Yangchen slumped to the side of her chair, propped up by the armrest, and covered her eyes with her fingers. Her breath came harder, louder. She knew her face was reddening. "I . . ."

Heat traveled from her chest to her skin. Along her scalp and temples, sweat began to bead, the shaved areas an exposed canvas. "I . . ." She tried again. "I . . ."

"Have been working too hard," Chaisee said. She slapped her knees and rose. "We've all been working too hard. I'd like to call a morning recess. For the entire assembly."

"I'm sorry?" Ashoona was confused by her sudden change in attitude.

"We can pick up in the afternoon," Chaisee said, resolute. "Everyone, take a break and leave the hall. Go see your friends and families. We become so focused on business that we often lose sight of what's really important."

A moment to rest and gather herself. Yangchen's only source of mercy was her foe.

Iwashi was the first to take Chaisee up on her offer, no longer wanting to have anything to do with his present company. He left his seat and stormed out of the room so quickly his bewildered attendants could barely keep up. With a wave, Chaisee sent her followers after them.

The dam burst—precedent had been set. Yangchen watched the assembly screech their chairs over the floor and file out of the building, some of them unsure of what to do with their newly granted free time.

Ashoona glanced back and forth between the Avatar and the Zongdu of Jonduri, sensing the tension in the air. But in the end, he followed his trader's instincts. Pursuing the matter wasn't worth the effort. "Friends," the elderly man said with a bow before exiting the hall with the remaining members of his retinue.

Once emptied, the floor was as peaceful as a meditation chamber. "Come," Chaisee said to Yangchen. "Join me upstairs for some fresh air."

# EXTRACTION

**IN A TESTAMENT** to his skill, indifference, and arrogance, Kavik's brother had left no particular instructions on arranging a meet. *Trust me,* again. Always, *trust me. I'll be able to find you.*

At the break of dawn, before the light over Taku finished lending the city colors and the skyline stood gray against the clouds, Kavik walked into a small, empty park, the stumpy intersection of five small streets, and sat down on a bench. There he waited.

The neighborhood seemed to be caught in a transition, several of the ground-floor businesses in the middle of failure while fresh ones were just getting started. A drooping banner above a run-down storefront promised a new komodo-chicken restaurant opening soon. He couldn't have been the first person to notice the supreme irony that it hung over the chipped signboard of an older komodo-chicken restaurant.

*Hope springs eternal,* he thought. After all, look at him. About to go another round with the one person he knew he couldn't beat. Songbirds flitted and chirruped in a nearby tree. Kavik threw his head back, closed his eyes, and let the sun warm his face. He had to make sure his features were exposed from every angle.

After half an hour had passed by his estimate, his patience paid off. The bench creaked with extra weight. Kavik had never subscribed to theories about masking one's presence or reading auras, but if there was ever a person who could control exactly how much trace they wanted to leave upon the world, it was his older brother.

"If you need to nap, nap," Kalyaan said. "You look like you haven't been sleeping."

The two of them kept their gazes on a dry, crescent-shaped pit with a small arching footbridge that would have been pointless even after the water feature was finished. "And you can rest easy?" Kavik snapped. "After what you've done? The nightmares you've been party to?"

"I have no idea what you're talking about," Kalyaan said. He smoothed his hair back. He wore it much longer than he used to; soon he'd be able to mimic the styles popular in the Fire Nation. "Are you still hung up about Bin-Er? That place wasn't our home."

*Spirits sucking on seaweed.* "Don't give me that!" Kavik yelled through a constricted chest, straining to keep his voice down. "I saw the island where Unanimity was created with my own eyes! I saw what you and Chaisee did to those people!"

"Right, so here's a lesson for you. Listing things you've learned doesn't earn you a confession from whomever you want." Kalyaan looked equal parts amused and insulted. "I'm not a two-copper street thief who'll fold under pressure just because the magistrate points her finger and shouts '*I know you know what I know!*' Have a modicum of respect for me, please."

A flutter, perhaps that flimsy hope Kavik sought, tickled the back of his throat. He could be forgiven his desire for a brother who was still human.

But like always, Kalyaan kept talking and ruined it out of sloppiness, superiority, both. "What I *can* say is that it is extremely difficult to gather a large number of folks in a secluded area for an extended period of time in secret without compensating them adequately. Perhaps these . . . people you're so upset on behalf of made the choice to do . . . whatever it is . . . out of their own free will. And received fair payment in return."

It was difficult to take a swing at someone sitting next to you, but Kavik tried anyway. He nearly dislocated his own shoulder for his trouble. During the conversation, Kalyaan had snaked a few strands of water from a hidden skin around Kavik's waist from behind the bench without him noticing, cuffing his dominant arm in place.

Kavik swore and kicked dust at his brother. In his mind he saw the chair with straps, that horrible chair the Avatar had buried deep within the earth.

"Hey! Take it easy!" Kalyaan relaxed his grip on the water and the pressure melted away from Kavik's wrist. "What's gotten into you? You never used to be this jumpy."

"Maybe it's because I found out I was related to a monster!"

"My boss doesn't tell me everything about her operations. It's called compartmentalization of information. A practice you and the Avatar should have kept."

The White Lotus valued opacity in the manner he described. Yangchen simply trusted the people she thought her friends. "We're going to burn you," Kavik snarled.

Kalyaan leaned forward, finally interested.

One of the surprising difficulties in blackmailing someone was informing them they were being blackmailed in the first place. "If you don't hand over Thapa, the Avatar is going to tell

Chaisee that you originally joined her organization as Zongdu Henshe's plant," Kavik said.

"Ah" was Kalyaan's only response.

"I'm sure you're handling Thapa in the city, because we can't find him." Flattery might season the dish Kavik was trying to serve. "I admit defeat and so does the Avatar. You've beaten us at tradecraft, so we've moved onto dirt. Give us Thapa and your secret stays safe for now."

"And does the Avatar know that by making good on her threat, she'd be handing me over to a person who will in all likelihood have me screaming for death for days on end? Weeks?"

"She doesn't care."

"I don't believe you. She's the Avatar. Air Nomad principles and all that. Coercion and threats of violence are off-limits."

"She doesn't care," Kavik repeated. "You and Chaisee have cost her more than you'll ever know, and she wants to see you bleed."

"Do *you*?" Kalyaan said. "That's the real question here. Do *you* want to see me suffer? You know you're going to have to testify before Chaisee for this plan to truly work. If you do, you might as well be the one holding the skinning knife."

He was right. The other challenge to burning someone was setting the table for the audience. You couldn't just hurl a story through a window at a stranger; you needed access to the person holding the stick, and once you had it, credibility. Master Lio's true identity was the evidence, the torch that would set Kalyaan alight, and only his word would suffice. He would probably have to deliver the news in person to Chaisee and dredge up their old life in the North. Without Kavik, the accusation would merely look like a ruse by the Avatar.

"Look me in the eye and tell me you'd be fine selling me out," Kalyaan said. "Tell me you'd be able to live with yourself knowing you were responsible for the untimely end of your own flesh and blood."

Kavik stilled his face, knowing that was a tell in itself. Trying to hide from his brother was futile. "I'd be fine seeing you get what you deserve."

"Blow me out to sea," Kalyaan muttered. His hands came up, then down on his thighs with a clap. "You'd really do it, wouldn't you? Not because you want to, but because the Avatar wills it so. She's convinced you your purity is at stake, and it doesn't matter to her that the decision would haunt you for the rest of your life."

As the sun rose, so did activity throughout the neighborhood. A few blocks down the street, people on their way to work crossed briskly from one corner to the other, existing only in a thin slice of perspective. A puppeteer could make a crowd on the cheap by dragging a bystander across the stage, dipping them out of view, and then repeating the cycle.

"Do you know why you haven't caught up to me yet?" Kalyaan said. "It's not because I'm better at sneaking around, following people, any of that. It's because you're incapable of making decisions of your own free will."

"Oh, go soak yourself."

"No, I mean it. You're constantly looking over your shoulder for approval. You can't choose a path when there's no outside party to judge you. There's a guru named Shoken you should read; you're a perfect example of his 'Fettered Man.' "

"What, in contrast to you?"

"Yes. When I told Chaisee you were my brother, there was no one to pat me on the head and say *Good job, you made the right move.* I just took the risk on my own."

In the distance, a porter pulling a heavy cart overladen with carrots and cabbages made it through the diagonal of an intersection before Kavik could summon his voice. "Wait, what?"

*"Wait, what?"* Kalyaan mocked. "Chaisee knows you're my brother and a spy for the Avatar. Your plan to burn me isn't going to work. I came clean to her about my origins a while ago and she forgave me for working with Henshe. I've become the role. The Zongdu of Jonduri's man, through and through."

Information, that strangest of coin. Kavik and the Avatar hadn't counted on a precious secret being given away so freely, and now the floor had dropped out from under him. A few moments ago, the one thing he and his brother agreed on was Chaisee's unyielding capacity for harming those who betrayed her. "You're lying," Kavik said. "Chaisee would never let you slide. She'd have killed you on the spot."

Kalyaan shrugged. "I don't know. Why wouldn't she show some leniency to the father of her child?"

*Everything I do, I do for family.*

Kavik dropped his head into his hands. His own choked scream of frustration bounced back into his face.

"Sorry." Kalyaan slapped him on the back. "You're no longer the baby of the family. Harsh stuff, but you'll get used to being an uncle."

As Kavik shook, Kalyaan circled his palm, warming him with friction as if to help him fight off a bout of nausea. "You and the Avatar can't burn me. You have no fuel for your fire. Just goes to show, honesty really is the best policy. I truly believe that now, which is why I'm going to tell you what'll happen next."

Kalyaan leaned into Kavik's ear. "Chaisee's not the heartless person you think she is. She accepts wayward brothers-in-law and wants us to be together. You're going to come with me, right now, and we are going to leave Taku. We'll figure out a way to collect our parents, and then all of us are going to live out the rest of our days happy and free, completely untouchable to the rest of the world."

"You've gone mad." Kavik pushed his brother away. "You've completely lost it." Kalyaan couldn't be the one with the stronger grip on reality here.

"Nah, I just have faith in the woman I love. She'll be handling your boss shortly enough." He thumbed in the general direction of the convocation hall.

Yangchen. She was in danger. Kavik leaped up from the bench, but Kalyaan grabbed the back of his neck and slammed him down hard enough to send a jolt through his tailbone. "No, no, no running off now. That would make this a kidnapping. You're not turning me into a kidnapper."

He made a motion toward the komodo-chicken restaurant. A man stepped out, thin and reedy. Tael. Behind him followed six men with the bearing of association headkickers.

Kavik realized he hadn't assigned himself enough value. He could make both Thapa and his brother. He'd seen the island where Unanimity had been trained and spoken to one of its assets in development. He was a wealth of partial information and Chaisee would benefit from having him under her control, if not killed.

He'd played right into the enemy's hands. Gifted them the chance to grab *him*.

The association members formed a half ring around the bench. "Fancy seeing you again," Tael said. "What's the matter? No greetings for an old friend?"

He didn't know how much Kavik hated his guts. Tael was the one who'd forced him to dispose of his former broker's body in Jonduri, and he'd murdered a member of Kavik's mission team in cold blood. Kavik leaned over and spat on Tael's foot. Honesty being the best policy.

Tael's face darkened while Kalyaan laughed. He knew Kavik had nothing in his arsenal left except the weapons of a younger sibling, tantrum gestures and refusals. "I'm not going anywhere with these rat-pigs," Kavik said to his brother. "What are you even planning to do with me in the first place? Keep me prisoner until I come around and forgive you?"

"*Prisoner* is a relative term," Kalyaan said. "I'd get you a nice room somewhere. Henshe had it pretty good in his cushy quarters at the Northern Air Temple. You know, before I put an icicle through his kidneys."

"Boss-boss," Tael said, his eyes fixed on something behind them.

Kalyaan glanced over his shoulder and Kavik caught a rare expression of surprise on his brother's face. "Well, what have we here?" Kalyaan muttered. "The Avatar doesn't run with such an unsavory-looking crowd."

From the other side of the park, a group of men and women, seven in total, converged on the bench from different directions. One of them was Do. The White Lotus had tailed Kavik to the meeting with his brother without telling him, not in the group show of force the association used to intimidate warehouse workers but through separate routes and stations, each unnoticeable, like true professionals.

The sight of backup should have heartened Kavik. But if Do's squad had followed him out of concern for his safety, they would have told him in advance. There was no reason to leave him in the dark. Unless—

Kavik balled his fists. The White Lotus wasn't here for him. They were here for Kalyaan. His employers had given up on Thapa and changed their focus to snatching his brother.

Kalyaan could tell them how to make more of Unanimity, one

wrecked body at a time. He could give the White Lotus the keys to power greater than any nation could summon. Compared to his brother, Kavik was simply the bait. They hadn't informed him they'd be watching his back because they didn't want him tipping off their true prize.

Two different abduction plans had collided. Kavik could see Kalyaan's pages flip, the calculations dancing behind his eyes. "Well, this is about to turn into a cluster," he said to Kavik. "Do these friends of yours know Feishan's in Taku?"

"They do." Kavik got up again, unimpeded this time, and did a quick spin to see how much danger they were in of being discovered. Around them, the windows of the upper floors were dark or shut. Pedestrians continued to travel the main thoroughfares a few blocks away, distracted by their business. Not a perfect bubble by any means.

"Can they be discreet?" Kalyaan asked.

"They can."

The association men fanned out, pairing off with an opposite number in the White Lotus. With exaggerated motions, Tael twirled his finger around in the air and then pressed it to his lips.

Do nodded and flicked his hand toward the ground. A thin dagger of fire shot out of his wrist. Kavik knew from their sparring sessions that Do preferred the heel of his hand as the source of his flame rather than the ice-pick grip used by most other practitioners of the technique. It allowed for a more forceful thrust, a deeper cooking of the victim's internal organs.

Knives dropped out of sleeves. The Earthbenders on either side pulled sharp slivers of pavestone from the ground; the Waterbenders drew liquid blades and garrotes from hidden pouches under their clothes.

"Don't move," Kalyaan said, rising, and suddenly he was the protective big brother again, the one who would shield Kavik from the storm with his body. "Keep your head down and stay still until I tell you otherwise. I'll get you out of here."

*Remain seated in the audience. Pretend not to be a part of the ugliness.* It was too late for that. The two lines of killers closed around them.

# THE PITCH

**YANGCHEN FOUND** Chaisee in the room where they'd played their fateful game of Sparrowbones. The Zongdu of Jonduri leisurely circled the walls, leaning her nose close to the scrollwork, examining the chop seals of the artists. "I'm trying to determine the fakes from the genuine articles," she explained before Yangchen could ask what she was doing. "These are mine now, or will become mine soon."

"Was there a deal struck behind my back?"

"Yes. I took on a chunk of Iwashi's personal debts, off the books. It turns out he's not very liquid, and one can only steal so much from Taku's coffers."

Somehow Yangchen was not surprised that Iwashi ended up the same as the shangs of Bin-Er. Exactly as rich as others were willing to treat him. "I have you and Master Lio to thank," Chaisee said. "The two of you didn't have to work him over so hard. Your skill and ruthlessness drove Iwashi right into my arms."

"You do always seem to come out ahead, no matter the scenario." If Yangchen recalled correctly, Chaisee's score line after the game had concluded was breakeven. Officially, she owed nothing and was owed nothing. But rather than chasing gains on paper, she'd exploited the hole Iwashi dug for himself and cut the back-channel deal. "I admit it. You're better than me."

Chaisee pursed her lips. "I don't understand. Better at what? Business? We're partners in business, friends and equals."

Yangchen wanted nothing more than to speak plainly for once, to stop pretending and cut through the curtain of lies. Getting Chaisee to admit the game was taking place at all might have been the only victory left to her, pathetic as that was. "At manipulating people. Information. Can we drop the act? Or are we to circle each other forever?"

But Chaisee and her iron discipline wouldn't relinquish even the tiniest patch of ground. "You seem to believe we're at odds. And worse, you've imagined your pride is at stake. Avatar, if there's one thing I've learned over the years, it's that you should never bring your pride to the table. Swallow your pride at every turn." Chaisee tipped her head side to side. "Some helpful advice to a young woman whom I greatly respect and view—forgive the presumption—almost as a little sister."

Yangchen flicked her arm out. A gust of wind snapped the doors to the balcony open, breaking the latch. The wooden frames banged against the walls.

Chaisee did not flinch in the slightest. "I did say I wanted fresh air." She strolled out to the railing and leaned her hands on it, breathing deep enough to be heard inside the room. Yangchen took the lesson to heart, shoved her pride down her gullet, and joined her.

Time, and more importantly how much of it one had left, could change a city's shape. The vista of Taku loomed as a menace, each block of apartments a hostile party, each open window a gateway through which Thapa could deliver annihilation. And that was only the view from this side. Yangchen turned her back to the rail and looked up. The spire of the convocation hall blocked out much of the sky, and through the archways she could see the city's great gong, the bronze catching the fire of the sun.

"I don't think it's fair," Chaisee said out of the blue. "Avatarhood. Never seemed fair to me."

Yangchen had heard this complaint countless times in every life she could remember. Whispers from envious students at bending schools, the stunned reactions of sages who'd never entered the Spirit World. The Avatar was adored across the Four Nations, so the refrain went. The Avatar was special. "You're right; the privilege of bending more than one element is indescribable," Yangchen said dryly. "I've been an unappreciative prig."

But Chaisee surprised her yet again. "Oh no, you mistake me. It's not fair in the other direction. To you and your predecessors. The injustice you face is simply awful."

The older woman wrinkled her nose. "Some carnival show of politics like the Platinum Affair happens, and history declares it's the fault of a child who had no choice in their anointing? Tosh, if you ask me. The people of the Four Nations feel entitled to think you're responsible for every stubbed toe and bad harvest in their life. As if you personally controlled the chain of events that make up history."

Yangchen knew exactly what Chaisee was doing. The veiled threat in one hand, the sympathetic remarks in the other. She was trying to turn her. She was trying to turn the Avatar into one of her assets. Her boldness knew no bounds.

There was hardly any difference between this conversation and the one she'd had with Kavik in his bedroom. How did one best soften the target? By telling them a story they wanted desperately to believe.

"Perhaps humanity should bear greater responsibility for its own fate," Chaisee said. "I've always believed in bettering my position, and that the burden to do so is mine alone. I'd wager that if the Avatar didn't exist, we ordinary mortals would act less foolishly."

"And yet I do exist."

"You do. And you must be accounted for." Chaisee drew another deep breath. "Avatar, in our final afternoon working session, I'm going to propose a change to the shang system that will cause quite a stir. I would appreciate your complete and unwavering support in the matter."

"What are your demands?"

To the bitter end, the edge of the cliff and over, Chaisee's discipline held. "Not a demand," she said calmly. "A path to a better future. I wish for the office of zongdu to become lifetime and hereditary."

Yangchen could hear the last tile click. She could finally see the combination completed. Her opponent aimed high, went for the largest hand. "Under such a regime, I would remain in control of Jonduri and all of the trade that flows through it," Chaisee said. "Upon my death, the title and responsibilities would pass to my heir."

"What about Taku, Bin-Er, Port Tuugaq?"

"Not my concern." Chaisee gave her a sly smile. "I could run all those cities just as well. But I'm not greedy. Controlling every sanctioned point of contact between the Four Nations feels like an overreach."

Yangchen understood the sentiment. Chaisee had managed to dominate both Henshe and Iwashi by unofficial means; there was no reason for her to have her name stamped everywhere on the map. "I think you'll find this arrangement appealing the more you consider it," she said. "I am the most competent official to hold this position in the history of the shang system. I have a vested interest in teaching my own flesh and blood to be equally diligent. I would provide a bedrock of stability in uncertain times."

Yangchen did consider the scenario. Not only from her own perspective, but from the memories she could plumb as well. To try to carve out a land for oneself from the established Four Nations in the current day and age would be the greatest of follies, except . . . this was how you'd do it.

Slip into an in-between place to lay your foundation. Focus on amassing not territory but wealth. Prove your usefulness on the world stage to the powers that be.

And most of all, protect your little fiefdom with the threat of disproportionate retribution.

"The terms would need to be ratified by the Earth King, Fire Lord, and Chief of the Water Tribe," Chaisee said. "Your passionate endorsement with the heads of state will again be required. But I foresee few objections in the end. I simply make everyone too much money not to get my way."

The Zongdu of Jonduri, in her moment of triumph, held up her finger and yawned into her elbow. "Apologies; you don't get much sleep as a new parent. Even with the time away from home, I haven't caught up." Yangchen waited while she blinked and rubbed the skin under her tear ducts.

Chaisee exhaled, collected herself, and resumed where she left off. "I would not ask you to go against your own aims, Avatar," she said. "No fresh tragedy would sprout from your acquiescence. The Four Nations would not change for the worse; in fact, there are upsides to our relationship continuing."

"You mean to imply that you're a known quantity. A rational actor."

"Exactly. Better I remain a fixture in your era than a rotating crop of fools. There are many favors we can do for each other."

A good asset delivered consistently over time. With Unanimity in her possession, Chaisee could extort the Avatar forever. She could write a personal and secret history to her own liking, out of view of the larger world. Chaisee reached out and patted

Yangchen's hand. "Take the gift I've handed you. Allow me to secure my legacy. And then, who knows? Together we might work on yours."

Everyone could win. "I would only have to ignore the steps you took to arrive here," Yangchen murmured.

"What's done is done and can't be undone," Chaisee said with a raise of her shoulders. "Let's not assign too much weight to the past when the future is all that matters."

No one would know if Yangchen took the deal on offer, except her and any of her successors unfortunate enough to have a strong memory. And that guilt, that sacrifice had never been an impediment before. Bearing the weight of knowledge silently in this case would save the most lives. Help the most people.

Yangchen layered her other hand atop Chaisee's. "I think we can ultimately come to a solution."

# *CHOOSING SIDES*

**THAT WAS** the trouble with younger siblings, wasn't it? Tell them to do one thing and they'd immediately do the opposite, was how the complaint usually went. Ignoring his brother's commands, Kavik leaped over the back of the bench into the fray.

He was on a team. The White Lotus might not have been the only team he was on, it might not have been the perfect team, but it far outranked Chaisee's association, whose flag he'd burned long ago.

One of Tael's squad was a Waterbender. Kavik reached out and felt around for their common weapon, quickly frisking the target from behind at a distance with his bending. He found the concealed ring-shaped tube full of water around the man's waist and pulled.

He'd been hoping to burst a seam or twist the spout around, but instead he ended up yanking the wearer backward, dragging him across the street. Kavik cursed the quality craftsmanship that was apparently to be found everywhere in Taku and worked the still-trapped water as best he could, pulling the ring bladder up the man's torso, forcing his arms above his head like a child refusing to change clothes.

Kalyaan tackled Kavik to the ground. While he kicked away his brother's attempts to restrain him, Kavik constricted the loop of water with all of his might, compressing the association man's neck against his own shoulder, blocking the blood flow to his head. His victim passed out as the pouch burst, spraying its contents everywhere.

Kalyaan managed to twist one of Kavik's arms into a hammerlock. *"You numbskull!"* he hissed. He hauled Kavik up right before a tiny arrow embedded itself in the dirt with a *thff,* narrowly missing them both.

One of the non-benders on Tael's side racked some kind of mechanism under his shirtsleeve and pointed his wrist at them again. Kavik had violated neutrality. Now he was fair game.

As if to reassure his underling, Kalyaan quickly plucked the arrow out of the ground and water-whipped it into the leg of a White Lotus agent. The young woman stumbled in surprise and keeled over, retching violently. The tip had been poisoned.

Three sharp knuckle jabs laced their way up Kavik's spine, and suddenly the world slowed, the chaos smothered under a blanket of numbness. He could have made out each flap of a dragonfly-hummingbird's wings. His legs were teetering stilts, liable to collapse at any moment.

Kalyaan grabbed him by the hair and shoved his head down, leading him through the fray in a broken rhythm, stutter-stepping through halts and fits, wrenching him this way and that like a doomed ice-dodging ship. He heard bodies come together in tight embraces, the ensuing grunts and coughs, the strain and muffled cracks of bones breaking, the wet squelch of sharpness cleaving flesh.

Kalyaan stopped them short. A man collapsed like a fallen log across their path, his life spilling from his neck. Kavik couldn't tell which side he belonged to, nor make out who dragged him away behind cover. Friend and foe blurred in a sick treaty of cooperation. *Don't get caught* the highest law of the land.

Kavik had been caught, though, the first and only loser by these rules. He tried to raise his head, resist Kalyaan's seeming insistence on him not looking. He saw Do and Tael stalking each other through the struggle. They came to grips inside each other's pocket, mutually, horrifically vulnerable. A quick exchange of feints led to a single trapped limb and then it was over without a proper start. Do slumped to his knees, his face white, his lips pressed together in a grimace. Tael kept the knife embedded in his chest like a handle and quickly clamped his other hand over Do's mouth and nose to suffocate him faster.

Do locked eyes with Kavik as he died in silence. With one last spiteful glare, the Firebender raised his fingers. A thin orange jet lanced outward and seared Kalyaan's arm, loosening his grip. Kavik stumbled free.

The White Lotus agent had given his life to his cause. Kavik couldn't waste the chance by looking back. He fled, if flight could describe his lurching, crumpled escape to the far street corner.

He rounded the bend into an alley. Before he could take another step, someone grabbed him by the shoulder, turned him around, and slammed him against the brick wall. Tael. His brother's hound had run him down.

The knife pressed to Kavik's windpipe was sticky with Do's blood. Kavik could read Tael's face even through his lingering daze. The association man was considering whether this family spat was worth the hassle, and whether an on-mission accident might not be the cleanest exit for the parties involved. The boss-boss's little brother was an ever-growing liability. Why not show some initiative?

Kavik couldn't raise his hands to defend himself. He sucked on his cheeks. Meeting death with a stupid face was the best he could do.

Tael recentered his grip on his knife so he could better draw the blade across Kavik's throat, a practiced butcher. "Spit on me, will you?"

*Well, yeah, if you're going to be a slow learner about it.* Kavik blew out the only source of water he had, the saliva in his mouth, focusing the moisture into tiny needles of ice with his lips. The shards sprayed across Tael's eyes.

The association man recoiled with a scream, the first real sound of pain anyone had made yet. Surely someone would notice.

Kavik left him behind and scraped along the alley wall in the direction he thought the city might be, the real city full of normal people who went about their normal business without a care, and not this world of unclean spirits behind him. The morning sun shone through the gap ahead. If he could reach a busy street, slip inside a group of clerks heading to their jobs, then he'd be safe, shielded by witnesses—

His shoulder, instead of landing on brick, met empty air. The alley had a door alcove, deep enough to hide an ambush. The person who'd been waiting in the recession sank his knife into Kavik's exposed flank.

*Huh,* he thought. *Felt like getting punched.* A warm trickle ran down his side, the flow of blood almost embarrassing. The most private, intimate part of him was leaking everywhere.

"I told you exactly what I would do if I caught you betraying the Avatar," Jujinta muttered into his ear. The note of satisfaction in his voice was unmistakable. A man of his word. He extracted his blade from Kavik's body and walked away into the light.

# CASUALTIES

**KAVIK KNEW** if he went down, he wouldn't get back up. He had found a measure of balance over his feet and so there he stayed.

Behind him, Tael's shrieks suddenly went quiet. "Too loud," he heard Kalyaan mutter. "What are you doing standing there like an idiot? We have to get out of here. Now."

Kavik tried to speak but the wound in his side opened wider. It no longer hurt like a punch. He turned around slowly, clutching his body, blinking through the searing pain. The outside of his leg was wet with blood.

His brother swore like they were young again. Kalyaan ran forward and dragged him back into the shadowed corner of the alley. Their parents would be so disappointed in them. Two boys with bad judgment.

And yet it was the Avatar whom Kalyaan cursed. "Spirits take her," he growled. "I *knew* something like this would— Hold on. I've got to move you. This is going to hurt." He grunted as he lifted Kavik onto his shoulders.

"I'm sorry," Kalyaan said. "We have to— I have to find a place to treat you. Someplace safe and clean." *But not in public,* was the unspoken part. He ran, jostling the wound, and Kavik bit his own hand to muffle his scream. His blood dripped down his brother's back.

They'd traveled like this through a blizzard once, bound to each other by Kavik's weakness. That was a long time ago and he was a lot bigger now, but Kalyaan's strength still prevailed. The ground flew under his older brother's feet.

One of the houses close to the park must have been a suitable location, because Kalyaan soon came to a stop. He kicked the door until the latch snapped and forced his way through, taking care not to slam Kavik's head against the jamb. The air inside was pungent and bitter, and through watery eyes Kavik saw jars of medicine stacked against the wall. A beaded curtain separated the tiny room from the back. Kalyaan had found the waiting area of an apothecary.

He laid Kavik down on a bench the long way. "You're going to be okay," Kalyaan said, stroking his hair with a bloody hand, doing his best to sound fully in control. That was the trouble with older siblings. They were full of it and made everything up as they went along, just like normal people. "I'll find bandages and clean water, and I'll get you fixed."

"We've got plenty of both," said a familiar voice.

Akuudan came in from outside and shut the door behind him. He planted his feet in the exit, an impassable human barrier. Tayagum ducked through the hanging beads. The grim, tight smile on his face was anything but a smirk of victory.

"Hello," he said to Kalyaan. "I'm told you know who we are."

Kavik wanted to cry out a warning. His brother was dangerous. Tayagum and Akuudan were two, yes, but they were older than Kalyaan and their fighting days were over. They were support, supply. Innkeepers. Before he could speak, Kalyaan's arms whipped out, a watery glint of sharpness aimed at their throats.

Akuudan and Tayagum reacted faster than their age, faster than their size, faster than anybody Kavik had ever seen outside the Avatar, and suddenly their histories came roaring into alignment with the present. They were former quartermasters of the Water Tribe, chosen to protect a pay chest full of platinum in the middle of a foreign army. They would have had to have been some of the best close-in fighters of the entire Water Tribe.

Tayagum not only dodged the water Kalyaan sent at him but added to its speed, flinging it into the ceiling behind him so hard it punched a hole through the wood. He wanted the weapon gone, refused to fall into the back-and-forth pattern of combat between Waterbenders. Akuudan rammed Kalyaan into the wall with a clear shield of ice extending from his empty shoulder.

*Akuudan's also a Waterbender.* Living with them, all of their behaviors had made it seem like only Tayagum could bend. They'd kept that surprise hidden the whole time from Kavik in case they needed an advantage. They'd never fully trusted him. Not from the day they'd met.

Akuudan flipped his shield into a liquid cocoon around Kalyaan before Tayagum ripped the water away, revealing a series of rawhide bindings wrapped around Kalyaan like bolas. The restraints must have been hidden in the ice.

When rawhide lost moisture, it shrank and became hard as wood. Tayagum had dried the bindings in a feat that would have made the White Lotus proud. Kalyaan's limbs were bound tight. He slumped back against the wall to keep from falling over like a worm. He couldn't bend anymore.

Akuudan backed away from him and plodded over to check on Kavik. The swirling arm of water extending from his body rolled back into its hidden source. "We got him?" he asked his husband.

Tayagum crouched over Kalyaan's slumping form and gave the confirmation. "We got him."

Kavik swallowed the fresh smear of pain in his abdomen. "I need help," he gasped. The raw walls of his muscles abraded against each other. "Jujinta—he went off plan."

"No, he didn't," Akuudan said. "Why do you think we were waiting here for you?"

For a brief moment Kalyaan thrashed, trying his bindings. He understood something dark. "Come on, fellows," he said, straining for composure. "Are we really doing this? My brother is wounded. He's bleeding out."

"Shh," Akuudan said. His hand loomed over Kavik, a threatening creature emerging from his long sleeve. There was little light in the room. Kavik could barely see his brother.

"You know what we want," Tayagum told Kalyaan.

Kalyaan rolled his neck as if no request could be more unreasonable right now. "You don't need to do this," he said. "You've won. You caught me."

"We haven't won," Tayagum said. "There's a big difference between holding a prisoner and getting them to talk. You taught the Avatar that lesson pretty good, and the two of us, well, we've known it for a long time. Did a stint in King Feishan's worst cells, and the interrogations we went through? The story alone would turn your hair white."

His frown contained a hint of pride. "Still, neither of us ever cracked. I'm hoping you're not as tough. This is your last chance to spill. Thapa's location, Chaisee's plan of attack. Give us the goods."

No answer.

"Not even a crumb, huh?" Akuudan sighed. "All right. If that's the way you want to play it." He made a show of examining

Kavik from one angle, then another, his brow furrowed in diagnosis. "Let me see how bad this wound really is." He clamped his hand, solid as a tree knot, over Kavik's side.

The explosion in his core stole Kavik's breath away. Deep crimson welled between Akuudan's fingers. The teary whimper that escaped Kavik's lips didn't do the agony justice. "Hmm, blood's dark," Akuudan mused. "That's not a good sign."

"What are you doing!?" Kalyaan screamed. "He's your teammate!"

"Is he?" Tayagum said calmly. "From our perspective, he's already betrayed us once. Little stoatweasel's always running around, sneaking off to meet with people we don't know. Seems to me like the two of you could have been planning to escape Taku together."

"No!" Kavik pleaded. "I wasn't trying toaaAGHHH!"

Akuudan squeezed again. This time Kavik had plenty of air, enough to howl and wail like he thought he'd never do again past a certain age, as if pain were a trial one outgrew. His kuspuk bloomed red.

Kalyaan tried to get up but the older man caught him and slammed him back into the wall. "The Avatar!" Kavik gasped, latching on to any words that would save him. "She'd never let you do this!"

"Who says she knows what's happening right now?" Tayagum said. "Crazy things go on during missions. Real heat of battle stuff."

"Ah, I bet she can guess though," Akuudan said. "You saw that look she gave us, when she ordered us to get the information at any cost. She absolutely knows the score. And if she's anything like me, she is sick . . . of this miserable . . . stinking . . . family." With each pause he twisted his hand back and forth, grinding deeper into Kavik's flank.

Kavik convulsed and snapped the back of his skull against the bench, almost hard enough to knock himself out. "I don't know where Thapa is!" he heard his brother shout. "Chaisee kept his location to herself! She didn't trust me with the final steps of the plan!"

"*Then what good are you to us?*" Tayagum roared back in his face.

Kalyaan's collapse was final. "Please," he begged. "I know the signal for Thapa to attack the convocation hall. He moves on a specific command. Three gong strikes at the wrong hour."

"Come on now; does that seem worth your brother's life? How long between the signal and the attack? What's his escape route? Give us more."

"I don't have any more!" Kalyaan screamed. "I swear!"

"Not great," Tayagum said. "But it'll have to do." He looked over his shoulder and called out, "Did you get that?"

"I did." Jujinta's voice was unmistakable behind the bead curtain. "I'll deliver the message to her." He took off, his footsteps growing faint.

Akuudan reached under the bench and began to stack rolls of bandages on Kavik's chest, redness already seeping into the edges of the cloth. "I'm envious," he said. "Your brother chose you over the mission. I guess there really is no stronger bond than family."

# BLINKING FIRST

**YANGCHEN LOOKED** into Chaisee's eyes with honest admiration. The Zongdu of Jonduri had simply given herself so much . . . permission.

If license to act freely in this world were a currency, then Chaisee had built a hoard to make the Avatar jealous. How many men and women in the entirety of the Four Nations could claim to be as unfettered as her? Monarchs and gurus and few others. No wonder Chaisee read so much Laghima and Shoken. Only those exalted minds could equal her in certainty of purpose.

Yangchen couldn't claim such greatness. Lines had been drawn all around her in a cracked-glass web. To cross any one of them would condemn her as a bad Avatar, a bad Air Nomad, a failure by innumerable past and future standards. No direction led to a clean getaway.

She took one last look at Taku, the deep green harbor, the gentle slope of its hills. Iwashi hadn't been completely hands-off in his duties; like the caretaker of a miniature topiary, he'd made decisions to prune and allow certain growth, favoring tidy businesses and refined industries that fit the image of prosperity embraced by all four elements. Viewed from this angle, by an audience of a blessed few, the cityscape was a harmonious balance of sea and wind and fertile earth, warmed by the sun. A painting of perfection.

What a crock.

Yangchen could fly. She saw things from above. And Taku, like every great success, was an elaborate piece of stagecraft.

She knew that outside the city limits, paper mills belched noxious odors into the sky as vats of slurry stewed in alchemical fixers. Farther down the trade routes, silkpillars died by the thousands of millions, boiled in their cocoons to unravel their threads. Entire villages of workers along the famous Perfume Trails had permanently damaged their senses of smell and taste from mixing batches of product by hand.

No one ever liked to look too closely at writhing, screeching humanity, not even in the most benign circumstances. The Air Temples had an expression regarding outside visitors who were shocked and disappointed by the incredible volume of chores the monks and nuns had to busy themselves with to support a few hours per day of meditation and study. *Weak eyelids.* Enlightenment was a muscle, and the world was too heavy for most.

Yangchen reached toward the door of the balcony, her fingers splayed. She quickly closed them into a Crane-Fish Beak form. The brickwork of the wall pinched shut, defying the solidness of baked clay and mortar with a snapping, grinding noise. She gave her hand a twist, and the wall locked itself into a spiral as tight as the petals of a flower in the cold.

She'd moved quicker than Chaisee could react. The zongdu startled away from the trickling dust. "What are you doing?" she said. "We had privacy enough."

Yangchen didn't reply. She leaned back and punched a gust of wind up at the great bronze gong, knocking the metal so it rang, sending a deep clashing buzz through the convocation hall and into the heart of Taku.

The act wasn't easy with her native element. Air normally pushed against surfaces; it didn't strike or make an impact. She punched again, harder, and a second reverberation rolled over the city. Under different circumstances she might have paused there to give Chaisee a chance to respond. She'd demonstrated sufficient proof of knowledge.

But in this world, Nujian was dead. An entire island of people had vanished. And Yangchen had swallowed her fill of half measures. For emphasis more than anything else, she leaped straight up and angled an overhead kick at the gong for a third sharp gust, a heels-over-head strike.

She finished the flip by landing on all fours, cracking the balcony floor under her knuckles. A sheet of rock sprouted from the ground below, a landslide that defied gravity. The stone lapped over the entire platform, trapping the two of them firmly inside the walls.

Light filtered through minuscule cracks in the stone like the gaps between fingers. They'd become two insects in a giant's cupped hand. Yangchen could see her fellow prisoner. The normally unflappable zongdu pushed on the twisted bricks blocking the doorway, trying to get back inside.

"What nonsense are you playing at?" Chaisee shouted. She pounded her fist over each section of the wall in turn, searching for weak spots, methodical even while her fear grew. "Release me this instant!"

*Are we going to behave?* Yangchen directed the silent question at herself with more than a little sarcasm. Now, in the crucial moment, she couldn't afford losing her surroundings to old fears.

The confined space had no terrors for her. She imagined her former selves backing away from the present, wanting to stay clear of her folly. Leaving her still Yangchen. "Do you know what makes an Air Nomad an Air Nomad?" she said. "The ability to sit quietly with oneself, anywhere, any place, without want or plan. I thought the two of us might try that together."

Chaisee wheeled on her. "We can't stay here!"

"Why not?" Yangchen had chased the complete picture for so long to no avail. Now was the time to see what willful ignorance might reap. "We shouldn't be in any danger. This space is no different from a hermit's cell. Certainly, no harm will come to you by *my* hand."

Yangchen leaned closer, her grin uncontrollable. "I happen to know that Thapa requires a little bit of time to work up to a really large blast. I might be able to save us before then, if you give me his location."

With trembling hands, Chaisee made gestures of calmness. A few strands of loose hair brushed behind her ears, a deep breath. "So this is your game? Betting it all on who blinks first? I didn't paint you as such an irresponsible leader."

Her nimble mind would reach for any thread it could to weave together a safety net. "Think about the situation you'd leave behind, Avatar," Chaisee said, trying to outpace the last few falling grains of sand in the hourglass. "Taku in chaos. The Four Nations in disarray. You don't want to depart this world bearing such heavy regrets now, would you?"

Yangchen stared at her before bursting into laughter.

Chaisee startled backward. Yangchen's shrill howls bounced and redoubled inside the small enclosure. *Regrets?* Threatening the Avatar with regrets was like trying to drown a fish. She knew that now. Yangchen would be doomed to an eternity of reflection upon her errors, no matter her choices.

"I *can't* leave this world," she gasped as she wiped a tear from her eye. "I'm trapped! I always come back! Haven't you heard?"

If she were bound to this rock, then she'd use her chains as a weapon. "You on the other hand, Zongdu Chaisee. Think about what *you'd* leave behind."

The whites of Chaisee's eyes grew.

"A forward-thinking person like yourself would have made plenty of assurances for your sudden and untimely absence," Yangchen said. "Your organization can survive without its head until it finds a new one. And you've probably drawn up contracts to leave money where you see fit."

That much was certainly true. The wealthiest individuals paid considerable attention to how their riches would live on past them. But there was a deep difference between planning for one's death and facing it.

"I'm sure you can trust your subordinates with your legacy, given how exemplary a leader you are." Yangchen giggled; some tales were too hard to spin with a straight face. She wasn't *that* good an actor. "I'd bet the world that your son will be well taken care of by all of those men and women . . . *you've paid*."

Chaisee cast her head down. "He's under the hall," she whispered.

*No. No, no, too soon. I need to see you mean it.* Yangchen crossed her arms and remained where she was.

"Didn't you hear me?" Chaisee's warble was the first note of true desperation Yangchen had ever heard from her. "There's a basement under the floorboards of the convocation hall! Thapa is sealed inside! You have to extract him!"

"I'm sorry," Yangchen said calmly. "You've fed me so many lies that I can't take your word at face value anymore. I go down there, find nothing, you take the chance to escape. I won't fall for your tricks."

*"What is wrong with you!?"* Chaisee grabbed her robes and yanked her close with the strength of a person who finally had something to lose. *"There's no more time!"*

She searched the Avatar's face in confusion. An understanding passed between them. Despite her earlier advice, Chaisee did have some pride remaining in her after all. Because the last of it crumbled away before Yangchen's very eyes.

The Zongdu of Jonduri sank to her knees. She lowered herself, still clutching Yangchen's robes, and did as so many crowds had done before in this era and eras past.

"Avatar Yangchen," she begged. "Save me. Please."

Hidden from witnesses, the two of them could reach their nadirs together. Chaisee the adherent. The follower. And Yangchen, a statue in an alcove. "I made a mistake," Chaisee said. "I put us in danger. This is all my fault. My doing."

They were most of the way there. A true declaration of repentance had a crucial ingredient. Was the zongdu insightful enough to grasp it in time?

Chaisee raised her head. Tears welled in her eyes. "Please!" she cried. "I'll do anything to make it right!"

*Good enough.* Yangchen leaped straight up, bursting through the top of the enclosure, the stone shattering around her shoulders.

She air spouted higher and higher, past the gong she'd struck to call forth Thapa from his hiding place, the roof of the hall shrinking under her feet. The effort was easier than normal, even for a master of the technique, as if her very body were emptier.

From up here, Taku was so miniature and unreal. She was tempted to take a step out of the whirling funnel to see if she could follow Laghima into the nothingness of legend. Another day perhaps.

Yangchen focused her attention below and committed the real irresponsible, self-destructive, unforgivable act of today. With the man who could kill her undoubtedly moments away from doing so, she entered the Avatar State.

The hall was an architect's model. On an earthen plate, it could be swiveled to the side. The centerpiece of Taku shifted in accordance with Yangchen's will, following her body's command. A tectonic drift, localized to a single block. Surely everyone who could see her was screaming in terror.

The posts of the building snapped like twigs. With borrowed power, she shunted the entire hall, Chaisee still inside, to the edge of the street. The building drooped in front of a crowd of bewildered onlookers like a damaged cake, a ridiculous sight. A once proud landmark nudged to the left.

Once the excavated pit of the lowest floors had been revealed, Yangchen fell out of the sky and landed in the western side of the foundation, which just so happened to be roughly the length of an airball court. Even the decapitated load-bearing pillars to the left and right resembled the footposts of her people's game.

The eastern side had been converted to a squalid burrow, full of filth and half-gnawed rations. A sole occupant stood keeper. Thapa. Chaisee had stashed him under the target location itself, outfoxing Yangchen and anyone else who might have known that one of his chief advantages was range. No wonder they hadn't been able to find him.

The vibrations of the gong had reached him in his hole, though, a signal that could have penetrated any location in Taku. The Firebender breathed in and out, head lowered meditatively, completely unperturbed by the havoc Yangchen had caused. He seemed determined to carry out his orders, heedless of the circumstances.

Thapa inhaled one last time and looked up at her. There was

a glassy, distant sheen to his eyes, from hunger or isolation or something else she couldn't identify. The selfish cunning that normally oozed from the man was nowhere to be found in his blank expression.

He'd finished the lengthy buildup for his technique. There they were, the Avatar and Unanimity, two great powers on opposite ends of a wavering scale, straddling the pivot of the world.

"Don't," Yangchen said. "You have—"

Thapa leaned his head back, far enough to give her a look up his nostrils. His stomach caved inward.

*You have a choice*, was what Yangchen was going to say. But apparently Thapa felt compelled to continue down his destructive path, just like Chaisee and Feishan and every shortsighted being Yangchen had ever pleaded with. He threw his head forward and let loose the ability he'd worked so hard for, survived and betrayed his comrades for. All that power had to go somewhere.

The distinct *pop-pop* of Unanimity sounded.

*No matter*, Yangchen thought, strangely at peace as she brought her hands up. *This is all right.*

She'd made a choice of her own, long ago.

# APPETITE FOR BITTER

### BEFORE TAKU

The cave in Taihua, as far away from the Northern Temple as could be reached in a single flight, was just a cave. No Air Nomads or gurus had ever resided there as far as Yangchen knew, and there were no accommodations to keep out the cold.

A campfire, easily seen from afar, would have been a bad idea. So when Yangchen returned to the isolated mouth in the mountains on Nujian, she saw Yingsu huddled against a rock, warming herself with the Breath of Fire technique.

Yangchen couldn't help feeling strange, watching someone who possessed such extreme abilities use the most rudimentary of skills. It was easy to forget the woman was also a Firebender who could perform the basics. *She wouldn't cook her food by blowing it up.*

Yangchen hopped off Nujian and landed on the ledge jutting from the cave while he loitered higher in the ridgeline. In the faint dawn sun, half of Yingsu was a looming shadow. "How's the monk?" she asked as she stared across the valley.

"Mingyur?" Yangchen sat down next to the Firebender and rubbed her eyes. "I ruptured his lungs and eardrums. I nearly killed him."

"You saved his life," Yingsu said. "I don't know how, but Thapa would have blown him to bits. I'm not exactly sure what you did with the—"

She searched for words, expanded and contracted her hands in an attempt to describe what she'd witnessed. She'd have some difficulty there. A void was invisible by definition, and Yingsu had never been on the receiving end of the forbidden airbending technique that had neutralized Thapa and Xiaoyun in Bin-Er.

Yangchen, lacking any other option, had tried to snuff out Thapa's blast with a sudden, violent version of the maneuver, centering the vacuum on the pinpoint terminus of the shot.

And spirits be praised, it had worked.

Not without cost, though. Mingyur had been caught in the radius of the bubble, subject to both the sudden, instantaneous lack of air and then the battering turbulence of the winds rushing back to fill the empty space. Yangchen had inflicted almost as much damage on him as the shockwave of a real explosion. She'd innovated a worse version of an already deadly technique.

"You got him to ground," Yingsu said. "Covered him long enough for Thapa to give up and retreat." The Firebender frowned as she processed the events. "He must have escaped with help. I can't believe his rescuers would let him take a shot at me and Xiaoyun."

"I don't know," Yangchen said. "Maybe he fit their needs better and they didn't want you anymore. You could have been demoted from asset to loose end. There's no way to be sure."

Yingsu swore and kicked her heel at the rock below. Yangchen watched her carefully. The danger they'd faced together, the attempt on her life by her former comrades, seemed to have changed Yingsu's attitude toward the Avatar who'd kept her prisoner for so long. Key pieces were flipped in moments like this.

"So Xiaoyun is really dead?" Yingsu asked.

Yangchen nodded. "So are you. You played a convincing corpse." The opportunity to deceive the world had presented itself in the hospital, and she was glad they'd taken it. "Right now, I am the one person who knows you're alive. It'll stay that way, provided you live discreetly and avoid trouble from here on out."

"You would really let me go free?"

While the Firebenders remained in her custody, Yangchen had spent every single night trying to decide what to do with them. She hadn't been able to find a solution until now. Ironically, Thapa's escape and betrayal had simplified things for her.

"If you keep your head down," Yangchen said. "Try to cause trouble with your ability, and you'd raise a flag to many dangerous people throughout the world, including the group that just tried to kill you. Being hunted is no way to live."

Yingsu made a low grunt. "Where would I go?"

"I have friends like you who were treated like pawns and suffered for it. I set them up with new lives. Keep in mind I could place you anywhere in the world. Air Nomad privileges. I can fly over borders, wherever you might want to settle. Which island in the Fire Nation do you come from?"

"I'm from the Earth Kingdom," Yingsu said, causing Yangchen to sputter in surprise. "I mean, at least some of my ancestors were Fire Nation, obviously. But I come from a village of mountain guides in Kolau. I always thought the reason I survived Unanimity was because I had good lungs, was used to breathing thin air."

She gazed over the terrain with the universal haggardness

of a person whose adventure hadn't turned out the way she'd hoped. "My parents tried moving to new parts, but we got caught on the wrong side of the Platinum Affair and weren't able to return."

*Just like Kavik.* The rocky terrain surrounding them would have been familiar to someone who grew up in Kolau. Yangchen waited for the barbs of homesickness to hook themselves into the Firebender. "There's a catch," she said.

"Hmph," Yingsu snorted. "And here I thought you were different than the other team."

*Not different enough.* "I want to know exactly how many people in the world can do what you do," Yangchen said.

"I couldn't tell you for certain." She saw the glare Yangchen was giving her. "No, really. Thapa, Xiaoyun, and I were the first to complete our training on the island. But there were other groups behind us, still in the earlier stages of the program." She shuddered. "They were younger."

There would be time for anger later, Yangchen decided, tamping down the rising heat inside her. Right now, she needed a clear head. "Then tell me where this island is so I can check for myself. You don't have to be exact. The stars at night, landmarks, which way the wind blew. If you knew what direction you set sail from. I have to go there."

"They took care to keep us in the dark," Yingsu said. "But lucky for you, orienteering is in my blood. I can tell you where to search for the camp." She paused.

"What?" Yangchen was wary. Revealing what you wanted was always the most vulnerable part of any negotiation. She wouldn't be surprised if one of Thapa's former allies had learned a thing or two from him about holding out for more compensation.

But Yingsu had a different need in mind. "You said you didn't fully trust your companions. If suddenly you know where Unanimity was developed, then it becomes obvious you learned from a firsthand source."

"Someone could deduce you were still alive." Clever of her to make the connection. Yangchen thought it a shame she couldn't make Yingsu an aboveboard member of the group. Chaisee had wasted her potential on destructive power instead of harnessing her smarts.

This *was* a problem. And the solution was ugly. "I . . . could create a ruse," Yangchen muttered. "Run it on my own team. Have them complete a fake mission and claim that was how I learned about the island."

The advantages of pulling such a trick were many. A mission to nowhere, attacking a useless target, would not only keep a valuable source like Yingsu hidden from the White Lotus. It might also convince Chaisee that the Avatar was hopelessly chasing dust on the wind and lull the zongdu into a false sense of security, right before Yangchen actually struck out for the island. The ideal patsy would even present itself in Taku.

"But I'd have to lie to my companions," she considered out loud. "More than I already have. Even an easy errand has risks."

"Is this the same group who helped you take me and Henshe and the others down?"

Yangchen didn't respond. In Bin-Er, Kavik, Jujinta, Tayagum, and Akuudan had all voluntarily run into mortal danger for her sake. Taking advantage of their loyalty had to cross a line.

"I'll assume that's a yes," Yingsu said. "They'll be fine. If you can't trust your friends, then at least trust them to be competent. Your people are skilled."

Yangchen didn't want to dwell on the issue anymore for now. She had time to decide how low she would sink. "Stand," she said to Yingsu. "There's another task I want from you as part of this deal."

The Firebender didn't correct her language, implying that

the bargain had already been struck. A good sign. She rose, and kept rising, and rising. Yangchen had to take a step back. She'd forgotten how tall the woman was. "Well?" Yingsu asked.

"I want you to try to blow me up."

"*What!*"

"You're going to perform your technique, and I'm going to see if I can repeat the trick I did to save Mingyur on command. I want to be able to completely nullify Thapa if I see him again, even if he's attacking me directly. You're going to be my practice partner."

The ledge in front of the cave was fairly long, about enough space to hold an Agni Kai, should the notion take them. Yangchen walked to the far edge and turned around. She'd seen Yingsu's control with her own eyes, how small and focused a blast she could make as opposed to Thapa's and Xiaoyun's over-the-top explosions. By her estimations, this exercise was feasible. Only half a folly. The advantage she stood to gain by succeeding was immeasurable.

The Firebender stared at her from across the flat plane, still in shock. "Do you have a death wish!? I'm not going to shoot you point blank!"

Yangchen counted on her fingers the reasons why she should do just that. "I saved you from bleeding out in Bin-Er, I saved you from Thapa, and I hold the keys to your chance at ever living in peace. You are so deep in my pocket you're covered in lint. If I want you to attack me, then you attack me."

Pivoting this burgeoning relationship back to matters of debt could have been the wrong choice. But Yangchen needed to extract as much value as she could from her erstwhile prisoner while she had the chance, for a reason she would never admit to anyone.

*I could have just killed you.* Had Yangchen simply disposed of the three Firebenders with the same ruthlessness that Kavik's brother had shown Henshe, then all of her problems would have been solved.

By the scales of logic, she should have done it. She should have denied Chaisee the opportunity to steal back her assets. She'd passed over the chance to eliminate them in the heat of battle, when she would have been justified by the unfolding chaos. *I was defending myself and Bin-Er.* A much bleaker act would have been to lose her prisoners in the mountains once she found them unwilling to talk. A terrible burden on the spirit, but on *her* spirit, the one the world thought a reasonable sacrifice for the greater good.

It would have all been so very convenient. Another Avatar would have decided to, easily. This she knew for a fact, from having lived through so many similar moments.

But she hadn't acted on the impulse. And now the notion that the world would have been better off had she made the rational choice to eliminate three highly dangerous people would forever lie with her in bed. It would sit with her when she meditated, sup from the same bowl at mealtimes, and dye every sunset from here on out.

*I need to know my mercy was worth something,* she thought as she looked at Yingsu. *I need to know that keeping you alive until now wasn't a mistake. That there are merits to forgiveness and clemency. Or else I have nothing left to stand on.*

Or else there was no point in being Yangchen anymore.

"What's the matter?" she taunted. "Afraid you'll kill the Avatar? You weren't such a coward in Bin-Er."

Yingsu worked the skin of her forehead with her thumb. Yangchen could guess that her headache came in shades of orange and yellow. "How do you know I won't go for an immediate lethal shot and escape by myself?"

Yangchen gestured up at Nujian, still floating in the air. "He's carrying your supplies and shelter and will flee if you do me in. An experienced mountaineer like you would know your chances of walking out of here unaided are slim to none."

Yingsu's mouth flattened. "You are a horrible little girl, you know that?"

She did. Quite well in fact. The Firebender sighed when she realized Yangchen wouldn't relent. "Come on," Yingsu said. She pointed at a patch of level ground lower down. "We need twice as much distance for this to have a chance at being remotely safe."

# THE BURIAL

**AT LEAST** *I've left the Avatar State,* Yangchen thought as she parted her hands, the suction between her palms a model for the larger vacuum she wanted to create. If she perished here, she would have a successor, a guarantee better than the one Chaisee had tried to secure. The Avatar enjoyed a permanence that normal human beings like the Zongdu of Jonduri could only envy from afar.

She knew what to look for, from practicing with Yingsu. The thin streak of vapor, the little rings that gave a tell of how far away the blossom would be planted. The key was not to be distracted by the sound.

*Tear the cloth. Rend the garment.* Yangchen ripped her arms wide, the muscles in her back straining. Creating a lack, an absent space was hard enough when she had time. Benders with only a basic understanding of negative jing thought air didn't resist. Not true. Air would fight you plenty.

There was a pulse between her and Thapa, barely detectable. The beat of an invisible heart.

And then nothing.

The only sign of an outcome was the dirt and debris wadding itself into a perfectly circular pile halfway along the basement floor, a breeze blowing toward a center point to fill the void. Yangchen and Thapa blinked at each other, equally surprised. The collision between two of the most powerful benders to currently walk the Four Nations had resulted in a whimper.

Yangchen's calm was gone. She swallowed a retch of fear, forcing the livery sourness back down her throat. Her mind raced uncontrollably over all the ways that could have gone wrong. How she wouldn't be able to do that again. Not reliably. Not forever. Her reflexes were at their peak; they'd decline as she got older.

But she did succeed. She'd managed to surround Thapa's nascent burst of purest positive energy with her emptiness. She had embraced the void, only she'd placed it outside herself. Laghima's teachings modified to suit her need.

The blankness that seemed to encase Thapa sloughed away from his eyes and shoulders. He looked at Yangchen, incredulous and angrier with each passing second, as if he only now comprehended his situation. She managed to smile. *Ties go to me.*

With a furious snort, Thapa sucked in another breath and hurled his head forward again. This time without buildup.

He wasn't supposed to be capable of that.

Yangchen was saved only by her tendency to over-prepare. She'd made Yingsu stretch her speed to its limits when they'd practiced, just because. Just in case. Her mantra. She emptied the air again, a knee-jerk reaction born of surprise and fright.

Another whicker, the soft huff of a blown-out candle. Yangchen and Thapa both reeled from the exertion of using their most powerful techniques at a finger snap. The cost of waging war over nothing itself.

Thapa shook his head and put his hand to his nose. It came away glistening red. With alarm, Yangchen noticed he was bleeding from his ears as well. Not her doing this time, not like how she'd injured Mingyur. Thapa *wasn't* capable of firing again so quickly. Not without destroying himself from the inside.

"Stop!" Yangchen shouted. "You need help!"

Thapa inhaled again, churning his blood into a scarlet froth around his nostrils. But this time his chest failed to reach the size it had during his other attempts. Instead of lunging forward he jerked to the side, clutching his neck as if his pathways couldn't handle the energies traveling in or out.

A tiny, incandescent spark burst over his head. *Pop.* Then another, and another, like a cloud of attacking fireflies. *Pop-pop-pop-pop-pop.*

*I'm sorry.* She screwed her foot into the ground. The circle of basement floor around Thapa dropped away, plummeting deep into the earth, taking him with it. She didn't know how far she'd lowered him before the quaking earth knocked her off her feet and a roaring red glow came hurtling out of the tunnel she'd created.

Stones and clods of dirt came raining down. She had no strength left to bend them away. She merely shut her eyes and let the earth pelt her. The least she deserved.

She lay there until the bombardment ceased, and then a little while longer. Moments of rest had to be grabbed when they could.

Eventually, Yangchen rolled over and got to her feet. She had a duty to perform. She stood up straight. Pressed her hands together and whispered a funeral benediction for Thapa. Life was sacred. The loss of it had to be recognized. She would never stop believing that.

When she was finished, she did a slow turn, searching for a way out. She found the stairs behind her. With the entire convocation hall snapped off, the steps looked like they led nowhere. She trudged up the creaky wooden planks until she reached the street.

A small crowd had gathered. The citizens of Taku gawked at her. She didn't know how much they'd witnessed. Surely most of them would have been distracted by the moving convocation hall or remained clear of the area out of common sense. At the very least, the events hadn't played out the same way as in Bin-Er. She could blame the spectacle on a different spirit. Her lungs hitched in a bad imitation of a laugh.

Yangchen staggered past members of the confused crowd. She didn't care what they thought of the Avatar, emerging from a hole, covered in dirt. They could weigh in as they saw fit.

And that included Earth King Feishan, who stood in the middle of his subjects, disguised in commoner's clothes.

His Majesty was furious. Frozen in silent rage. He'd come to Taku to obtain firsthand evidence of a conspiracy, secret dealings behind his back that could threaten his grip on power.

Well, today he'd gathered plenty. Feishan never lacked for intelligence, and Yangchen could tell he was fitting the pieces together in his mind more or less correctly, all the way back to the first reports of explosions in the sky over Bin-Er. It would no longer be possible to deceive him.

Yangchen bumped past the Earth King without acknowledgment. *I could sleep,* she thought.

# TRUTH

**"EASY NOW,"** Akuudan said to Kalyaan in the darkness. "One hard shake and the kid starts bleeding again."

"You'd better kill me," Kalyaan replied coldly. "If the two of you have any sense, you'll cut my throat right now."

"Oh?" Tayagum sounded interested. "And why's that?"

"Because every moment you let me live is another chance I'll escape. And once I do, I won't just kill you. I'm going to *butcher* you. The spirits will turn their eyes away from your remains. There won't be enough left of your corpses for the *scavengers!*"

"Listen to the big talk," Tayagum said. "Maybe we should check those bandages again."

"*NO!*" Kalyaan screamed.

Kavik had had enough. He opened his eyes. "Stop it," he said. "All of you, stop."

They were supposed to maintain the ruse until Jujinta returned, but he didn't want Kalyaan to experience any more of this. He was still Kavik's brother. The cruelty had to end somewhere.

He struggled to his elbows and hissed. The puncture in his torso was real, but the wound was nowhere as deep or dangerous as they'd made it appear. He looked over to see Kalyaan sitting on the floor, the rawhide biting into his arms and legs. The bindings still held.

"I'm not dying," Kavik said. He reached into Akuudan's sleeve and pulled out the jointed straw hidden inside. A trail of sticky bloodlacquer squirted from the tube, adding to the dried patch on his torso. "See?" he said. "Fake." Most of it was, at least.

Kalyaan blinked once, all the time he needed to realize that he'd been had. He listed to the side like a ship blown by an unexpected gale. His worldview probably needed more than a few adjustments.

So did Kavik's. He had never beaten his older brother at anything before, and now a crushing uncertainty lay heavy in the air. The two of them were lost in uncharted territory again.

The only thing Kavik could be sure of was that he found no pride in the moment. Not when he'd played this dirty. Not when he'd exploited the one bond that hadn't broken since their childhood in the North.

And yet, he knew he'd make the same choice all over again if he had to.

## YESTERDAY

*"Let Chaisee win,"* the Avatar repeated, quoting Kalyaan while her team stood by her in her bedroom.

Kavik didn't know if he still counted as a member of that group. He'd just come back from meeting Do and Ayunerak, and the others had arrayed themselves like a jury. Yangchen had the same hollow look she'd worn the first time she'd cast him from her company. Nujian was still a fresh wound.

He waited for her to pass sentence. Repeat offenders were always treated harsher.

Yangchen swung her legs off the bed and planted her feet on the floor, hunching over. "She's already won. We're out of time."

Her knee jogged up and down. "We have to shift to damage control," she said. "Feishan's already here, which is bad enough. But I can't let Lord Gonryu and Chief Oyaluk enter Taku with Thapa still under Chaisee's control. I need suggestions."

"We send them messages," Akuudan said. "Warn them away from the city. Easiest, most straightforward solution."

"Yes." Yangchen puttered her lips. "Let them know a potential threat waits to ambush them in Taku. We'd keep the rulers of the Four Nations from harm. Long enough for them to return home and declare war on each other. It's an option."

"You passed off Bin-Er as the work of spirits, not humans," Tayagum said. "Claim there's a spiritual disturbance and that the convocation needs to be canceled. If anyone has authority over such matters, it's you."

"I don't know how well that story took," Yangchen said. "Feishan certainly never bought it in full. But it makes the list."

She looked around the room and made a rolling motion with her hands as if begging them to speak faster. "There are no rejected ideas here," she said. "We are desperate."

Kavik couldn't keep up with the discussion. He could barely process the fact that Yangchen hadn't permanently banished him from her presence. "Wait," he said. "You can't give in like this."

"Didn't you hear me?" The bags under Yangchen's eyes were deep and dark. "The game is over. We've lost. There's nothing left to do except grovel in front of Chaisee and pray she doesn't hurt us anymore."

"That's just it," Kavik said. "Up till now we've been playing for breakeven. Reacting to the enemy. We haven't tried to hurt them back."

He remembered how the momentum during their Sparrowbones session with Iwashi had only changed once they stopped worrying about the impending losses their side would suffer and instead focused on what the enemy stood to lose. The way to beat a cheater was to outcheat them.

"My brother is Chaisee's right hand, and he's in Taku," Kavik said. "We attack her through him. And we go after him through me."

Tayagum bristled, and the hostility that Kavik had been expecting finally reared its head. "You're full of it. We know how you sided with Kalyaan in Jonduri at the most critical moment. You think we're so gullible to believe you won't cave to his interests again?"

"I won't," Kavik said. "In fact, I'm going to burn him. Or at least threaten to."

He paused to reflect on whether his voice wavered. It hadn't. "I'm the only person in the city who can lure him out of hiding. Once I do, I'll let him know that I'll spill his past as Henshe's plant to Chaisee. We all know what she does to plants."

"You'd be threatening him with torture and death," Jujinta said.

Leave it to Jujinta to remove the gloss in one stroke. Kavik swallowed. "Yes. He'll have to flip to our side and give up Thapa."

There was a pause, a good sign that his pitch was attractive enough to consider. "Give us the room, please," Yangchen said to the others.

They filed out without complaint, even Jujinta. Being alone with the boss was normally a privilege, but not now, clearly. Once it was just Kavik and Yangchen, she wasted little time. "Is this a ploy in service of the White Lotus?"

"No. We cut them out of the operation. It's like you suspect; they're more interested in seizing control of Thapa than stopping him. And if Kalyaan falls into their hands, I don't trust them not to use what he knows to expand Unanimity."

Yangchen's knee had stopped bouncing. "What's different this time? Huh?" Her growl was angry, the issue was personal. "You feel bad about Nujian? Did the island shame you into taking action? The guilt finally get to you? I tried telling you once before that we had to fight for people whom we had no connection to, complete strangers, and you didn't buy it. You picked your brother. Family above all else."

"You have to trust me," Kavik said. "Like you did with Iwashi."

She threw her head back and laughed. "That was for *money*. A lot of money, granted, but still a pretend match with made-up rules. This is for the world. This is for my—"

She caught herself and pulled back, mortified. Any number of words could have finished her sentence. Her reputation, her legacy, her spirit, her conscience. Her ability to sleep at night. He wanted so badly to tell her that those were all worthy causes.

"I've been thinking about a piece of advice Jujinta gave me," he said.

Yangchen frowned. "He told me I have to balance the books," Kavik explained. "That's what matters. Actions and nothing else. How I feel, how you feel about me, is irrelevant."

Kavik had long since come around to the opinion that Jujinta was a sage in disguise. His words of wisdom could halt even the Avatar in her tracks. Her anger dissipated, leaving only a husk of exhaustion behind.

"I can't tell when you're lying, Kavik." Her voice was dried out and withered. "You're that good. Few people have ever fooled me as badly as you have. I made one of the most consequential mistakes of my life banking on you, and here you are, asking me to do it again."

The collapse in her shoulders told him everything he needed to know. She would give in, not because she believed in him, or had any inclination to welcome him back into her embrace. She was simply that desperate.

And in a twisted way, he didn't care. At some point in their lives, everyone needed to be carried home. *Let me do this for you,* he thought. *You shouldn't have to bear the world alone.*

Yangchen scrunched her eyes. Kavik could tell she was summoning enough strength to enter the whirlpool once more. "Let's say you do manage to bring your brother to the table," she finally said. "A threat can't be empty. If Kalyaan doesn't cave, or if he stalls for too long, then what? Are you going to follow through and serve him up to Chaisee on a platter?"

He had an answer ready.

"If it comes to that," Kavik said. "First, we'd resort to the backup plan." He explained what he had in mind. In general terms. Sugarcoating as much as possible.

"*No.*" Yangchen snapped upright. He'd shocked her back to alertness. "Are you mad? We're not doing that."

"Kalyaan has one weakness," Kavik said. "Me. I say we take advantage as much as possible."

One truth had traveled with his family, surviving the journey from their home in the North, to Bin-Er, then Jonduri, and now Taku in a circuit around the shang cities. Kavik's brother loved him and would always protect him.

They could exploit that love.

"The kind of ruse you're talking about is reprehensible," Yangchen said. "Little better than actual torture. I can't be a party to such a scheme."

"You'd certainly be tainted if you went along with my plan," Kavik agreed. "It's almost like you'd have to atone by spending the rest of your life working to bring balance to the Four Nations. You might even have to keep going after you die."

Yangchen stared at him, her eyes wild with disbelief at his impudence.

"What?" Kavik shaped his lips into the most punchable form he could muster. "Did you have different plans in mind for your next life?"

She flung her blankets at his face and stomped out of the room. It wasn't long before he heard her giving fresh orders to the others, asking to see the maps of Taku again. Someone tore open the bag of buns. Not even the Avatar could fight on an empty stomach.

He smiled to himself. *Glad to be of service.*

## TODAY

When Jujinta ducked back inside the apothecary after delivering the message to Yangchen at the convocation hall, the mood was anything but triumphant. He glanced around at Kalyaan slumped in the corner, trussed like a roasted bird, Tayagum trying to extract Akuudan from the bladdered vest full of bloodlacquer that had gotten stuck, Kavik applying a patch to his very real, still very painful injury. "Have we stopped pretending?"

They must have looked like a real collection of master spies. "Yes," Kavik said. He shifted wrong and hissed from the jolt that ran up his spine. "Did you have to cut me so deep?"

"I told you it was going to hurt for real. What did you expect?"

Kavik supposed Jujinta had played his part perfectly, making the wound appear serious enough to fool Kalyaan's experienced eye but not so grievous as to kill him. He didn't want to think about how his former partner learned to halt his blade at exactly the right level. Trial and error required errors.

So much effort and they still hadn't achieved the victory he'd been aiming for. They could only arm the Avatar with more information and hope she could use it to gain a better position against Chaisee. At the very least they'd be leaving the city with Kalyaan in tow.

"What do we do now?" Jujinta asked.

Kavik grimaced. "We remain patient and—"

The gong of Taku struck.

They were nowhere near the hour mark. At this distance from the city center, the metal was a low, contemplative hum. The heads of everyone in the room collectively snapped upward.

A second toll.

Kalyaan began laughing. "You piddling amateurs. You've given the whole game away. Your fumbling Avatar has led us all to our—"

"Stop talking," Kavik said. He flung his soaked bandage at his brother and frosted the cloth over Kalyaan's mouth. They needed to hear.

The third ring sounded.

Akuudan shuddered. "That's it," he said, despondent. "It's over."

"No," Kavik said. He pushed himself off the bed, limped over and reached up to place his hand on the man's shoulder. "Believe in her." *Even if that's all we have left.*

He beckoned Tayagum and Jujinta closer. They seemed to understand. Together the four of them closed ranks and formed a circle, arms bracing each other. Kavik had huddled with his mother and father like this once as Unanimity shredded the skies above Bin-Er. This time the Avatar's companions shrank from the quiet, waiting for its end, each passing moment another strike.

Kavik worried the inside of his lip until he tasted salt and copper. He could hear Tayagum and Akuudan beseeching Tui and La the same way parents would ask for their child to come home safely. He could feel Jujinta rocking in place, adding his fervor to their plea.

As for himself, he simply counted. Slowly.

Somewhere around one hundred he found the courage to speak. "I don't hear explosions," he murmured.

"I thought I felt the floor shake for a moment," Jujinta said under his breath. "But I could have been imagining it."

They waited longer. Two hundred.

Hope began to pump through Kavik's veins, thawing and cracking his frozen body. If the command to Thapa had been delivered, and no detonation happened, that could only—well, probably—mean one thing.

Three hundred.

Tayagum was the first to call the results of the contest, unafraid to tempt fate. "You know what?" he said to Kalyaan, who glowered furiously at them over his gag. "I think our boss just beat your boss."

Kavik thought so too. He let out the longest sigh of his life, his chin falling to his chest.

Only when he raised his head again did he realize he and the others were still holding each other in a tight embrace. No one let go.

The victory had curdled into awkwardness. "So . . ." Kavik said. "Are the four of us square?"

He was met with a round of icy stares. "You have got to be kidding me!" he cried. "After everything we went through?"

A bizarre gulping noise came from his left. Jujinta was laughing. *Laughing.*

Akuudan and Tayagum broke out into grins. They reached for him at the same time, their hands fighting over who could muss Kavik's hair harder.

"I hate you all," Kavik grumbled.

# THE PATH FORWARD

**TWO PLAINLY DRESSED SAILORS** met at the Taku docks and boarded one of the lighter crafts. The afternoon provided fine conditions for a cruise, and had an unfortunate calamity not befallen the *Bliss Eternal*, they would likely have seen the hulking pleasure boat gliding off the coast, its giant banner lapping in the breeze.

One of the pair knew what she was doing. Though she hadn't needed to travel by water much recently, she knew how to cleat the halyard, adjust her heading, trim the jib sheets. Memories guided her hands with swift sureness. Sailing had changed little throughout the eras.

There was a good chance the other member of the party had never been on a boat before, outside of the floating feasts that were sometimes held on giant rafts over Lake Laogai. Yangchen couldn't be sure. This Earth King got around more than his predecessors.

Feishan was content to let her do the work of maneuvering the skiff. Sometimes, when they met in secret like this, a little power struggle would ensue to see who would break the silence first. Today set records, especially since Yangchen took them out to sea without airbending the sails full or pressuring the hull with self-made waves. She thought it important to experience life without bending sometimes.

Once they were far from the coast, Taku a smear on the hills, she lowered the sails so they might drift in place for a while. Feishan took a sniff of the sea breeze and probed his teeth with his tongue. "Do you care to explain yourself?"

Yangchen didn't like it when he spoke to her like an employer, a superior officer. Not only did he lack the right to do so, but such language and tone couched their relationship in reasonability. Extracting reason from Feishan was an occasional victory, not a constant.

Yangchen shrugged. "How much did you see?"

*"Enough to know you were lying!"* He shouted loud enough for her to smell his breath. "Passing off lights and sounds over Bin-Er as the work of spirits! And now this! Do you take me for a fool?"

"No." The leaden weight in her stomach ever since Unanimity had been unleashed in Bin-Er came from knowing that with enough time Feishan would eventually put together the truth, or a reasonable model of it. He was smart enough.

The truth. Yangchen had fled the truth for so long that she was certain her mind had split along the cracks. Now was the time to glue her perspectives back together. Now the truth could finally serve *her* for once.

"Through my own investigations I came to learn that Zongdu Chaisee of Jonduri secretly developed a bending technique capable of leveling a city," Yangchen said. "This was the force that decimated Bin-Er."

Feishan leaned back against the wale. The revelation was sudden, large, but he looked nearly satisfied to hear it. People like him *wanted* to see enemies around every corner; assurances that he was in no danger and could rule in peace would never be fully accepted.

A normal person might have immediately asked *why*. Power, influence, wealth. Chaisee had all those in her official capacity as zongdu. Why would she remain unable to sit comfortably with the resources and talents she'd been blessed with, the accomplishments she'd earned?

But the Earth King was cut from the same cloth as Chaisee. While the two of them would have rarely spoken, Feishan probably understood her mind like closest kin. He didn't need to plumb the depths of her reasoning. "How?" he asked instead.

The sudden mildness, the casualness of his body language, failed to distract Yangchen from the gleam in his eye. She continued giving her statement. "She was building a position where she could assassinate you and Oyaluk and Gonryu in one fell swoop. I put an end to her plot. The business with the convocation hall. Zongdu Henshe was her coconspirator and she murdered him to cover her tracks."

Feishan could not have cared less about the fate of Zongdu Henshe. The surest tell that the Earth King was sniffing interestedly around the bait, swiftly reconsidering his priorities, was the fact that he did not upend the skiff in a tantrum. An attempt on his life? Water under the bridge. "Where is Chaisee now?"

"Gone. She fled Taku after her plans failed."

"And you *let her*?"

"She's wily," Yangchen said. "And I'm not a bounty hunter." *Not in this life, anyway.*

Feishan rubbed his jaw. He'd trimmed his beard since she last met with him in Ba Sing Se, a mistake in his disguise. No commoner would have applied such an edge to their facial hair. "The man I saw you defeat was a practitioner of this technique," he said.

Her gaze reached over the horizon. *Defeat* was a nice word for him to use. Some interpretations would have it that she'd killed Thapa, even though she hadn't crushed him with earth, even though he'd created the blast that had ended his life. A temple elder could weigh in, if she ever recounted her deeds, submitting herself for judgment. After her own death, she might not have a place next to her people. They'd set her likeness aside, far from the nuns she'd grown up with.

Feishan seemed to take her empty quietude at face value, an Air Nomad regretting an act of violence. "Who else have you told?"

"No one," she said. The White Lotus had learned about Unanimity through Kavik, and the rest of the team had seen it firsthand.

They bobbed in the water, rolling with the waves. Another boat sailed closer with three people on it, but still small enough in the distance. Not a concern so long as they played their parts. "This is rather nice," Feishan said, indicating the peaceful seas, the sun that drenched their faces.

"Mmm," Yangchen responded. The two of them, a pair of world leaders, free of their identities and burdens, relaxing in companionable silence.

Mere skin wrapping the guts. Inside the two of them, wheels spun in turmoil. Yangchen cycled furiously through scenarios and outcomes, knowing that Feishan was doing the same, adjusting to her adjustments, their plans tangling with each other like fighting serpents. They weren't basking in the moment; they were thinking too feverishly to speak.

Yangchen had the advantage of the first move, being the holder of the truth. Now that she'd dropped it like a boulder on Feishan's head, she could watch the ripples and guess where they would travel.

This Earth King treasured power above all else, even more than riches. He was both pleased and obligated to chase it, the same way Chaisee's self-imposed standards compelled her to grow her ventures to the point of overreach. Now that Feishan had learned such a powerful weapon could be brought forth by human knowledge, his own obsessions would force his hand.

The Zongdu of Jonduri represented his best lead at obtaining information that could tilt the axis of the world forever in his favor. He would hunt her down across the Four Nations till his last breath. He would never give her a moment's respite.

Striking a deal, selling the secrets of Unanimity wasn't an option for Chaisee. Not with Feishan as a customer—the Earth King would simply kill her upon completion of the transaction. To remain one step ahead of the hounds, she and her family would have to live the rest of their lives in anonymity, moving from place to place, never settling long enough to attract undue attention.

Perhaps a cruel fate for a person who wanted stability and status for her bloodline. But then again, that was basically the life of an Air Nomad. It was all a matter of perspective.

"Now that you know who was responsible for Bin-Er, you can stand down the troops you are currently using to menace Chief Oyaluk and Lord Gonryu," Yangchen said. "All twenty divisions of them."

"I have only ten divisions in offensive positions," Feishan said lightly, still pretending this was a leisure cruise.

"You have twenty." If ships were easier to count from the skies, armies were child's play. "It would be a show of goodwill to recall those soldiers and their transport fleets far away from the strategic ports of the continent. You're known as many things but not yet a peacemaker. A show of good faith would burnish your image, and I would make sure history gave you your due. People might speak of you in the same breath as the Avatar."

Feishan mulled it over, which lent weight to Yangchen's theory that he found the prospect of being loved genuinely appealing.

His observers in Bin-Er would have told him about the crowds cheering in adoration for her, and the Earth King was a jealous man. Popularity was the one victory that had eluded him so far.

While dreams of being known as Feishan the Benevolent wandered through his head, Yangchen readied her next move. There would never be a better time. "I have a further proposal," she said.

There was a world where righteousness alone fueled her impending speech. *The shang cities are deeply corrupt, cause much suffering, and benefit only the powerful few. The system was deemed necessary only because of the Platinum Affair. Return to normal relations with your fellow rulers and dissolve it immediately.*

And then there was the world she'd been born into, over and over again, never that much different each time.

"I have been diligently managing Bin-Er on your behalf," she said. "A substitute zongdu, if you will. But two of my peers turned out to be traitorous conspirators. Of the others, Iwashi is deadweight and Ashoona will retire soon. The shang system, from which you profit so greatly, is vulnerable to the base desires and compulsions of the human beings who control it."

Before launching into the crucial part of her pitch, she paused to check within herself for a lump in her throat, rising bile. Any sign of guilt. *How bad do I need to feel right now in order to live with myself?*

The answers would have to come later. "I believe it would be better if the entirety of trade flows between the Four Nations were managed by a single, neutral, incorruptible party that not only you but Chief Oyaluk and Lord Gonryu could trust."

"You," Feishan said, catching on immediately. "*You* want to run Jonduri and Port Tuugaq in addition to Bin-Er."

Yangchen gestured back toward the coast. "Don't forget Taku."

*A hand either opens or closes.* Jetsun's words. Yangchen needed to be the one holding the reins of power in order to let them go. "Your endorsement of my proposal in front of the other rulers during the ratification would travel far in this matter."

Feishan had little reason not to see the wisdom of her argument; she'd done well for him in Bin-Er. But then again, reason wasn't why he'd closed his borders. Reason wasn't why he'd purged his court. "You think I'm some spineless merchant willing to pay tit-for-tat," he said.

Perceived insults and grievances seemed to lend the Earth King strength the same way Yangchen's past lives flowed through her limbs and ignited her eyes when called upon. His breathing quickened, as if he needed air for his imminent combustion.

"I haven't forgotten that you've lied to me about Bin-Er," he said, his voice low and stalking. "I believe you lie still. You intentionally let Chaisee escape, didn't you? A woman who wanted to murder me, released without so much as a slap on the wrist. I've taken the hands of entire families for less."

They both knew he wasn't threatening the Avatar's person. That was neither possible nor necessary. "I know you favor the other rulers, especially Oyaluk. You beg and plead on his and Gonryu's behalf not to conduct open hostilities. Which means they're weak. They're afraid. This scheme of yours is just another shield you hope to raise over them."

Feishan licked his lips. "They never really paid for trying to depose me. Cutting off relations—what a halfway measure on my part. I needed to make them bleed so much more. But I couldn't retaliate properly back then; I was still recovering from Nong's rebellion. Back then, I didn't have, say . . . twenty divisions ready to attack at my command."

He waited for Yangchen to blink. But she'd had her

fair share of staring contests recently. She was warmed up. "Starting a conflict would not be in your best interests," she said, letting his bluster melt away from her shoulders like thin snow.

To the paranoid, facts seemed like threats. "Why?" Feishan snarled. "Because you'd let the other nations know about this bending technique?"

"No," Yangchen said, standing up on the bow of the skiff. "I would simply hand it over to them." She flicked her wrist, sending a gout of water into the air. The signal for the crew of the other boat to attack.

A thin streak of vapor ripped through the swells, cutting a furrow across the sea. The water bloomed a hemisphere of heat and light and noise, the *pop-pop-BOOM* pattern backed by the additional hiss of water boiled to steam in the blink of an eye.

A wave came rushing for them. Feishan screamed as Yangchen threw her weight against the hull to lift the opposite end high enough so the skiff could ride the surge instead of capsizing. A sailor's instinct as opposed to a bender's, but it did the job.

Feishan had never come under fire from Unanimity. She would grant him the experience. She called for a second blast.

Tayagum and Akuudan hadn't liked the idea of Yingsu bombarding the Avatar, but at this point there was precedent. *Come on,* Yangchen thought. *Really let us have it.*

Yingsu obliged. The next shockwave spun the boat in a pinwheeling circle. Yangchen looked at the terrified Earth King holding on to the lashings for dear life, sea spray dousing them both. *Understand that this is what I saved you from. Believe that this is what I could give your enemies.*

One last bluff. She'd never permanently hand over Yingsu to be exploited by the Fire Nation or Water Tribe, which meant the truth wouldn't get her completely across the finish line.

Too bad.

As the boat churned its message into Feishan's innards, Yangchen reflected on what she'd learned from the Earth King's negotiating style from their encounters, as well as the epiphany she'd shared with Chaisee in the darkness, wondering how long it would be before Thapa rendered them both to dust. When playing the game, sometimes you didn't want your opponent to respect you as smart, rational, and clever. Sometimes you wanted the opponent to believe you were completely unstable and utterly reckless.

Yangchen leaped up to the top of the mast, using it as a lever to rock the vessel back and forth, throwing her weight around to keep the bow pointed forward into the waves.

"Don't worry, Your Majesty!" she shouted down at Feishan as another blast from Yingsu sent the waters surging underneath them. "We won't sink! I've got our balance under control!"

# *RESPITE*

**FEISHAN WAS RIGHT** about one thing; Yangchen had indeed let Chaisee go free. Her and Kalyaan both.

"I can't believe you did that," Ayunerak muttered, leaning her forehead against her hands. The Executor of the White Lotus sat across from Yangchen in the same Agna Qel'a safe house they'd hidden in the last time Yangchen was here, while Kavik stood at the window as lookout. The society didn't have an unlimited budget, nor would they have wanted to burn more secret locations than necessary.

There hadn't been time for the three of them to meet in Taku, not with Yangchen busy outlining to a stunned audience her plans for each shang city in turn. So they'd postponed their conversation until her return to the North Pole. The "alignment of intelligence between trusted allies," as Ayunerak had pitched it, had taken nearly an entire lamp's worth of oil to finish. The petering moss wick cast only a sputtering light around the room, inking the occupants in dramatic swathes. Especially

Kavik, who looked more like a regal, shadowy sentinel than he possibly deserved.

"Every time I think you've reached the pinnacle of reckless-ness, you surprise me further," Ayunerak said. "If Feishan finds Chaisee, he'll extract the secrets of Unanimity from her one way or another."

"She won't be easy quarry," Yangchen said. "We all know how smart she is. And she has resources she can draw on in her flight."

Ayunerak, a sharp mind herself, figured out the puzzle in a flash. "You turned her," she said. She leaned back, taking her weight off the table, her face a battleground, surprise warring with frustration. "You flipped her into an asset."

The move was only possible after Chaisee had been fully stripped of the leverage provided by Unanimity. The conver-sation had been quick and taken place in the dark. Lengthy follow-ups would be needed, but those could take place later, in safe locations. Yangchen had to give Chaisee the immedi-ate boon of collecting Kalyaan from Taku and her child from Jonduri before disappearing, or else her incentive to cooperate would be lost.

Love could sometimes be a weakness. Mercy could sometimes be cruel. The important matter was that Yangchen had sworn twice, once to the former zongdu and then later again to Kavik, that she would not let Chaisee's son come to harm.

Ayunerak saw only the trove of information that had slipped through the White Lotus's fingers. "She's dependent on you now. Her hidden accounts. The dirt she must have on her business and political contacts. Her research. You've snatched it all in one fell swoop."

Yangchen didn't know why the Executor was so envious. There was no quick victory to enjoy. She needed to unwind

Chaisee's networks, settle the issues of her organization. Make restitution to her victims where possible. The project was monumental.

*Though Chaisee's money will certainly help,* Yangchen thought.

Having little else to reprimand Yangchen with, Ayunerak resorted to morals. "Are you not concerned about punishing her for what she did?"

Not concerned? The question of justice was like a burr in her throat. Chaisee's fate would remain in her hands until Yangchen or Feishan left the mortal world. She'd be a wedge, splitting and lengthening the crack between Avatar and Air Nomad. Yangchen was more concerned than anyone else in the world. Living with her choice was her own punishment.

She had no answer to give. But Kavik did. "Retribution is for amateurs," he interjected, his eyes still focused out the window, like a professional. "I believe you told me that once, Executor."

Yangchen could tell Ayunerak wanted nothing more than to hurl her agent into the nearest body of water. Instead, the Lotus decided to preserve her dignity by getting up to tend the qulliq. A fine example of maturity from their elder.

Yangchen and Kavik made the journey along the canals by foot, their hoods pulled over their heads. The moon was not out and Agna Qel'a was a blur of darkness against the canvas. They walked a zigzag route and at an exacting speed that left them in a perfect gap between the latest night patrols. But if one overlooked that fact, they could have pretended to be a pair of youths, enjoying each other's company on a leisurely stroll.

"Thank you," Kavik said quietly, after they gained enough distance, from a corner below the blind spot of a watchtower.

"For what?"

"My brother will live. If you hadn't stopped him, he would have pushed his luck too far one day and gotten killed. He made out better than he deserved, but then again, he always does."

Not the sort of statement the boy with a wounded hand, who had been haunted by Kalyaan the untouchable phantom, would have made. She heard a rustle from under Kavik's hood, as if a smile had rubbed his cheeks against the fur. "I'm just grateful my nephew will have a family."

"Yes, well . . ." She trailed off, not wanting to spoil the warmth of the moment.

There was another factor that had led Yangchen to her decision. She had simply run out of space in her head to wage battle. The harsh reality was that she couldn't keep fighting both zongdu and Earth King in their respective arenas. She'd needed help, from sources who could be counted on to do exactly as she'd hoped.

They'd been sitting at the table to her left and right the whole time.

By pitting Feishan against Chaisee in a great hunt, her opponents could burn time and resources trying to outthink each other for a change, giving Yangchen room to breathe. It wasn't a perfect solution. But it was one she could watch and manage. She could break even while the other players traded hits back and forth and cheat toward one of them or the other as needed.

"So you're the zongdu of everywhere," Kavik said.

A gross oversimplification. But beyond her wildest hopes, momentum was indeed heading in that direction.

Yangchen's message to the shangs of Bin-Er those many months ago, when Henshe was still alive and she hadn't yet heard the name of Unanimity cross his lips, had failed to take root. That was because she'd been asking people with power to give it up willingly. Throwing lifetimes of evidence and experience and appeals to humanity in front of a group who could dismiss her with an unexamined *no*.

This time her approach would be different. She would dip her hands, would let the streams of money and power course through her fingers. And then she'd divert those flows accordingly.

Provided they didn't rot her to the core. "With the resources of every shang city at my disposal, I can fix, actually *fix* the problems in Bin-Er *and* Taku *and* many other places across the Four Nations." She felt the need to defend herself. An Air Avatar touching money. "I couldn't end the Platinum Affair. So I'm going to own it instead."

Here was another reason to leave Chaisee and Feishan to each other. Her plate would spill over with the duties of managing the entire flow of trade and communication between the Four Nations for the conceivable future. She might even need Chaisee's counsel. Another dilemma to face. Whether advice could be cleanly taken from a dirty source.

"You don't have to convince me," Kavik said. Another rustle of a smile. "I know you'll do the right thing."

They arrived at their destination, the entry passage to the Spirit Oasis. The lesson on taking help where she could also applied here, tonight.

*Taking* help. She didn't want to force him to do this, regardless of whether he understood or believed he was being forced. *You're holding a knife to my brother's conscience,* was how Kalyaan had put it. She'd regretted asking Kavik to join her as soon as he said yes.

Yangchen put her hand against the wooden door, barring the way. "You know how dangerous this could get," she said.

"I'm the one who saved you from that fog the first time, in case you forgot," he said. "So, yes, I think I have some idea."

"You don't have to do this. You're back in. My good graces,

you have them. You've more than proven yourself to me and the others. The books are balanced."

He leaned in, brushing the edges of their hoods together. "Look at me," he said softly. "I'm not doing this out of compulsion."

*Liar.* Kavik could have been hiding any feeling or motive under his face. "No," she said, shaking her head. "You still feel indebted. I'm calling it off—"

"Spitting spirits, you are so annoying! I want to help you because you deserve it! Do I have to tattoo the message across your skull?"

There. That was the part of him she recognized. That was the part of him she could work with. She mustered herself and pulled open the door. "Let's go."

There was no requirement to face a partner on the grassy center island of the oasis when hoping to make contact with the Spirit World. Yangchen had proven that. But sitting down with Kavik, as a duo, felt much more balanced. The eternal koi circling each other in the sacred pond showed the way. Best to give and take. Push and pull.

Yangchen squared her breathing. The blossoms of the osmanthus and satsuma layered bitterness atop sweet in a gentle pattern, far superior to the distilled, driving perfumes of Taku, now that she had the comparison. Kavik adopted her cross-legged posture, though he kept his hands at the ready instead of touching his knuckles to each other.

Together they waited.

This time, her entry into the Spirit World took place the right way. If there was such a thing.

Ayunerak would have had no grounds for criticism. Only Yangchen's spirit made the journey. She had a partner watching her body back in the material realm. She slipped across the boundary as easily as she did the first time with Jetsun and found herself in a blue forest that glowed with luminescence. She began to walk with a singular purpose, as Shoken had taught, ignoring the whispers of the trees, the dancing eyes she knew were watching her from every direction. She held only one image in her mind. Jetsun's prison. The talons of stone enclosing the mist.

She was intruding. There was no escaping the label this time. The Spirit World could shift in reaction to outsiders, and the landscape itself seemed to have decided that there was only one fitting place for an intruder. She found herself guided toward her destination, roots as thick as barrels undulating out of her way, branches unfurling like fingers to point out where she could find her punishment. When she breached the forest's edge to find a plain studded with giant thorns, there was even a small path of matted grass, as if victims had been dragged along this route to their eternal torment before.

She kept going.

The ground underneath her feet grew barren, tilted, familiar to her. She didn't slow, barely blinked, until the canyon loomed large ahead of her. Inside the walls was the thick, still soup of vapor. The spirit that held her sister.

She descended the slope, steadily this time, watching as the fog enveloped her. Instead of digging into her skin like before, the mists slipstreamed around her form, granting her the thinnest of berths.

Her suspicions had been founded. *My past lives, the weight of them all at once,* she thought. *They're too much for you. They're too much for me as well.*

The next part she knew would hurt. To venture deeper into the fog would mean ignoring the cries around her. Yangchen steeled herself and marched forward amidst the wandering shadows.

She turned away from the shrieking woman who tore her hair out in clumps, somehow always having more to fill her hands. She narrowly avoided the clutches of a petitioner begging an invisible judge who just wouldn't listen, why wouldn't she listen.

A mourner at a never-ending funeral, a test-taker watching his dreams crumble over and over again before his eyes. The doctor who couldn't save the one patient who mattered. Yangchen stumbled past the endless suffering. Her resolve began to crack.

*I can't handle this. I can't handle this.* The fog didn't need to infect her mind to torture her. It could just show her humanity, bare and ripped open. It could show her the truth. History repeated itself. Each of these lost souls once had an Avatar, but their agony reflected a world perpetually falling out of balance.

Yangchen fell to her hands and knees. She wanted to weep, for the past and the future alike. No victory in this struggle would ever last. She crawled forward blindly, like a child, unsure of her dimensions or her route or her reasons for being here, only knowing that she was sinking under the weight, falling lower and lower.

Her hand landed on someone's leg.

She looked up in surprise. Before her lay a sleeping man, sprawled out on the ground.

Yangchen jerked back, expecting him to bolt upright and awake to his nightmare, but he remained still, breathing in and out in a deep rhythm. She hauled herself around to look at his face. Though his hair was unbound and disheveled, his lips were relaxed in an unconscious sigh.

She did not know the rules of this place. But everything she'd seen so far told her this man was an anomaly, the closest thing to a signal she'd found in the swirling noise of terror and chaos. Yangchen rose to her feet and staggered in the direction she thought he might have come from.

Not far away, she found a woman with torn sleeves curled up on her side, using her own arm as a pillow. And then another sleeper, and another. A trail of bodies, not corpses, but men and women who looked like they'd simply laid down to rest where they were.

She hurried, trying not to step on torsos or trip over tangled limbs. A hope she hadn't tasted in years rose in her throat. She fought the flutter in her chest, not allowing herself to believe the wisp of orange in the mists ahead, not daring to speak until she got closer, taking one denying step after another, until she finally came upon the Air Nomad woman sitting calmly on a flat rock in the lotus position, her eyes closed in meditation, looking exactly the same as she did when she first guided Yangchen into the Spirit World under the imposing stone fingers of a giant's hand.

"Jetsun?" she asked, the name coming out a choking sob.

Jetsun opened her eyes. Not once while her sister was alive had Yangchen ever confused or surprised her. Today was no exception. No matter which realm they met in, Jetsun would always see her, understand her, recognize her, deeply and completely.

"Yangchen," she said. "What are you doing here?"

Yangchen rushed forward and threw her arms around Jetsun, nearly tackling her off her perch. They wobbled back into balance together as a single mass.

*"I'm sorry."* Those words became the universe. She would gasp them until the end of time. "I'm sorry, Jetsun. I'm sorry. I'm sorry . . ."

Jetsun rubbed her back until a warm patch had developed over her skin. "For what? The spirits brought me here after I returned you to the physical world. There's nothing for you to be sorry about."

Her question broke the endless loop. It occurred to Yangchen that maybe she should have shown more caution, in case she hurt Jetsun again somehow, if contact between them were forbidden. But when she pulled away, her sister's shawl briefly stuck to her face, glued by dried tears.

"How do I free you?" Yangchen said. She didn't want to speak of her sister's death in the mortal world. Jetsun would already know what had happened, that this form was only her spirit. She knew everything.

"Free me from what?"

"This place!" Yangchen shouted. "How do I free your spirit from this place?" They needed to leave. They could flee until they reached the canyon's limits, climb to a better portion of the Spirit World where there was light and grass and anything but the shrieking of the condemned.

The condemned. Her distress might have been a beacon to them. A ghastly apparition staggered up behind Jetsun, draped in bloody nightclothes. The hiccuping man Yangchen had encountered the last time she was here, his queue wound around his neck like a noose. He lunged forward with wild eyes and Yangchen tried to shout in warning.

Jetsun shifted and caught the man as he fell over her. She cradled him on her rock, carrying his weight as easily as she would a newborn. "There now," she soothed, brushing the side of his head with the back of her hand. A warmth flowed from her fingertips, as solid as it was invisible. "You can rest."

His spasms gentled. Slowly, gradually, his muscles released their tension, and his eyes drifted shut. Jetsun rose to her knees and with great care lowered him to the ground behind her platform.

Yangchen had to get up and look. The fog had thinned enough that she could see a field extending into the distance. Dozens of people lay on the canyon floor. Quiet, no longer screaming, no longer shaking with agony.

"Jetsun," Yangchen said, utterly bewildered. "What are you doing here?"

Her sister thought it over. "I suppose . . . I'm reliving the worst day of my life? Watching my greatest fears. Dwelling on my deepest regrets."

The noise that came from Yangchen's stomach wasn't a laugh. It was the expulsion of a darkness that had festered within her for years. Her sister was immune. The tortures that existence could summon had no hold on Jetsun and never would. Yangchen felt like she was drowning in relief and envy and gratitude.

There was a saying so ancient that none of her lives could remember the origin. *The true mind could weather illusions without being lost. The true heart could touch poison without being harmed.* Jetsun's spirit was so mighty that she could share her peace with others, just as she had done with Yangchen in the world of the living.

"I feel so bad for them," Jetsun said as she looked over the still bodies. "I can ease their pain for a time, but they inevitably rise again and wander off. As if some part of them sought out their own punishment and suffering."

She turned to Yangchen with a smile. "I imagine you're able to do the same in the human world, no?"

"No." For the first time in her life and afterlife, Jetsun was wrong. "No, I can't."

Yangchen began to shake. The truth came pouring unstopped from her lips. She babbled near incoherently. "Jetsun, I'm no good at this. I'm ruining everything."

This was the real Yangchen. The frightened child who could admit the world was too big to grasp, too heavy. The fool who thought she could make a difference, the fraud who told others so. "Jetsun, I don't want to do this," Yangchen whispered hoarsely. It had all been a lie. The idea that she might be worthy of the mantle. The notion that she could have any real impact. "I don't want to do this anymore. *I don't want to do this anymore!*"

She keeled over and curled up on the stone. "I keep losing parts of myself," she wept. "You. Nujian. I can't hold it together. I don't know if the world is worth it. It never changes. It never learns."

Jetsun shifted so her lap was under Yangchen's head. She brushed strands of hair out of Yangchen's face and didn't answer.

Together they sat. Existed.

"You know I hated you sometimes, right?" Jetsun said.

Yangchen's eyes popped open. "What?"

"Frequently, I hated you," Jetsun said, matter-of-factly. "You were a little terror. A nightmare. I used to tell Abbess Dagmola that you'd ruined my life and I'd drop you off the cliffside when no one was looking."

"*What?*"

Jetsun sighed. "I would say such things out of anger, because I felt like I wasn't my complete self around you. Taking care of you was exhausting. I never had space. Being your guardian tore chunks out of me; because of you I ended up in a different shape than I would have untouched."

She tugged on Yangchen's earlobe. "But I loved you too. I loved you more than I hated you, loved you more than life itself. Believe me when I say that you were *always* worth it."

Jetsun pushed Yangchen off her lap without ceremony and bade her stand up. They met eye-to-eye, the same height, and she smiled with pride. "Sister, no longer little. You're afraid of failing. You're afraid of every success that might slip through your fingers, every missed chance. You're so afraid of what the voices will say." She smoothed Yangchen's shawl. "Don't be."

"But—"

Jetsun hushed her with a glance. "In this fog, there are so many people here I can't help. I've only encountered a few out of the many. Shall I abandon the souls within arm's reach?"

The twinkle in Jetsun's eye, the upturned curl of her lip. This couldn't be the last time Yangchen ever saw them. "I think I'm where I need to be," Jetsun said. "Just like you're where you need to be."

She leaned over and whispered into Yangchen's ear. "Your friend needs help. *Wake up.*"

Yangchen opened her eyes. She was back in the oasis. But all was not well.

She'd thought the fog had avoided her. But really, it had flowed by like water finding its level, until it found the point where the barrier between realms was thinnest. An extension had broken through, but not for her. Kavik's form was wreathed in the vapors.

That cocky smirk she knew so well lay plastered over his face, a mask of triumph. But tears streamed from his eyes. "The *Sunbeam*," he repeated, again and again. "The ship you're looking for is called the *Sunbeam*."

*They seek out their own punishment.* By the rules of this twisted spirit, Kavik believed the worst moment of his life was when he betrayed the Avatar.

Yangchen quickly bent a sphere of water from the sacred pool and encased Kavik from head to toe, like he'd done for her patients in the mountain hospital. The lungless scream of a predator denied prey echoed through the cavern.

But she was louder. *"LET HIM GO!"* Yangchen roared back, vibrating the air so hard that the waters rippled and icicles fell from the walls. She'd lost two friends and protectors already. She vowed there wouldn't be a third.

The spirit's grip on Kavik suddenly vanished. She fell down, the winner of the tug-of-war. Kavik's body dropped beside her, his shroud of water splashing her, and he choked to life once more.

She let him roll around on the grass, hacking and coughing until his lungs were clear. Once he came to a stop, she flopped down on her back next to him. They were both too tired to even sit up.

Yangchen stared at the vaulted ceiling of the ice cavern. "Are you all right?" she asked.

Kavik's panting slowed and he took a gulp of fresh air. "I don't— I don't know what happened there. Did you save me?"

"Just returning the favor."

She heard his head roll to the side, toward her. "Did you find your sister?"

"In a way." Yangchen blew out a long breath. The journey had been so arduous, and yet small words, short answers, were all she could muster. Perhaps that was enough. "She'll be fine."

Neither of them rose. Yangchen wished she hadn't seen the fog open the window into Kavik's vulnerabilities. There needed to be an effort on her part to trust him. Instead, she'd been given the ultimate assurance. She'd been granted a certainty she didn't deserve.

"I used you and the others as part of a ruse in Taku," she said, her confession an attempt to balance the scales.

He took the revelation in stride. "I suppose that's only fair, at least where I'm concerned. You have to apologize to everyone else, though. Especially Jujinta."

She would. She would beg the most honest and scrupulous member of their team for forgiveness. "I did it to protect Yingsu," she added.

Kavik's surprise lifted his shoulders off the ground. He took a moment to try and piece the implications together. "Is she joining up?" was all he asked in response.

"I don't know. Maybe." The Firebender seemed to have appreciated making a difference on behalf of the Avatar instead of being exploited by a zongdu. Sometimes purpose was better than money. Yingsu would certainly make a formidable addition to the group.

But in the end, everyone had to decide for themselves.

Yangchen squirmed in place, dreading her next question. "What will you do now?" she asked.

"I'm getting out of the game," Kavik said. "According to Ayunerak, the heat's off me in the North. I can finally go home. See my parents. I asked the White Lotus if they could set me up as a healer's assistant. I'd enjoy that life."

Yangchen was the one who'd given him a taste for the job. "Don't do it," she said.

She didn't care how shameless it was to demand he abandon a noble calling. Yangchen grasped between them for Kavik's hand, guided by his warmth. Finding his fingers, she gave them a squeeze.

Then she let go and smacked the back of her hand against his.

"Stay with me," she said. "I need you by my side. There's so much work to do, and I want you with me until it's finished."

Kavik's laughter pierced the Spirit Oasis. Yangchen had willingly delivered him the victory. She knew he'd been waiting for this moment since the day they'd first met.

"Tell you what," he said, smacking her back. "I'll sleep on it."

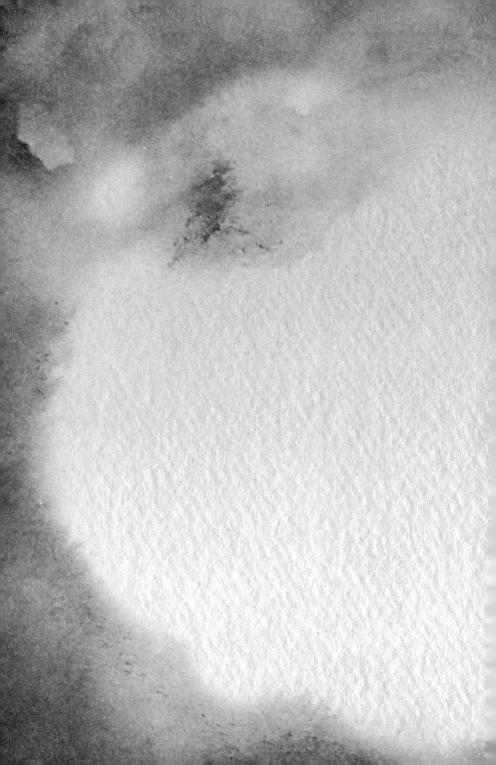

# ACKNOWLEDGMENTS

I'd like to thank the familiar crew, without whom these novels wouldn't exist. Anne Heltzel for guiding my craft. Andrew Smith for creating the possibility. Stephen Barr for being my champion. Joan Hilty and Jeffrey Whitman for steering the way. My family, whom I never told about my writing until the day I knew I was going to be published but who probably had an inkling that I'd end up doing something off the beaten path eventually. And of course, Michael Dante DiMartino and Bryan Konietzko for creating the world we've all lived in for so long.

Let me talk about that last part. I started working on *The Rise of Kyoshi* in 2018. As of writing these acknowledgments, it'll be five years that I've spent writing novels in the Avatar universe. That's an eighth of my life, currently. More years than I spent in college. I've worked on these books longer than I've stayed at any single company at my day job. Half the time my partner has known me, I've been writing for this franchise. It's given me career highs, mental ups and downs, and perspective on being an author that I never would have gained elsewhere.

But the show first aired in 2005. It's old enough to vote. My five years might seem like a long time to me in retrospect, but it's only a brief slice of the universe's long life, a life kept vibrant by the love of so many viewers, readers, and creatives. Like the cycle of the seasons, new stories will continue to grow forth and inspire us all. I'll be watching and reading, grateful for the time I shared with Avatar.

Thank you.

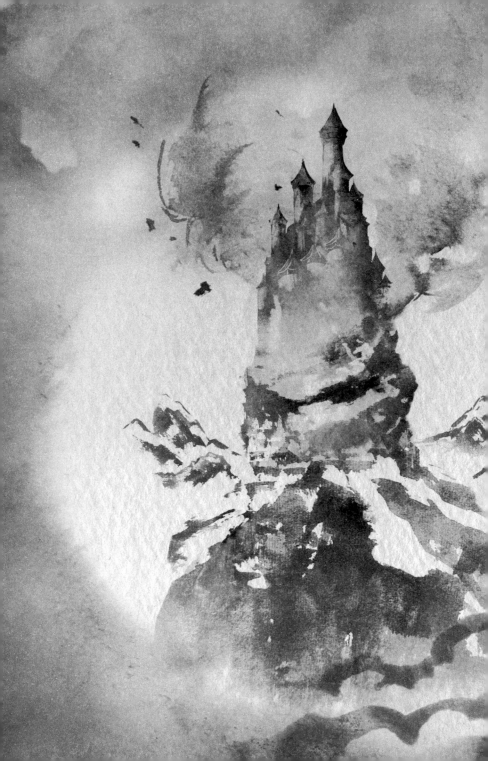

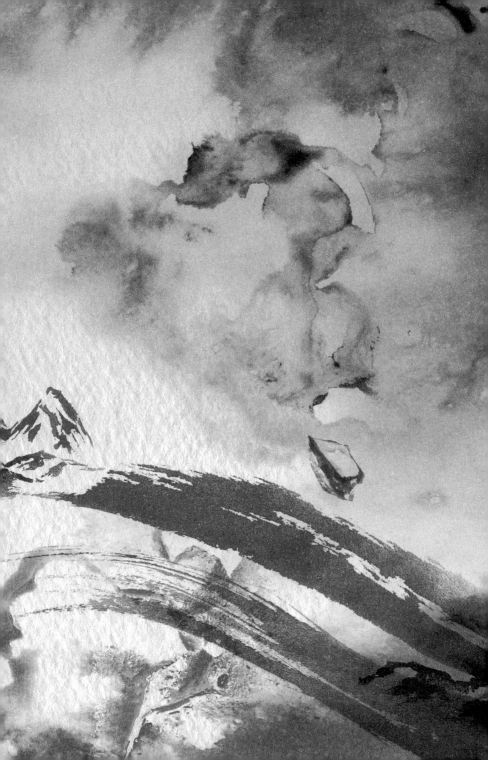

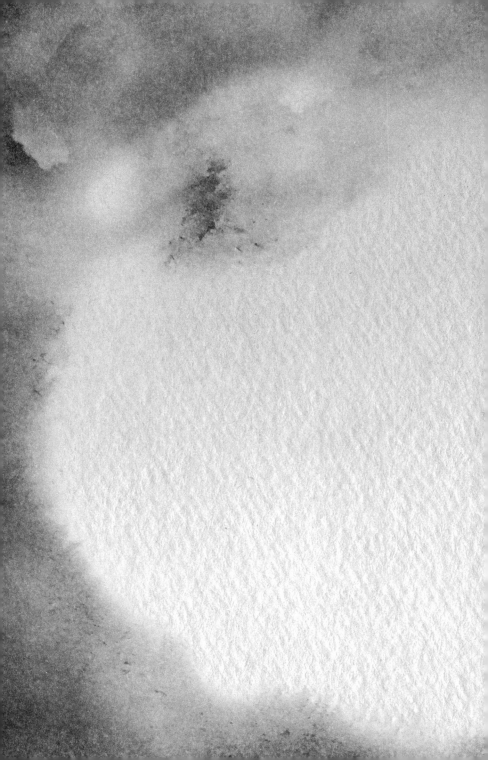